Howdy to my fans and friends!

Well, here we are at book number ten in the Chet Byrnes series. I get to visit with many folks with that newfangled invention called email, and I should have a new web page—another newfangled invention—up at www.dustyrichards.com. (And what does that gosh-darned WWW stand for anyway?)

My Facebook page is another place where you can keep track of my personal appearances and book signings, and all future releases. I like email and Facebook a lot, but nowadays my phone hardly ever rings. That's progress, I reckon.

The Byrnes Family Ranch series can be found on audio from Recorded Books, if that's your pleasure. They sure do make for nice gifts.

Horses, dust, cactus spines, rattlesnakes, and bawling cattle—welcome to the American frontier. The good men who fought the outlaws were a tough breed. They prayed and lived during turbulent times amid hardships few modern folk could ever imagine. They are our history—even in fiction—and are part of why we have America today. People like Chet Byrnes made it a better place to live, breathe, and raise our kids.

So swing onto the saddle and hope that horse don't buck you off. Until the next adventure, thanks for visiting with Chet Byrnes and his boys, and I sure hope you enjoy the ride.

Dusty Richards
Springdale, Arkansas
February 2016

*Read all the adventures in the
Byrnes Family Ranch Saga . . .*

DUSTY RICHARDS

DEADLY IS THE NIGHT

P

PINNACLE BOOKS
Kensington Publishing Corp.
www.kensingtonbooks.com

PINNACLE BOOKS are published by

Kensington Publishing Corp.
119 West 40th Street
New York, NY 10018

All Kensington titles, imprints, and distributed lines are available at special quantity discounts for bulk purchases for sales promotions, premi-
ums, fund-raising, educational, or institutional use. Special book
excerpts or customized printings can also be created to fit specific
needs. For details, write or phone the office of the Kensington sales manager: Kensington Publishing Corp., 119 West 40th Street, New York, NY
10018, attn: Sales Department; phone 1-800-221-2647.

PINNACLE BOOKS and the Pinnacle logo are Reg. U.S. Pat. & TM
Off.

ISBN-13: 978-0-7860-3667-7
ISBN-10: 0-7860-3667-2

First printing: October 2016

10 9 8 7 6 5 4 3 2 1

Printed in the United States of America

First electronic edition: October 2016

ISBN-13: 978-0-7860-3668-4
ISBN-10: 0-7860-3668-0

PROLOGUE

Ortega Morales reined up his powerful bay horse and studied the distant desert horizon for a dust cloud. The stout gelding under him was hot and sweaty, but he still had lots of strength if he called on him for more effort. The afternoon heat waves warped the cactus mesquite scene clear down into Mexico. He reached through his field glasses, hoping to see a trace of the rustlers, when the two teen boys with him slid to a halt beside him. The pair, Ronaldo Maguey and Filipe Sanchez, were tough enough boys and knew how to use the pistols they wore—still they were not *pistoleros*. He would have felt better with more experienced men, but they were all he had and would have to do. There was no time to go back to the ranch for more help to take on these rustlers.

At a water hole, earlier that morning, they had found fresh tracks of two dozen, or more, cattle being rounded up and then driven south. The horse tracks indicated as many as six or more riders herded them and bound for the border. His boss, JD Byrnes, said to let those people who lived down there have a few beef, but he didn't want rustlers to take a single one.

When Ortega would cull the mustangs on that end of the ranch, he drove many of the culls to the Lady of the Church village for the people to slaughter and have to eat. He knew it would be a friendly place, but there were no allies there armed and ready to help him arrest the thieves. These rustlers would all be tough *hombres* and there was no time to send for help. The job of handling them rested on his shoulders. He must catch and hang the thieves and then take charge of the cattle and return them to the ranch.

His plan sounded easy enough, but after several years of riding with Chet Byrnes as a deputy U.S. marshal, he learned these situations never turned out either easy or simple. He and his two men rode farther south and finally heard the cattle bawling in the distance. He held up his hand for them to halt.

"Sounds like they've stopped at the Lady of the Church village."

The boys nodded. Looking grim-faced, he made sure they all understood the situation. "Boys, taking on these bandits might be tough and there's only three of us. You guys will be in the cross fire if they choose to fight. If I can get the drop on them, it will be over, but I will need backup if that does not work. When we get closer I'll give you my plan."

"Ortega, me and Filipe are ready to do anything you need for us to do."

"Fine. We can take them."

Ortega booted the bay on until they were on the

crest and could see the dust made by the cattle milling in the pens. Being herded together with other cattle not known to them upset the social order of who was boss. That would be a good distraction for Ortega and his men's arrival.

Through the glasses he could see a half dozen sweaty horses hipshot at the rack in front of the *cantina*. Then he spotted one horse hitched down in the grove of huge cottonwood trees by the cattle in the corral.

"They left one guy with the cattle. We need him hog tied and gagged."

Ronaldo dismounted. "We can come along down there like two guys going to town. Get him tied and gagged, then you can bring our horses off the hill. There's no windows in that old *cantina*. They won't see you coming down if you go east a little."

"I'll wait till you get him bound up and do that. Good plan."

Ortega checked the loads in his pistol. They were a while getting down there but he finally saw them coming through the grove. They were horsing around like boys do in a push and shove on their way to town. They came up close to the man and Ronaldo cracked him over the head with his gun butt. The man's knees buckled and the boys had him down, tied, and gagged when Ortega pushed his horse off the east side of the hill leading the other two. Good work. They would do for help.

Their horses were soon secured in an empty corral. He gave them his orders. "I am going in those front doors gun drawn and tell them hands up. I will probably have to shoot at least one to enforce my order. Ronaldo, you go around back. Don't shoot anyone unarmed, but if anyone with a gun in hand comes out, shoot him down. Savvy? And you need to take some cover in case they shoot at you."

"I will have it covered."

"They don't deserve a blink of your eye. Shoot them. Filipe, you come in after me. There will be lots of gun smoke in there, but shoot anyone still armed and left standing."

"I'm ready."

"So am I."

"Let's do it."

Ronaldo headed around for the back door. Filipe trailed him, coming up beside the solid front of the building staying out of their line of sight. With a nod to his partner, Ortega went through the batwing doors and shouted, "Hands high or die."

One of the men standing at the bar went for his gun and Ortega nailed him. Next he swiveled, cocked his gun, and shot the short one trying to get up from a table and draw at the same time. Then Ortega took a bullet in his left leg and that toppled him to the floor. Filipe shot two other men who were rushing over to shoot Ortega. His belly on the littered dirt floor, Ortega saw one of them headed for the open back door. He aimed the pistol and shot at him, but Ronaldo cut him down from outside in the open space.

Filipe was there on his knees with a smoking Colt in his fist. "How bad are you hit?"

Ortega managed to sit up and shake his head. The pain in his leg was real sharp. "I think we've got them."

"Yes, sir."

He could see the boy was shaking hard. He wanted to reassure him the fight was over. "Filipe, I'd cross any river with you they had."

"Oh, I'll stop shaking after a while, Ortega. I've never been in a gun fight before."

"He all right?" Ronaldo demanded of his buddy.

"No, he's shot."

"There ain't a one of 'em left, boss."

"There's one with the cattle—" Ortega managed to say.

"Yes. What about him?"

"Hang him before you leave here and then take the cattle back up into the ranch."

Ronaldo swallowed hard. "We will. The bartender sent for the doc. We can do the rest. I'll go find a buckboard to get you back to the ranch. What can I pay him?"

Ortega dug in his pocket and came out with some bills for him. "Whatever he asks. Filipe, get me some tequila to drink. This leg hurts bad."

When the doc and some help arrived, they laid Ortega across two tables, cut off his pants leg, and the doc removed the slug and gave it to him for a prize. The physician poured alcohol into the wound that set him on fire. Bandaged up, the doc straightened and said, "Keep the bandage clean. Don't walk on it a lot till it heals."

Ortega couldn't believe the man's lack of any concern. Why, his leg was still bleeding through the bandage, the pain was much worse, and his doctor just went over to the bar, downed a shot of something, thanked the barkeep, and left.

Ronaldo was back. "This man says he can get you back to the ranch. I paid him twenty dollars. His name is Diego. We made you a bed. Can we carry you out there and send you home?"

"Sure, but first, get me two bottles of tequila. I will need them to stand the pain and the ride." By then, because of the pain, his vision was groggy and he had no energy left.

He knew he had to leave immediately. If he stayed any longer in Mexico, and those men's leader found out where he was, killers would be sent to get him. At the ranch he would have his wife Maria and a lot of protection. He'd much rather have JD worry about him than the boys, though they had damn sure earned their pay that day. His men had done one helluva job. He was deeply proud of them.

Some of the men now in the *cantina* remembered him. They carefully carried him to the conveyance and laid him on the bedding. Crossing themselves, they wished him well. He thanked them.

His vision swirled, but going past the pens, Ortega saw that the last rustler swung on a rope in the cottonwood grove. His eyes closed, he prepared for a long rough ride that would jar his pain-filled leg. There were only tracks that made for a road northward, and Diego wasted little time pushing for there. If the man didn't wreck, they'd be back at the main ranch by dawn.

His driver stopped routinely to check on him, give him a drink of water or tequila. Ortega finally figured out as day shifted to night, the man was real concerned about him dying on the way.

Each time the man stopped he asked, "Are you still breathing good?" and then gave him a drink. It was almost funny. If he had not been so pain stricken he'd have laughed. And at each stop Ortega would tell him he was and the man would store the bottle not to break, climb aboard, and drive on. The many stars were a blanket over his head when he periodically woke up by being rolled around on the rough road they were driving on. But Diego made good time despite the darkness, trusting his horses. In the predawn light, over the rattling rig's sounds, Ortega could hear windmills pumping water. He figured they were almost at the ranch when the dogs began barking. They were there.

A sentry shouted, "Who are you?"

"My name is Diego. I have your man Ortega and he has been shot."

"Mother of God. Is he alive?"

"*Si.*"

At that point Ortega fainted. Next he knew his wife Maria had climbed on the buckboard, kissing him and begging him to talk to her.

"I—am fine—now—you are here."

"Oh, thank God. It is your leg?"

"He took the bullet out down there."

"Where are the boys?"

"They are fine. They sent me home. They are bringing the cattle the rustlers stole back to the ranch."

"Good God. You all right?" His boss JD climbed on the buckboard bed with them. "What happened?"

"Rustlers took about thirty head of cattle at the last waterhole—we found tracks—"

"For heaven's sake, JD, carry him into the house. The poor man must have ridden from Mexico in that rig. Put him on our bed. Here, Maria, I'll help you down." It was JD's wife Bonnie so concerned for his care. The lovely blond lady had taken charge.

He was lifted by a half dozen men, carried inside through the concerned crowd, and set on their large bed.

"Have you eaten?" Bonnie demanded.

"No, but tequila helps the pain."

"Get him some and a glass, Juanita. We'll fix him some food while you two talk. Everyone except JD and Maria out. Let the poor man get some rest. JD will tell you all about it once he hears the whole story."

"You recognize any of them?" JD asked.

"No. Thanks to the two boys that were with me, they are all dead. But I knew if their boss got word that I was a patient down there he'd send killers after me. I couldn't have defended myself. I knew I had to leave fast. Ronaldo and Filipe arranged it with Diego."

"You did the right thing. Can you tell me anything more?"

"I can. We caught up with them at the Lady of the Church village. They'd penned the cattle and six of them went to the *cantina*. We saw they left one man to guard the cattle.

"Those boys slipped down there into the grove of cottonwoods, hit him over the head, and gagged him. They really are great boys." He took a break to squeeze his leg.

"I thought if I busted in the *cantina* with my gun like Chet did a time or two, they'd give up—and I'd have the drop on them. Didn't work. One of them shot me in the leg while I gunned down two. Filipe shot two or three more and Ronaldo got one going out the back door."

"You're lucky to be alive." JD shook his head at the actions his man had taken to get control.

Ortega shrugged the comment off. "After the snooty doctor took out the bullet, doused it with alcohol, and bandaged it, he said not to walk on it and left. Ronaldo found the wagon man. Diego did a great job getting here last night and not turning over. I owe him more money."

"I'll do that. I think he's eating now."

Ortega forced a smile. "I think he was afraid I'd die before he could get me here and didn't want my death on his hands."

JD was laughing as Bonnie delivered Ortega's tray of food.

Then JD turned to Maria who had been sitting quietly the whole time the story was being told. "You can feed him. We will leave you two alone. I must go tell the people the story."

Ortega groaned in pain.

"Bonnie has some laudanum. After you eat I will get the bottle. You have some and you will be able to sleep after that," his wife promised him.

"That might be the best idea. That rattling ride last night didn't help me much, but I'll recover quick now I am here."

She leaned over and kissed him. "I worried all night knowing something bad had happened."

"It was a real long ride. I may be out when the boys return, but you wake me and tell me. I think they are fine, but I want to know they are all right so I can stop worrying."

She agreed. "Now eat."

The laudanum made him sleep for the next three days. He would waken long enough to eat and empty his bladder and bowels. The boys returned unscathed and they were treated as the heroes of Diablo. The ranch had a *fiesta* and *fandango* for them.

Maria changed Ortega's bandages every other day and told him he was healing. But when not drugged with the laudanum, he still fretted. Who had sent those rustlers? His name? Maybe later he would know. When he was better he would worry about the man in charge of the rustlers.

After a week, JD, Bonnie, and Maria decided Ortega could be moved back to his own home. He apologized to Bonnie for taking over her bed for so long. She hugged him gently and kissed his forehead. "We care about you, and you are such a great foreman this ranch needs you well."

"I need to be here, too."

They carried Ortega, sitting on a stretcher, over to his place, him shaking his head about the fuss being made over his move. All the children lined up along the way told him to get well. In his own house and bed at last he kissed his wife. "Thank you, Maria. It is so good to be back here."

"*Si.* So good and you are healing."

"I am and it can't be quick enough."

"They say it was Buster Weeks's men you tangled with. Rumor is he has put a thousand *pesos* up for you to be dead."

"Nothing cheap about him, is there?"

She laughed. "He is serious I bet."

CHAPTER 1

His day started with a loud bang. The sound of a loud rifle barking close by had Chet Byrnes sit up in bed and reach for his six-gun. Covers thrown back, he set the weapon on the blanket top of his cot and jerked on his pants. Listening intently, he began to hear voices of the men in camp. They sounded, to him, as being excited but not from a raid. Boots finally on, he stuck his head out of the tent. Armed men were gathered about thirty yards away. Their breath steamy, he could see and hear one say, "By God, that's one damn biggest grizzly I ever saw."

He slapped on his hat. A bear had invaded Stage Coach Central at Center Point that early morning and obviously the night guard shot it. Chet's jacket on against the cold, he joined them.

His man and stage line superintendent, Cole Emerson, a tall twenty-some-year-old, greeted him. "Jock shot a helluva bear this morning. Did it wake you?"

"I thought the Indians had raided us."

Everyone laughed. It was one huge boar bear, and

if he'd been mad Chet wouldn't have wanted to have to face him.

The night guard, Jock, spoke up. "I tell you, boss man. I see him in de dim light and I know my pistol no kills him. So I went and got that .50 caliber from the office. It was the right gun, no?"

"Jock, if you'd shot him with a pistol, you'd have been his breakfast right then."

"I am not so dumb, huh?"

He hugged the man's shoulder. "You are a great hero. Thanks from all of us."

Wrapped in a blanket, Val, Cole's wife, soon joined them. "Wow that is one big bear."

"Where's Rocky?" Chet asked about his four-year-old son that she cared for.

"He's fine. I made him stay in the house until I found out what had happened. That is a grizzly?"

"Yes. Jock went and got the big rifle from the office."

"Well, I'll go get your son dressed and let him see the big bear."

"Thanks," Chet said to her. Val had been Cole's wife for several years and they had no children. So when an ex-love of Chet's back in Texas died of pneumonia, the dead woman's daughter wrote him and told him about his young son back in Texas that he never knew about. She offered the boy to Chet. So Cole and Val went back to the land he left over a two-family feud, where no one knew of his connection, and they brought the boy back. Val asked if she could raise him and he agreed. Chet had just married his current wife, Elizabeth, and she thought it a good idea, too. His other son, Adam, by his first wife,

Marge, was at the Camp Verde Ranch with Rhea and Victor. Chet had lost Marge in a jumping horse accident.

Elizabeth, who he called Liz, was at the home ranch in Preskitt Valley expecting their first offspring at any time.

"They have breakfast ready in the mess hall," Cole said. "I had a thought about the bear. I am going to have him mounted and hang him in our office building."

"Great idea. Hannagen can come see the biggest threat to his stage line since we stopped the raiders."

"You going up to the west place and see Lucy?" Cole asked him.

"I'd like to but I really better go back and check on Liz. Hannagen and I are still checking more on building that telegraph line across northern Arizona. He thinks the government will pay a large part of the costs."

"That would help. The last bid you got was a million dollars?"

"Maybe higher than that."

"They are building stage stop structures at the first two stations east of here. Station number two coming from Gallup, New Mexico, is next. The Navajo trader with all the wives has his own at the first one. You know he is a real smart businessman."

"He has four wives and that may be the reason."

Cole looked to the sky for help before they went inside the mess hall. "I don't need three more."

"Nor do I, buddy. One is enough."

"Our buckboards are running right close to time each day. It is all working smoothly, but we haven't had much of a winter so far, and that's probably why the big bear came out and wandered around."

Chet agreed. The two went through the line for scrambled eggs, side meat, German-fried potatoes, and pancakes on their plates. A boy brought them steaming coffee in mugs and asked if they needed cream and sugar.

Cole said, "Thanks and no."

"Is your man Drew getting things done on the Colorado River side?"

"We are building two stage stops over there. The other two have them, so by spring we will be ready for those stagecoaches."

"You are doing great so I'll head back. I'll stop at Robert and Agnes' at the sawmill and be sure our log-hauling operation is doing all right."

Cole smiled between bites. "That boy is a helluva manager, isn't he?"

"Yes, he is. He makes money every month that he can haul logs, handles his own business, keeps books, orders his own needs, and has good men working for him. He is very efficient in his superintendent job."

"I heard they now have a baby girl?"

"Carolina is her name. I laugh when I think about his wife. She's a dedicated Mormon but she makes him coffee." Chet had wondered when they were first married how that would work out, but when Robert set his mind to things they always worked well.

"He takes her to church, too."

"Oh, they have a sweet life and she loves that big

house. Not many young people in Arizona have a setup like that to live in."

"Hey, Val and I appreciate our house up here, too. But mostly we appreciate having the boy."

"I know. You tell Val that the new baby coming will not change things at our house. Rocky will be here with you two. Liz and I have discussed that and we think he is better here since he lost his mother and you two replaced her."

"I will tell her. She's been worried it might change things."

Chet shook his head to dismiss any concern about the boy's future custody.

"Good."

Spencer and Jesus joined them.

"Well, Jesus, you'll be home with Anita shortly," Cole said, teasing his longtime partner at guarding Chet.

"I remember you getting back to Valerie whenever we got back from a job. Whisk and you were gone."

"When we'd get back from business, Cole would hightail it to his wife in town," Chet said to the new man on the team.

Spencer nodded. "I don't blame him. Both these guys have sweet wives. Me, I am still trying to convince Rebecca Franks back in Preskitt that we can have a life together."

Chet knew the woman they rode back with on the stage a while back, Rebecca Franks, who Spencer rescued from the brothel, was not convinced she could return to normal society and not be scorned by that same society.

"Well, good luck, Spencer. I sure don't regret marrying Val, and her past never comes up," Cole said. "Of course you know the three of us have been together for years. I hired on and helped Chet take the first herd to the Navajos. A bunch of Apaches attacked us. They weren't more than boys. I shot one and Chet captured another. He told me to bring him along as a captive, and he went off to see about the spooked cattle. The buck drew a knife and I had to shoot him. When I caught up with Chet, he asked where the Indian was. I said dead. That he drew a knife on me. I think he almost laughed and shook his head. I wasn't sure I wouldn't get fired for doing that."

Chet nodded. "That was our first trip to Gallup with a herd, and we learned a lot. Sarge took over running it after that. He has the whole thing down to a routine. We bought that Windmill Ranch since it is a quarter of the way over there. We mix the cattle before the drive so they don't fight over who is boss on the trail, and that saves lots of work driving them."

"Sarge is married to your sister, right?" Spencer asked.

"Yes. She was married before and her husband was with us," Chet explained. "Good guy, he got killed in a horse wreck. They'd been married a year and a half and they lived in the big house on the Verde place. She was expecting a baby. I don't think he was even buried and Sarge came to see me looking very serious.

"'When it is proper may I court your sister?' he asked. I was taken by surprise and said sure, but she needs some time to find herself. Then I asked why he didn't court her before her first husband did? He said, 'I didn't think I was good enough for her.'"

"He'd wanted her all the time?" Spencer asked.

"You don't know Sarge. He's a deep thinker. That really mattered to him," Cole said.

"Don't ever say a word about it. But he politely waited on her hand and foot every chance he got. Best we can tell she finally asked him if he really wanted her for his wife. He said, 'Oh, yes.'

"They must have talked about her condition and the baby not being his. He said it didn't matter; it would be his child. She said, 'Then let's get married; if you want me now in this condition, I know you will want me after the baby gets here.'"

They laughed.

"How did Cole get Valerie?"

"Val and JD's wife, Bonnie, had gone to Tombstone for the bright lights. Two wild girls going off to see the wild world. They were good friends. Jenn is Bonnie's mother. She has the café in town and has found half or more of my men for me. You met Jenn. When Bonnie left, she did not write her, and Jenn was upset and worried about her welfare. We were going down there anyway, so I promised to check on her. Val had quit the business and she was working in a café. She hated the business she told us. I offered her a job with Jenn 'cause I knew Jenn needed help and she was a good worker. We bought her a stagecoach ticket to up here. She has always been grateful."

Cole began his side of the story. "Val was working for Jenn at the time. I kind of set in to convince her

I was serious. She said she had gotten religion and would not simply live with me. I said I didn't expect that and we got married."

Jesus came in explaining, "Chet hasn't told you it all. After we had put Val on the stage back to here, some white slavers kidnapped Bonnie and planned to sell her in Mexico City. We got on their tracks about halfway down there—just the three of us— and Chet decided we didn't have enough manpower to get her out of their hands, so he went to this powerful *hacienda* man and offered him three head of the Barbarossa young horses for her safe return. No questions asked. It worked. Though we did sweat it. And when we got her we ran like hell for the border."

Chet nodded. "When I'd originally met with her in Tombstone, she told me she didn't want to go home and was pretty set on staying, but when we got her back, she was ready to go home.

"I think Bonnie realized she would never be a real person in that business, just a slave and that her life would have no value to anyone except what they could get from and for her."

"JD got serious and she married him. We all wondered if they would make it." Jesus shook his head. "But they finally found themselves, right, Chet?"

"Tell you how serious the two of them are. They get on their knees every night and pray out loud before they go to bed."

"Wow," Spencer said. "I'll have to meet them. I love Valerie. She is a great breath of life simply being on the scene."

Cole said, "She's changed my life."

Spencer agreed. "I can see that just being around you two."

"Speaking of changing men's lives, we need to head back home. There is still no word on the telegraph wire deal and Cole has the buckboards running, so let's the three of us head home tomorrow."

Morning came quickly the next day. Frosty after breakfast and on stiff-acting horses, they set out for the south. Spencer drew the bucker and he made some stiff-legged hops before he got him out of them. Everyone waved his hat for the pony to buck some more but he quit.

They stopped and spent the afternoon with Robert, wife Betty, and the baby girl.

Betty made them lunch and then they rode for the Verde place. They arrived late, but Rhea got up and fed them. Because Rhea was excited for any news, they told her all about Robert's baby girl Caroline and how Rocky had grown some more. There were plenty of beds in the big house for them to sleep on, and at breakfast the next morning, Tom was there with Victor to talk about their operations. Vic told them the new place they bought east of the village was really going to help expand their hay business plus some corn he wanted to plant the following spring.

Tom spoke next. "I know you probably don't realize it, but the large number of range cattle are becoming a big problem. I don't even recognize the brands on these cattle. They must have driven them up here and turned them loose. They break in when we feed hay. What can we do about them?"

"Drive them down in the Verde wilderness I guess."

"There are really a lot of them. What say we get the ranchers together and all of us purge them out?"

"Sounds good to me. Want to set up a meeting to talk about it?" Chet asked his foreman.

"Up at the home place you mean? To have a meeting? They'd come to a meeting up there and listen to you."

"I don't know about that, but we can try."

"Something needs to be done. How is Liz?"

"Fine when I left her. You tell Millie hi for me."

"Millie's good. Said to say hi to you and Liz."

"I'll get the gathering deal started when I get there."

"Yes. We need to do something soon. Those cattle are a big pain." Tom shook Chet's hand and left to give instructions for the day to his ranch crew.

"He's a great boss. I never worked for a fairer man," Spencer said.

"He can work cowboys there is no doubt. I'm pleased having him run this big ranch that's for sure. His wife loves their big house even with her daughter gone and married. They are up at Windmill right now. Sarge is teaching him how to drive cattle and feed the Navajos."

"Wasn't Millie mad at you about that deal?" Spencer asked.

Chet shook his head. "She got over it. She got married at fifteen. So did her daughter."

"I'm seeing having all these businesses is not just a matter of being boss, but you get into things I'd never dreamed about being in charge of."

"Part of the job."

Jesus shrugged. "He gets it all done."

"What about that boy on the east place you just bought?"

"He's doing good. He'll have his hay land fenced and ready to mow come next spring. Have corrals built and I'll need to find him a set of cows and bulls by fall."

"You think that place will be operating that soon?"

"It sure will if he has his way."

Spencer shook his head, taking a short rein on his horse that had bucked leaving Center Point the last time he stepped in the stirrup. He damn sure wasn't taking any chances about him this time.

It was past noon when Chet dropped out of the saddle at the yard. A stable boy took Chet's reins, and he looked wistfully at the back door for his wife to come welcome him.

Instead a very serious looking Monica came out, arms folded, and he hurried to see what was wrong.

"She all right?"

"Come inside. I'll tell you what happened. She'll be fine I think."

"What's wrong?"

Monica shut the door and faced him. "She lost the baby last night."

She caught his arm. "The doctor was here. He says she will be fine and he had no idea why the baby died. Things like that happen. But he gave her a sedative and told her to rest."

"Thanks. Sorry I was not here."

Monica agreed and said, "I will have your lunch. Those men need to eat?"

"No, they are going to check on their women."

"Good. Go look in on her. Maybe best she sleeps for a while. Come back and eat."

"I'll do that. Thanks, Monica."

Upstairs he quietly slipped in their bedroom. Her small form was under covers on her side and she breathed easy. Her face looked quite pale to him sleeping there. That might have been because of a loss of blood? He didn't know enough about an abortion or miscarriage to understand what happened. But she was alive and breathing. He'd not disturb her and quietly left the room.

Downstairs with lunch on the table, Monica brought him a letter from JD. Usually Bonnie wrote them with newsy things about the ranch operation and their life. This was in his handwriting.

Dear Chet

Today they brought Ortega Morales back from the border in a buckboard. He'd been shot in the leg by rustlers down by the Lady in the Church village. He tracked some thieves down there herding about thirty head off the ranch. With two boys they shot six or seven of them, and after he was shot they hung the last standing one. A real brave deal but what you'd expected from him and our men. One of the boys with him took charge, got a doctor to remove the bullet, and hired a buckboard to bring him home while they drove the stock back.

Ortega was wounded, was lying on his back in a buckboard all night for the ride home. You know there are no real roads between here and there.

What a ride from hell that must have been. He is recovering and will be all right.

Your old buddy Buster Weeks is behind the rustling down here running some outlaws—now with seven less—but there's plenty more down in Mexico that need work. That is the best information I could get on the situation.

Bonnie sends her love to you and we pray that you and Elizabeth are doing well.

Have any answers let me know?

JD and Bonnie Byrnes

"Is it bad news?" Monica asked him.

"Bad enough. His foreman, Ortega Morales, was shot by rustlers in Mexico by that bastard Buster Weeks's border bunch. He's recovering and they've got the cattle back, but he expects more trouble."

"What must you do?"

"I guess go see when I am sure she is all right."

"And I suppose they can shoot you then?"

"Monica, I need to lead these people."

"I know that. Toby came by going to town and asked if I thought you'd be here later. I told him I had no damn idea."

"You must have been real upset to swear at him?"

"Yes. The doctor was here and examining her and I had no idea what was happening."

"This thing that happened to her? Ever happen to you before?"

"Yes, and it's not any fun, I can tell you. Liz really wanted the child. Me, I didn't care and it turned out well for me that I lost mine."

"I do know how badly she wanted one. This will be a blow to her."

Monica left the kitchen crying. How heartfelt that tough woman could get amazed him—she really cared about Liz and her feelings. How did he comfort her? Damned if he knew.

He went in the living room to read the *Miner* last issues.

His ranch foreman, Raphael, knocked on the back door. Chet came back and opened the door.

"How is your wife?"

"Fine. Come in. She is sleeping. How are you?"

"Fine." Then his man laughed and unbuttoned his wool coat. "All the women are wondering how she is doing? They are burning candles at our shrine for her."

"It must be working."

"Good. They all love her so. I will tell them not to worry."

"Is anything else wrong?"

"No. Everything is going well. How about you?"

"Rustlers shot my foreman at Diablo. He's mending, but it sounds like I better ride south and check it all out. He's a tough guy but you mess with those bandits long enough one of them will shoot you."

Raphael agreed. "One of them even shot you?"

"They did once and I was lucky. Well, someone needs to check it out. She gets better I'll go south and find out what I can do about them."

"I have some good men that know that country."

"I am certain. JD has some, too. But thanks for thinking about me."

"I consider you my friend and you know that. If there is anything I can do, call on me."

"Yes, I will. Everyone good in the crew?"

"Everyone is fine. That girl Lisa you found with the rustlers who married Miguel is a real leader of the women. She has them sewing clothes for the children. Your wife provided the material, thread, scissors, needles, and buttons."

"I saw her leading them older women at the *fiesta*."

"She is not bossy. They will do anything she wants them to do. I think she was a real good thing to come here."

"Yes, she has been. I better go see how my wife is doing."

"Tell her wc all are praying for her."

"I will. *Gracias*. I will let you know when I plan to leave."

His wife was awake when he got back upstairs. Her dark eyes wet, she stared at the ceiling from under the covers.

"Liz, I am so sorry I wasn't here."

He settled on the bed beside her. "I know how much you wanted it."

"Oh, Chet, there was no way—nothing I could do to keep it in me."

"You didn't do it. That was God's thing. No one can change whatever the plan he has for us. You can't do anything but suffer the consequences. It was not to be. I consider you the neatest wife and person a man could have. I wanted nothing to happen to you. How do you feel?"

"Weary. Thanks, I love you, too, and I so wanted a child."

"I know that well. We will strive ahead. Monica has taken this as hard as you have."

She nodded that she knew.

"Anything I can do for you to make you comfortable?"

"Hold me for a while. I will clear my mind of this tragedy somehow."

"We need to get on with our life. You are important to me. Raphael told me you are helping the women make some nice clothes for the ranch kids."

"I want them to be proud. They are learning to read and write. Maybe they can't afford new clothes, but they can make them. Even the little ones smile and beam wearing new clothing. Lisa asked for my help and we laid out a plan. Those women know how to work hard. You know that from the way they work our events. Let's get up. I need to stop hiding. I am your wife and very proud of that, so I must get on with my life."

"You strong enough?"

"Yes."

"I'll wait for you. I don't want you getting dizzy going down the stairs."

She shook her finger at him. "I am fine."

"That's all I ask."

She dressed quickly, brushed her hair, and led him downstairs. Monica met and hugged her. "Are you all right?"

"I am fine. I think I am hungry."

"Supper will be ready in a short while."

"I can help."

"Why don't you—"

"Monica, I am getting on with my life. Chet, go read your newspapers."

"Yes, ma'am."

Their conversation going away sounded like a mother-daughter argument.

He read the papers. Nothing stuck out. She came out and asked about JD's letter.

Carefully he explained to her what he had read.

"It said he was going to recover?"

"Yes."

"I suppose you need to go see about it?"

He agreed.

"You and him were close working in the Force together?"

"Yes, Ortega is a hard worker. They have repaid me all the money I loaned him, and he and his family have a working ranch now."

"When will you have to leave?"

"If you are well, in two days."

She nodded. "I will be fine. A little defeated but I will be well."

"I will send word to Jesus and Spencer that we leave at midnight Wednesday."

"Fine. Supper is about ready." She dropped her voice. "Monica is better."

He rose and hugged her. "Thanks."

The time flew, and with things close to wrapped up Liz saw him off under the stars at the stage depot.

The others were hugging and kissing good-bye. Both of the other women came over and spoke to her as the men loaded their saddles and war bags in the back rack.

Chet waved at his wife and climbed aboard facing the back. Jesus took a place beside him and Spencer rode in the backseat. In a clatter of hooves, with driver Pike Moore shouting at his teams, they went rocking off to Hayden's Ferry.

"Your wife doing fine living in town?" Chet asked Jesus.

"She says at first it was different, but she says she really likes her privacy now she has it. The lady next door walks to the store with her. The merchants treat her very politely. And she attends church twice a week. So far she says it is fine."

"How about your lady?" he asked Spencer.

"We had a long talk the past two days. She promised to give us some more time. She really likes your wife. When she learned about what happened to her, she asked if we should go see her. Then she changed her mind and said you were there and she didn't need us."

"You think she will find her a place in your life?"

"I really hope so. But who knows—her life with me is not wild partying and raising hell with men."

"A woman has to decide, I guess, whether she wants a real life and family or just a good time."

"I've been around several crazy women of the night. She doesn't act like that even when we're alone. But I guess they act like other women, too, when they aren't raising hell. I'd say she hasn't found a track to run on in her life so far."

"Good luck."

Jesus chuckled. "Yeah, mine never wanted to marry me and now she says she really likes it."

"Good for you. Chet, is your wife okay?"

"Disappointed. But she comes up fighting. It bothered her the whole time she was not pregnant. Now she lost it she's slipped back some in her disappointment. But we have each other. I have two sons. She really wanted one. We'll just have to wait and see what happens next."

"I can't believe your story how she came to you to buy a gold horse and ended up marrying you."

Jesus shook his head and laughed. "It happened. I was there. But the best part was her wading in the Santa Cruz River and him afterwards drying her feet and she thought he was like Jesus and the apostles before the Last Supper."

"How was that?"

"She asked if she could wade in that small river. I said yes. There she was, pretty as any woman I ever knew in the golden sunlight, shafts coming down through the giant cottonwood leaves, her kicking water and wading around like a ballerina. I was in such awe and she came out saying that I sure had lots of patience to put up with her foolishness. I had gotten a towel to dry her feet so she could put her socks and boots back on. That was all."

"Man, I could see her doing that. Well tell me—" They hit a large bump and had to regain their seats. "Then what happened?"

"She asked me to bathe her. That was hard but it didn't seem out of order to her. She later said, "I know I was bold but I wanted you to see me as I was." Later we danced the night away and then took my bedroll and made love in the hay. I can't forget the night every time I am around hay."

"Did you commit to her anything?"

Chet shook his face. "We said we'd write. I was on the go and no letters followed me I guess. I thought she had gone back to her *hacienda* for good. When I got back to Tubac she'd written two letters to me. Boy I was elated. She had a plan to have guards take her to the border. Could I pick her up there? I said I'd send Jesus to go get her, and Ortega's wife Maria told me I had to go get her myself. If it was her and I'd sent some guy to go get her, she'd have gone back home."

"Were you married right off?"

"No, she had a large *hacienda* she had left her brother-in-law to run. But she wanted to see if we were really made for each other. So in time we were married in her church."

"Tell him about her husband," Jesus said.

"Three years before we met, some bandits came to the *hacienda* and knocked on the door. He went to answer it and they gunned him down. She met two of them on the stairs and gunned them down and shot the third one coming back in the house stepping over her husband's bloody body."

"That is tough. She really had things hard and was strong enough to win."

Chet stretched his tight back muscles. "In the first

place her husband kidnapped her from a dance and then took off. Married her in a small Catholic chapel and took her back as his wife to his *hacienda*."

"I'd say she was used to short courtships."

"She told me later that she worried I'd think badly about her boldness, but she feared she would lose me forever in the short time we would be together that day and night."

"You are a lucky guy. You pulled up roots in Texas and came here and haven't had a bad day yet."

"The day I got shot I thought was going to be my last day."

"I've never been shot. But I never have been in law enforcement, either."

"It will damn sure make you a lot more cautious."

"I bet so. I need to talk to JD's wife—her name is Bonnie, right?"

"She will tell you she does not miss the fast life and will even tell Rebecca that, too, if you think it will help."

"I don't want to lose her, but I fear she may go back. There's lots she's never told me, and I fear about her past."

"You want some time off?" Chet asked.

"No. I am who I am. I wanted this job and that is how I'll earn my living until you get tired of me. I am not going back to construction or being a cowboy unless I have to. With this job I can afford to support her. It might not be enough for her, but we won't starve."

"Good luck," Chet said, grateful that Spencer was staying with them.

They reached Hayden's Ferry, caught a meal, and reloaded on the southbound Tucson coach. They made Papago Wells and later in the night, Tucson. Chet got them all rooms and made plans to meet them for breakfast. Then he fell into bed and was asleep fast.

CHAPTER 2

His coffee the next morning in Tucson tasted good and the *huevos rancheros* with fresh pork sausage filled the gap in his belly. "I want to talk to my attorney, here, Russell Craft, about Buster Weeks and his gang. See what he knows about his activity while we are here. Lawyers hear a lot others don't get to. You two can rest or see the town. We can meet for lunch at Jesus's cousin's café. All right?"

"Sure. Or we can go down to the *barrio* and maybe learn something, too," Jesus said.

"Good idea. Tomorrow we can go to Tubac and see if the Force is there. The women will be there, and they will have horses for us to ride over the hills to Diablo if the men are not there."

Chet found Russell at his office, and he greeted Chet with a smile and handshake. "I don't see much of you anymore?"

"I have been building a stage line from Gallup, New Mexico, to the Colorado River."

"I read you had some problems up there. That parallels the route planned for the railroad."

"Yes, it does. Too many problems starting up, but we've solved them for now. We are using buckboards now for the mail, but in a short while it will be a stage line."

"That train may never get there at the rate it's building track."

"You are right. Things are about at a standstill."

"What can I do for you?"

"I am having old problems return. My foreman on the Diablo was recently shot by some of Buster Weeks's so-called employees from across the border. What do you know about him and his dealings?"

"Not very much. There are some Arizona warrants out for his arrest, but he pays officials well enough in Mexico to remain at large."

"They foreclosed on his ranches above Oracle?"

"Yes. And he was not in good shape financially when he lost his hold on that place. Old Man Clanton's hold on the beef markets for the army and the Indians in this area is very strong, and you have the only other large cattle sales Clanton doesn't have in the territory."

"I never understood why the government does business with him, but he must have connections. He also knows how hard the Navajo Agency is to get to, to deliver cattle to from down here, and besides that they have four delivery points to serve up there, not just one."

"Oh, I've never heard a bad word about your deal. In fact, it runs so smoothly you actually scare people off who would love to have it."

"Good. That's the plan. My brother-in-law Sarge Polanski is a real hand at cattle delivery."

"Must be. As for Weeks and those two ranches, two banks split those ranches of his.

Arizona First has one; the Tucson Territorial Bank has the north one."

"Any idea what they would have to have for them?"

"Not much. Bankers don't like cactus spines in their boots. You know what I mean?"

"Yes. Price them. I'll be back. Get a guaranteed list of the cattle, horses, any assets owned, and the private land in each. I might be interested if I could make them work."

"No problem. That might be fun. I'll try to get you low dollar. You will be back when?"

"I hope in a week, but however long it takes, it takes. I'd like to get this Weeks's rustling stopped so ranchers can go on with their business and not get shot at."

"I understand that nephew of yours is really shaping that place up."

"He really has taken an interest in it."

"I met them at a social thing here in town. He has a very lovely wife."

"Her name is Bonnie."

"Yes, I remember. Well, he must really work hard. They don't attend many things up here."

"He takes his job real seriously. Thanks for your time. I was in town and wanted to drop by. And know that I am very serious about considering those two places."

"Next time you come by I'll know all about them. Good luck with Buster and his deal."

They shook hands, and Chet left to arrange for a buckboard ride down to Tubac.

After lunch Chet and his men took the hired buckboard, loaded down with their gear, for the Morales Ranch at Tubac. The stock dogs welcomed them when they arrived and two of the men's wives hurried to greet them. No sign of Roamer or the others.

He hugged and kissed both women on their cheeks and thanked them for the warm welcome.

"We always are so glad to see you. We can fix some food in a hurry. I imagine you are tired. How is your lovely Spanish wife Elizabeth," Bronc's wife, Consuela, asked.

"Doing well when I left her."

"Oh, she is so pretty."

He soon learned that his three-man team had gone to check on a smuggling of gold bars operation coming across the border, so that federal agency in charge could get the matter under control. Gold ore could be imported to be smelted with no taxes, but on gold bars there was a U.S. tariff in place.

The Morales women fixed them lunch and Chet said they'd go to see about JD and Bonnie in the morning if the men were not back. Both of the wives were friendly and as usual glad to see them. Jose's wife, Ricky, had a new baby and Chet told them about his loss. They said to tell Liz they would pray for her and understood her sorrow.

Chet could see that even with Maria gone, the place was still running well.

Before, Maria, Ortega's wife, did the cooking and kept the camp, but they had built her a fine *casa* over there at Diablo so she could join her husband. Since then the other two women had taken her place and they knew how. He was pleased that his men had a good haven to come rest there like in the old days.

In the predawn they ate breakfast, saddled horses, and prepared to ride over the desert range of mountains that separated the ranch from Tubac, the old Spanish capital of that region before the United States Government bought the land. The small community sat on the Kings Highway to Mexico City. The border was perhaps forty miles south of there. There was a large Catholic church and mining activity on the mountain east of the village of Tubac, which sat beside the shallow Santa Cruz River going to join the Gila River north of Tucson.

The trail west was single file over the desert mountain range and steep enough in places that the horses were sweaty when they reached the top of the divide. The men rested them in the cooling breezes that the canyon lacked.

"There is a road out of Tucson that goes to the ranch. You have to avoid this range of hills, but it is longer, so this is a shortcut," Chet said to Spencer, who was making his first trip to the Diablo Ranch.

Jesus spoke up, "This man they talk about, Weeks's foreman, Masters, tried to ambush us on this trail coming up here one time."

"You guys have had lots of fun, haven't you?"

Chet nodded. "And tough times. But a stagecoach guard shot Masters a few months after we took over the ranch, when he tried to hold up a stage east of Tucson."

"No one missed him, I bet?"

"Not the Diablo Ranch people," Jesus said. "He raped and got many of their wives pregnant. They hated him. They were glad when Weeks and Masters were gone."

"Sounds like one nice guy," Spencer said as they mounted up again.

"He sure wasn't. And he was a liar," Chet said as he led the way downhill on his horse. "That place had set empty for years. They slipped a deed into the county courthouse files that included the headquarters where we are headed for today. No one had any idea how it got in there, and I hired my lawyer to object since the man who owned it was in California and had a legal deed for all that land. We won the case and bought Weeks's cattle after a certified count was made. It of course was way short of the bank's inventory."

"Nice guy. What about the other ranches he had?"

"We may go look at them when things settle down here."

"You have never seen them?"

"No, but we have crossed them and they look like great desert grassland to me."

"He lost them, too?" Spencer asked.

"The banks foreclosed on him for nonpayment I understand. Then they split them apart so each bank has one of them."

"What do they want for them?"

"My lawyer Russell is looking into it for me. We may examine them when we go back to Tucson and before we head home."

Spencer shook his head. "More ranches. How many are you going to buy?"

"Only the ones that touch mine," Chet said. He and Jesus laughed.

Spencer smiled. "Sounds like more work to me."

"He will find it," Jesus said.

They reached the Diablo Ranch about noontime. Blond-headed Bonnie saw them coming and shouted, "JD, your uncle is here."

A cheer went up. Someone rang a schoolhouse bell and Chet grinned. They were at last at Diablo, and the fun times would begin.

Off his horse, he swung the slightly pregnant Bonnie in a slow circle and kissed her. "You look lovely, darling."

"No. I am, as you can tell, with another baby—but very happy and so glad you came. We will have a *fiesta* tonight with all my *companeros*."

"Yes, of course." He threw his hat in the air and the lined-up workers and wives plus children shouted hurrah. JD was hugging and patting his back so glad to see him.

"How is—" Then he saw Ortega with Maria at his side on one crutch crossing the yard to join him.

"*Compadre*, so good to see you are up. How is your leg?"

"Getting better. Now we both have been shot, huh?"

They laughed and he kissed Maria on the cheek. "You look beautiful."

She blushed.

"Come to the house," JD said after meeting Spencer and sharing handshakes with Jesus.

Boys took their horses and they went toward Bonnie's large house to talk things over. She was already busy making plans for the night's event with those who he considered the leading workers' wives. She soon finished and joined them, hugging Chet's arm and leading him, with the others following, to the dining room table where she left them and went off to order lunch.

JD told them the rustler story and the fact he had learned they were Weeks's men who had died in the gunfight, the one that the boys hung as well. Before the story was over someone had fetched the two boys who were with Ortega and brought them to Chet. Chet stood up and shook each of their hands.

"We are very proud of the job you two did in Mexico. You have broken the rustlers' desire, I hope, to come and steal our cattle. Thanks so much for taking care of my old *compadre* here and getting him safely home. You are men now, and I am so glad you work for all of us here at the ranch."

They thanked him and excused themselves, beaming as they left.

The day continued. Chet took a *siesta* and woke up with music coming from the pavilion JD had built to hold such events. When he got up and went into the kitchen, he found Bonnie busy frosting cakes with two girls helping her. She stopped and asked him how he felt.

"Oh, I'll be fine. Long stagecoach rides make me

stiff for a while. I don't sleep well being gone from my wife, either."

"Did the doctor say why she lost the baby?"

"I think he told her he did not know but that it happens often and was not her fault. She's taken it hard."

"I am surprised you left her."

"I couldn't do any more for her, and she told me to go because she knew I wanted to know all about the rustling. She also said she wanted me to make sure Ortega was really okay."

"We appreciate your concern and are always glad to see you."

"I think, in time, she will be fine. Depressed yes, for now, especially since she'd never carried a near full-term baby before and to then lose it."

"I'd be sad, too. The rest of us have been lucky. Robert's wife had a girl?"

"Caroline."

"We never hear much about them. She's Mormon?"

"They get along fine. She told me none of her girlfriends have anything like her big company house and none of their husbands have his income. Betty is happy and makes coffee for him and for me when I go there."

"Big tall blond girl. I recall her from the dances I attended down at Camp Verde. She was quite pretty."

"Yes, she is a darling. Her family and friends were opposed to her marrying him because he was not a Mormon. But they have a great life together."

"That sounds great. Lucy and Shawn?"

"We have not heard about her baby. It should be here."

"Your sister?"

"Susie is fine. Her boy is growing, too."

"I hate being isolated from everyone, but I love this ranch and all the things happening here. The good things anyhow. You know we will have our own oranges and lemons next year and even some grapes they say."

"The place looks so well planned and well kept. I am proud of all he gets done."

"Those two men together have made some real strides in the cattle sales since you told them they needed to do that."

"I noticed in the ranch books that you did that, too."

"They have butchers in town that want our cattle, and the Globe deal is taking more since they saw our quality. We don't deliver them any skinny stolen Mexican cattle."

"That's what they needed to do. I knew they would when they realized the cost of ranching and how many we had to sell."

She looked around to be sure they were alone. "JD takes more time for me now, too. He is relaxing more about the ranch operation, letting others do the work. He is managing people now and is handling the job well. I think you should know that. And more important, he plays with his son a lot and is a much better husband to me. You know what I mean?"

"Still praying together?"

"Yes. Every night and God bless him he lives that life now, too."

At the celebration, Chet danced with some of the wives, spoke with some of the hands he knew, met others, and the music went on and on. Jesus joined him.

"I think some women have Spencer in their web tonight," Jesus said.

"I noticed there were some women around him."

"We've all found someone at one of these and never saw her again, huh?" Jesus asked.

Chet nodded. "I met one in New Mexico coming west with the family one night at the Bernalillo Ferry across the Rio Grande. They were having a celebration and invited me. Lovely widow woman—never saw her again. Her name has even evaporated."

"Did you and that tall Navajo lady ever have an affair?" Jesus asked him.

"No, but we thought about it. She had deep concerns over her people and she didn't want to give that up. I saw what she was doing, and linked to a white man would only have diminished her power among her people. I understood that."

"She is six foot tall, too."

"Every bit of that. Liz even asked me if we had an affair in the past when she met her for the first time up at Center Point. I told her no and why."

"What comes next?"

"A good plan to watch the south end of the ranch with more help stationed down there. Mexico is lots stricter on anyone crossing their border, and any raid we'd make down there might bring us more trouble. We will reinforce the southern border of our ranch and stop any more invasions into our side."

Jesus nodded he understood. They'd figure a way to stop the stealing of cattle.

CHAPTER 3

The next day he and JD set up a three-camp idea on the border, each manned by three men to keep an eye on the goings and comings of any rustlers until any threat was over. That was the best solution they could figure out for the time being.

This plan was going to work, JD agreed. Chet and his men planned to ride into Tucson and, using the Force's horses if they needed, look at any of the ranches Russell found for them. Later when they returned to Preskitt Chet could hire boys to have them taken back to Tubac. That all set they went on visiting. Much later that morning Spencer came out of hiding—hungover and no words were exchanged about his absence. He agreed to the border guard plan and after supper they turned in early for a quick start to their ride into Tucson.

The next morning Bonnie and two of the wives had made them a fancy casserole breakfast of scrambled eggs, sausage, onions, sweet and hot peppers with cheese, and Arbuckle coffee plus sweet rolls. They left stuffed full for the ride to Tucson.

They arrived late that evening, put the horses up, ate at Jesus's cousin's diner, and slept in hotel beds. After breakfast the following morning, Chet met with his lawyer Russell in his office.

"Well they have that ranch north of Mount Lemons sold to an eastern buyer. That has the house that Weeks built for his wife. You know her?"

Chet shook his head. He did but didn't even want to talk about her destruction of Reg.

"I'll think of her name in a minute. She's a big man around town's daughter. A very attractive woman. They have a ranch up near Hackberry, too."

Chet finally admitted, "I know about her. She was the one who really messed up my nephew Reg. I guess she messed up Buster, too."

"Well after she left him, he and all his deals went to hell. I knew he was over-financed but I figured he'd climb out of it. After she left him, I think he fell off the wagon and went to staying drunk, not minding his business and so it all failed."

"I will think of her name. As I said, she did the same thing to my nephew. She's a black widow. He was running our place up there near Hackberry and when she spurned him he ended up committing suicide."

"I didn't know about that, but I do know that when Weeks lost her he lost his way. That house place had a great view of all the country north of Lemon. I think it's what sold that place so quickly and that the bank might come out with very little loss. On the other hand Rob Nye at the Tucson Territorial Bank has the number two ranch. I don't think much besides the ranch land is up there. I heard the ranch houses are old adobe jackals and nothing as nice as on number one."

"The banker want to sell it?"

"He is no cowboy. Acted like he'd sell it cheap and cut his losses. But you can talk to him. He'll be in his office. Nye's an on-the-up-and-up guy to me."

"I'll do that. Thanks. What do I owe you?"

"Nothing. Come by more often to talk and tell your lovely wife I said hello."

"I can do that."

A young man met him in the Tucson Territorial Bank lobby and asked if he could help him.

"I'd like to see Mr. Nye. Is he available?"

"I think so. Let me check. Who may I say is calling?"

"Chet Byrnes of Preskitt."

"Nice to meet you, sir."

In a short while he was ushered into Nye's office. A large portly man rose up and shook his hand firmly. "Nice to meet you, sir. What can I do for you?"

Chet took the seat indicated before the desk as Nye sat back in the chair. "My lawyer told me you had Weeks's ranch number two for sale north of Oracle."

"Number two is right. They got the gold and I've got the shaft. He tell you they have a buyer ready to pay full price for number one because they've got that damn fancy house that he fixed up for the rich bitch he married and who shortly after that divorced him?"

"He did. Weeks is not the only one she screwed up. My nephew had the same fate and he never even married her."

"I would not have kicked her out of bed. But she's something else. Originally, in the second ranch deal, Weeks messed me up on it by bringing his cattle from the first place onto that land, joining with the cattle already there, making the herd look big. My men are bankers. They're not cowboys and never noticed different brands while they were counting the cattle. I thought they'd got a good count, but it was two herds."

"So what do you have left?"

"A count short of a hundred cows. Probably all culls. I have a good man running the ranch. He made a list of the cows and he reported many were old ones. You may go look but there is no *hacienda*-like setting for the headquarters, only some jackals. Seriously, there is a solid title to all the lots of land with it, but it is all cactus country. The deed calls for thirty sections."

"Is it a good deed? That's over twenty thousand acres."

"I know that part is good. We double checked the deed and it is all legal."

"I am interested."

"What would you do with it?"

"That is a big ranch. Let me go look at it and I'll be back. What was the first ranch's size?"

"As I recall like four sections."

"And they never offered this buyer your place to join it?"

"Not to my knowledge. I have the most land but I don't have the headquarters."

"As I said, let me go up there and look. We, maybe, could partner on that place or something."

"I have been to that house Weeks built on Mount Lemon. He spent a fortune on it. It has running water, a boiler to heat water for bathing, and lots of glass, which cost a fortune to get freighted out here. Mexican floor tile and lots more. He made a castle out there for her."

"Did she live in it?"

"For about a year I think and then she divorced him. She left after that and went up to their north place. You know anything more about her?"

"I have no idea, just rumors from the cowboys that work for me."

"Go look at my ranch. I have heard all about your ability to make ranches work." Nye showed him the land map of the place, and Chet wondered how it became deeded land. A U.S. Government land swap that had, no doubt, been made years ago.

"That big maybe you could find a way to make it work?"

"So far I've made all my others work." He rose, shook Nye's hand, and went to find his men.

He found them at the café.

"Well, boss, what now?" Jesus asked.

"I am posting a letter to my wife, telling her we are taking a few more days. Then we are riding up north of Oracle to look at a ranch."

"How big?" Spencer asked.

"Thirty sections."

"Wow, that is lots of land."

"All desert the banker says. They have some jackals for headquarters. He said Weeks spent a fortune on the house up on Mount Lemon's back side for a woman he married and who divorced him in a year.

That is why the rich eastern man is buying the place. There are only four sections in it."

"How did they get so much land in the other ranch?"

"The federal government has made some land swaps. The ranch Lucy and Shawn run was one that Bo bought for me. Obviously the government wanted some piece of land somewhere else and the owner of that got the land out here for it. Nye is satisfied the deed is good. How Weeks found it I don't know. But he obviously got it for a song and then mortgaged it to Nye along with livestock they counted twice. The other bank got the smaller place with the great homestead."

"Counted twice?"

"Yeah, they did that to Nye and I bet Weeks did it to the other banker, too."

"How?"

"Nye told me his bankers didn't read the brands. They counted legs and divided by four."

Everyone laughed and shook their heads as full plates of Mexican food were brought over by the girls.

"You need more let us know," the lead waitress said. "The boss says you are such good customers, to feed you more."

"*Gracias,*" Chet said.

She and the other girls left them to eat their lunch.

After an early breakfast the following morning, they rode north with bedrolls on behind their cantles. Jesus had some good beef jerky and dried fruit for them to eat. Canteens full, they left Tucson behind and went around the mountains for Oracle and on north.

This region had saguaros, prickly pear patches, lots of grass, plus yucca stalks. It also had the century plants that bloomed once in a lifetime and died. Apache squaws used to dig up the plants and make a weak beer out of the roots. Chet never knew how, but he heard stories from some Apache army scouts who told him this is what the squaws did. An occasional patch of tall gnarled cottonwood marked the watering spots for wildlife and livestock in washes and even where springs popped up.

He was impressed when he saw several tanks of mortar and rocks had been built below a spring to water stock, too. There was plenty of grass and he liked the rangeland. The cows they saw when they reached what he considered the property line bore the W—W brand. They were old longhorn cows with great horns, and the bulls were mixed in with the longhorn stock. Certainly not the genetic route to better beef cattle, a big factor in what their offspring were worth on any market.

"Them cows have lots of age on them," Spencer said. "I'd be surprised they can still have calves."

"There was talk about old longhorns in Texas that were able to have calves until they were thirty-five or older."

"These are getting close. Why so many old ones?"

"He probably bought them as cheap cows to mortgage. Bankers are not cattle graders."

"He always has been a damn crook, hasn't he?" Spencer asked.

"Taken the easy way to go."

Near dark they reached the shabby headquarters and met the foreman Nye had told him about, Frisco Johns, a squat-built Mexican who greeted them with a big smile. "What can I do for you, señor?"

"Mr. Nye said to come meet you. My name is Chet Byrnes. The good-looking guy is my man Jesus and that other *hombre* is Spencer who rides with us."

"You come to look at the ranch, señor?"

"Yes. For several reasons. One is what can be done with it? The second one how to do it and what can we do to get that done?"

Amused by Chet's words, Frisco smiled at him. "Most *gringos* come here ask where the ranch house is?"

"I can see that. Where should it be?"

"The man who owned it before Weeks bought it never lived out here. He and his wife lived in Oracle and his *vaqueros* lived out here. He said his wife thought this place was too close to hell for her to live way out here and too far from town to drive for groceries."

"You worked for him?"

"As a boy, yes, but I left when he got too old and my uncle who ran it retired to Mexico. I came back here later to run the ranch, but when Weeks bought this place he fired me. Said I made too much money and he hired boys in Mexico for little money to be his cowboys. He fed them beans and paid them ten dollars a month.

"I talked to Señor Nye when his bank repossessed it, and he hired me and I found some good men to work, but now there are only eighty cows left. Before we ran four hundred cows and had grass. But now—

"Come inside. My wife will fix all of you some food. We can talk more. There is hay and water in the big pen for your horses."

"I can put up the horses," Jesus said in the last red light of sundown.

"No. One of my men, Baca, can do it. Come, the three of you, be my guests."

Chet thanked the man taking the horses. Then they went inside the adobe house.

A bright-faced woman with a straight back greeted them. She was considerably younger than her husband, her dark hair pinned severely back, but her smile was warm and she was very attractive.

"This is Rosa. Rosa, these are Señor Byrnes, Jesus, and Spencer."

"Chet, ma'am, and nice to meet you."

"Welcome to my house. I don't have much company so it is a pleasure to meet you three men. Why are they here, Frisco?"

"Señor Nye sent them to look over the ranch and see what could be done with it."

"Did you tell them to go to Apache Springs and start all over?"

"Where is that, ma'am?" Chet asked.

"He can show you. Long ago the Apaches used it as a shrine or something. Everyone is afraid the Apaches would come back and burn him or her out if they built there. But now they are about all gone, who would care?"

"That danger is past."

"I can show you the place tomorrow," Frisco said.

"Good idea. Thanks, Rosa."

She smiled. "See, Frisco, I told you someday a smart man would come here and believe me."

He laughed. "She has said that for years."

"You two have been married for years?" Chet asked.

"Yes. Bandits killed her family in Mexico. I found her." He turned to her. "You were how old?"

"Thirteen. He really did save me or I would have died."

"I told her she could not live with me. She said marry me. I had no one. But I said I can't I am old enough to be your father."

"I said he was not my father and had no family to stop him."

Frisco agreed with her story and continued, "So we went to a priest and told him to marry us. He said no she is too young."

She came back. "So I said, no problem. I would go on living with him as his wife anyway. So he married us."

"That was a lie, but he married us. And we have been man and wife for fourteen years now."

"No children?" Chet asked.

"Not one ever lived."

"My wife lost one before I left Preskitt. She was married before, but her husband was killed and they never had any children."

"That is a shame but nothing you could do," she said, motioning for them to sit at the table. "The *frijoles* are hot."

"And we're hungry," Jesus said, then bowed his head and crossed himself.

"You have a wife?"

"A new one, Anita, yes, and she lives in Preskitt."

"I bet you men have pictures of them. After supper show me them."

"I don't have one of mine but she is a nice lady," Spencer said.

Chet showed her his wife's photo and she oh'd and ah'd. "My, such a beautiful woman. Where did you meet her?"

"Tubac. She came by our camp looking to buy a horse, and after that we were married."

"And your wife?" she asked Jesus.

"Anita was her maid."

"Wonderful stories. And yours?" she asked Spencer.

"We met on a stagecoach going to Preskitt."

"Oh, my, not one she-lived-next-door stories among you three." She laughed and took a seat.

"See, she has no one to talk to out here but me," Frisco said. "And she knows all my stories."

"Hey, she's a great cook and a sweet lady, you better appreciate her while you have her," Spencer said. "Good women are hard to find."

They all laughed.

He offered them hammocks set up in the yard and they accepted. She promised she'd have breakfast ready at daylight.

They woke early, saddled the horses, washed up, and ate her breakfast of oatmeal with raisins and brown sugar. Chet had a plan that three of Frisco's *vaqueros* joined them.

Chet told Frisco he wanted each of his men to

ride with a ranch hand and see as much as they could. He and Frisco would go to the springs Rosa had talked about. She cheered at that announcement. The hands laughed.

For a while, there was nothing but some hills. Chet and Frisco rode side by side until, all of a sudden, they rode up a canyon lined with huge gnarled cottonwoods. There were lots of places for a big house and a spring-fed lake in the middle. Most would've called it a cow tank, but it was natural and maybe covered an acre or more. The water spilled from the spring into a real long man-made rock and mortar trough that could be accessed from either side for animals to drink. The water went out the end of the structure and disappeared in the ground.

Yes, this cove would make a great headquarters. It would need a road cut into it and some arranging, but it would be so much better than that dust bowl where they built the original, where Frisco's jackal stood.

"Did Nye ever see this?"

Frisco shook his head. "He was not interested in spending a nickel more on this place."

"How much to build a road into here from the current one?"

"Five hundred dollars."

"Do it. Rosa will have her wish."

He shook his head. "She will be hard to live with until it is built."

Chet laughed and clapped him on the back, returning to their horses. "Ah, a good wife. We are lucky we both have great ones."

"You are a much different man than I expected

to meet. I have heard about the big ranches you own and how tough you are. I don't doubt you could be tough, but you didn't come up here and insult me, push me away, or swagger around like Weeks always did."

"Why do that? If I take on a business I want it to make money—fair enough?"

"I see that. You listened to my wife. Most men would have scoffed at her words. You turned your ears up to hear her part. But you knew women many times will make their men do what they want. The present ranch headquarters looks like a place in Sonora you'd find in the desert. This looks like Fort Huachuca."

Chet nodded. "The cottonwoods and with a large two-story house with sleeping porches."

"What will you do now?" Frisco asked.

"Tell Nye to spend some money. Build a headquarters to show people and buy three hundred mother cows to stock it along with a dozen good bulls. Cull the barren cows. In two years he can sell this place for a fortune to a real rancher."

"If you believe that, then why not buy it yourself and I'll do the rest for you here."

"Where will you get the cows?" Chet asked.

"Socorro, New Mexico. I can buy half to three quarter Hereford and Shorthorn cows up there next fall. Cost twenty-five dollars apiece. None over five years old and bred to a good bull. Now, the road will cost you five hundred dollars or less. How big a house?"

"Six bedrooms."

"I can get some good carpenters up here from

Mexico. Cheap but I really would need a *gringo* to buy the material. If I tried, they would rob me. Do you have one like that works for you?"

Chet nodded. "We can talk to Spencer. He could do it and knows building. Tonight we will ask him."

Frisco grinned. "*Gracias.* I came here because I love this ranch. My family has run this ranch for many years. I would like to run it when it is stocked and a real ranch."

"If I buy it, you will have that chance to make it work."

"*Gracias.*" They shook hands to seal the deal.

That evening he spoke to Spencer and Jesus. "Frisco wants to run the ranch if I buy it. But I would need a construction supervisor for about a year to build the headquarters over at Apache Springs. Frisco is afraid they would cheat him buying material and the like. He can get all the help we need from Mexico."

"Who will ride with you?" Spencer asked.

"Jesus and I will pick up a hand if we need one. Get the house up and you can come back to us. What about Rebecca?"

"She can marry me and be my wife or go her own way. What was this springs place like?"

"A cottonwood tree canyon with maybe an acre or more of natural lake in the center, spring fed, and has a hundred-foot-long watering trough below it someone built years ago. It is a place where the headquarters should have been built."

"Can I go home and ask her first?"

"We have time. I can get a construction man if

you don't want it. We can ride by and see the springs place on the way going back."

"I damn sure want to see it. And Frisco wants to be the foreman here I bet?"

Chet nodded. "I don't figure you want to sit up here and simply be the boss."

Spencer chuckled. "You know me too well now."

"If I can make a deal with Nye when we get back to Tucson, then you decide after we get home. I think this ranch can be a really damn good one."

"Those cows that I have seen are all old. That is no problem. We will buy three hundred cows in the fall over at Socorro, New Mexico. Frisco knows how and when. Meanwhile you put up the headquarters building and we can sell it if we want, or keep it and make it bigger."

"It is damn sure a real grassy place."

"I think the same. Jesus, what do you think?"

"I like it. More water development would help, but we can do that in time, too."

"Good. We will look at things on the way out. Next day see what Nye will take for it. Then we'll know what to do?"

"What is it worth today?"

"I think anywhere from ten to twenty thousand for the land."

Jesus nodded in agreement.

Rosa made them breakfast early and told them to come back and bring their women. She wanted to meet them.

Chet shook the men's hands and thanked them for their help. He told Frisco to look for a yes or no answer at the Oracle post office. The man smiled. "Good to meet you, *hombre.* I will look for it."

They rode off but didn't make it back to Tucson that day, due to delays like looking around and stopping at the springs. His men agreed that the spring's site would make a real salable ranch headquarters. The next day they rode into Tucson, put their horses in the livery, and had lunch. Then Chet went to find the banker.

"Well." Nye closed the office door. "What did you think?"

"Tell me the bottom dollar you'd take for the ranch?"

"Twenty-five thousand."

Chet shook his head. "Too high."

"Twenty?"

"No."

"Fifteen?"

"Twelve thousand," Chet said.

Nye shook his head. "You are a man that I know makes money and I know you can operate ranches. What will you do with it?"

"It is going to require lots of money. Frisco said you didn't want to spend any more money on it."

Nye nodded. "But I can't give it away."

"I'll leave you with an offer of ten thousand dollars for thirty days, clear title and the cattle."

"You offered me twelve once. You are getting cheaper?"

"I'd pay twelve today like this—three thousand now and three thousand every year on January first until the twelve is paid off."

"I'd do that on fifteen thousand. No interest, huh?"

"Thirteen?"

"No. Fourteen and the way you break it down—your deal. You know you are robbing me now."

"Draw up the papers. I will be here in the morning to sign them for fourteen at that same payment schedule."

"What in the hell are you going to do with it?"

"Make it a working ranch."

"Can I have your ranch bank account on it, so I can make some money?"

"I can't move the Diablo one over here. Those folks have been good to me, but I will put this place to bank here."

"What will you call it?"

"Apache Springs Ranch."

Nye shook his head. "We can do all that paperwork tomorrow. I think a master of the arts of finance has scalded me. And I went to college to learn all that."

"Just think, you won't have owning it on your mind anymore?"

"How many men do you have with you?"

"Two of my men who always ride with me."

"Meet me and my wife Helena at the Bull's Head Restaurant at seven thirty. I am buying supper for you and your men."

"We can't dress up. We have no dress clothes with us."

"Tell them you are my guests. It will get you in."

"I heard it was a real fancy place?"

"They take money like the rest of the places. Enough said, see you then."

Chet joined his men. "We have a ranch."

"How much?" Jesus asked.

"Fourteen thousand."

"Wow. You did good."

"I told him to accept it or my next offer was ten."

"And he did," Jesus said. "Well, Spencer, the job building the house is in your pocket."

Spencer looked concerned. "I don't know what Rebecca will say."

"Guess we will learn that later," Jesus said. "Where are we eating?"

"With him and his wife in the Bull's Head Restaurant, seven thirty."

"In our clothing?" Jesus asked in shock.

"We are his guests. He has the money to pay for us he told me."

"I always wanted to eat in there. Tonight I will," Jesus said. "No one I know will ever believe that I ate there."

"I will," Chet said, and they laughed.

CHAPTER 4

Two days later the ranch deal was settled and they rode the stage home. Chet sent Frisco a letter—telling him they'd bought it. A boy was hired to take the horses back to Tubac. The day presented some light rain and cooler weather in their travels. But moisture was a treat to ranch people. So little fell on the territory every drop was appreciated.

He wired from Hayden's Mill about their return. Three buckboards met them. Anita on one for Jesus, Rebecca on another for Spencer, and his own wife, Liz, on the seat of the third one. All were dressed up for the cold spitting snow.

"How are you feeling?" he asked, climbing aboard.

She held the reins. "Very good. Better now you are back. Your things loaded. I can drive. You can tell me about what happened and how Ortega is doing."

He kissed her on the mouth. "Drive on. He is healing fine and they are setting up some guards on the south end to stop any rustling there. We are waiting to see if news of those rustlers' deaths will stop further cattle thieving. And I bought another ranch."

"I expected that. Tell me about it." They rode on under the stars back to the ranch.

Liz said she was interested in seeing it. He agreed to show it to her. "It is a grassy desert ranch, and has a great foreman to run it. His wife, Rosa, asked me to bring you down there. She is a lot younger than he is. Bandits slaughtered her family but she survived the attack. He found her in Mexico and wanted her to go, I guess, to a church shelter. She told him no, she was going with him. He said then she had to marry him. They asked a priest who said at first she was too young. Thirteen I think. She told him that was no problem that she'd live with him anyway. So the priest married them."

"She sounds like a good woman." Liz chuckled.

"Oh, she is very nice and funny, too, despite her isolation. She even told me where to build the new headquarters."

"More money." She shook her head. "I understand you spend money to make money. You also have two long letters from Hannagen at the house, but I did not open them."

"Why not open it?"

"I figured you'd be home sometime and you had to answer them, not me."

"How is Monica?"

"My usual mother, she didn't want me driving into town without a guard."

"You should listen to her."

She elbowed him, but their thick clothing kept it from doing much but making them laugh as she hurried the team through the night to get home. The piney smell in the air made him grateful to be back. That and a small amount of her perfume had caught his nose. Home would be great. Having his wife to sleep with again would be, too.

Monica greeted him and turned on her heels. "Food is in the oven. I will have breakfast early for you."

He ate a portion of the beef and potatoes; then they went to bed with his whiskers and all. She told him he could fix that in the morning.

Next morning he was up before dawn, leaving her sleeping. Monica had breakfast ready along with a thousand questions. He stopped her with a question of his own.

"My wife acts like she is over the matter of the baby. She looks much better. Is she really okay with everything?"

"Yes. She said it had to be behind her. You two had a life to live and she would not miss any of that."

"Thanks." He sipped on his coffee. "I thought so. Hoped so, but wanted to be sure. And I appreciate all you do for her while I am gone, and for us when I am here. Now I need a bath and a shave."

"You need clothes up there?"

"No, I've got some out. I'll be fine. It is good to be home."

"Better to have you here." She poured him more coffee.

"The ranch all right?"

"Fine. Raphael says it is a mild winter. I agree."

"Oh, we will get some big snows, but for now that is holding off."

"Are you off on another wild goose chase soon?"
He laughed. "None that are planned right now."
"Good."

He took the bath, shaved, and regretted his too long hair as he was drying it. Maybe he'd get his wife to cut it. She was better than most barbers. Dressed and in his chair he read the two letters from his stage line partner in Gallup.

Letter one explained the action congress was taking on all telegraph lines proposed nationally. They wanted more of them to connect the U.S. from coast to coast. Many lines were too crowded with messages to really be effective. Others like their project needed to be funded by the government to ever get them affordable for ordinary people's usage. The rest of the letter contained reports from further hearings on the proposed law in both houses of congress.

Hannagen pointed out that since they planned to follow the railroad's eventual route it was an even more feasible project than most that would be used for years.

Letter two contained a bill to be introduced in both houses of congress for ten such projects in the west. Their own route was listed as number three in importance in the list of needed lines, a fact he was excited about, especially with them funding it. This did not mean ready to go. Funding was still needed. That would come from the budget committees. They had nothing until the bill was passed by both sides. Hannagen felt it was going to pass through both houses, so they better be ready to move on everything. Fast.

Meanwhile Chet needed a money account set up at Nye's bank in Tucson to run his new ranch. He also needed an answer from Spencer Horne about him taking the superintendent of building job.

Liz was dressed and came by to kiss him. "Any news, good I mean?"

"Hannagen thinks the bill will pass in this session. The bill to sponsor the telegraph line."

"More work?"

"Yes, more work."

"What happens today?"

"I need to see Tanner at the bank about setting up another account in Tucson for the new ranch project."

"Who is going to run the deal down there?"

"I asked Spencer to build the headquarters, but he is going to ask Rebecca, first, if she'll go along. Yes or no he might decide to do it anyway."

"I tried to talk to her, and she told me she couldn't talk it out. It was too complicated and she said she would simply need to figure it out. Figure out what she really wanted to do with her life. But she did thank me for asking."

"I guess that may be her way."

"I could not believe she would even want to go back to her old life. But I am not her, nor will I ever be that mixed up."

"Obviously it is something that really bothers her."

"She said when her husband was killed that she had no money and felt it was the only way to go. Spencer talked her into quitting before she even started working, but now she feels perhaps she should not have done that."

"He's going to find out what she intends to do before he gives me his answer about the ranch headquarters building. This man Frisco wants to be the foreman but thought they might skin him on buying supplies to build it. They won't touch Spencer. But it may all lie in her answers if she'd go along or not."

"Then who would ride with you besides Jesus?"

"I can get someone until he gets the place built. It was provisional. He'd come back with me if he wanted to after the job was completed."

"I think you sure need a good second man to back Jesus. Let's run into town. Eat lunch at Jenn's. She will want to hear about the baby and what you can tell her about her daughter who is expecting again."

"She really is. And she laughs about it if you can imagine that."

Liz nodded she knew. "I can. She is very dedicated to JD and their life."

"Absolutely so. That ranch has turned the corner financially. Finally."

"I will get dressed. Has Raphael been here?"

"Not yet. But he must be busy."

"I know he wants to talk to you."

"I can catch him later."

"I am going to get dressed for the cold."

The weather had warmed up some by then. Solar heat on their left side going in made their clothes seem much too warm as they got to town.

Chet arranged to set up an account for the Apache Springs Ranch and for a money transfer to Nye's bank to start it.

Tanner was excited to talk about his own news.

"Confidentially, Kay and I were married quietly by the JP, and I really appreciate having a wife as good as she is. Marriage is a great experience."

"Well, best of luck to you both." Chet didn't approve of her and the things in her past but it was not his choice, and he really liked Tanner. Poor man probably never had a woman in his life before her.

"Thanks. I saw how happy you are with your wife. I never believed I'd ever find one, so I am sure pleased to have her."

"Good. I'll tell you more about the new ranch later. Liz is waiting."

"I will be anxious to hear about it. Thanks for all your business, Chet."

Back in the buckboard he went by Bo's land office and they both went inside.

"How are you, Liz? And I see you finally made it back?" he said, appraising Chet.

"I sure did." He shook the tall man's hand. "How are the wife and boy?"

"Amazing. Absolutely amazing. He is growing like a weed. He'll be walking soon I'd bet."

"Well, I bought thirty sections of grassy range north of Mount Lemon last week."

"Did you get it cheap?"

"Fourteen thousand."

"You stole it. Need anything from me?"

"No, it has a good deed and I think it was a bargain. What else?"

"I bought five more homesteads all complete by the new east place. What's wrong with that country?"

"Too isolated. No place to earn a dime."

"I guess you're right. Three more for Sarge and two for Shawn up there."

"They've been notified?"

"Oh, I don't buy them unless I have one of them look at the place first. Then I send them a letter so they know they have been purchased."

"My checkerboard ranches."

"Hey, some day they will all be worth much more than I pay for them. Having this deed land wouldn't be a bad idea."

"I am in full agreement. Keep up the good work."

"Tell me what the place ailed from that you bought down there?"

"No headquarters and isolated but it has grass and water."

"Show me on the wall map where it is at."

He went over and traced the line of the road out of Oracle. "See this place?"

"That is deeded land. You must've done well. Boy it is all in one block, too."

"I call it the Apache Springs Ranch."

"Come have supper with us one evening. I know my wife wants to talk to Liz."

"Set a time and date with her and we will do that."

"I sure will."

"We better get back home." His wife agreed and they left for the ranch.

When they got back one of the boys put the team up and Raphael joined them. Chet invited him in to talk with him. A chill was beginning to set in as the sun slipped down.

"Is anything wrong?" Chet asked his man.

"No. But you one time said I should pick a man to learn my place. I have such a man now who could do that job. He is young but he will learn how. My bones are getting tired. I get up sore and maybe in my mind I forget some things. I feel it is time to start turning my job over to that man, but before I do, I want him to learn by riding for a time with you."

"Who is he?"

"Miguel Costa who is married to the woman Lisa Foster that you brought back here. She already has settled enough to lead the other women. He and she make a good team together."

"Will it make the others unhappy? He is younger than most of them."

"Some but they are not foreman material. You have to tell them how to do it every time. That is not a foreman. They need to be helpers."

"Proceed with your project. If you think he would be good, then I agree."

"*Gracias*. I will prepare him for it and tell him he will be riding with you."

Good. With that matter settled, he went back to look at his books. They needed to be brought up to date. More money had shown up from the Navajo Cattle Sales script redemption. The government was shortening the time they must wait for their money. That was all right as well.

He ate supper with Liz and then worked a few hours more. She filed the papers he recorded until she finally coaxed him to quit and go to bed.

"Everything is fine so far."

"Biggest thing happening is the Diablo cattle sales that are covering their costs down there at last."

"So now we will have a new ranch to drain us."

"Not drain but grow into another paying operation."

"I understand that, too. You do well at this business and all the traveling, but I like you home with me, too."

"I try."

"I know."

Now all he needed was to hear from Spencer and his decision, so he could move on it and get to cut out a real ranch down there.

They went off to sleep in each other's arms.

CHAPTER 5

Spencer was on the porch waiting for Chet when he got up the next morning. Bundled up in a long tailcoat and more clothes on under that against the frosty morning, Spencer rose to his feet when Chet told him to get inside. Monica who'd overslept came hustling into the kitchen and looked hard at Spencer. "What're you here for?"

"To tell the boss man I'm taking the job."

"What will Rebecca do?"

He shook his head wearily. "I guess go back to Texas. She has not decided what she wants to do."

"Really?"

"I told her I had a job to build a ranch headquarters and we'd have to live down there until it was done, that we would be roughing it for a while but I'd get the bunkhouse done fast, for us to have a home. She said that wasn't the way she wanted to live. Made me sad but I gave her the money for her fare back home and told her thanks."

"But you are still going to build the ranch headquarters?" Chet asked.

"Yes."

"You want anything out of that house in town hauled out here and stored?"

"No. The landlord can have it."

"We need to notify him to find a new renter."

"I can do that," Spencer said. "Some things don't work is all there is to it."

"I have an account started at Nye's bank for the new ranch. Write me your plans as you go."

"Can I talk to you alone?"

"Sure."

They went in the living room.

"I want to know something. There is a widow woman named Lucinda Marcos down at the Diablo. Her husband got killed in a horse accident a year ago and she has two small kids. Would it be all right for me to go ask her to marry me and live on the new ranch while I build it?"

"Fine with me. Do what you have to do and explain it in your letter when you get started."

"I'll buy a wagon and team in Tucson, get her and the kids, and get back up there."

"No. I'll pay for the wagon, harness, and team. You just make sure you get a good one. You will need it for supplies anyway. Buy an army wall tent and what you need to set up a camp for living quarters. Keep me informed how things go."

Spencer shook his hand. "Thanks, I can do that."

"Breakfast is ready," Monica announced.

"We're coming."

They ate breakfast and Spencer left for town to close things up.

"What did he find out?" Liz asked when she came down to join him.

"Permission to go get a widow woman from Diablo and marry her."

"So soon?"

"I think he already knew the last one wouldn't stay with him."

"Rebecca sounded very much undecided about staying with him or going somewhere else when we talked." Liz shook her head in disappointment.

Chet agreed and hugged her. "He has his own life to live."

She agreed.

Late in the afternoon a man on a weary horse reined up at the barns and told one of the stable boys that he needed to talk to Chet Byrnes. A youth ran to the house and told Monica a man was there to talk to the *patron*. Monica took the boy to the living room, where Chet was finishing the books.

"You know this man?" he asked the boy.

He shook his head.

"I better go see who he is."

Monica frowned. "I'd wear a gun."

"I can do that." He strapped on his gun belt from the hook, put on a jumper against the cool air, and went outside.

The man, in his rather shabby dressed appearance, got up and came over. "My name is Harry Olson. You never heard of me I bet, but I've heard of you, Mr. Byrnes, and I rode up here to see if you could help me."

"What sort of a problem do you have, sir?"

"My wife Marcella was kidnapped by some outlaws.

I reported it to the law and they said she'd probably run off with them."

"Where do you live?"

"Maricopa County. Between Hayden's Mill and Mesa."

"The law told you that?" Chet could hardly believe a lawman would do that.

"A deputy sheriff told me that when I said I knew someone had kidnapped my wife. I know it was a kidnapping because the neighbors heard her screaming that day and then she was gone. They told me so. She'd've never left me on purpose. She was kidnapped."

"Any idea who they were?"

"If I had, I would have gone after her myself. Instead I rode up here."

"You eaten anything lately?"

"Some jerky."

"Come with me." He went up the porch stairs, making sure the man was following him.

At the door he stopped. "Aw, Mr. Byrnes, I can't come into your house."

Monica was standing in the kitchen doorway, blocking it, watching.

"Come on, Monica. Harry has not eaten a meal in the long ride up here. Fix him some food. Please?"

"What?"

Chet was hanging up his gun belt and jumper in the hall. "Anything you have."

"Breakfast?"

"Fine."

"I didn't—" Harry started to say.

Chet sat him down at the table. "I don't know what we can find out about your wife's kidnapping, but we could go down and try to investigate her disappearance."

"I'd sure appreciate it. I heard you rounded up many criminals, and they said you lived up here. It was a further piece than what folks said it would be, but a man on the road pointed your place out to me."

"You farm down there?"

"I do, sir. I raise hawgs. Fatten shoats and butcher them and I smoke some hams. Lots of Mexican people live around me and buy my meat. No big business but we don't starve."

"How old is your wife?"

"Eighteen."

"You been married for a long time?"

"No, sir. About six months. Marcella has been a great wife and never minded our hard life. She really dressed up my house. Nothing like this one though."

"Where did she come from?"

"Texas."

"How did she get here?"

"She was the second oldest of eleven kids. They came there by wagon. Her paw wanted to raise cotton. He rented a farm by me. I courted her and she accepted my proposal. We got married in the Good Will Church.

"That deputy said she just run away. Said that women did it all the time. Marcella would never run away. I swear she'd never do that."

"Where were you when they kidnapped her?"

"I went to buy some barley at Hayden's Mill for my hawgs. That trip took me all day to go and come back with my wagon loaded. When I got home Marcella was gone. There were three horses' tracks in my yard and around the house. My neighbors heard her scream but never saw them when they did it. I trailed them east for a while but lost them in the dark."

"Why would they kidnap her?"

"I don't know." He shook his head. "Marcella was real pretty."

"She not have any jewelry or money?"

"No. I am a hawg farmer. How could I have any money for that?"

"Could you have anything worthwhile they might have wanted?"

"Nothing but her. Nothing is missing that I could see."

"My man and I will be there in a few days. I need to close up some business here first. I can't promise you anything, but we will investigate and do all we can to find her."

"Thank you, sir. I will ride home and wait for you."

"No. When you finish this food, you won't leave yet. My foreman, Raphael, will find you a bed and you are to get some rest. In the morning, he will see you are fed, have a sound horse to ride, and have food to supplement your ride home."

"I didn't come for charity. I just want her back." He looked close to crying. "I am grateful, sir."

"Harry, I want you to know we might never find any trace of her. The trail is cold by now and their purpose unknown. But we will look."

Harry Olson rode a ranch horse for home the next day. Chet hoped he didn't freeze to death going back. He and Jesus would be there in two more days. Looking at a cold, cold trail. That would be all he could think about. They'd try . . .

CHAPTER 6

He and Jesus took the Black Canyon Stage to Hayden's Mill. The driver unloaded their saddles, rifles, and bedrolls on the ground. Jesus went to rent them horses. A cold north wind with sand bits on the drafts stung Chet's cheeks while he stood there guarding their gear pooled on the ground.

The agent holding on to his celluloid visor came out and told him bring their things inside.

"I am sorry, Mr. Byrnes. I hate he dumped your things out there. You're one of our best customers. I'll help you get your things into the depot inside." Soon all their stuff was inside. It took Jesus twenty more minutes to arrive with the horses he rented. He complained, "They aren't much."

They saddled them and took to the road. Late afternoon they found Olson's hog farm.

"I knew we were close." Jesus wrinkled his nose.

Smoke ascended from the tin chimney of a sheet iron–covered small dwelling. Harry welcomed them in, and Chet could hardly believe what he saw. The interior was all very clean and neat, freshly painted with bright curtains. Those must be her marks on the place.

Olson looked as shabby as he did in Preskitt.

"Have you learned anything?"

"Not a thing."

"Tomorrow I want to ride east. Meanwhile Jesus will talk to the Hispanic neighbors. Maybe he can learn something. I will need a picture of her."

"There is one we had made."

"I won't lose it."

"It will be all I have of her."

He brought the small-framed picture out wrapped in a towel. Chet agreed that she was a very pretty girl. Jesus looked at it and agreed she was, too. Finding her with no more than a picture would be like spotting a needle in a haystack, but Chet knew, somehow, they'd try.

Olson fed them beans and apologized he had no skills at cooking. Jesus made the oatmeal at breakfast and they parted. Olson and Chet rode to Mesa and showed her picture to many but got no information. They rode back at dark. Chet had bought some fresh beef from a butcher on the way back for Jesus to cook along with potatoes.

They ate heartily while Jesus told them he had talked to one of the women neighbors. She had seen two men leading a horse the day Marcella was kidnapped. The horses they rode were bays, but the animal they led was a paint.

"She never saw your wife riding it. But she said she thought it was funny that they led around a paint with a saddle on it. They may have gone east like where you found tracks and taken her that way."

"She describe them?"

"*Gringo* cowboys she said."

"After they heard her speak, others said, 'Oh, yes, I saw them.' So two cowboys was all I learned."

"Wish we'd had the paint horse information where we went today. More might have seen her, if they went east. We will go east of Mesa tomorrow. Maybe someone saw them over there or saw the paint horse if they went that way."

They left early and were well east of the Mormon settlement town when they dropped off a ridge down onto a ranch. A middle-aged Hispanic woman came out on the porch, shading her eyes against the low winter sun in her face.

"Good day," Chet said. "A week or so ago did two men water their horses here with a woman on a paint horse? Maybe her hands were tied to the saddle horn."

"*Si*. I told Tony when he came home that night someone should go see about her. She had been crying. Those men didn't care about that. Tony said later I should mind my own business. Such things got people shot."

"We care about her. Where did they go?"

"North."

"You ever seen them before?"

She shook her head. "They were *gringos*. I could see she was a prisoner and that hurt my heart, but I could do nothing." She held her fist to her chest.

"May God bless you, and we thank you for this information."

"I will pray more for her safety now that you are on her trail."

Chet saluted her. They rode north, crossed the Salt River below the temporary irrigation diversion dam, which cut the river's flow to half. By forcing part of the river water into a ditch used long ago by Indians to irrigate the farmland west of there, it made an easy crossing now.

"I can't believe she saw her," Olson said. "Oh, my poor wife. With her hands tied, too."

"It is a bad deal, but it really makes Jesus and me believe your whole story. We are a long ways from your farm and she saw them. It is not a feather in the wind. We will find her, Harry."

He was crying. "I swear these bastards have to be caught. Thank you—for helping me."

Jesus rode in close. "It is time to hope. We have a trail from here, Harry. I think we will have more luck. With less people around, there will be more witnesses seeing three strangers as standouts."

Chet added, "And they will give us more information. The kidnappers will think they got away with it and will get careless. They probably took her through Mesa in the dark. It may take us time, but we are on her tracks."

"How will I repay you?"

"You worry about finding her. Jesus and I need no rewards."

"No one has ever done anything this big for me. I appreciate both of you. How did you know her hands were tied?"

"If she went with them freely, her hands would not be tied. You have been very honest with us."

"All the time I only told the truth."

"Yes. I know and believe you. Today I wish we knew why they took her?"

Olson agreed. "Me too."

"We need to ride up to the Indian agency at Fort McDowell. Then see if they saw them passing through there."

Olson nodded. They camped at the McDowell Agency that night, and a Mexican woman vendor fed them supper for fifteen cents apiece. She agreed to make them breakfast at sunup.

Chet bought the horses some corn from the subtler and they fed them in feedbags after watering them in the Verde River. The day had warmed, but he knew it would be cold in the low ground. They had good bedrolls. No one had seen the three passing because the road to Rye didn't pass close to the agency, and no doubt they'd went on rather than stop and draw attention.

Dawn they ate a large flour tortilla wrap filled with hot meat and beans. Chet paid her well and they rode north to Rye and Sunflower. Witnesses there at Rye had seen the three Chet sought pass through. The woman rode under a blanket for warmth on her shoulders. One man said he knew she was a prisoner but he had no way to help her. Those two men were armed and he thought them hard cases especially if they'd been challenged.

The next day they stopped in Sunflower. A man told them the older guy's name was Rodney Pierce from back in Texas. Chet wrote it down. After they rode on he asked Olson if these men might have known her from there.

"She and her family left Texas when she was

sixteen. She never said she had a boyfriend back there."

When they remounted, Chet said, "Olson, she did not go with them because she wanted to. Even if they knew her, in my mind, she didn't want to go with them without a struggle."

He nodded. "I regret every day that I did not take her with me to Hayden's Mill."

"They might have killed you for her."

"Yes, they might have."

"They are not ghosts. They leave prints, and when they stop we will get them."

"You two believe that?"

"Damn right. There is a fork in the road ahead. One goes to Holbrook, the other one goes to Mormon Lake. We need to learn which way they went."

Near the Y in the road they spoke to a man driving a freight wagon, with the two teams of big horses hauling some hardware to a rancher, south. He'd said he came from Holbrook when they asked him.

"Two men on bays and a girl on a paint. Have you seen them on the way here?"

"Two days ago. They had her hands tied to the horn."

Chet nodded. "That is his wife, Marcella. One man's name was Rodney Pierce."

The man shook his head. "Sorry. I knew she was in trouble. But feared doing anything in case it was a marriage deal."

"She is this man's wife, not his. We have tracked them from Mesa."

"Sorry. I saw a problem and didn't solve it."

"Mount up. We'll catch them," Chet said to his pair.

"I didn't catch your name, mister?"

"Chet Byrnes."

"Glad to meet you, Chet Byrnes."

"Your name?"

"Sam Coffee's mine. I sure wish you luck finding them."

It began to snow that afternoon, so they decided to stop at a small store with a wood stove and to sleep on the floor in their bedrolls. Their horses were fed grain and were stabled in an empty shed.

The storekeep told them how the two men stopped and bought some supplies. One of them stayed outside with a girl. He saw her hands were tied to the saddle horn and that she was crying.

"Oh, I pray she lives. She is such a wonderful wife," Olson cried.

"Mister, I'm ashamed I didn't stop them. But in the end I didn't know if I could stop them short of being shot myself."

"I know, but so many have seen her plight and not done a thing."

"Go easy, these guys must be tough. Normal people have to draw back when they might lose their lives. That is why Jesus and I are here."

"Oh, Chet, I'd never found her trail—just makes me sick she is being so mistreated."

"We will get her free."

"I have been praying for it."

Chet clapped his shoulder. "That won't hurt. We are making progress."

Jesus agreed. The storekeeper's wife fed them a

hardy stew for supper and oatmeal for breakfast. Chet paid her for the meals, over her protest. The next morning, they rode out with it still snowing. It finally let up around mid-day but it turned colder.

At this rate, they'd be two days getting to Holbrook, by Chet's calculations. They built a pine-covered lean-to facing the campfire to sleep under that night. The horses were fed grain and tied to a line between two trees. A bitter night, but they heated water for tea the next morning and ate more jerky. Saddled now, they rode on. The sun warmed and the snow turned to slush when they reached a place to overlook Holbrook, on the bank of the Little Colorado River, shining like silver in the sun.

They looked at all the horses in the fields and pens for a paint. They found several but no bay horses with them. When they got into the town they looked hard at the various ponies at hitch rails. Then Jesus spurred his horse up an alley as something caught his eye. Olson and Chet reined up and Jesus soon waved at them to join him.

"Think that is them?" Chet asked with his coat swept back from his gun butt.

The saddled horses looked worn out, tied in the alley and standing hipshot. They obviously had not been fed. Where were the men and girl?

"If you have to shoot at anyone, be careful, they may use her for shield. Olson, guard these horses. Jesus, you go that way. I will go this way."

Chet charged his horse through the wet snow in the alley's shade. At the next street he saw two men begin to flee. They had a girl ahead of them. He fired a shot in the air.

"Hold up. I'm a U.S. marshal."

The man on the right half turned and shot back at Chet, the shot too wild to do any harm. They kept running. He charged the horse after them and closed the distance. The one on the right tripped and the girl fell with him into the snow. Chet shot the other one still running. The bullet struck him in the back. He straightened and then fell facedown. Chet jumped off the horse on the back of the other man scrambling for the gun he'd lost, and he knocked him out with his pistol.

Jesus stepped off his sliding horse and jerked the shot man to his knees. He drug him by the collar.

"Who—who—are you?" she asked, looking white in shock but trying to gain her feet.

Chet helped her up. "Marcella, we brought your husband, Harry, with us. I am a U.S. Deputy Marshal. That is Jesus Martinez, a deputy. We have been coming to rescue you."

She hugged him crying. "Is he all right?"

"Tired as we are but he's fine. How are you?"

"Tired, too. I didn't think I'd ever get away from them."

"Why did they kidnap you?"

"Zeke, the one you shot, he said he wanted me to marry him in Texas. I didn't want him. He found where my family lives near Hayden's Mill. Then they came to get me and take me back to be his wife."

"Who is the groggy one?"

"His brother Rodney . . ." She looked wide-eyed as Harry hurried to her.

"Yes, that's the man who loves you, Marcella. He's coming for you. Go meet him." Chet took off his hat and scratched the top of his head. He watched her run to hug her husband.

Been one helluva chase. He saw the local law was coming on the run toward them.

"Now it is over, partner. What do you think?" he asked Jesus.

"Glad it could end so good. Boy I could use a bath, shave, and a good meal."

"So could I. You the marshal here?" he asked the man as he reached them.

The man behind the mustache nodded.

Chet told him his name and that they were law enforcement men and that the two men were to be held for trial on kidnapping charges and transported back to Phoenix. "The man over there has been shot, but it should be minor."

"I can handle it from here. Thanks, Marshal Byrnes, and nice to meet you, sir."

"There are three horses in the alley over there. I am claiming them and will have them put in a livery. We will come by and give you names and all the information at the jail tomorrow. We've been on their trail near a week now. We are tired, dirty, and hungry."

"Where did you start at?"

"West of Mesa a week ago."

"Why did they kidnap her?"

"One of them she said she turned down back in Texas. He decided he'd kidnap her and take her back to Texas to be his wife."

"Take him to doc's," he told his deputy, pointing to the wounded one. "I got this other one. I'll lock him up. Glad you caught them. I had no papers on them."

"There aren't any. When Harry reported the kidnapping, a Maricopa deputy decided that it was not a kidnapping but that his wife had just ran away."

The marshal looked upset. "How did you get involved?"

"Her husband rode to my ranch at Preskitt on a worn-out horse to get me to help him."

"Brave guy, huh?" The marshal shook his head, impressed.

"He damn sure is." Chet reloaded his pistol as the sun went down behind him.

Jesus went to put all the horses up. Chet turned to them. "You two lovers come along. She needs a new dress, some long handles to fit her, and a coat. You get some new underwear, britches, a wool shirt, and new coat. Let's go find them."

"I don't have—"

Chet shook his head, smiling. "I know I don't have to do this, but my wife will pay for them."

"Huh?"

"If Liz was here she'd do that for you two. I know her well."

The girl laughed, then she shook Harry some. "Silly. His wife is buying it. You get it?"

"I guess. Damn it, I am so glad you're safe I can't even think."

"Harry, I would never have stayed with him even in Texas."

Chet chuckled. "We knew that, too, and that's why we kept tracking you. Let's go shopping."

They agreed. Later, carrying their clean clothes,

they went to the Grand Hotel. Chet ordered them the honeymoon suite and hot baths immediately. And a large meal for the two of them to be delivered in one hour in their suite.

The two were frowning at him.

He ignored it and had the porter show them their suite. Then he said, loud enough for them to hear while marching upstairs, "Make it two nights. We have to make reports to hold the outlaws tomorrow and will leave the next day for home."

Marcella ran back down the stairs, over to him, and pulled him down and kissed his whiskered cheek. "Thank you so much, Chet Byrnes."

He winked at her and smiled; then he arranged for rooms for him and Jesus. His partner soon joined him and they went out to eat.

Over supper, Jesus smiled. "What would have happened to her if we had not run them down?"

"Probably would have been forced into being his wife and if she tried to escape, murdered, forced into prostitution, or taken into the white slave trade."

"I had sure wondered if the deputy had been right, until that rancher's wife said her hands were tied. I will stop and thank her on the way home. It was so strange. You mentioned it and she said, yes, she was tied to the saddle horn."

"At first, I was not so sure he was rambling, either, but we knew he had told us the truth after that."

"Exactly. I felt bad even doubting him after that."

"We were lucky, but I'd still gone on this search because of his ride to Preskitt was not a foolish trip when the deputy discounted his story. He needed help."

"All the horses are being fed for the ride back. I bet Rocky could ride that small paint horse. He is really broke."

"I bet he'd love it. He says the pony is too slow."

"I wonder how Spencer is doing."

"And the widow woman he took with him. What was her name?" Chet asked Jesus.

"Lucinda Marcos was her full name. Her husband was Roman Marcos. He was killed a year ago in a roping accident during roundup. She is a lovely lady."

"I figured you knew the whole story. I remember that she had nowhere to go after he was killed, so the ranch continued to pay her his wages."

"She appreciated it and works hard on ranch events with Bonnie. She will miss her when she leaves with him."

"I hope both of them are happy together."

"I hope so, too. Spencer's is going to build a great headquarters."

All the paperwork was finally done, and now it was only their long ride back. In due time he'd be back to Preskitt and with Liz. It couldn't be soon enough.

CHAPTER 7

The snow melted in the warmer weather going home. The Olsons were like honeymooners riding side by side, but they kept up and she cooked the meals all the way back. The snow was melting fast when they got off the higher elevation.

When they reached the store, the man who had noticed her tied and crying shook his head and had to hug her. He apologized to her for not helping her.

"Oh, they might have shot you. These men and my husband found me in the end and I am so grateful you worried about me. What you told them helped them find me."

The storekeeper hugged her again. "He is a lucky man to have such a lovely wife."

"I am the lucky one. God bless you."

They kept going home. After they crossed the Salt River they reached the Bar K W and rode up the drive. The rancher's wife saw them coming and ran out to greet them. Marcella got down from her ride, and both women hugged, then kissed, with the rancher's wife uttering, "Hail Mary" the entire time.

After that the two of them danced in the dust.

"You are safe at last. I prayed so hard for you, my dear."

"Yes. My name is Marcella. They spoke about you and knew you were worried about me. I thank you for that."

"My name is Anna. My husband calls me Duchess."

"Nice title. You know they learned who had me when you described me with those men?"

"I felt so bad. You looked so sad on that horse." She hugged her and cried.

"I am fine, Duchess. You saved my life. Be happy. May I come to see you after I get my life straightened out—some day?"

"Oh, yes, do that."

"I will. Now we must get home. His pigs must be lonesome for him."

Duchess laughed. "Like Tony. His cows would miss him, too."

They rode on to the Olson place. They dropped out of the saddle at sundown. Olson rushed off to check on his pigs that a neighbor had fed while he was gone. He came back satisfied they were fine.

Chet waited outside on the porch for him to talk about his business. "If you had more money could you expand your hog operation and make money?"

"Of course."

"You ever made up a business plan? It would show me how much money you would need to do that and how you could repay the loan."

"Marcella could do that. I'd help her."

"Jesus and I will go home tomorrow. When you get it done mail it to me."

"Yes, sir."

"I want you to become a success at this place of yours."

Olson smiled and hugged him. "I can never repay you for finding her. But I can make our hog business much bigger and make enough money to repay you."

Chet nodded and they went inside.

After breakfast, Olson told Chet, "She says we should bring that plan to you at the ranch when we get it done. She wants to meet your wife and see your ranch. We will take the stage this time."

"Good. My wife, Jesus, and I will be glad to see you. Wire me your plans before you leave here because the stage arrives up there at midnight and the ranch is six miles east of there."

"Oh, thanks. Be careful and God bless you."

She hugged and kissed both of them.

They rode off in the morning for the stage stop. They left the paint out at their place; Chet planned to get it up to his son later. They sold the horses back to the liveryman and took the next stage home.

CHAPTER 8

Liz told him on the ride home from the stage stop office he had gotten a telegram from Hannagen that their project had been okaycd by all parties in congress and he needed to start planning it.

"I should have checked with him. I was within a day's ride over there at Holbrook."

Liz shook her head. "I think from what you told me it was a great miracle you even found her."

"Duchess made the difference. That lady is so neat. I don't know how you will ever meet her, but her testimony to us made the difference. You'd love her."

"What does the telegraph company need from you?"

"I need to find a surveyor, poles, wire, glass insulators, and explosives to blast the holes out of rock for them. Plus a crew of hardworking guys to stretch it four hundred miles."

"Is that all?" She laughed, going to check on Monica in the kitchen.

He frowned after her. *Is that all?* He needed lots

more and would have to find it. He better wire
Hannagen for more information and get ready for
finding poles and two contractors. The poles would
have to come from up there where the pines were,
around Center Point, on the rim. And he'd need an
army of wagons to haul them east to Gallup and start
there. Unless they needed to start from over on
the Colorado River at the same time as the eastside
started so as to meet in the middle. Then he'd have
to bring the wire and material overland from San
Francisco and send the poles over there.

He better get the how and where they'd start from
from his partner before anything else. He immediately wrote Hannagen his letter requesting where to
start and mailed it.

Liz and him, the next day when the temperature
warmed up, rode over to see May and Hampt.

They were welcomed by a very pregnant May who
was excited they'd come to see them. She gave them
a full report on his nephew and her stepson Ray who
was attending college in St. Louis and how he might
not come home the following summer vacation, instead touring with a music group he played the
piano for.

"I got him into playing and he was such a natural
at doing it. He has gotten better and better at it. His
brother Ty never played an instrument in his life but
he is the real horseman. He is the best at training
horses. You have both seen and know that."

"Yes. That gray Diablo horse is still one of the best
broke horses I own."

"Tell her about Bonnie," Liz said.

"She's with a baby again," Chet said.

"She's like me, fertile." Then May blushed.

"Fertile men around here." Liz laughed and that made him feel better; she was taking such things more like her old self.

Chet shook his head and went to meet Hampt who had just ridden in—and probably had seen them coming.

"I heard rumors you bought a new big ranch?" The big man stepped off his horse and hitched him.

"Yes, in that grassy desert country north of Oracle. Thirty sections."

"Wow, is it a good place?"

"Bank repossessed it. The cows Weeks had on it are old enough to vote. We're culling them, and my man over there says this fall he can buy us young cows at Socorro carrying half or better British breeds in them for twenty-five dollars a head plus bred back."

"Why so cheap?"

"There is so little market over there for anything, and people need money to live on over there, too."

"Now that the Apaches are not very much of a problem, I bet you can drive them through their land as a shortcut."

"I bet so. Even hire some Apache boys to drive them is all we'd need to do that."

"Hey, get your horse. I want to show you a real set of cows I have now."

"Thought you'd never ask."

Hampt laughed. "You really must trust me. You hardly ever come by here to check on me."

"Hampt, I'd trust you with my life. You know that."

"Where's your guardsmen today?"

"Spencer is down at Oracle, picking up a wife at

Diablo and taking her to the new ranch house site at the Apache Springs Ranch that he is supervising."

"Who did he marry?"

"You recall hearing about a cowboy called Roman Marcos working for JD that got hurt and died from his injuries in a roundup accident last year?"

"Yes, I heard about it from Bonnie's letter to May. Big shame. He had two kids?"

"Yes, Spencer knew all about it."

"Didn't he have a woman?"

"She went back to where she came from. I don't know any more than that."

Hampt laughed. "Me either. Start looking and tell me I am not about to have all white-faced cattle on this ranch." He waved his hand at the long string of white-faced young cows that raised their heads from the hay they were eating to check out the riders.

"You are coming on. They look real good, too."

"I am busting my buttons over them. Glad you got to see them."

"My last trip to the Verde, Tom said that those range cows that were dumped up here needed to be driven out?"

"We moved three hundred head of cows plus calves I bet down into the Verde River wilderness a week ago while you were gone after that man's wife who got kidnapped. They won't ever find those cows down there I bet."

"Everyone agreed to do that, didn't they?" Chet asked.

"Yes. Everyone agreed. All the ranchers were upset about these people that drive cattle on others ranges and don't check on them or anything. The situation needed to be controlled."

"Bet they won't do a damn thing, either, at the next legislative meeting."

Hampt shook his head in disgust. "They've got too many paid-off legislators in their pockets."

"See any other problems?"

"No. Now tell me more about what Spencer's doing?"

"You know I bought a new ranch north of Oracle. One of Weeks's outfits the banks repossessed. W Bar W is the brand. There is a man named Frisco whose family ran it even before Weeks bought it. He will stay and run it. He is married to a much younger woman he rescued in Mexico. She is a very neat lady and funny.

"Spencer is building new headquarters at a new site on the place. The previous owners did not live on the ranch and they looked like many Sonoran places we saw down there, just adobe jackals and pens on a dusty flat. There was a big spring in a cottonwood canyon that we chose for the home place."

"That woman he met on the stage left him?"

Chet nodded. "Rebecca was not happy I guess playing the wife role. Spencer paid her fare back to where she came from. He went after the widow woman I mentioned with two kids on the Diablo Ranch he met when he was down there."

"So your ranch operation expands some more."

"Yes."

"Hey, you need any help holler."

"I will. You know that I trust you and count on your leadership."

"You know I won't ever forget you hiring me when you came here the first time from Texas."

"Hey, I feel like you are my brother."

"That makes me feel good. Do you ever miss him?"

"You have done a good job filling his boots, my friend."

"You know my thoughts. May and the kids are all one big blessing to me. This ranch is a job, well, like heaven."

"Good thing, pard. You earned it and more. I better get home."

"Elizabeth doing all right?"

"You saw her. Thank God she has a good attitude about things."

"Tell her that she is in my prayers. I wouldn't want to say anything to upset her."

Chet clapped him on the shoulder. "I will, and now I'll go up, get her, and head for home."

"Who will help Jesus?"

"A young man from the Preskitt Ranch. Miguel Costa is his name. I think. Raphael really likes him, wants to train him to replace himself, but first wants him to ride with me and Jesus for a time."

"I don't know those *vaqueros* that well, but on that last cattle drive with those unwanted cattle, they really worked hard. My men said I should borrow them more often to help us."

On the ride home, he buttoned up his coat. Liz did, too. The weather had turned colder. When he dropped off his horse in the yard, a stable boy came, on the run, and took both their horses.

Chet went to the house appraising the buttermilk-looking sky for future developments. It was going to snow. And soon. The moisture would be good and his operations were braced for it with plenty of hay. No telling how much or how long it would last.

Liz ran to use the facilities and left him with Monica.

"Well, no one rides with you anymore?" Monica asked with her hands on her hips when he stepped onto the back porch.

"I simply rode to Hampt's and talked to him."

"The rules say someone would ride with you wherever you go."

"I had Liz with me. I will try to do right the next time."

"You better. And choose a man to take Spencer's place."

"I think Raphael already did."

"Good. Supper will be ready soon."

Liz was smiling as she came into the room. "It's good to be back, Monica. It is getting colder out there."

"I worried about you being out in it."

"Thanks. But I am not a baby."

"Supper is ready. Will it snow?"

"I think so."

"Let's eat. I am starved," Liz said.

After the meal he read the newspaper as the fireplace crackled. Curious about the weather, he parted a curtain. The yard was white beyond the covered porch, and lots more big flakes were falling. They might be in for a real one. Wind was out of the east. Strange direction, he thought, for it to come in from.

"Think it will snow much?" she asked.

"No telling until we wake up. Let's go to bed."

Lying in bed, he listened to the wind in the eaves. This storm had grown, in the last few hours, to a bad one. No telling how much snow had fallen or how much they'd have in the end. *Well, sleep tight, folks. It's just another obstacle.*

CHAPTER 9

Chet woke early, dressed, and went down to the kitchen. Monica was feeding small sticks to her range fire. She straightened. "You have a big shovel?"

"No need for it yet, it's still snowing."

"How much?"

"Several feet is what it looks like. I don't know what the record is, but I bet we've beat it for the most ever. Damn sure a big one."

"When will it quit?"

"I have no idea."

By noon it stopped but remained cloudy. One of the hands had cut a crossing from the big barn, through snow half as tall as he was, to the house. It took over two hours to get it done. Raphael was his first visitor on this new highway.

"I think someone took revenge out on us. Where is Sarge and the cattle drive he is on?" his foreman asked.

"He should be close to the New Mexico border by now. He has some haystacks and a setup over there. I'd bet the snow is not that deep there."

"I hope not. Do you need anything? I will send some boys over here to move more firewood in by the fireplaces."

"Good. How is everything else?"

"We are working to feed the stock. I dread the cold that will come next."

Chet agreed. "Make sure everyone is safe and is accounted for when you end the day. Someone could get lost and die from exposure out there."

"I will tell everyone to do that. I never saw so much snow in my life." He tipped his snowy hat and left the house.

Liz joined him. "How long will it take to melt if it warms up?"

"A week or more. There is lots of the white stuff out there."

She shook her head warily and laughed. "What a mess it will be."

"People unprepared are going to lose lots of cattle on the range."

"I never thought about that," Monica said. "How will we do?"

"Better than them. We have lots of hay."

She nodded.

"We've worked to have that extra supply for years like this."

"I never think of those things. That is why I cook and you run ranches."

He hugged her. "We appreciate you."

The next day he helped fork hay on some big sleds that Raphael had bought somewhere as a bargain, prepared for this day. The first horse team had tromped out a way to the open country where the bawling cattle stood waiting. They looked great in the bright sunshine as forage was forked off for them.

"We may lose some cows that didn't come in last night ahead of the storm," his foreman warned him as he watched Chet throw some more hay. "You know that my boys can do this. Fork off the hay?"

"I know, but I wanted to help. Not sit and worry about the other places and what they did not do right."

"We are doing all we can. We had an old barn where I kept the dry wood, but the snow collapsed the roof in. Now, instead, I have boys cleaning the snow off of the other woodpiles so we will have the wood." He shook his head. "I hope we don't get more."

"Me too."

They had unloaded two of the sleighs and were going back for more. Chet rode one sled back. By evening Raphael had a head count and felt he'd lost no more than three head.

As Chet stood before the living room fireplace warming his backside, Liz asked him about his man Toby at the new east place.

"Soon as we can we need to take some food over there. Toby, his wife Talley, and his hands who are clearing brush may need something to eat."

It was almost a week before they could get into town on the one lane opened on the road. Chet with Miguel drove a big team to get supplies that the ranch needed and plus the ones he suspected his man on the eastern division would need when they could get there. It was a slushy mess but they made it, loaded the wagon bed with all the things from the mercantile, and headed home.

Reports of people lost and killed from the storm filled the *Miner*'s pages in the issue he brought home. Several more were unaccounted for and still unreachable out in remote places. When he returned Raphael told him they almost had the road off the mountain cleared to Camp Verde. He said he thought Tom and some of his men were making progress from the lower end. But the sun only shone for a few hours a day on those slopes, due to the winter angle, which slowed the melting.

Chet thanked him. They tarped down the supplies, needed at the upper ranch, in the wagon and he thanked Miguel for his help.

"When will you try to go to Toby's place?"

"Even if they have the road to Camp Verde open, that mountain across the valley may still be blocked on the far side, so it will be hard to get to them."

"When you get ready to go, simply send me word. I am very pleased to be asked to accompany you," Miguel said.

"I am certain we need a report about the second mountain before we leave here."

"I can go check it if you want a report."

"Give it another day."

"Sure. Lisa said for you to tell Elizabeth hi for her."

"Can do. It's turning colder again. Won't help our melting any."

Miguel agreed and left him.

"How is your new man?" Liz asked him on his return.

"Sharp. I can tell he's excited to go to work."

"Could you see why Raphael chose him?" she asked.

"I think he's carefully watched them all. Miguel reminds me of Jesus a few years back when he first joined me."

"I will sleep easier now that you have Miguel, since Spencer Horne is your building superintendent and not with you." She laughed. "And he's married by now?"

"I don't know about that but maybe. He will write and tell us if he is."

"This snow is bad business, isn't it?"

"No one has seen the like of it down here. Up at Center Point they get this much snow, but down here this is unusual."

"I wonder how Cole is doing?"

"They planned on snow problems. It is in their postal contract as a thing of nature."

"I am still thinking about Toby. So you don't know if you can reach him even with this side open?"

"That north rim may have more or less snow than this one."

"How will you know?"

"If this side gets thawed out enough not to slide a wagon off into the canyon, we will check that road on that far side."

She hugged him. "I'll be glad when it melts."

"So will I."

A cold spell put it off two more days. The third one came on warmer, and a cowboy on a caulked shod horse rode up from the Verde Ranch. He reported the narrow mountain road was really thawing and he felt they could make it down safely by mid-day.

"Has anyone seen that north road to the east ranch?" Chet asked.

"Yes, sir. Toby is at the Verde Ranch with a wagon. Tom made him wait till it thawed and sent me to tell you about conditions."

Thank God they must be all right. "He say anything was wrong?"

"No. Toby said that they were getting low on a few things, but nothing serious. Said he'd stock more next time. He's a tough enough guy. Some of us thought he was a kid. He ain't."

Chet agreed. If the devil wanted Toby, he'd only get him kicking and fighting to get loose.

Miguel was there with Lisa at his side. When the others moved away from Chet, they joined him.

"How are you, Lisa?" Chet asked Miguel's wife.

She smiled and shook her head. "Fine. I never saw so much snow in my life."

"You're not alone. Thanks for all your hard work around here."

She nodded. "That same thanks to you for my chance to be here with him."

"You did well. Miguel, too."

His man laughed and nodded. "We going north?"

"Just to the Verde tomorrow and see how things are going down there. Toby made it there and will come here today. He can go get anything he needs in town and then stay here overnight. We can leave Jesus and his bride at home for our trip."

Miguel smiled and nodded. "What horse do you want tomorrow?"

"One of my roans."

"I'll have him saddled."

"Tell a boy to saddle them. You and Lisa come to lunch today."

"We accept," Lisa said, smiling, and took Chet's arm. "I will go along and talk to Elizabeth."

Miguel smiled and fell in with them. "Did it ever snow when you were in Texas?"

"Not much. I can recall a dusting or two."

"Must be like Mexico. There was only snow on some real high mountains."

Chet agreed and showed Lisa inside the back porch.

Liz met and hugged her while the men washed up. Monica served them roast beef, rice, gravy, and biscuits.

"I should have made tortillas with those two here," Monica said.

Miguel shook his head. "I like your biscuits. I can eat tortillas at home."

"Maybe you will eat them at home," Lisa said.

"Fine."

"We get hooked up on the telegraph business, he might not get to eat them very often."

She frowned. "Are you finally building one?"

"I understand that the government is going to be committed to help us build one across northern Arizona," Chet said.

"If you go you will need a cook, too?"

"I'll need lots of things. You putting in to cook for that crew, Lisa?"

"He goes. I can go."

Miguel smiled. "Only if she will bake some biscuits."

"I bet she can do that. We will find her an oven or a Dutch oven."

"When?" Liz asked.

"When they tell me they have it all ready to start."

She sighed. "I still want the job."

Toby came back from town, and in the sundown's last light agreed to stay overnight. The boys put up his team and grained them. Chet accompanied him to the house for the heaping plate of food Monica had kept warm for him in the oven.

"Now, tell me about your ranch operation," Chet said.

"We measured it," Toby said, waving his fork over the plate of food. "And Talley says we have forty acres of hay ground that's brush free. We will have it fenced before the grass breaks out. That family you sent me almost have the corrals built. They will build the big barn next and we will be ready for spring. I got worried with all the snow, about supplies, so started out. Told Talley I worried it might snow again and then we'd be in tough shape. Of course I have two big bull elk hanging in the meat cooler that we built earlier so we'd not starve, but it would be rough."

"Good thinking and action. I may have a source of cattle, next fall, for your place."

"Where?"

"Socorro, New Mexico. Man told me ranchers over there have to sell several cows to meet their debts. You may have to find a route to get them over here, but if they come to the sale we can buy them."

Toby smiled. "Now you're talking. I'll find me an Apache that knows the way."

"That's a good idea."

"We've been working hard. I'll be ready."

"Sounds that way. You be careful going back."

Toby yawned big. "Thanks. I can sure stand the sleep tonight though."

"Anything else I need to do?" Chet asked him.

"Talley said to tell you hi. She thanked you and your wife for all you did for the two of us. She likes the house now that it is repaired and thinks we'll have a great ranch to run someday soon."

"Be careful going home."

"I will, Chet. I promise."

The next morning, Chet and Miguel were about to leave when Jesus rode in. "I am coming along, too."

"Good. We're going to the Verde Ranch today. You know Miguel. Let's ride. Anita is fine?"

"Doing very well she tells me. She has plenty of wood thanks to Raphael and enough groceries so I am glad you have a place for me."

"A house can get small after a while, even a big one."

Jesus nodded as they rode out for the lower place.

Mid-morning they stopped at the big house to see his son Adam. Rhea and the boy answered the door and Chet swept him up. "How is my big man?"

"Fine, Daddy. Where is Liz?"

"It was too cold for her to come today. Did you have fun in the snow?"

"Yes."

"Good, I'm glad someone did. Where is Victor?"

"Him help feed cows. They bawl a lot these days."

"I bet they do. I need to find Tom," he said to Rhea. "Is everyone all right down here?"

"As far as I know, yes. We had less snow than you

did they say, but it was a mess. I don't know how Toby made it over here from where he lives. But he's tough, isn't he?"

"Yes, a very determined young man. He's heading back home today with supplies."

"I have some coffee made. Tom sees your horses he will be here."

He hugged her. "We have all day."

"You said it was too cold for Liz to come?"

"Yes."

"Is she sick?" Rhea asked, concerned.

"No, she's lost a little spirit over her loss, but she's doing all right."

Rhea wrapped her arms around herself. "I love her. I'm worried because before that happened she was with you in your travels, all the time."

"Losing the baby that late disappointed her."

Tom arrived and they drank coffee together.

"We had less snow but it was still three feet deep. Our cattle were close and we didn't lose any. The Herefords were fine. The men that stay over there and feed them ran out of about everything but beans before we got them re-supplied. I don't think we have to worry about the free grazers cattle being here anymore. Most of them starved or will, and many local folks that don't put up hay are in the same shape. What about Sarge?"

"He planned to leave early for this month's delivery and he has hay stored there. All we can do is hope he made it and that it isn't as bad over there as it was up at Preskitt."

"Cole was set up for that kind of weather, wasn't he?"

"Yes. But I'd bet they had more snow at Center Point than I did."

"That road to the rim north of here has got more sun than this side. But I figure on top it's deeper than a tall mule's belly. Robert has plenty of horse feed. We sent him lots last summer. I imagine he had food stored since he knows how it snows up there every year. The snow will be gone around here in two days the way it is melting now."

"I wanted to come by and be sure everything clicked down here. Now I hope Shawn and Lucy are okay."

"They put up lots of hay. I know that. Have you heard from Spencer Horne?"

"I expect a letter once the stage gets through."

"He's building a headquarters on that new ranch?"

"Yes. I bet they don't have any snow down there."

"Safe bet. What about Suzie? She has ample supplies, doesn't she?"

"Yes, she keeps well supplied. Isn't your married daughter Sandy staying over there with her?"

"Yes. Her husband, Cody, is working for Sarge this winter."

"Well, he'll get broken in then. Sarge has a good hay stock on hand and we have two months' supply of cattle over at the Windmill now, don't we?" Chet asked.

"That's right and I have another bunch for the third month here, thank God."

"You're right keeping that many head in back supply in case we get in a bind. Good job."

"I worry all the time we'll get caught short," Tom

said. "But I still don't want too many on hand, either."

Satisfied that the rest would have to wait for a big thaw to see him, he and his men rode back to Preskitt Valley after lunch.

Waiting was a letter from Spencer that a ranch hand had fetched from town.

Dear Chet,

I made the trip to the ranch. Lucinda Marcos accepted my offer to marry her. I brought her out to the church at San Xavier. A father there, after some persuasion, married us. Then we went to Tucson and I bought her and the children some new clothes. I ordered some things I'd need from the mercantile that were to be hauled up to the site. We also got food, supplies, a tent to live in, cooking gear, and some tools.

Frisco and the cowboys had made me a road (little rough) in, but we are set up at the headquarter site. He has a contractor coming with some boys and a road grader to make the road in better. More later.

Spencer Horne

He looked up for his wife. "Sounds like he has it all in hand down there."

"No report of a wire or anything from Gallup?" Liz asked.

"The whole world may be under a blanket of snow. No, nothing at all."

"If they expect you to build that line overnight, someone needs to be getting things ready."

"I agree. But it is their job to get the material lined up, my dear."

"I know that. But I am thinking one day they will drop the whole thing in your lap."

"They might." *God forbid it.*

A warm spell with lots of rain swept in and snow went to vanishing, but the rivers swelled and the Verde River became a half-mile wide, in places, from the reports he got from the lower ranch. The creeks around Preskitt belched lots of water and several bridges were lost. They simply floated away. He wondered how Leroy and Betty Lou were doing in flooding water on Oak Creek on the fruit farm. He hoped they were smart enough to be prepared. He couldn't go check on them until all the water went down.

The sun came out finally and Chet drove Liz into town. They had lots of mail. The one he opened immediately was from Sarge, sent from Gallup, New Mexico.

Dear Chet,

We made it fine to here and fed hay a few days—made all our deliveries on time—except the two most north ones and we did them only a day late with more hired help. No one was hurt except their feelings. The Agency gave us an A. I am heading back to the Windmill Ranch. I know it must be a mess all over.

Sincerely yours,
Sarge

Chet handed her the letter and laughed. "He said no one was hurt—except their feelings. No telling who or what that was all about?"

"Now if Lucy and Cole would write we'd know all about everything."

"There is a letter from Bonnie here."

"What did she say?"

"Dear Liz and Chet,

"I am going to kill your man Horne. He swept in here in a big wagon and took my best helper Lucinda off to marry her. Now what will I do for help? I should make Chet come here and make him help me with the fiestas. No. I am kidding. Those two left here as excited as kids at a birthday party. I know he knows by now what a great lady she is and they should make a good pair. I asked Spencer, before he left here, if he thought it was cooler up there at the new ranch than down here and he said maybe.

"They must be settled up on the ranch by now. All we hear about is how deep the snow is up where you are at, and how many cows starved to death in the territory. I told JD you all had feed for them anyway. Hope nothing froze off. We are all well and busy ranching.

"Love,

"Bonnie and JD"

"No letter from Gallup, either?"

Chet shook his head, putting the rest of the mail into a cloth sack. "Not yet anyway."

On the way back to the ranch they saw meadowlarks searching the muddy-surfaced road for anything to eat. The sun's glare off the snow was so bright it hurt his eyes even under the shade of his hat. Still, a much better day than those past snowy ones.

"Keeps thawing out I may go check on Shawn and Lucy."

"I'd love to but it still would be cold and the house would be warm the entire time I am gone."

He shifted hands with the reins. "I don't blame you for not coming. Stay home and warm."

"Good. Be careful crossing the Verde. I don't want to lose you."

"I will do that. But it should be down by then."

"There is still snow on the rim, melting, to feed it."

"I realize that. I'll send word to Jesus. We should have stopped by and I could have told him, but I can send a boy in to tell him when we will leave. We still need to get packhorses ready and get all my thick underwear out."

She hugged her arms to her body on the buckboard seat. "I will shiver for you."

They went over the hill to the ranch and he sent word to Miguel to meet with him. Raphael would take care of getting word to Jesus.

"We are going to the upper ranch day after tomorrow. Get some packhorses and what we need to camp out on the way. I've sent word to Jesus about our plans. He knows what food supplies we will need. It may take two weeks to make the circuit."

Miguel nodded. "I can do all that. I've been splitting firewood and getting in shape."

Chet's back muscles hurt from simply driving home from town. He lifted her by the waist off the buckboard. "How about before bed tonight you rub my back?"

"Whenever. You stiff?"

"Enough that I'd appreciate a back rub."

"I'll give you a good one." She laughed and shook her head going into the house.

That settled, he went to find Raphael and tell him his plans. Things might be on the move at last, but that depended on the snow's depth up there.

CHAPTER 10

The three of them, with three packhorses, rode out breathing steam in the cold morning air. The sky was clear and Chet was anxious to get on the way. He had no regrets about leaving his wife behind, save not having her along to keep him warm at night. She did not need the exposure, though she was back on her things-to-do list.

He could smile at her concern for every person on earth and especially their "people," like the little cross-eyed Hernandez girl that she had the eyeglass man fit with glasses so she could see normal. Her family had treated her like an invalid since birth, but Liz saw the problem and had an answer. Now the little one ran and played like the others, and she idolized Liz for that. All part of having a family to help each other he called it. Every bit as good a deed as finding Harry Olson's wife and getting her away from those kidnappers.

They stopped long enough to tell Tom they were going north to check on things and would camp on the rim that night. His foreman said everything was going good and had a report that Toby made it home safely. Chet told him about Sarge's success and that Spencer was married and at the new head-quarters living in a tent.

Tom laughed. "Be careful. Millie sends her best."

There was still lots of snow on the rim as they made camp. They slept in their bedrolls. Early the next morning, Chet and Miguel loaded and saddled stock while Jesus stirred the oatmeal and boiled the coffee. Then they hit the saddles to get to Robert's, hold the baby girl Caroline, and drink Betty's hot coffee.

She reported the snow had been bad but they were still hauling logs Robert had skidded to the logging roads before the storm hit. More good plan-ning by his man in charge. Robert was still out working when they left, and Chet and his men rode on to Center Point where the snow was still three feet deep on the sides of the road.

It was after dark when they reached headquarters. Cole came out to greet them. Valerie and Rocky, all bundled up, joined them. Miguel and Jesus gave the horses to the stable boys and they all went to Cole's house to talk. Valerie had *frijoles* cooking on her stove, so they didn't starve.

Large logs in the fireplace warmed the big tight-built house, and for the first time in three days Chet felt warm again. Rocky asked Chet about a new horse and his father told him they would have a paint horse for him at Preskitt in the spring. Harry was going to send it with someone who would be riding up there then.

Cole told them the buckboards were moving

again. Chet saw how weary he looked. He'd have to take these things easier. He couldn't fight record snowfall.

"We're going out to see Lucy and Shawn. Thought they needed checking on."

"I have not heard a word. But the mail is moving again."

"We promised them an impasse here in winter, but it is the same across all the places north of here, too, I'd bet."

"Your other places working?"

"They seem to be. Jesus and I rescued a woman that had been kidnapped. The law told her husband he believed she had simply run away."

Cole shook his head. "Jesus and Byrnes to the rescue, huh?"

"Boy we had to ride from Mesa to Holbrook to find her, and it was as cold going there as it was when we rode back from the north rim that time chasing the outlaws and that woman we saved."

"Kathrin. She married Ben Ivor at the mercantile in Preskitt."

"She comes to help you, too," Val said.

"Yes, she does. They've had two kids since then, too."

"I lived in Preskitt and I never had any kids there," Val said, shaking her head.

"Her not having kids was the cause of her husband marrying two sisters in Utah and her leaving him," Jesus said to Miguel, who'd not heard the story.

Miguel quickly agreed. "I have been in their store and she is a nice lady."

"Ben's first wife left him and went back east. She hated Preskitt and the West. Ben and Kathrin make a good couple. But that was the coldest ride I ever made. And we had lots of prisoners to guard."

Chet smiled. "Jesus never forgot the trip back. He's right. It was cold. But I don't think there is enough gold in Alaska to ever coax him to go up there."

His man shook his head.

Cole looked at the new man. "Miguel, some of the best days in my life, I spent with Jesus and Chet. You can count your stars they will be for you, too."

"I am grateful you three brought Lisa back so I could marry her. Thank you."

"Miguel, Chet Byrnes has saved all of us," Val put in. "We all love him for it. Oh, I'd cry every time Cole rode off but Chet always brought him back. And in the end we have shared in his success, too."

"Valerie, I have heard a lot of praises about Chet, but the greatest thing I ever heard was when Raphael told me I was chosen to ride with him. 'My son,' he said like I was his boy, 'you must guard him with your life and he will do the same for you.'"

Chet spoke up, embarrassed at the talk, "Eat your beans. We have some cold days left to get over to the north ranch."

"How is Liz?" Val asked.

"Great. Ready for the snow to melt, too."

"That won't happen up here until March, will it?"

"You can't tell," Chet said, busy eating. "Someday anyway."

"No telegraph in the works yet?" Cole asked.

"Hannagen says congress passed our part, both

the law and budget committee, but finding the money is like our cattle script—it takes time with Washington."

"Maybe in the spring you can start?"

"I hope so."

The next morning he hugged his son Rocky good-bye and they rode west. The sky was clear and he figured it would be above freezing by mid-morning. Large ravens followed them as if expecting a handout, but when they got nothing they gave up.

They stopped at the first stage station west that evening. It was the one that moved his operation over there to qualify for relay status. The place comprised a wagon yard, store, café, and bar. Many freight rigs were parked there anxious to move on but waiting for better conditions, especially the eastbound ones.

The man in charge, Ralph Thomas, put them in two guest rooms rather than the bunkhouse used by the others staying over. They spent the night and rode on to the ranch the next day.

Approaching the headquarters they passed men forking hay off two wagons to a long line of cattle. The workers waved as if surprised to see them coming.

"He has a large herd," Miguel said.

"They had a big herd that Lucy and Reg had gathered from maverick cattle running loose up here and he still wanted more. We brought two hundred more cows from Hampt's place to add to them a year ago or so. It helped Hampt's operation and ranch to recover a lot."

"Lucy's brother-in-law Bennie got a little behind operating this ranch, too," Jesus said.

"I didn't realize he had not hired enough help, being thrifty. But he does fine working for Cole on the west end. Looking at the cattle, Shawn and Lucy have done well. There are lots of cattle up here."

When they rode up to the house place, Lucy in a long coat was standing there holding the new one. Liz would be jealous about that. He couldn't blame her, considering their own situation.

"What's his name?" he asked from the foot of the stairs.

"Clem Eubanks. How did you know it was a boy?"

"I guessed it by your smile."

Shawn rode up skidding his horse to a sliding halt. "Wow, Jesus, how are you doing?"

"Miguel, meet Shawn."

"Where is Spencer Horne?" He shook Miguel's hand. "Nice to meet you."

"Up at the Apache Springs Ranch building us a new headquarters."

"Where is that?"

"Shawn, let's get them inside. I want to hear the whole story, too," Lucy said.

"Why sure, honey. Hitch your horses, guys; we can put them up later."

Inside, Lucy's younger sister, Hannah, took the baby after showing him to everyone.

Seated at her large dining table, Lucy told them the boy was two weeks old but they had no mail service so her letter was probably still at the Hackberry post office informing them about his arrival. Her daughter came into the room and climbed up into

Shawn's lap like she belonged there, which warmed Chet more than anything.

"Well," Lucy said to Chet, "what brought you to Hackberry?"

"We have been everywhere else. Robert and Betty have a daughter, Caroline. Liz and I lost ours."

"Oh, I am so sorry. How is she?"

"Fine. Disappointed, but busy. It was too cold or she'd have come along with us. Other news— Spencer is married to a lady from the Diablo Ranch and he is building headquarters on the newest ranch, which is perhaps a long day's ride north of Tucson. It was part of Weeks's ranches he lost to the banks."

"He's the man that had the phony claim on the Diablo Ranch," she explained to Shawn.

"I knew him from the Force. He was not a nice guy," Shawn said.

"Ortega was shot by one of his men rustling our cattle. He's fine now and the rustlers are dead. But Weeks is still operating his rustling operations down in Mexico."

"Ortega is a helluva great guy," Shawn said. "Glad he survived."

"Yes, he is. We saw your cattle being fed. They look great. You have enough hay?"

"Plenty. We really poured our hay making on after I got up here. I hired two other hay crews that had mowers and stackers. Bought some grass standing and we have the hay. I think the cattle are doing great, but if there is anything wrong point it out to me."

Lucy said, "Before we started feeding hay, he and

the men rounded up almost a hundred and fifty mavericks this fall."

"That is amazing. Do you have all of them now?" he asked Shawn.

"Chet, this land up here is so vast there were still lots of wild cattle. I can't say but we, maybe, only got the tamest ones. I'd like to corral some distant water holes so when they go in to drink they have to stay in there until we brand them as ours."

She put in, "That would require some more cowboys to check on the traps a couple times a week."

"I think we can make that work. So the work is to build them and then patrol them?" Chet asked.

Lucy nodded her head. "There isn't much to do up here."

"Last time, you had ranchers complain that you were catching all the wild cattle?"

Shawn dismissed it. "They might complain, but they don't try. They're too lazy."

"How do you want to start?"

"Is a dozen traps too many?" Shawn asked.

"Fine. Get what you need built."

Chet winked at Lucy.

"There, Shawn, you have your traps."

He nodded, pleased.

"Is your hay equipment at the Verde place being repaired?"

"I have the blacksmith doing it here. He's good, cheaper than hauling it over to Camp Verde and back. I'd like to ask for three more mowers, racks, and stacker for next year."

"I will have them up here by then. You will have lots of hay equipment this season."

"Traps and with roundups we will have two hundred more head by this time next year."

"Mother cows?"

"Yes, I want six hundred head of them by then. Since I got here we have fenced most of those homestead places Bo has bought for you. They all will make hay for us to cut. The rest will be fenced before the grass greens."

"Chet, you didn't send a boy up here. He works like a horse and those men who ride with him, just as hard. Come back next spring. We will have our largest calf crop ever," Lucy said.

"I don't doubt that for a minute."

Spud burst in the house, threw his hat aside, and unbuttoned his thick coat. The short man was smiling from ear to ear. "Boy, you and Jesus look so damn good to me. I've been calving cows all morning. Next year we won't have no more snow babies— them damn bulls are all going to be put up so the calves come when they have a better chance to live."

"Don't believe a word he's saying. He only lost one calf. He calves most of them in the sheds. But he's right, we are putting the bulls up until later," Shawn said.

Spud hugged Chet and Jesus as well. Then he shook Miguel's hand. When he sat down Lucy's daughter left Shawn and was already climbing into Spud's lap. "Him is me Spud."

"You have more boyfriends than I can count," Lucy teased her.

"They all mine."

After hearing the kidnapping story, Lucy and Hannah fed them a large meal for supper. He explained about stocking Toby's eastern ranch and the Oracle one with cows in the fall. How Sarge, despite the snow, made it to New Mexico and got his cattle there on time. Then he described the Diablo Ranch improvements, told them about Bonnie and JD, their plight, and how his Force was still operating in the south.

"Miguel, how did they get you to help them?" Shawn asked him.

"You know my foreman Raphael at the valley ranch?"

"Yes, I have met him."

"He said, 'Miguel, I have chosen you to ride with the *patron*. See him tomorrow about the new job.' I did and told my wife Lisa I was concerned how to please him. She said, very forcefully, 'All you have to do is be honest and be yourself. You are smart enough to learn the rest.'"

"Lisa was one of the women who came back with us from the stage-raiders shoot-out in Colorado. She's a good girl and she told you the truth about me."

Miguel said, "That rich rancher's son held her like a slave. She feared for her life the whole time she was with them. I am very proud she is now my wife, and she works hard to help all the people at the ranch. She thinks our boss is such good man to have given her another chance."

"He's a good man," Lucy said.

"Jesus and I are proud Miguel joined us. Raphael and I go back to when outlaws stole some good horses, shot the ranch foreman and his jingle bob man. He and I were tracking them. I left him there to protect the bodies because we knew another posse might be coming so I went on. The deputy leading the second posse wouldn't let him go and catch up with me. He has regretted it ever since."

Jesus smiled. "I bet that desk deputy won't tell him that today. He was too nice back then and uncertain. Today he runs the ranch."

Chet nodded in agreement.

The next day they rode with Shawn and saw how good things looked and how orderly set up things were. Spud bowed out to work on cutting out any cows close to calving. He had one pasture-born one but he was stout and after a few tries to catch him, Spud left him with his momma. "Hell, he'll make it."

Spud's wife Shirley lived in a log house on a homestead close to the ranch, so they stopped by to see her. She invited them in and served them coffee. She was very happy to see them come by.

"He told me before he left you'd come by and I was to be sure to tell you how badly he treats me and what poor conditions we live in up here."

They all laughed with her.

"I have learned a lot about orphans since I married him. All the orphans you have saved, and other not so well treated."

"What's that about?" Chet asked.

"Well several of us have had such poor treatment from others that anyone nice to us is grand."

Chet told her he understood.

More snow melted each day. When they rode into Hackberry, Chet met the black blacksmith Deacon

Moore again. The man showed him how well he was rebuilding the farm equipment for the next season. Chet thanked him and agreed that Shawn's decision to keep the work here was a sound one. They had more than enough work at the Verde Ranch blacksmith shop.

Back at the ranch, Shawn took Chet aside and told him how he was so proud to have Lucy as his wife. They were a team, and her daughter was like one of his own. "Chet, if I had planned it could not have come out any better. She is such a wonderful wife and we love each other. I wanted a chance with her. I got it thanks to you. I'm very happy and so is she."

"Good. And all on the ranch is working well."

"Yes. And Spud is great. He gets more done than two big men. I see why you sent him to help me. He is a hardworking super person, and he knows these people up here. The crew respects him like they do me. I first wondered about his wife, Shirley, but Lucy and I love her. She had made a bad decision to run off with that guy, but she's solid now. They make a good pair."

"Things look good. I am certain the four of you will succeed."

It took them five days to get back home. A ranch hand drove Jesus to town in a buckboard. Lisa came over to hug and kiss her man. Then she thanked Chet for taking him and bringing him back in one piece, and standing on her toes, she kissed him on the cheek.

"I did that to make Liz jealous," she teased, and they both laughed.

Only a step away, his wife also laughed. His arm secure in hers she shook her head. "Lisa can be a devil."

"No. She came here one. You turned her to angelic."

"Have you already forgotten how you said I needed to stop her cussing and I'd have a great daughter?"

"You did that to her."

She squeezed his arm. "I agree we did."

He wondered what was holding up any action on the building of the telegraph. Things must be fuzzy about the money involved or they'd be chomping at the bit for him to get poles and a pathway going. No telling. At least he was home to stay for a while anyway.

"How is Lucy's baby?"

"His name is Clem. He's a large boy. Shawn and Lucy act very solid together. No tension. It's like they've been together forever. The little girl crawls all over him and Spud."

"That sounds heavenly."

"It's nice, but I am happy to be back here with you and glad most of the snow is gone."

"Amen."

CHAPTER 11

A couple drove up in an unpainted wagon. She wore a worn shawl against the chill over a wash-faded dress that looked patched. He had a gray mustache and dismounted in the stiff manner of having arthritis when he came down off the wagon. The horses were longhaired and had not been brushed lately.

The man helped the woman down and they headed for the back stairs.

Monica was standing beside Chet. "Here comes more trouble, as if you need any."

"Who is it?" Liz asked from the kitchen, taking the browned biscuits out of the oven.

Reaching out a hand to shake, Chet said, "Hello. I'm Chet Byrnes. What can I do for you?"

"Claude Cannon and this is my wife, Edna. We hoped to talk to you, sir."

"We are about to eat lunch. We have plenty of food. Need help on the steps?"

"No, sir. We will have to take our time but we can climb them."

"Come easy."

Monica set plates for the newcomers. Liz looked at her for an answer. Monica shrugged. Both visitors washed their hands, apologizing for the timing of their arrival at mealtime.

"No problem. Come on in. That is my wife, Liz, and this is Monica who runs the house."

"Good to meet you all."

Everyone seated, Chet gave a prayer and they nodded amen.

"Mr. Cannon, why did you come?"

"We have a daughter named Cary. She's seventeen. Despite our warning her she has left with a worthless no account devil of a man."

His wife, tears slipping down her face, said, "I fear he will kill her when he tires of her."

"Where did they go?"

He said, "I think he took her to Tombstone."

"Where do you two live?"

"We live near Hayden's Ferry. Harry Olson told us you might help us. He and his wife heard about our problem. He told us how you had rescued his wife, Marcella, from those kidnappers."

"His wife was kidnapped. Your daughter left with this man. There is a difference."

"No. We think he drugged her to get her to go," his wife said.

"Who is this man?"

"Charles, but they call him Chuck Hadley. He never works and we think she was drugged and he is taking her to sell her in the white slave trade."

"Do you have a picture of her?"

His wife brought an oval portrait, sealed in a tin-type, out from her pocket. The girl looked like a lot of teen girls in braids. Pale skin but not a real beautiful girl. Still, she had white skin, and they would fetch a higher price on the list of such traders.

"You know teen girls disappear all the time. Most never come back or are never seen again."

The father nodded. "The only chance we have is for you to try to find her. A few years ago, I'd gone down there myself to find her or be killed. But I am no good at fighting or with a gun anymore."

"I will go look. How long has she been gone?"

"Five days."

"I better have someone to get hold of Miguel and send word to Jesus. We can catch the stage at midnight."

Liz stared at him. "You just got home."

"Time is all-important in these cases, Liz. We will go look for her, but I can't promise anything."

"Oh, thank the Lord. Sir, I have no treasures to give you, but I will pray for you every day that I live."

"I don't need that. But what we may find could break your heart. You understand that?"

The Cannons both nodded solemnly.

"Excuse me."

He went outside and asked one of the stable boys to go find Miguel. The boy nodded and ran off. Back inside, he told them they must stay for the night, but he and his team would be ready to pull out at midnight.

Miguel was there shortly.

"Someone has taken their daughter, they think, to Tombstone. They suspect there's foul play. We are going to check on where she might be. We are taking the stage at midnight."

Miguel nodded. "I will send someone to go tell Jesus."

"Yes. He can meet us at the stage."

Liz excused herself to prepare him a war bag. Monica showed the worried couple a bedroom where they could sleep.

Chet and Liz privately discussed his plans. "Two and a half days to get there. We won't stay long if we can't find her, but we will look everywhere we can and be thorough."

"So, I can expect you back in a week?"

"I don't know how long, but I will be back as soon as possible."

"I know, and I know you have a big heart. You also have a good record of recovery. I hope for her parents' sake you find her."

"So do I."

At the stage office, he hugged Anita. "I am sorry I need Jesus again so soon."

"Oh, I know. He is always ready. I expect this after being with you two so long. I should have married him two years ago. Even with all his trips with you, I have found it is a nice way to live."

Lisa was also there, waiting in the cool night, and he talked to her. "I am stealing your man again."

"That is okay. He really likes his job and I am his strongest supporter. You are challenging him to do more than herd cows. He is learning. He will some-day be a Cole Emerson and run something for you."

"I think so, too."

"Good. Be careful; we all need you."

When he and Liz were alone: "Lisa is learning to deal with all this, too, isn't she?"

"She doesn't miss a thing. Bet you noticed that she has him wearing a cowboy hat like Jesus does. Not a *sombrero.*"

"That was her change?"

"I bet it was. I will find out." She chuckled.

They left off on another trip to save a girl. Like looking for a thumbnail-size gold nugget in a stream. It would take lots of pan swishing. Maybe they'd find her. He hoped so.

They had a two-hour layover in Tucson late the next day, so the men ate at Jesus's cousin's café. Then they rode the stage to Tombstone. It was after ten o'clock when the weary travelers arrived. He got two rooms while they went to the *barrio.* If there were anything on the wind, they'd know about it before the night was over.

He made rounds of the saloons, spoke to some men he knew, showed them the picture of the girl, and asked for their silence in not telling the world. No one had seen her at any of the parlor houses. A new girl working, someone would have seen or heard about her. But Hadley might not be there with her yet, depending on his mode of transportation. She'd been gone a week by that time.

He went to bed before midnight and in the morning met Jesus and Miguel at the small café they knew served a good breakfast. In those early hours, the night chill remained. But still much warmer than the mornings at home. The biscuits were hot enough to make a little steam when opened.

"Nothing about her last night. I might have to put a reward out for her return," Jesus said.

"Good idea. You know, Chuck Hadley may not be here yet."

Both men nodded.

They rented some horses and checked in some places in Fairbanks and Charleston. But no one knew Hadley by that name or had seen the girl. Chet had hoped someone knew something, but so far nothing had turned up.

Day two a man on the boardwalk stopped by him and under his breath asked if he'd found the girl.

Chet shook his head, ready to cross the street.

"Would you pay two hundred dollars for her?"

"Sure. How do I get her?"

"Tear two one-hundred-dollar bills in half. When you get her you pay the rest to the one delivering her."

"When?"

"I will leave word at the hotel where to get her. All these men that sell women are tough and will kill you if you try anything."

"I want her alive or no deal."

He nodded and stepped off to cross the street. Chet saw he was not a cowboy or businessman. Plain work clothes, no hat, he guessed him around thirty years old with brown hair. He didn't know him.

He tore two one-hundred-dollar bills in half and put half of each in an envelope. Stuck the remaining parts back in his wallet. How would he get the first halves to the snitch? What was this man's position in the deal? Time would tell. Jesus and Miguel were still off somewhere. Maybe someone would be in the lobby. No sign of him. As he stepped outside a man standing in the dark stepped closer. "I made the deal. But he wants a hundred more."

"I'll find someone else." He figured it was a stall for more money.

"She is very nice. She might get hurt if you wait too long."

"Two hundred was the price."

"Give me the money."

Chet handed him the two halves in the envelope. "I want her unharmed."

He nodded and went away. Chet went into the hotel to sit and wait.

The shakedown for more money was part of every deal everywhere and every time. That much money would buy her. Mexican women were available for much cheaper.

Jesus came by him in the lobby and went upstairs. Since Chet did not talk to him, he knew there was something about to happen. Miguel did the same and went upstairs. The new man learned fast.

The snitch was back. He showed himself in the doorway, then went back out. Chet rose. He hoped his boys had figured things out. Once he joined the man, the guy led the way down the block and stopped at an alley.

"Third door on right. It isn't a trick; he needs the money."

"I can kill you if you've lied to me," Chet said, and paid the man ten dollars.

The man took it like he expected it. "No. He wants the money."

Chet twisted the knob from the side to open the door. Nothing. He stepped inside and saw a candle on a table. On a bed he could make out a form wrapped up in a sheet—either sleeping or dead. A masked man stood in the shadows.

"If she's dead you are, too."

"Not dead. Give me the money."

He really wanted to give him a bullet, but he took the second halves out of his wallet, handed them to the man under the flour sack mask, who had reached forward. Chet then stepped over to the bed. The man ran out the door. There was a scream. Chet knew his men had him.

His ear to the girl's mouth he could feel her breathing, but it was slow. What had he given her? Damn.

"We have him," Jesus said.

"Ask him what he gave her."

"Nothing."

"I don't care what you do to him, Jesus. We need an answer or she might die."

"Just laudanum."

"Is she naked?"

"Yes."

Nothing he could do to dress her, so they'd take her in the sheet.

"Miguel, can you carry her. We need her taken to a doctor."

"I can. She is small." He bent over and soon had her wrapped in the sheet and in his arms.

"Any of you seen a doctor's office?" Chet asked.

"A house, block west," Jesus said.

Miguel did not act overburdened with her in his arms, and they started for the doctor's house.

"Good. Jesus, bring this scum along."

When they arrived at the doctor's house, Chet hurried up the porch and knocked. A bald man came to the door. "Yes?"

"A young woman has been drugged and we need your help to save her."

"Bring her right in. How long ago was she drugged?"

Chet turned to Hadley. "When was the last time you drugged her?"

He shrugged. "About an hour ago."

"He do this to her?"

"That and he sold her."

"You law?" the doc asked, shaking his head.

"Yes, U.S. marshal."

Doc nodded at Hadley. "That the son of a bitch did this to her?"

"He did and he's going to prison for doing it."

"Can't give him enough time."

"Agreed. My name is Chet Byrnes. That is Jesus Martinez and Miguel Costa. My deputies."

"You live in Preskitt, don't you?" Doc asked.

"Yes."

"She live up there?"

"No. She lived at home with her folks at Hayden's Ferry."

Doc shook his head again.

"Her parents drove clear to my ranch and asked for my help. Said he'd kidnapped their daughter."

"Most lawmen would have said they had more important things to do."

"Not me. Now, what about her?"

"Let her come out of it naturally. She'll have a hangover. My wife can dress her, and I think, besides feeling bad at first, she'll recover. You putting him in jail here?"

"Not here. Too many men escape from it. I'll put him on the stage up to Benson; they will hold him there until they can take him up to Phoenix for trial."

Jesus nodded. "I can do that."

"When she can travel we'll stop there and fill out the papers. They can hold him without bail until then."

"Wait up there or come back here?" Jesus asked him.

"Depends if she can travel."

"I can take him up there on the late-night stage and take the noon one back here."

Chet agreed. "Handcuff him."

"Mister, I won't do him no harm."

"Hadley, you won't do anyone harm where you're going. Handcuff him."

While Jesus hauled him off to the stage depot, the three men went out on the porch so Doc's wife could dress her.

"You need some sleep?" Doc asked him.

"I can wait until she wakes up." He didn't feel, until she woke up, that she might be all right.

When she finished dressing the girl, the doc's wife came out onto the dark porch. "She is reviving some."

"Let's go see her," Doc said.

He spoke to her and checked her heartbeat with his stethoscope. Unplugging his right ear he nodded. "What is her name?"

"Cary."

"Cary, can you hear me?"

"Yes."

"Cary, you are safe. Hadley is on his way to jail."

"How?"

"Cary, I am Marshal Chet Byrnes. You parents asked me to find you."

"Oh, God bless them. I didn't know if anyone would worry about me. He had me so doped up I didn't know where or who I was." She began to cry. "It has been the worst time of my life. Two other men raped me and then told him they wouldn't pay what he wanted, that it was too much."

"You know their names?"

"Arnold is one. Lake is another."

At the names, the doctor added, "I bet it is Aaron Arnold, he owns a cathouse. Tyron Lake is another shady character hangs around, he's a gambler, too."

"Those men both raped me."

"Cary, you'd have to testify in court that they did that?"

"I would do it." She gritted her teeth and fists. "Where is Hadley?"

"On his way to jail up in Benson by now."

"Good. I did not deserve any of this." She began to weep.

Doc's wife came to sit on the bed and comfort her. "Darling, your worst fears are over. This man will have them punished."

"But I have nothing. No clothes. Nothing."

"Ma'am, when the stores open would you take her and get her some clothes so she can travel? A rickshaw would take you to a dress shop. She will need two dresses, shoes, the rest. I will pay for it."

"That's very nice of you. I could do that."

"Get a new dress for yourself."

"I couldn't do that."

"I insist."

Before he left her, Chet went over his plans of how they'd take her home as soon as he had both men arrested for her rape. She solemnly nodded and he kissed her forehead. "Things will be all right."

Cary smiled, her eyes shining in the light of the lamps.

Next he and Miguel went to sleep upstairs in some empty bedrooms. Chet woke in a few hours and found Miguel waiting downstairs.

"You get any sleep?"

"I am fine."

Before they went for breakfast he learned she was sleeping, and Doc's wife said she was going to be all right when the final effect of the laudanum wore off.

At the meal in the one-counter café, the two had eggs, bacon, and soda biscuits with a bowl of flour gravy and good coffee. Chet was hungry and enjoying it all. Miguel even smiled.

"You ever have a case like this before?"

"Similar. But most women don't want to testify. It can be a brutal thing when the defense lawyer tries to make her out as little more than a *puta* in the courtroom."

Miguel nodded that he understood.

"There may be a way to stop that. If Hadley would sign a confession that they did that to her, then the prosecutor would have something more than her testimony. If the men knew that, they might make a deal to plead guilty and save them some prison time. It might work."

"Would Hadley sign it?"

"I think he can be convinced. All the crimes are on his head, and he can't afford a fancy lawyer."

"Who are these other men?"

"I don't know them. But we will before dark. I need to find the town marshal, Virgil Earp. He will know them."

They found Virgil in the Alhambra Saloon. He smiled and nodded when Chet spoke to him.

"Good to see you. What can I do for you, Marshal?"

"This is Miguel. He rides with me. Miguel, Virgil Earp."

"Glad to meet you, sir."

"My pleasure. I know you aren't here to drink."

"No. I want to arrest Aaron Arnold and Tyron Lake."

"What for?"

"The rape of a young woman being sold into the white slavery."

"Wow. That is serious."

"Where can I find them?"

"Heaven on Earth Whore House is two blocks over. Arnold keeps some thugs on his payroll. Be careful there. Lake is sleeping with a doxie in the Belle Hotel at this hour. I could take you over to the hotel so you can arrest him, and we can put him in a cell in the city judge's office until you get Arnold."

"I would appreciate that."

"I'll be back," Virgil said over his shoulder to his brother and some others.

They walked the blocks to the hotel.

"Lake is in what room?"

"Two-oh-four."

Virgil asked the desk clerk for a key to save kicking in a door, and the young man kindly obliged.

They marched upstairs. At the room, Virgil said quietly, "Draw your guns."

He unlocked it and it swung open. Chet pointed his gun at the startled man who sat up in bed. The naked woman with him screamed.

"U.S. Marshal Byrnes. Tyron Lake, you are under arrest for rape of a minor and dealing in white slavery. Make one wrong move and I will shoot you. Get up and get dressed."

"You can't—"

Miguel jerked him out of bed by the arm. "He said get dressed or go naked."

Then Miguel picked up the short-barreled Colt

on the nightstand and shoved it in his waistband, holding his own in Lake's belly.

"All right. All right."

"What am I going to do?" the woman asked, shielding her body with a sheet.

"How the hell should I know? They can't prove a damn thing on me. My lawyer will get me out in a few hours."

"You are going to jail in Tucson. Tell him to go there."

"Huh?"

"You heard me. Get your shoes on."

"Earp, he can't do this to me. You stop him right now."

"I can't do a thing but cooperate with the federal law."

"You're going to pay for this. All of you."

"Handcuff him and check around for other weapons. We don't want her shooting at us on the way to that cell."

"Get Leon Newburg over to the county jail, he'll get me out on bond," Lake told her.

Chet didn't bother to tell them that he wasn't using county facilities to house Lake. They hustled him out and in fifteen minutes he was locked in the single cell at the city judge's office. Lake was screaming his head off.

Virgil, outside the cell, softly said, "If you are not quiet, I will chain you up and gag you."

"You can't do that—" But Lake shut up.

"I'll be back for him after I arrest Arnold."

Virgil nodded. "He will be here. I can come along if you want."

"We can handle it. Thanks."

Virgil nodded. "Good luck, then, is all I can say."

Miguel went to check on Jesus's return and was to meet Chet on a corner a block from the house of ill repute. It was after twelve and the Tucson stage should be there if Jesus caught it.

Fifteen minutes later, Miguel met him there alone.

"The driver told me he couldn't catch the night stage. There were no seats. They had an armed guard riding shotgun."

"Well, Arnold has bouncers working for him. They may try to block his arrest. Get ready to catch hell."

His man nodded. "I'm backing you. I am sure we can do it."

They walked up the wide stairs to the veranda of the house. Chet knocked on the door, and a black domestic teen maid invited them in.

"How may I's help you?"

"We need to speak to Aaron Arnold."

"I am so sorry but he be asleep and does not want to be disturbed."

"I am a U.S. marshal. Show me his room."

"Oh, I can't do that, sir."

"What room is his?"

Miguel had his gun out.

"Show us." Chet shoved her toward the stairs.

She tried to retreat in wide-eyed fear.

"Show us the room he sleeps in."

"Don't shoot me."

"Keep going to his door." He waved her on.

She was shaking and he feared she might faint, but instead the young maid led the way. The parlor was empty and she was taking fast steps until they reached the second floor.

"Now where?"

Trembling, the girl pointed at a door and fell to her knees weeping. Chet nodded at Miguel and told him to smash it open with his boot. It required a second try. As the door flew open, Chet fired a shot into the ceiling. "Hands high or die!"

In the boiling gun smoke, a man with a hairy chest sat up in bed with his hands high. The woman next to him was screaming into a pillow for him not to try anything.

"I am U.S. Marshal Chet Byrnes. You are under arrest for the rape of a minor and white slavery."

"You must be crazy—"

"No. Get up and get dressed, or go to jail in your underwear. I don't care. Get him out of bed and be careful. He may have a gun handy."

Someone was coming up the stairs. Chet could hear his approach. "Watch him."

Chet came out the door and met the half-dressed man holding a pistol in his fist. "Drop the gun."

The man didn't. Chet shot. The shock-faced man went rolling backward down the stairs in a cloud of black powder and sprawled out at the bottom. Two more men appeared.

In that cloud of gun smoke, gun cocked, he ordered them to raise their hands. Chet then asked Miguel, "Is he dressed?"

"We're coming." Miguel brought Arnold out cuffed and carrying his shoes.

"Arnold, one trick and I'll shoot you."

"Get my lawyer down to the courthouse," Arnold shouted to the robed women onlookers. "Do it right now."

They went past the wounded guard who had not moved since his fall.

"Don't do nothing," he said to his henchmen. "This sumbitch will shoot me."

"What should we do?"

"I told you. Get my lawyer to the county court-house."

Chet and Miguel swept him out onto the porch.

"Keep walking," Chet told his prisoner.

Arnold walked barefooted ahead of them. Miguel was watching behind them.

"This is not the way to the courthouse," Arnold complained.

"We aren't going there. We're going to Tucson where you can't buy your way out."

"Who are you? You son of a bitch."

"I am the man that's going to slam you into jail for rape and white slavery. Better see all of Tombstone you want right now. It will look different when you get out of prison in twenty years."

As they walked toward the cell holding Lake, they saw Jesus coming toward them on a buckboard. Jesus made the driver stop and then got off.

"Well you found a ride but you still missed all the fun." Chet laughed.

"Sorry there were no seats for me. I owe Frank Herman here a ten-dollar fare?"

"I can pay that." He dug the money out.

"Who's he?" the rancher driver asked with a toss of his head.

"Aaron Arnold under arrest for raping a teen and white slavery."

"Hmm. You think you can get him tried here?"

"No. But in Tucson I can. You have another buckboard to take them to Tucson?"

"I can get another to do it."

"How much?"

"Twenty bucks apiece."

"How long to get ready?"

"An hour. Where will I meet you?"

"City hall. We have another prisoner there, him, and a third one in the Benson jail. Plus our gear."

"I've got a big rig and four horses for forty bucks."

"Sounds better to me. Get them."

"You expecting any gunplay?"

"No."

"Why not?"

"First people we shoot will be the prisoners."

"Good idea. I need to go get that outfit. I'll be back."

Chet paid him the ten-dollar fee for Jesus. "Thanks. See you at the city hall."

Jesus explained about the stage. "They had a shotgun guard plus six passengers coming back from Benson last night. No room for me, so I hired Hank there to bring me back."

"Good idea. We have Lake at the city judge's cell.

Aaron here had an armed guard that I shot. But we want to move fast now. You two put him in the cell and I'll meet you there. I may buy Cary a stage ticket to Tucson and have her meet us there when she can travel. The doctor's wife took her to get some clothes and shoes. I better go fix on that."

Jesus and Miguel took the prisoner to the cell while Chet cut back for the doctor's house.

Cary and Doc's wife were back and the doctor's wife was fixing her hair.

"Cary, we have Hadley, Lake, and Arnold in custody and must take them to Tucson. I hired a wagon to take them up there. I will get you a ticket on the stage to Tucson and either I or one of my men will meet you at the stage station there. Can you do that? Ride the stage by yourself to there?"

"I will ride with her," Doc's wife said.

"Sorry I don't know your name, but if you'd do that, I'd gladly pay you and for your ticket."

"My name is Della, and no, you have done enough. You are a brave man doing what you did for her."

"Della, your ticket both going and back will be paid for."

"I have read about things you've done for other people. If Arizona had more men like you we'd be a state already."

"That's why I do them."

"I understand that. We will be in Tucson in the morning. One more thing? I understand you have a wife?" Della asked. "Does she have an address where I can write her? I want to thank her, too, for letting you do these things."

"Her name is Elizabeth Byrnes. Post Office Box Fourteen, Prescott, Arizona Territory. She would hug you. Good day. See you tomorrow in Tucson."

They both agreed to see him there.

He ate a bean and meat flour tortilla meal from a street vendor while he walked to the judge's office, washing it down with a bottle of sarsaparilla from another street vendor. His men, with their prisoners, were ready to go.

"How about Cary?"

"Della, the doc's wife, is bringing her to Tucson. She looks nice in her new dress. One of us will meet them at the stage depot and take them to our hotel."

Frank Herman drove his big Conestoga wagon, with his hoof-stomping big horses, into town and halted the teams. The prisoners were loaded over the high tailgate with Arnold swearing they'd never get them to Tucson alive.

"Arnold, you have a will written?"

"No, why?"

"Anyone attacks us, I will shoot you first and them second. You better pray they don't try anything."

His threat shut the loud mouth up. They rumbled out of Tombstone, stopped over at the Benson jail, loaded Hadley, and were on their way. The grade going west was steep and hard, but the big horses were on their toes and pulled through. They finally emerged over the crest. The wagon was not as comfortable as a stagecoach, which had suspension that helped over the rough spots, This rig had none, but they were making good progress.

Chet doubted they could get a mass of riders to stop them, but he was on edge and would be until they arrived at the Pima County Courthouse. The jail was still many hours west of their location.

It would be a long night.

CHAPTER 12

At dawn, when they came off the last high spot in the highway and headed down hill through the forest of saguaros toward the sleeping town of Tucson, Chet decided he could sleep for three days when it was over. He only hoped they'd let him do that. Tossed around and shaken by the crude ride, he was ready for the last of an estimated forty-mile journey from Benson.

He admired Frank Herman's driving. He never let up on the horses, making it the fastest drive he possibly could. And seated on a spring seat, he'd taken a bigger beating than Chet suffered in the wagon bed.

At last with the sun peeking in an orange fire ring from behind them, they rattled through narrow streets for the courthouse. Frank reined his horses to a halt at the front steps.

"You are here."

The three lawmen clapped and cheered. Someone came out of the jail and let down the chained-up tailgate. "What have you got?"

"Three rapists and white slavers. I am deputy U.S. Marshal Chet Byrnes."

"We've got plenty of room for them. They must have wired ahead. We have bailsmen and lawyers inside anxious to bail them out."

Chet shook his head. "They are too big a risk to run for Mexico to allow them out on bail."

"Whatever you say, sir," the jail guard said.

The prisoners were unloaded and then his two deputies stepped down.

Chet took the lead and parted the crowd in the lobby. They were soon back in the jail portion and the handcuffs were taken off. The prisoners were ordered to completely undress, shoes and all. They made them walk naked clear of their clothes and put on striped uniforms.

They were asked their names and who to contact in case of death. Barefooted, they were marched back to the cells. The sheriff, Ben Deloris, was there. He asked Chet and his men to come into a side office for a conference.

"Marshal Byrnes, you stirred up a hornets' nest. What is the situation?"

"Chuck Hadley kidnapped a young woman, Cary Cannon, up in Maricopa County. Her parents, Claude and Edna Cannon, came to my ranch at Preskitt Valley and asked me to try to get their daughter back. Claude thought the man who took her intended to take her to Tombstone.

"My two deputies and I began to look for her in Tombstone and a snitch got me a chance to buy her. Hadley wanted two hundred dollars. After he took my money my men arrested him. She was heavily doped. We took her to a local doctor.

"When she woke up she said besides Hadley raping her, two other men had also raped her and, afterward, each man declined to buy her. That made them accomplices to white slavery and kidnapping. She said she would testify against them."

"What a horrible story. Those other two have strong lawyers and are demanding them to be bonded out."

"Hell, they'd simply run to Mexico. Do I need to talk to the judge?"

"I am setting that up. When did you sleep last?"

"Two days ago."

"I know you brought them here because the Cochise County jail is not escape proof, and they would have enough pull there to get out on bail."

"Arnold runs a whorehouse and I shot one of his guards while arresting him. Lake is a gambler and no doubt a white slaver. Hadley is a worthless lazy bastard who courted a young girl and then kidnapped her to sell her."

"I have sent for Judge Kimble. He won't let them have bond after hearing you."

"Sorry I am causing you so much trouble."

"Hell no. Those three bastards have no right to be loose to do it again."

"Exactly."

"What do you need to do next, besides sleep?"

"Get some of that. Della, the wife of the doctor who revived Cary, is bringing her to Tucson on the afternoon stage. I need to meet her."

"How about you sleep. I will send a deputy with

one of your men to meet her. Where would you put her up? And what next?"

"Feed both women first, and I'll get rooms at the Congress Hotel for all of us. Della may wish to stay. Send a telegram to Claude Cannon, Hayden's Ferry. Tell him his daughter is safe and in Chet Byrnes's care. Send the same wire to Elizabeth Byrnes in Preskitt with the same note."

"I can take care of all of that."

Chet put some bills on his desk. Deloris shoved it back. "We can handle this. You obviously have done enough. I will handle this and see about the judge."

Jesus came in. Chet told him how to handle the women and the hotel. He agreed to take care of it. "I should pay Herman."

"Give him a hundred and thank him."

Jesus approved, took the money, and went to get Miguel. All that handled, Chet slouched in a leather chair and closed his eyes for minute. Deloris was back. "The judge is in his chambers. We are going up the back stairs."

"Madhouse out there?"

"Worse than that. Kimble is a tough judge, but he's fair."

In the judge's room, Kimble nodded as Chet stood before the bench.

"Tell me all about this matter of the arrests you made in Cochise County."

Chet slowly reconstructed the reason he went there, how he found Hadley and trapped him into accepting payment for her. Then how he arrested

Lake and then Arnold as rapists and accomplices in kidnapping and white slavery.

"Marshal Byrnes, I know your reputation in enforcement is very strong. You have asked my court not to allow bail to be extended to any of the accused in these charges. Why is that?"

"They reside less than ten miles from the Mexican border. They will take a powder down there first chance they get. They are all able to do that. Arnold owns a whorehouse. Lake is a gambler, and I believe research could prove he had been involved in other white slavery before or why would Hadley have let him use her body?"

"This young lady will testify?"

"She will and I believe a smart prosecutor could get Hadley to testify, too."

The judge said, "These kind of trials are tough on innocent girls."

"I told her that, but she has been abused and wants them punished."

"Is there a chance they'd plead guilty to a lesser charge?"

"I hope no one accepts it."

"I will not set bail on them. They may go to a higher court, but your argument is good enough for me. They are too great a risk to receive bond."

"Thank you, sir."

"No, after hearing your story and the difficulties, I thank you."

"I am going now to get some food and rest."

Deloris stopped him. "Avoid that mob downstairs. Go out the back door. Your men have gone to get her."

"Thank you."

"There will be a grand jury assembled. They may need you to testify."

"I understand."

"Get some sleep."

"I will as soon as my men and the women are safe and settled."

He joined his bunch, Della, and Cary at their usual family café.

"Those reporters didn't find you?" Jesus asked.

"No. I left by the back door thanks to the sheriff. Judge has refused them bail."

"Hurrah."

"You ladies all right?"

Della nodded.

"I had a telegram sent to your folks that you were all right, Cary."

Cary looked pleased over all they'd done for her. "Thanks. I am sure my folks have been worried."

"I had a wire sent to my wife, too."

"We already ordered. The waitress is bringing you some food and sarsaparilla," Jesus explained to him.

"Do we have beds?"

"Yes. At the Congress Hotel."

Della said, "I am going to stay an extra day if she needs me."

"Thanks, Della. She can use the security."

"This food sure looks great," he told the waitress.

"Oh, señor, you always say that."

"It's always good."

He thought how really good it had been as he fell across the bed and went to sleep in his clothing.

CHAPTER 13

First light the next morning Chet woke uncertain of where he was. A hotel in Tucson. The prisoners were in jail. His head pounded with a headache. He felt like he'd been run over by a wagon and team, but he got up, straightened up his clothes, and hitched on his gun belt. Another day, another dollar. He'd much rather been home for this one.

His men and both women were in the lobby waiting for him.

"We going to the restaurant around the corner?"

"Let's go to Sue's," Della said. "She has a good place to eat. Doc and I eat there whenever we are here."

They agreed and went a block farther. The coffee was good, the platter of breakfast man-size, and they thanked Della for the suggestion.

"What will happen next?" she asked.

"We need to wait for the grand jury to meet. They will direct the prosecutor what to do next."

Chet bought a newspaper and laughed.

Tombstone businessman claims his competition lied about him and he was arrested by mistake. Aaron Arnold, through his attorney, John Freeze, says an over-zealous U.S. marshal busted into his home, shot his butler, and hauled him off without an attorney to the Pima County jail not allowing him any bail. Judge Gail Kimble ruled that all three men turned over to the county sheriff were too large a risk to release on bond.

Lawyers for the defendants are taking the decision to the Arizona Supreme Court.

"They won't hear from them for six months," Chet said, shaking his head. "Did that bouncer look like a butler to you, Miguel?"

"No, but he had a gun."

Chet smiled. "I like the businessman feature the best."

They went back to the hotel. The prosecuting attorney came by and went over the evidence. He told them they were calling in the prospective grand jury members and court would be held sometime soon.

"We all have things to do. Cary has not been home in some time. Della is staying here to help her but does need to get home. My men and I have jobs to do and family."

"I will call you all in the next two days."

"Good." He wired Liz he was tied up for another day or so with a grand jury appearance.

Court was finally called and he and everyone made their appearances. A couple members of the grand jury asked Chet if he thought the rape of Cary made them a part of the white slave trade charges.

"I believe they accepted being part of that criminal offense by raping her as a test whether to buy her or not and not reporting his offer to sell her."

"Do you think she was merely a prostitute and going to profit for doing it?"

"No. When Hadley sold her to me, she was naked and unconscious from laudanum. A state that he kept her in after he kidnapped her from her family's home near Hayden's Ferry about one week earlier."

"Mr. Byrnes, how did you get involved in this? Couldn't local authorities have handled it?"

"Local authorities offered them no help, so Claude Cannon and his wife drove from Hayden's Ferry to my ranch at Preskitt Valley to ask for my help in finding their daughter. I said I would try to find her. They had caught something that was said about Tombstone, so we started there. I made it known that I would buy her and was led to Hadley who sold her to me for two hundred dollars.

"We took her to the doctor. When she recovered she told us those other two men sampled her body, in Hadley's hope, to buy her. That to me was guilty proof by association. They never reported the crime. They used an innocent girl's body for their own purposes as a test whether to buy her or not. That makes me angry. She could have been my daughter or yours."

"Thank you."

He left the jury room.

A newspaper reporter followed him out of the courthouse. "Sir, do you consider your apprehension of these three men unusual for a federal marshal, stepping into territorial law and arresting them?"

"No."

"But, sir, aren't there county sheriff officers to handle such matters?"

"When outlaws cross county lines, they can avoid apprehension in the next county. A young woman was kidnapped in Maricopa County and taken to Cochise County by her kidnapper. There her kidnapper became involved in white slavery trade and two men tested her for that purchase. Those three men would have slid by the law enforcement in both counties had my deputies and I not apprehended them."

"Will they be tried in federal court or territorial court?"

"That is up to the prosecution. I merely arrested them."

"I understand you own several ranches across the territory. Why are you involved in enforcing the law?"

"Arizona will never reach statehood without showing America we are not a criminal hole for all such men as those I arrested here to hide in. I am for statehood and will do anything to move us there."

The reporter had to half run to keep up beside him as he wrote his notes. "Sheriff Behan of Cochise County says two of these men were illegally arrested in his jurisdiction. That they both are prominent businessmen and pillars of the community."

"Maybe he needs a new set of glasses."

"You don't agree with his assessment of Mr. Lake and Mr. Arnold?"

"I don't. Lake is a gambler by profession. Arnold owns a whorehouse. If we attempt to build statehood on those kinds of businesses, Arizona will never become one."

"Both are legal legitimate enterprises."

"I did not arrest them for that. By their treatment of that girl, as someone to buy, they broke the federal law that prohibits white slavery."

"Why?"

"They were involved in the crime. They are as guilty as Hadley was who kidnapped her and then offered her for sale to them."

"Both those men have hired high-price lawyers to defend them."

"That's legal."

"You don't object to that?"

"Not under the law for their defense."

"But you insist they are guilty."

"A jury of twelve men, presided over by a judge, will decide that."

"But you, personally, decided they were guilty."

"That is why I arrested them. And I consider them the scum of the earth for what they did to that girl."

"They have witnesses they say will show she's a wayward woman."

"Under federal laws you cannot sell any woman, wayward or not. The girl was kidnapped and he tried to sell her to three men I know about, Lake, Arnold, and me. The other two never reported him to Sheriff Behan about what he tried to do with her. That is what a law-abiding citizen would have done—reported the crime. They raped her and considered buying her from Hadley. They are accomplices to

the crime and the prosecutor will prove it to a jury.
Now I have more important things to do than argue
with you."

"One more question?"

"Hurry."

"Why did you not put them in the Cochise County
jail?"

"Look up the number of prisoners that have escaped from that jail."

"You are saying the sheriff of that county lets
them out?"

"That or he has a poor system of locks on his cells.
Good day."

He could already hear the Tucson newsboys hawk-
ing the next morning's paper. *U.S. Marshal says
Sheriff Behan lets criminals out of his jail.*

His crew was in the café seated at a private table
in the back.

"How did it go?" Jesus asked.

"I told them what I thought and they cold-faced
me. How did you all do?"

Cary shook her head. "I thought the same thing.
But I did not cry. They asked me if I ever worked in
a house of ill repute. I told them I did not. Why
would they ask me that?"

"Cary, I am sorry, but if the defense can make the
jury believe you have done that, then they can get
your testimony downgraded. But the law reads that
anyone involved in selling people, it does not matter
who they are, it is a crime."

"Della told me their raping me might not hold up
if they have witnesses. But you say it doesn't matter
about my role, that it was a crime to sell me."

"Exactly."

"I want them punished."

"So do we. That's why we are still here instead of home with our families. Right, Della?"

"Yes, sir. We all are here because we have a cause to prove."

The men nodded. "What will the judge do?"

"He promised no bail. That means they can't run for the border. When the grand jury decides their fate, we will know the next thing we must do."

"What about you, Miguel?"

"I am learning all about these legal proceedings."

"It gets complicated. Prosecutor Jacob is supposed to send us word here when the jury decides what the charges will be."

Jesus jumped in with news for Chet. "Elizabeth sent you a telegram. She is coming down here to help you."

"Tonight?" Chet asked.

"She left last night so she will get here tomorrow."

"So, Della, you will get your wish to meet my wife."

She smiled. "I heard that earlier. Cary and I both are excited to meet her."

Cary nodded.

"I hope the grand jury does their deliberation this afternoon."

"Will we all have to testify again?" Miguel asked.

"Yes, they may try them separately. No telling."

"Spencer found us here. He is getting some supplies and will be back to talk to you later," Jesus said.

"How is he doing?"

"Says there is lots to do. But he looks happy about his marriage."

"That sounds good."

"With the help Frisco sent from Mexico, he says he is learning more Spanish to be able to talk to his kids."

Miguel chuckled. "He has a long ways to go."

Chet smiled and drank some of the fresh coffee the waitress brought him. "You have to crawl to walk."

Miguel agreed.

"I am curious," Della said. "What will you do next after this trial business is over?"

"Go home, put my boots up, and rest."

"These two men tell me you get cases like this all the time. You and Jesus last found another woman kidnapped that the local law denied she was taken?"

"We also went to Utah twice."

"Do you keep records of all this?"

"No."

"You should. Someone needs to write a book about all your work so your children and people will know all the generous things you have done for the people of this territory."

"I'd be happy with statehood for Arizona."

"Amen."

Spencer returned. He hugged Chet. "Good to see you, boss man. The ranch headquarters is moving slow. The lumber is there and we do have a plan. In sixty days I promised Lucinda a bunkhouse completed enough to live in. It may be close. She is a darling and really helping me a lot. Best thing that ever happened."

Chet didn't tell him the woman, Rebecca, did not leave Preskitt on the tickets he bought her to go back home but was *housekeeping* there for a widowed man named Chandler and his two children. Chandler had some mining interest at Crown King and had more money than a deputy marshal. Luckily, Spencer now had himself a wife and that was a better sounding deal anyway.

Spencer left them after an hour's visit to drive his wagon of supplies back to the ranch. Things sounded like they were moving along well up there.

They received no word from the grand jury and went back to the hotel. Chet took a bath and shaved in his room. With his wife coming the wait would not seem so long. He met her when the stage arrived. They hugged and kissed. He had her luggage delivered to the hotel, tipped the deliverer, and they joined his growing circle at the café owned by Jesus's cousins, for supper.

The prosecutor, Jacob, came by and they talked in private. "The trial will start very shortly, and I believe all three will plead guilty to the white slavery charge. That is a federal trial and they can get from five to ten years at Leavenworth, Kansas, or the Ohio Federal Penitentiary, since Arizona has not built the state prison at Yuma and they'd have to serve time at some county jail here on bread and water and road-building in chains."

"You think they will plead guilty then?" Chet asked.

"I think you put the fear of God in their hearts that you were going to succeed in getting them convicted even if they proved Cary was a harlot. I don't believe that is the case, but that was their purpose from the get-go to get them off. But under the white slave law even a prostitute can't be sold, so by pleading guilty and admitting, they will get lesser years."

"Let me ask Cary what she thinks first?"

He drew her apart and told her they could save a long trial and get them behind bars for several years.

"They will go to jail?"

"Yes. Federal jail."

"I would appreciate not testifying. But I promised you I would even when you told me how bad it would be for me."

"We have won. Considering the high-price lawyers they hired we have won. They could not sell anyone into slavery or be an accessory to that and not face the trial and conviction."

"How did you figure that out?"

"I had that in mind when you woke up and you told me what they did to you."

"Thanks. Your wife is beautiful."

"She can help you. It is her way."

"She offered to help me. I may go back to Hayden's Ferry even after all this happened to me, but I really appreciate her offer to find me a new life."

"We can work that out later if you need help. I must tell the prosecutor that his plan will work for you."

Jacob thanked him. "Sentencing will be at eight a.m."

Chet promised him they would stay to hear the punishment.

With his wife in tow they all sat in the courtroom

and rose when Judge Kimble arrived. When all were seated, Kimble asked each prisoner to rise, and individually asked each if they were innocent or guilty of breaking the law concerning white slavery. They pled guilty.

"The crime you are charged with is a dire one. Many of America's finest men died fighting so that this rule became the law of the land. The law says no man shall enslave any one, black or white, and anyone breaking the law, including accomplices, and found guilty will serve up to fifteen years for violating that law. You three have admitted you broke this law. I accept your plea and sentence each of you to ten years but no less than six for good behavior."

A woman wailed and Chet thought she was Arnold's wife. Two lawyers tried to object to the length of sentences.

"Your objection is out of order. Their sentences will stand. Their destination to federal confinement is being decided in Washington, D.C."

"Your honor, may they have a few days' bail to settle their businesses?"

"Absolutely not. I consider them as severe risks of running away, and such action is not a practice in federal court after a guilty plea. Court is dismissed."

Chet hugged Liz, Della, and a teary-eyed Cary. His men were smiling. Jacob and his two assistants shook his hand and congratulated him.

"Supper tonight at the fancy restaurant where the banker took us."

"Can we go like we are?" Della asked.

Jesus squeezed her arm. "They will take his money I am certain."

She laughed. It didn't matter; Liz, Cary, and Della went shopping anyway. He knew that Liz wanted to help Cary all she could, and they were going shopping for warm clothes for the girl to wear home.

They were at the Mexican café eating lunch when the Chief U.S. Marshal Bruce Cline came to find him. The man had been out of town on government business and never had met Chet in person.

After Cline explained his absence, he told Chet how pleasing the convictions were to the service. This had been a very hard law to prove in the past, but his accomplishment would make more cases work for prosecutors.

Then he showed him three letters.

Chet read them quickly. There was a murderer, or a gang, killing ranchers across the state for their valuables. They struck mainly isolated ranches where the crime was cold by the time anyone found the victims.

"After I get home, I will investigate the matter."

"Thanks. Your Force works well, too. Keep the letters; they may help you."

"What did he ask you to do?" Liz asked.

"Here are the letters. Maybe you have an idea."

"I don't have to read them. My husband has a new assignment."

He kissed her forehead. "I guess so. Let the men read them."

"More work for you?" Della asked.

"Yes. U.S. marshals must find the jurors and set up courtrooms. They do little but serve federal warrants.

My job is to support local sheriffs and work on cases that cross county lines. I don't draw a salary. They pay my deputies, not me. But I keep working at it in the hope that, in the end, Arizona will become a state."

Della nodded.

Liz hugged his arm. "Can we go home tomorrow?"

"We can send everyone home. Cary can go with the men and meet her family at the Ferry. We will put Della on a stage home and you and I can go by and look at Apache Springs if you want."

Jesus interrupted them. "One of us rides with you two. That's the rules."

"To keep us out of trouble, right?" Liz said.

"Yes. Miguel will go with Cary. I will ride with you."

"Okay, that is settled. Jesus, you better find us some solid horses and two packhorses plus the gear and supplies we will need."

"When do we eat tonight?" Jesus asked.

"Seven at that fancy place Nye took us to."

"Come on, Miguel, it is past one now. We have lots to acquire, huh?"

"Can he do all that?" Liz asked.

"Yes. Good thing Della is going home tomorrow. Doc will think we kept her for good."

"Oh, no," Della said. "I have written Doc letters every day. I am so grateful to you, all of you. And Cary, my dear, good luck. Sounds like you will soon be home."

"Yes. I will write you. You have been like a mother to me."

"I feel like that, too. Doc and I never had a single child live, so you have been like a daughter."

Liz took Cary aside. "Don't worry, Cary, if things get too upsetting at your home, come to my house. If we are not there, just explain to Monica. She will look after you."

"I will be fine. You all are my family, too. I thank God a lot."

Chet then told her, "I am certain you would like your family to meet you at the ferry. Miguel can wait there if you don't feel secure."

"I think it will be all right. I have your wife's offer if I can't."

"Fine. We will wire your parents when the stage will get there and they can meet you," Chet told her.

"Thank you very much."

"No problem. We will be back up there at Preskitt in a few days."

"She is—your wife has been so nice to me."

"She's a great lady."

"Miguel told me about his wife, Lisa, and all she did for her."

"You would like Lisa, too. We are a big family."

She nodded, choked up by it all.

Jesus and Miguel had the horses, supplies, pack-saddles, a saddle for Liz, and the gear to camp along the way ready to go. They all met at the restaurant and were seated in the back, which did not bother Chet or anyone. They had a very nice meal together.

Della said she'd make Doc bring her to this restaurant on their next trip to Tucson. Everyone cheered her on. After an enjoyable meal, they went back to the hotel. Early breakfast at the café, Cary and Miguel went to the stage stop with Della who was sad at leaving the group.

Liz, Jesus, and Chet went to the livery stable and soon rode out north for Oracle. Chet figured it might take over a day to get to where Spencer was camped with his bride. The weather was pleasant but cool enough for jackets, and they made good time trotting the horses, all well broke ponies. She agreed with him that the rolling country was fine-looking rangeland.

Near dark they started up into the canyon and he told her they'd make it all right. The lamps in Spencer's camp appeared and Chet shouted, "Hello, Spencer."

He ran out to the edge of the light and waved them in. "Come on in. Lucinda, the *patron* is here."

Hugging his new wife's shoulders, Spencer Horne beamed his welcome. His men unloaded the pack-horses and helped set up the two tents under Jesus's instructions. Spencer helped his wife at the fire to fix more food. Her two children were bright eyed and excited about the company.

Spencer took a lantern and showed Chet the framework for the bunkhouse they had assembled so far. He had lots of the needed material, including the roof shakes, already on the site.

"I have the house framing ordered, but it will take a while to get that lumber up here. I have two sawmills on Mount Lemon cutting lumber for us, but they have to keep up the mining needs at Tomb-stone and that area first. Mining timber is their first order of business."

"I savvy. Liz wanted to see the area. Today she saw lots of the rangeland and agreed it would make a fine ranch. These headquarters will make it a property worth a lot more. I can't believe the ranch's developer's wife lived in Oracle and not up here."

Spencer agreed. "I am in love with this ranch. And I agree it is going to be a real good one."

"Well, I know you are working hard. Take a day off for her. It will be built in plenty of time."

"She is my source of energy. She loves it here."

"I believe in you getting this done. You have nothing to prove to me, but stop, take a breath, and enjoy this project. Have some festivals, do some things that are fun, and it will save you. Hear me?" Chet waited for his answer.

"I will. I have been wound up. I wanted this to be my work and I guess to show the world what I could do."

"You are. You can. Slow down. I saw you in Tucson rushing around. Next time, take her with you. Stay overnight in a hotel; have a nice meal. Let her shop. I will pay. It will be worth it. This place will be here waiting for you. Build some faith in your foremen and let them manage the crews. It won't all get done as fast as you might want, but it will be fun, not fury."

Spencer put his hand on Chet's shoulder, then dropped his head. "I will do that like you suggested."

"Good. I smell food. I am hungry. Let's join them."

"How did your trial do?"

"The three men pleaded guilty to the white slavery charges. They will be in a federal pen for no less than six years."

"What did their lawyers do?" Spencer was shocked that they actually pleaded guilty.

"I guess the lawyers explained that if they were found guilty of all charges, without pleading guilty, they would have to serve consecutive years and never get out."

Spencer laughed. "I never heard of that before."

"It was not done as a rape case. Those lawyers could make her out to be a whore in the trial. She wasn't one. But the law on slavery is tough all the way down including accomplices to it. Their raping her was a test to buy her. They never reported it to the law, so they were a part of the slavery crime. No matter how hard those lawyers might have talked down poor Cary in a trial, the law excluded no one from being held in slavery, black, white, or even prostitute."

"Thanks for explaining. I learned a lot riding with you. I will get this job done someday, but keep a spot open for me with you when I am done."

"I will. Take my advice, too."

He quickly agreed. "I can do that a lot easier knowing you are waiting on me."

Later at night on the side-by-side cots, Liz asked him what he thought."

"I spoke to Spencer, told him he was working too hard. I told him to slow down. He'd get it built and needed to enjoy it along the way."

"Good. He will listen to you. I am impressed he has so much done already."

"It will be done but he needs to smell the roses, take

her to Tucson shopping, go to a hotel overnight, not go at breakneck speeds."

"I thank you for bringing me by here. I agree it will be a great ranch someday."

He rose up and kissed her good night. Even sleeping in a cot was nice with her around. They'd be home in a week. Then this mystery killer business reported in the letters could be investigated.

CHAPTER 14

The trip home took them cross-country. They were floated across the Gila River by a ferry above the San Carlos Reservation, skirted Superstition Mountain on the third day, and cut northwest for the stage road to Preskitt. Three days later they rode out to the Valley Ranch.

A boy rang the school bell on the post, and everyone came on the run to greet them. Liz dismounted, laughing, and hugged the women there to greet her back one by one. Chet gave his reins to the stable boy and shook Raphael's hand.

"Miguel told us you found the girl and those men are going to jail."

Just then he saw Lisa run out of the main house to greet them. She was talking a mile a minute to his wife about how happy she was helping Monica. Lisa then came over and hugged Chet. "Oh, Miguel is so proud of getting to ride with you. I may not be able to make him as happy as you do."

Chet laughed and kissed her on the forehead. "He will come back to earth."

"Maybe. No matter. I am really very proud he made such a good trip with you and Jesus. Everyone looks up to him. I thank you, but you know we love your wife even more."

That was Raphael's plan. He wanted Miguel to be in a higher place than simply being a ranch worker so that when he retired, Miguel could take his place as foreman. Chet saw how the plan was working and it made him smile.

In the house at last, he took out the letters and re-read them. The oldest one came from a rancher's wife who wrote to the head marshal that someone needs to stop these killings. Parties unknown had murdered ranch families on both sides of her place and no one did a thing. She lived up near Snow Flake. Her name was Clara McClure.

He stopped reading and looked at his map of eastern Arizona. He had her area picked out. Then he read the next letter. This man lived north of her, closer to Holbrook. He wrote about a ranch murder near him. Then the last letter was a man living south of Holbrook, named Elliot Downing. He asked for help on the frequent murders in his area. As many as four incidents happened over in his part of the territory.

Maybe he'd write Susie a letter and Sarge could go investigate the situation. The other two were too far away for Sarge. He knew the deputy at Holbrook, Randall Cates. He met him on his last trip to Holbrook. He'd write him and ask about the situation.

"You reading those letters again?" Liz asked, joining him.

"Those people are so far away over there I'd hate

to ride over there for nothing, especially at this time of year."

"I know my husband very well. The telegraph building is not starting or he'd have wired you. If you need to go see what you can do, get your men and go."

"I will consider it all."

"Good, I am taking a bath."

"You suggesting I do the same?"

"It might not hurt."

"I am coming up right behind you." He laughed. A bath might be wonderful.

The next morning he and Miguel rode into town and met with Jesus at his house. Chet read them the letters and asked what they thought should be done about it."

"I think we better go and see about this," Jesus said.

"I am with whatever you two want to do," Miguel added.

Chet nodded his head. "Today is Tuesday. Let's ride out Thursday morning. Tomorrow, Miguel can fill your list, Jesus, with what we will need for two weeks to ride over there. Then Thursday we can head out unless it is snowing. In that case we can put it off for a few days."

Jesus turned to his partner. "Bring a buckboard in tomorrow and I will help you get everything."

"No problem. I will be here about ten?"

"Good."

Chet stood up at the kitchen table. "Anita, I am sorry. We are taking him away again."

"Oh, I knew that when I married him and from

before. He has plenty of stove wood split for me. Being with you is how he makes a living. And we have reunions every time he comes home. Have you heard anything from the girl you saved?"

"Cary is fitting in at home she wrote in a letter to Liz .I don't think her folks have much of a farm. But she will find herself."

"How many of the women who came through here can say that Monica taught them how to cook? I can."

"We all love her."

Anita nodded. "Please tell Elizabeth I miss her company."

"Come any time and visit her. She's home."

"She won't go with you this time?"

"I'd rather she didn't. It can turn bitter cold this time of year."

"She loves to go though."

"She never complains about it."

With a smile she hugged his arm. "She has you and she really is happy with you. She is a different person now than she was before you two married. She no longer has to be the boss like before you came along. And she likes that role. Some women would never like it."

"You sure hit the nail on the head. She likes being a wife."

"No. Being your wife."

Still smiling at what Anita said, Chet told them he'd see Jesus Thursday morning. Then he and Miguel headed home.

Miguel slapped his mount and they started off to the ranch. "I did not know Anita before she married

Jesus. She was house help, but she talked more today than I ever heard her talk before."

"She was Liz's maid then. Today she is Jesus's wife and she is fitting into that role well."

Miguel nodded. "My wife came out of a shell, too, after I married her. She worked hard before. Now she works hard and leads the others. I guess being my wife moved her a station up?"

Chet nodded. "I am glad she did that."

"Oh, me too. She is fun. She is what you call—she lets her hair down when we are alone."

"That's why you smile a lot."

"*Sí*. That is why."

"How lucky we are to have the great women we both have."

"Oh, yes. For Thursday, when we go, do you have any idea who these murderers over there could be?"

"Mean men that must be stopped or they will kill more."

Thursday morning the temperature was above freezing but not by much. One of the packhorses acted up some and Chet was about ready to trade him off before they left, but Jesus said he'd settle down and be all right. As they rode out under the cross bar for the Verde, he turned back for one more long last look at the ranch house. They might be gone a while on this wild goose chase looking for some murdering robbers who left no witnesses. They have to be mean devils. Hitting isolated ranches, they must have cased their victims carefully to make no slips, and not leave any trace of their identity but the dead people. Chet thought they might be matching wits with a smart person despite the cold killer mind-set.

They stopped briefly to see his son Adam, and Tom rode over to visit for a minute and then they rode on. Nothing was wrong at that place and while they'd not make Susie and Sarge's Windmill Ranch by dark they'd be up there before noon the next day. Camping out went well and at dawn they had eaten breakfast, saddled horses and the pack ones, and rode on.

His sister, Susie, came out on the porch, and the north wind swept her long black coat against the jeans she wore covering her legs under a dress.

Some hands came and took the horses as she hugged Chet and Jesus, then shook Miguel's hand. "Nice to meet you. You are married to Lisa, right? I met her at some of our get-togethers over there. She's a smart girl."

"I am proud of her."

"I know why. Everyone, come in. Sarge has gone to check on something, but he should be back soon. I will fix everyone lunch. Chet, how is Liz doing?"

"She is almost over our losses. Of course it hurt her. It is too cold for her to come along especially since we are looking for killers over east."

"It would be too cold for me. How are Bonnie and JD?"

"She's having another baby and she's really a good wife, making him a good husband. They will have fruit growing next year. And the ranch is already covering their expenses. Ortega was wounded by rustlers but he's getting well and they got the cattle back. The rustlers were killed."

"I guess it's tough going in lots of places. Sarge said he sees lots of desperate people, who have nothing, on his drives to the Navajos."

"I agree, but that is never an excuse to rob and murder anyone."

"Oh, no. That is who you are looking for?"

"Bad cases of murder. No details, either."

"Good luck. I'll fix lunch." She left shaking her head.

"You really provide your foremen nice houses. I saw Cole's at Center Point. I saw JD's, Lucy's, Tom's, and now this one. Oh, Robert has a good one, too."

"They're all hard workers. I felt they deserved a good home."

Miguel added, "Hey, I am happy at the ranch, so is Lisa, but maybe someday, huh?"

"Someday." Chet could see that Miguel didn't miss a thing.

When Sarge returned the two men sat before the fireplace and talked about snow and cattle drives.

"I know we didn't get the snow depth you did, but we did get snow and had our work cut out to feed the cattle. It was a good thing those places we set up came to good usage. Whew. Heck. Many of the Navajos couldn't get to any of those points."

"Good thing you started early."

Sarge agreed. "And now we have the cattle in place. I wondered if Windmill was a luxury to have. It's not. It was well planned and Bo keeps finding us homesteads to fence and use for our hay raising. If we can afford it, I'd like two more complete hay mowers. I can get part-time help to mow and stack it."

"I'll have Ben at the mercantile order them. I hope they can get them here by the time you need them. It isn't easy, but he's a top dealer he says and they try their best to serve him."

"I should have told you last fall. We have most of the land fenced and they make good places to cut and stack hay. I may be able to sell some hay if this winter keeps up."

"That is not bad."

"Tell me about all the other folk."

"Robert and Betty have a girl. JD and Bonnie are expecting again. They also expect some oranges and lemons next year. Lucy had a boy and Shawn, with Spud, have that place under control. May's also expecting and Hampt's getting along.

"We have come a long ways since we fed those starving Indians on the Verde River, haven't we? You even had to talk to General Crook about those people not getting food."

Then Chet told them about rescuing Marcella and Cary. Sarge knew about all the past things they'd accomplished since he'd been there, and even before when they had to take the Verde Ranch away from the crooked foreman who held it.

"You know anything about the ranch murders?"

"Only what I heard. They must be animals is all I can say. The deputy from over there came here and asked us if we knew anything. I told him only what I heard. We never saw anyone we might suspect. I don't even know anyone you could talk to about it who would know firsthand who they were or anything else in that situation."

"We may have a dead end but we'll look."

"I bet you find them. You're pretty damn sharp at solving those things."

Sarge leaned in closer, lowering his voice. "Who is that woman that drove Reg crazy?"

"A rich woman who married and divorced Buster Weeks. She drove him to drink before she even met Reg. Her father is very rich and they have a big ranch over by Hackberry. I heard her name but I don't remember it. She was the same one anyway."

"He must have lost his mind?"

"I agree."

"Susie wondered about him and his first wife. She thought that ended strangely. What happened? I caught a rumor about him on one of the drives, and the guy that told me acted like he knew all about Reg and her."

"Guess with him dead we may never know."

"I just wondered. We don't even live in the area but I knew him, and, of course, Susie knew him so much better. She said he was somehow different when he came out here and it wasn't all about the wife he lost, either."

"Susie would know."

"I was thinking, I need to send her over to your house more often. My schedule doesn't give us time to do much."

"This place will run without you for a few days. You have a good man under you. Use him and take her somewhere."

"Okay. But we are kind of far from all but Preskitt."

"Fine; come over to our house."

"You'd probably be gone."

"More than likely, but Liz and Monica and a whole

bunch of others you know will be there. It will be a good break. Oh, how's that son-in-law of Tom's doing?"

"Cody Day's a good worker. He sees things before they happen. I hope Tom don't call him back."

"Where does he and his wife, Sandy, live?"

"Over the hill at the closest homestead. It had a house we fixed up some for them. Being newlyweds they wanted some privacy."

"I will stop by and see her, and him if he's there, since I am the cause they are married."

Sarge laughed. "I heard the story."

Susie called from the kitchen. "Cody is bringing her over, Sarge."

"That will save you a trip." Sarge winked at him.

When they arrived, he visited with Sandy and Cody. They sounded happy about being there, liked the arrangements made for them, and Sandy thanked him again for all he did.

Chet reflected on how, at that boy's age, he'd run their Texas ranch's operations and, how he always complained, to himself, that he had no time to court a girl. He sure made up for it later. Life dealt some strange hands.

Chet and his men rode out the next day to get to Holbrook. They camped that night and then went on. Finally in Holbrook, his men put the horses up at the livery and were to meet him later at a diner they liked. Chet headed for the sheriff's office.

Randall Cates was the deputy. A man in his forties with some gray in his sideburns. In his office, Cates leaned back in the squeaking chair and tented his hands.

"What can I do for you?"

"There was a murder up here a few months ago?"

"Charlie Farrell. A bachelor. He had a small cow operation. Lived up in the Burner Canyon Country. They tortured him to tell them where he kept his money. He finally told them in a tin coffee can. They spilled a few coins but never picked them up. Then they shot him. I heard reports he had a few thousand dollars, but I doubted he had over a few hundred. He was an old miser and unless God gave him money he didn't have much. Who killed him? I suspect some drifting cowboy that folks saw riding through the country about that time. No names."

"Who got his ranch and cattle?"

"Good question. Robbie Clements paid the taxes, so he now owns the homestead. He owns the K Bar Three Ranch. I don't recall who got the cattle."

"Farrell have many cows?"

"I don't know. I never figured he had very many."

"What was his brand?"

"CFX."

"I'll try to remember that. Thanks. You think it was drifters that robbed and killed him?"

"Lots of things happen up here. It's a vast country. I gave the case my best. He'd probably been dead a week when his corpse was discovered. Good luck finding his murderers. I had none."

"You think more than one man killed him?"

Cates shook his head. "I don't know. I hope you can solve it."

Chet met his men for the late afternoon meal.

"Learn anything?" Jesus asked.

"The dead man's name was Charlie Farrell. He was

a bachelor. They supposedly got his money from a coffee can after torturing him. Another rancher, who paid the taxes, has his homestead. He ran cows but there's no count of them or who eventually got them. The deputy told me the brand was CFX."

"Boy, this sure sounds tough to me. What do we do next?" Miguel asked.

"Get answers to questions. What did that man pay for the place? Where are the dead man's cattle? That would be a start."

"We run questions down and get nothing sometimes. Other times we find we answer our own questions," Jesus said.

"How do we start?" Miguel asked.

"I want to know how Charlie Farrell died. That should be in the coroner's report. It may tell us something," Chet began. "Then I want to meet this man who bought his homestead land. Next we need to learn how many cows he owned and where they went afterwards."

"Chet, I thought a murdering drifter robber killed him?" Miguel said.

"In a case like this everyone around is a suspect. Savvy?"

Miguel nodded. "I am trying not to be too slow. This goes deeper than I first thought."

"You know the man's name who bought the place?" Jesus asked.

"Robbie Clements. He owns the Three Bar K I believe. No the deputy said K Bar Three brand."

"Where do we start?" Jesus asked.

"Here in the village. Quietly ask around what they know about Charlie Farrell. We need to know about the money he had. What was he like? Anything else we can learn about him."

Miguel said, "Let's do this."

"Good. We may be here a few days so first we'll get some hotel rooms, then supper."

Chet and his team were ready to investigate the murder of Charlie Farrell.

The next morning they met with the undertaker and read his report. His killer and-or others had burned the soles of his feet, until he probably told them where the money can was. That was what the undertaker had surmised.

Chet asked the man, "How old was he?"

"I wrote down sixty because there was no birth certificate to tell me his age."

"Okay. Thanks. You say here he was shot twice in the back of his head with .44/.40 rifle bullets you extracted from his skull?"

"Yes."

"The old man would have died from them instantly?"

"Oh, no doubt. Probably lying facedown on the floor. His hands were tied behind his back. I'd say they had the money and whoever shot him did it so he could not report the robbery."

"Most drifting cowboys, that the deputy suspected, would not be mean enough to do that, would they?" Chet asked.

"I agree. They'd probably left him tied and hightailed it for far away, spending the money in some whorehouse."

Chet laughed. "Probably so. You think he had much money in that coffee can?"

The older man, sitting in his chair, shook his head. "I have no idea. Farrell was the original skin flint around here."

"Other words he didn't give anything to the poor orphans and children's fund?"

He chuckled. "Whenever he got a coin I think it would scream 'Don't put me in the moldy purse.'"

"He have anything else valuable?"

"Not that I know of. He used coffee grounds twice they said. A guy one time asked him if they were weaker."

"What did he say?"

"Cheaper that way."

Chet thanked him, took his notes, and left. He met Miguel outside on the porch of the funeral home.

"You learn a lot?"

"Some. But it is all spread out and I don't have much at that."

"Tell me what you learned. Jesus will meet us for lunch now."

"The café he likes?"

Chet nodded and told him all that he learned as they walked the two blocks.

"What bothered you the most about what you heard?" Miguel asked, close to the entrance to the diner.

"The way he was murdered. I've been around several robberies. The Mexican bandits were the worst, but they shot with the people facing them and with pistols. This killer shot him twice, in the back of the head, with a rifle."

"That is real brutal. Maybe Jesus has some answers."

Chet hoped that Jesus had found out more.

Over lunch Chet asked Jesus, "What did you uncover?"

"Charlie never bought any liquor. But he did frequent the same *putas* on the regular times he came to town."

"At the red light house?"

"No, they charged too much, they said." Jesus smiled. "They were Mexican women around here."

"Get their names?"

"Yes one is Yolanda and the other calls herself the Ycllow Rose."

"Can we go talk to them?" Chet asked.

"I suppose so," Jesus agreed.

A woman who lived in that *barrio* section sent them down there to where one of the women they were looking for was working. The Yellow Rose was washing clothes in the Little Colorado. They found her on her knees in the water, beating her wet wash with a stick to get the dirt out. She stood up and the wet, thin dress she wore left nothing to the men's imaginations.

"Rose, I am the U.S. marshal and I need to ask you a few questions about Charles Farrell."

"I am sorry, but he is dead now, señor."

"We know that. Who killed him?"

She went into cussing the devil in Spanish and ended with, "He was such wonderful lover I miss him with all my heart."

"Oh, I bet you do. But what can you tell me about him?"

"Charles, as I called him, brought me flowers that

he had picked on the way to see me. It was as if he was courting me."

"That was nice. Did you ever think he had any money?"

"One time. He came by with his flowers and he was drunk—he said his brother had died and that hurt him. He was such a tender, how you say, man at most times. He only came drunk that one time. But it made his tongue loose that day, huh?"

"Go on, please."

"And that he—his brother—left him his gold mine and money."

"You believed him?"

"*Si*. It was my birthday and he gave me a one-hundred-dollar bill."

"He ever do that before?"

She shook her head. "Not ever again either. I only charged him a dollar a night. If you are interested I would treat you guys for that?"

Chet shook his head. "My deputies and I are happily married men."

"Oh, I treat lots of them, too."

They laughed.

"Was his brother's name Farrell, too?"

"I can't remember his name. He owned the Candy Cane Mine at Silver City. That was what was sold and he said the lawyer sent him the proceeds in cash by mail."

"Not many people knew about it?"

"No, he swore me to never tell anyone. But now he is dead. Who cares?" She shrugged her shoulders.

"I wished he'd given me some of that money before they robbed him."

"Anyone else ever talk to you about this?"

She shook her head.

"Tell no one else. Here is a twenty-dollar piece for your trouble."

She looked at it in her brown palm and shook her head. "I could entertain you a lot for this."

"No, you have done enough for it today."

She licked her lips. "You need me you can always find me. *Gracias* to you *hombres*, too."

They left her and hiked for their horses hitched in the tall cottonwoods on the higher bank.

"Wow," Miguel said, looking back to be certain no one was around. "So he was not a poor man."

Jesus agreed. "But who besides Rose knew that?"

"We need to find this Yolanda," Chet said, mounting up.

Jesus nodded. "She lives on the west side of town."

"You know where?"

"They described the house to me."

"Let's go talk to her."

Jesus agreed and led the way.

"Can we find out what the mine sold for?" Miguel asked.

"I can wire the U.S. marshal at Silver City, and he can find out and get me the answer."

They came to Yolanda's yard gate of the brown stucco house. It had signs of roses in the yard. Winter bare stems showed what it must have looked like in warm weather. Jesus went to see if she was at home.

A woman wrapped in a blanket stood in the half-open door and spoke to him. Chet heard her say, "Not now. Later after dark."

Jesus tipped his cowboy hat and nodded. He returned and they mounted up.

Amused, Jesus said, "She thought I wanted her body. I think she had business inside. Later tonight after dark, huh?"

"And it will be our turn." Chet chuckled. "We have done well. I want to talk to the banker next."

"What will you ask him?" Miguel asked, riding beside him.

"If anyone has paid off a ranch loan lately that surprised him?"

"They would do that, wouldn't they?" Miguel asked.

"Yes, and have a flimflam answer for how they did it."

"What is that, flimflam?"

"It means their source sounds made up—or a big fat lie."

"I am learning, Chet. Really I am." All three laughed.

He found that the bank president, Carlyle Worth, was a starched-collar kind of man, and he quickly took Chet into his office when Chet announced that he was a lawman.

"How may I help you?"

"I have a reason to believe someone paid off a mortgage on a ranch and it shocked you."

"Why is that, sir?"

"Over the past few months has anyone come in

and paid off a large loan and you didn't know how he did it?"

"What are you pressing for, Marshal?"

"There was a large unreported robbery in this area. A man was killed. The person that killed him gained a helluva lot of money with torture. Now I think he may have come in here and paid off a loan he had here."

Worth sat back in the chair. "Are you saying that old skinflint Farrell had lots of cash?"

"Why ask about him?"

"He's the only murder I have heard about this year."

"Do you think Charlie had any money?"

"A bucket of dimes, maybe, that the old bastard had saved."

"So, who came in with an unusual amount of money about then?"

"Deputy Randall Cates."

"Hmmm?"

"He exchanged a five-hundred-dollar bill for smaller money a week after the old man was shot."

Hell. Cates may have been involved. "I take it you don't get many of those around here?"

"I had to look up the treasury department's pictures of them. There is someone I didn't even know on it and the thousand-dollar one had a different unknown guy on it, but his was good."

"Did you ask him where he got it?"

"He said it was from his uncle's will."

"Any more?"

"Robbie Clements also got an inheritance, he said, but he paid me off with hundred-dollar bills."

"When?"

"A week after that. Those are the only two I know about. What else?"

"If I paid for the wire, would you secretly send a telegram to Silver City, New Mexico, and find out what the Candy Cane Mine sold for at auction?"

"Does that enter in your investigation?"

"Yes, and I will have more answers when you learn that amount."

"Are you close to something up here?"

"I am. There have been several murder-robberies across the eastern part of the territory. I don't think, right now, this murder is connected to any of those down in the Snow Flake area, but not a word to anyone until I have stronger proof."

"I would not tell a soul. Give me three days to get that price the mine sold for. I am pleased you came along and have to thank you for taking this case on. I believe you are about to solve it. Good day, sir."

He left the bank, met up with his men, and very quietly he told them all he heard from Worth.

"Doesn't that connect Cates to Clements?" Jesus asked.

"Strange, isn't it?"

"What comes next?" Miguel asked.

"We check on some cattle. If there was no sheriff's sale of Farrell's cattle, I want to know why. That is outright rustling even if he has no heirs."

"I'm wondering how Cates got a five-hundred-dollar bill," Jesus said.

Chet nodded. "We have more answers to get."

"With that north wind blowing, those range cows not being fed hay, they will be up in those side canyons out of that gale force," Miguel said.

"Good thinking. We ride tomorrow and check that out."

"Did that deputy think we'd buy that drifter theory and ride on?" Jesus asked.

"Might be what he dreamed we'd do. We need to see what this other gal knows."

After dark, they hitched their horses at a rack and went to her door. Chet knocked.

She cracked the door. "How many of you are there?"

"We just came to talk to you. We'll pay for your time. My name is Chet Byrnes and these are my men Jesus and Miguel."

"Come in then." She wore a black silky dress that flowed around her in the flickering candlelight as she showed them two facing couches. "Have a seat, *mis amigos.*"

She sat down, exposing lots of her stocking legs, and asked, "What do you need to know from me?"

"Was Charlie Farrell a friend of yours?"

"Oh, yes. But he is dead."

"What did you know about him?"

"People spoke bad of him. He always came to my *casa* bathed and shaved. He really was not such an old man as people thought he was. He just looked older. I considered him a stallion when we shared bodies. What else?"

"Does the Candy Cane Mine mean anything to you?"

"He mentioned his brother owned it. His name

was Howard. I met him one time when he came over here from New Mexico, and I entertained him for Charlie. Howard had more money than Charlie. He bought me a lot of roses to plant after we met."

"Did he tell you Howard had died?"

"Yes. He even gave me more money for rose bushes because he said Howard would want me to have them. He said his brother talked about coming back to see me. But he died. That's sad, isn't it?"

"Yes, it is." Chet leaned forward on the couch. "Did Charlie ever talk to you about his inheritance?"

She shook her head. "No."

"Did you ever hear anyone talk about it?"

"No. But I wondered how much those killers got away with?"

"You think more than one man killed him?"

"I knew how strong he was. One man, even armed, could not have subdued him."

"I thought he was an old man?"

"I told you, only in how he looked. He was much younger than he looked." She smiled, remembering. "He told me he was raised very, very poor and never forgot it."

"Well, we can't get him back, but we will try to get his killers."

"Do that for me."

"Maybe for everyone. I am going to pay you for your time, Yolanda. You have been a big help." He gave her ten dollars.

"I could treat all of you for such a price."

"Buy some more roses." He got up, hugged her, and they prepared to leave.

"*Via con Dios, hombres,* and I wish you much luck in finding those *bastardos.*"

"Same to you."

"Now I know who you are, señor. Someone told me a story a few years back about a man named Byrnes who hung two men who had raped a woman at Sunflower, huh?"

"They also had killed two good men."

"They deserved it, the hanging you gave them."

He thought so, too.

They rode back and put their horses up at the livery, then walked to the hotel. The desk clerk handed him a note as he gave them their room keys.

"What does it say?"

"You are asking too many questions. Get out of Holbrook if you wish to keep breathing. You are too nosy for your own good. Or else find a burial plot and we'll plant you there."

"Who wrote it?"

"No name."

"Be careful," Jesus said to him.

"I can do that. Let's get nosier and check some cows for brands."

They laughed and went up to their rooms.

Before falling asleep, Chet spent some time thinking about the threatening note sent them. Bold enough.

He got them up early. They went by the livery, saddled their ponies, then hitched them out front of Burl's Café and went inside. The meal went fast. To be friendly, the man who owned it came by and told them to be careful, that a wild bunch was running around and anything might happen.

"I think we can handle ourselves," Chet told the man.

"I can't afford to lose any cash customers." He was laughing as they left for their horses.

"You think he was in on it?"

Swinging into the saddle, Chet looked through the glass at the man inside, pouring coffee for his regulars.

"I think he's clean. Let's ride."

Two hours later they were in the Burners Canyon area. They punched up about six cows and were trailing them through some light juniper cover. Chet tried to read the brand.

Miguel said to Jesus, "Head that roan *vaca*. I can heel her."

Both men could rope. Hardly a boy who ever traipsed over the Mexican border to work in Arizona couldn't head or heel with a *riata*. They sped after the bovine, Jesus standing in the stirrups and twirling his loop over her horns. He dallied the leather rope around his saddle horn and turned off, swinging the angry cow in an open space for Miguel to catch the back hocks with his loop. The cow was laid down on her side in the grass, and Chet dismounted to check her brand.

He could see that someone had redone the CFX brand on her side to a K—3. Sloppy work, but a rebrand. They needed to check others. He took the head catch loop off her horns and Miguel backed his horse to give him time to remount in case she was mad when she got up and tried to hook at him.

Jesus was rewinding his *riata* as he rode off to find another. Chet put her in his tally book—roan cow, earmark changed, too. Then he shot his roan horse off after Jesus and Miguel. He saw that they had another one held down. Brindle cow, same brand change. Cow number three was mostly longhorn with stripes of black down her sides—brand changed. Six cows checked as they rode over the hill to a deserted house, corrals, and large shed.

"This his place?" Jesus asked.

"Could be—"

Someone began shooting at them. The slap of a bullet in the juniper boughs and then a rifle report followed. It came from a long-distance shooter but missed. The three charged their mounts for the ranch quarters and made for the big shed that was open. They bailed off their saddles once inside, and guns drawn, they rushed back to the door to see if they could hold off the shooters.

Jesus had his Winchester, and when a horse and rider with a smoking pistol appeared in the junipers across the way, he shot the horse. Rider down and scrambling, he wouldn't get far running. Chet shot twice at another horseback shooter that appeared. Got him.

With a break in the action, Miguel ran back, got his and Chet's repeating rifles with a box of .44/.40 cartridges, and brought them back.

Chet holstered his six-gun and levered a fresh round into his Winchester, so when another horse appeared he took him out, too. That left two afoot.

"What next?" Jesus asked.

"I guess more horse killing."

"Those bastards need to be stopped and taught a lesson—not to mess with U.S. marshals."

"I hear another horse coming off the hill behind us." Chet rushed to the back of the barn and fired five shots through a missing board and bat siding space.

"They've got three less horses now. I sure hope they don't have to walk home."

Miguel shot. "Got another."

"How many more are there?" Chet asked.

"They aren't showing up out there," Jesus said.

"I figure we need to ride like hell for Clements's place. He's probably already gotten his money and split this country."

Jesus frowned. "You know where it is?"

"Tracks, I've got a man can track them."

Miguel jumped on his horse, laughing. "Things can sure get exciting all at once with you two."

"Hell, this had been slow," Chet said, charging out of the barn after Jesus, Miguel following.

The tracking was easy. Even at high-speed riding the best Chet could tell was there were either two or three of them headed southeast.

He pushed the roan horse hard, crossing the open grass country. He could make out the three riders ahead and knew they were beating on their horses hoping to escape. One of the horses went down and rolled over. The other two never stopped.

"Get that one if he's alive, then follow our tracks. Clements's place can't be far from here," he shouted at Miguel.

"I can handle it."

Chet nodded and turned back to the chase. When he passed the downed rider his head looked in a strange position on his shoulders. He'd broken his neck. "Forget him."

"I saw him. He'll never ride again."

Not long after he could see bare, gnarled cottonwood trunks and a ranch house.

Chet pushed his hard-driving roan up beside Jesus. "They may be lying in wait for us to ride in."

"What should we do?"

"Rein up short and we can surround the place."

His man nodded and when he turned to Miguel, he nodded he heard him, too.

Damn. This close. Now they needed to tighten the noose on Farrell's killers. Why would anyone kill for money and take the chance of being caught?

He slid the roan on his heels short of pistol range and looked at the open door of the house. Any minute he expected a rifle barrel to appear. Instead a woman rushed out with two small kids trailing her and a bundled baby in her arms.

She was screaming at the very top of her lungs. "Don't shoot! Don't shoot! I have no guns. They're crazy."

A small child fell down and she stopped to grab his hand. Then, dragging him, she repeated her plea. With her looking, terrified, back at the house, he sent Miguel to get her to cover. His man spurred his horse to obey.

Someone came out with a six-gun looking as if he might shoot her. Chet took him down with a well-aimed .44/.40 bullet like they'd used on poor Farrell. Then a second person in the doorway shot at him. The bullet whizzed by, but Jesus, on his knee, took him out with his Winchester.

The last one came out on the porch with a money-bag in one hand and a blazing six-gun in the other. The two lawmen punched his ticket with four well-aimed rifle shots.

"That all of them?"

Chet nodded. "Unless they have another."

They reloaded their carbines just in case and headed for the house. Miguel was off to the left beside the corrals on his knees in the dust hugging the wailing woman, trying to comfort her. Both kids were crying.

Chet's ears still rang from the shooting.

"You his wife?"

"Common law one."

"He got another?"

"Hell, I don't know. That whole bunch's been crazy for eight weeks. Robbie wasn't any better. I don't know what they'd done but it must have been bad. You're the law, ain'cha?"

"U.S. Deputy Marshal Chet Byrnes. My deputies Miguel and Jesus. We are here to help you."

"Ruthie Ann Spaulding—he—he never married me. But I got rights, don't I? As Mrs. Robbie Clements?"

"I am certain you have common law wife rights." He turned back toward his man. "Jesus, go get that sack of money on the porch. That belongs to the estate of Charlie Farrell."

"Mrs., you want to go back to the house?" Miguel asked her.

"Not in all that gun smoke and those dead men."
She made a sour face like she was sick from it all.

"We can open the windows. These children need
to get to a stove. They don't have enough clothes on
for this weather. Come. I can carry those two big
ones. It is cold out here."

"Guess I ain't got any other option."

"No." Miguel hefted the oldest on his left hip,
then picked up the smaller one. "Chet, I can get our
horses after I get her settled in the house. Don't
worry, they won't leave."

Still shocked by all the bloody carnage in the past
few hours, Chet's brain felt numb. Surely all that
money was not worth this kind of dying.

"Do that. I better go help Jesus gather the
bodies," he said to Miguel who was already gone.

Boy, it was really too much and not over yet.
Deputy Cates had lots to explain before this case was
closed. Robbie Clements was dead. This woman
and her children needed to be provided for in the
courts. Part of the recovered money belonged to his
deputies. *Liz, I am sorry but I won't be home in a week.
There were still the murders south of here to investigate.* He
almost laughed, but it wasn't funny. Four more un-
solved killings—those he was sure were connected.
This one separate.

Everything settled down. A neighboring rancher,
Billie Ford, came by and offered to get some others
to help. By sundown, they had the three corpses
from the other ranch joining the dead here. Three
had somehow escaped. The undertaker arrived to
serve as coroner along with a justice of the peace
named Wiley Ostormyer. They told him that the

Yavapai County Deputy Sheriff Cates had resigned and left for parts unknown. Preskitt had been wired and another was supposed to be coming. Who knew when he'd get here?

The JP made the Clements ranch house his courtroom. He ruled, in all cases, that the deaths were justified. He made Mrs. Ruthie Ann Clements Robbie Clements's heir and the executor of his estate. An inventory was made of the ranch cattle. She had two hundred cows and assorted calves plus yearlings all wearing the K—3 brand, all of which were now hers along with his section of land and the Farrell half section he bought from the county tax office. All the horse stock belonged to her and everything mortgage free.

The JP decided that the marshals involved were entitled to sixty percent of the cash amount recovered.

Chet asked Jesus and Miguel to donate a thousand dollars apiece to the Farrell's two lady friends and put the rest in their own bank accounts. Even after the donations they each would have over twenty thousand to bank.

Miguel sat in shock. "That is more money than most men make in a lifetime."

Jesus nodded his head. "I have been riding with him for almost four years. No, more than four years. I have over twice that amount in my account in the Preskitt Bank. Someday I will own a large ranch. I am still learning."

"What will I tell Lisa?"

"That someday you both will also own a big ranch."

"How often has this happened?"

"Oh, several times. Cole will tell you he has a big bank account, too, from the days serving with him."

"I am shocked."

"Don't tell others; it will only make them jealous."

"I savvy that."

"You know when we chased those guys back to Clements's ranch, all of us could have been killed. Chet's been shot once on this job. He knows how dangerous it is, so with this money he prepares that it might be our widows' and orphans' fund."

Back at the hotel, Chet wrote Liz a letter that night explaining how they'd solved the one crime and settled everything from wills to widows. They were going south to Snow Flake next.

He never told her about the donations made to Yolanda or the Yellow Rose by his men and how the women both cried about Charlie's death when the men gave them the money. Nor did he tell her about the lanky boy in his late teens named Samuel Trent who moved in with Ruthie Ann Clements. The crazy kid followed her like a hound pup after a gyp. Nor did he mention how she went to town and how fine she dressed on her newfound wealth. He didn't add that he knew she'd never make a lovely lady in society, because she, as likely as not, scratched herself anywhere she itched in public. He saw her do it openly in town getting out of her new buggy.

They had to go south in the morning snowing or not.

I love you, Elizabeth.

CHAPTER 15

Light snow fell all day. They stopped for the night at a roadhouse for freighters who were headed south for Fort Apache. Chet felt cold despite his layered clothing that was usually sufficient to keep him warm. They had the horses put up and headed for the bar and diner for supper. In the big noisy room of people he felt the heat hit his face. He hoped he wasn't taking a cold. That was all he needed.

They ordered food—the man who waited on them said they had beef, potatoes, and carrots. That included bread and coffee. The meal price was fifty cents, which was double café prices in civilized places, but they were not there and this place had no competition. He unbuttoned his coat and rose to put it on the chair back. Sometimes these chases were hell. Chet recalled Jesus's complaints of that cold run, coming back from Utah with all the prisoners and Ben Ivor's second wife-to-be Kathrin. He was so pleased with the success of that trip he never noticed the low temperatures.

The coffee was not good. Their meals came in a

bowl as thin stew, and the bread was like the French made that you tore off in chunks and dumped in the liquid. It was not a select spot to spend the night when he could have been in his own warm house with his wife and eating Monica's meals. After he finished, he sat back, realized that Utah was Jesus's worst trip and this might be his worst so far.

Morning they had pancakes and thin sugar syrup. Chet didn't even try the coffee. They loaded the packhorses and saddled up to head south. Clear, cold mountain air swept his face and they rode. They reached the village of Snow Flake mid-morning and found the Yavapai County deputy.

Steve Knowles was the man in charge. After their introductions, Knowles asked, "What happened to Cates?"

"He resigned before we closed the Farrell murder case and left for parts unknown."

"Was he a suspect?"

"We have one unanswered part he played. He cashed a five-hundred-dollar bill around the time Farrell was murdered, and that drew suspicion on him. Nothing was done about it. It looked bad, but I had no evidence that large bill came from Farrell's money."

"Did you see it? The bill?"

"No, but the banker at Holbrook said he had to look up a picture of it. He didn't know the person pictured on it, but it was valid.

"We had a bloody shoot-out with Robbie Clements and his hired guns, and by the time we came out unscathed, Cates had gone."

Knowles shook his head. "Hell, they said that the guy killed was an old skinflint."

"His brother who died owned the Candy Cane Mine at Silver City, and Farrell received near a hundred thousand dollars in inheritance money."

"What was your take on it all?"

"I don't take reward money."

Everyone laughed.

"Well, you solved that one. Now I hope you find my killer. He, or they, have murdered four families. We are a pretty close-knit community here. Most are Mormons. We think we know everyone and can't find the loose maniac in our midst. I have four files you can read. I wrote everything I found or heard in them. I may not be the best investigator, but damn, Byrnes, I've done all I can do after each murder."

"No one doubts that. You may be matching wits with a smart killer, killers, or they may simply be lucky."

"You have a reputation of dogging down and finding killers. I wish you luck and I'll do anything I can to help. Just ask. I want this animal stopped."

"Thank you. Now, we should get settled. Is there a livery for our stock?"

"Matt Jepson will do that down the street on the right."

"Rooms and board?"

"Mrs. Halter is a widow with several bedrooms and she lives a block away. She will serve the meals you need if you tell her. I arranged all this so you'd be free to investigate when I was told you were coming to help me. I know you'd want the time spent here shortened as much as possible, so I prepared all I could."

"You are right. And thank you. Miguel can put the horses up. Jesus and I will start reading your notes."

Knowles nodded. "I will go with him. We will leave your personal things at Mrs. Halter's house, and put up the horses. I'll arrange for lunch here and supper with her tonight."

"Thanks again."

"No problem. I want this business solved."

Sitting across the desk from each other, Chet handed the case file marked number two to Jesus to read.

He opened file number one.

Forester Family Murder, June 1876

I received my first report about a grisly murder scene out on Pierce Mountain. Hans Peters, a cowboy at the D Bar S ranch, came in and told me the Forester family had been murdered. Axed to death. Him, her, and their two children. It had happened a week or so earlier he thought. I took six posse men and we rode up there.

To enter the house we wore masks because I knew the smell would be bad.

I felt, after several years as a lawman, I would handle it better. I didn't.

When we got back I asked each man that could write to give me his notes. They are in an envelope marked one in this file.

*The killer probably used an ax that belonged to the
Forester family. I don't know in what order he
murdered them. The father, Cy, had been decapitated
on a stump block, which may have been brought
into the kitchen for that purpose. His hands were
tied behind his back. I had no idea how many blows
the murderer did to sever it.*

*Both children were beheaded by the same method.
One boy was five and the other seven or eight. The
mother was naked and I suspect she had been
raped. Her hands and feet were tied spread-eagle
on top of the bed. The killer slit her throat, I think,
when he was done using her body.*

Chet closed the file. The killer or killers were
some kind of crazy mad people.

"How does that one read?" he asked Jesus.

Jesus had wet eyes when he dropped his file on
the desk. "They smashed the baby's head on a porch
post to kill it. The buzzards had consumed most of it
laying in the yard. But his dried blood was on the
porch post. Inside the house the father had his chest
chopped open and his heart had been removed.
Three children were cut into pieces. I couldn't read
what he said about the wife's death. No tracks to
follow . . ."

"Let's go outside and get a breath of air." Chet
stood up and shook his head.

"I don't know how Knowles is still sane after
handling two of these cases?"

Jesus looked pained. "Chet, there are two more
here yet to read."

"I know and reading them is going to be hell."

Jesus agreed, stretching his arms over his head. It had warmed up outside some and the sun sparkled on the bare cottonwood tree bark.

"We, somehow, must find him before he strikes again."

"You have any thoughts?"

"No. Knowles knows this land. He knows these people, but he has not found a suspect in the eight or nine months these four horrible crimes happened."

"You read number three and I'll read the last one. They can wait. There's a woman coming with a covered tray. I think she is coming with that for us."

"You must be the marshals. Deputy Knowles said to bring you two some lunch. He and your man are repairing a packsaddle and will be here when they're done."

"Thank you. My name is Chet Byrnes. And that is Jesus Martinez, one of my men."

"Nice to meet you. My name is Edie Halter. The deputy asked me to board you while you are here since we don't have a hotel or café."

"We're pleased you agreed. Let me have the tray."

"No. Please, just open the door. I carried it this far. I hope you like it."

"Hey, after weeks of our own cooking and not so good café food, we will be easy to please."

"I can see you are a flatterer. I am happy to be your hostess."

"You ever can come to Preskitt, my wife and I will show you a real good time."

"Keep talking. I'd love to see your house and the woman you married."

"Well, you are invited."

Jesus told her, "He is not joking. He has a great wife, and you will love the mansion."

"Here is your lunch." She set it on the table and uncovered blue and white dishes, shiny silverware, and the food, in two pans. It was a hefty load she had carried blocks to them. "The elk steaks were fresh cut, the rice and gravy is mine, and the rolls are still warm. Butter is in that dish. I am sorry I have no coffee."

"We understand. I bet they don't even sell it around here," Chet said, pulling up another chair. "Tell us what people around here think about the crimes."

"Honest," the fortyish woman said, still fussing to get things off the tray and set out it on the desk for them. "People around here hardly talk about it. We are God-fearing church people, and these crimes are near impossible to believe they've happened here where we live. And the fact no one has been able to find and stop them is scaring us all."

"Usually, by now, someone has found a culprit to accuse?"

She nodded. "Eat. You will need lots of strength to ever find them. I don't believe in ghosts or spirits, but they may be here."

Chewing on a tasty bite of elk, he shook his head. "There are no such things in this world. There is a human behind these attacks. He, or they, may not be human in mind but they are living, breathing beasts. Edie, we are here to find the beast. Me, Jesus, and Miguel."

"I hope you can. I can speak for everyone in the region. Free us from this curse."

Finished with lunch, they thanked her. Chet said they'd bring her tray back later but she said she'd take it herself now and have their supper ready at six p.m. if that suited him. She pointed out her house to him and took her tray back.

Miguel and Knowles rejoined them.

"We repaired a packsaddle. It will be all right."

"Good. You can read any one of these," Chet told Miguel. Jesus was already into number four—three people murdered. They beheaded the man and their son of twelve, then used the wife's body and slashed her throat. Just like the Forester one.

Miguel lowered his head, pushed the file away, and admitted, "I am sorry. I can't do this."

Chet pulled the file back to himself. "Knowles, were these four families good LDS church members?" He referred to the Church of Jesus Christ of Latter Day Saints, or Mormons.

He shook his head. "No. None were members."

"Were these women common law wives?"

"They might have been, why?"

"I want to know what they had in common."

"They were people who lived on the fringe. You know what I mean?"

"I think the fact they were not Mormons might attract a killer who had a mind-set they were not worth letting live. The common law wife thing could also be a point."

"No one that went to church would ever do it."

"I am not accusing anyone. But a mentally upset person could use that for an excuse to do this."

Knowles shook his head. "I am not defending my church, but I have not seen or heard anyone talk like that."

"I believe when you get to looking at these four crimes they are all near alike."

"I have found nothing suspicious about anyone. That is the problem."

"Let's look at the location of the murders on your map."

"I have them marked. They are around the outside edge."

"Places where you wouldn't be seen much when traveling there? Could you get a buggy or wagon to all sites?"

"I saw no tracks of them at these places."

"Maybe they parked off away some, so you would not see them. People do strange things. A man murdered a woman I knew, and she managed to write his name on a bed sheet with her own blood before she died. We found it."

"Chet, I scoured those sites for any clues, like if a note fell from a pocket or jackknife dropped. I found nothing."

"The killers must be real careful. That means they are very smart or you'd have found something. So far there have been no slips. "

"Right."

"These reports you made are as well done as any I ever read on any crime. I see the problem is these murdered people are outside the normal way of living. They are doing things that might be very sinful in the eyes of zealous ones."

"I thought they fell victim because they lived off by themselves."

"I agree with Chet." Jesus nodded his head. "They want to clean up the—"

"The sinners," Chet added.

Knowles nodded. "If he was a killer bear I'd bait him. But how?"

"Do you have more living like those murdered?"

"I never really thought about them. There are some more out there, but I have not thought about going out there and checking on them."

"Let's split up in pairs and start checking on any possible sinners in the morning. We must note anyone suspicious, maybe leaving town because they are going out to find those fringe people. We have to disregard what a good person they seem to be."

"Won't that warn the guilty party we are looking for them?"

"If we knew names we could watch closer," Jesus said.

Knowles dropped his chin. "Chet, you have me convinced those people were murdered for not living their lives like the killer expected them to."

"Now we need that person to slip up."

Knowles added, "And before they murder someone else. I simply hope it works."

They agreed and Chet's bunch headed for Edie Halter's house.

"I never noticed the dates those murders happened. The first was in June."

"Why would you want to notice that?" Miguel asked.

"Moon phases? Events at the time?"

"That might trigger them to murder?"

Chet nodded. "Hey, I did not want to push you on the file?"

"You didn't. I did not want to admit I cannot read. Lisa is teaching me and maybe next time I will be able to read what you give me."

"Miguel, I did not hire you to read. You are a good support to our team and I am glad you are learning reading. That will help you in the rest of your life."

Miguel smiled as they hung their hats and coats up on the pegs in the back-enclosed porch. Washed, they climbed the inside steps into her home and into the food smelling kitchen.

After the sorry meal the night before back up the roadhouse, this lady's food was going to be a great change.

It was too early to for him to even suspect anyone in the case, but this was not the first challenge they had to solve with no clues. They would do all they could, and hopefully stop those gruesome murders.

CHAPTER 16

That evening when his men went upstairs to bed, he stayed and spoke to his hostess, Edie.

"May I ask if you had any further thoughts about these crimes?"

"Terrible. I still can't believe anyone doing such horrible things to other humans."

"Edie, I believe those people murdered were all sinners in the eyes of this killer or killers, and in their tormented minds, living in sin. If someone had robbed them they might have been shot so the robbers could not be identified, but they would not have been so ritually murdered."

"Oh, my Lord, then the killer was not a drifter?"

"My theory is that the killer is upset these people were not churchgoers and were not legally married. He was cleansing the earth by doing these ritual-like murders."

"So he could be a neighbor and thinks he's doing God's work?"

Chet nodded. "Will you think of anyone with such a conviction?"

"I will consider it. They would have to have a strong belief about that to murder them."

"They are too willing to reset the world's clock."

"I heard you were a good man coming with answers and now I see it."

"Not good enough ones so far."

"Oh, I bet you find them."

"Please, really think about any individual around here who is so deep in his own convictions to take things into his own hands this way."

"You want a zealot?"

"That is what the Bible calls them."

"I will search my mind. I have seen some men shake their fist in anger when they hear or see people they think are not good Christians. I will find you some names to check out but for heaven's sake don't tell a soul I did it."

"I won't. But you be careful, too. He will be crazy and would hurt you if he even thought you were helping us stop his business of cleansing the land of non-Christians."

Later in his bed, under the covers, his mind flipped through a hundred names that could be suspects—not one that he knew by face. What a mess? It would not be easy looking through this small population for a clever deceptive person with a mean-purposed killer's mind.

But the killer had made or would make a slip. Right now he was doing a damn good job of keeping under cover. Tracking him down would be a challenge, but somehow he had to or there would be more horrific killings for him to feed off of. This situation was unlike any one he'd ever taken on, but all criminals make mistakes and he damn sure would find them.

CHAPTER 17

Their hostess fixed a big breakfast spread for the men well before the winter sun came up. No doubt she, at one time, had a family. His curiosity was aroused eating her flapjacks and homemade syrup. He'd have loved a hot cup of coffee, but since the beverage was not allowed by Mormons her well water in a glass had to do.

The men were talking when she came back to the table bringing another stack. "You men going to quit eating on me?"

Jesus spoke up, "No, ma'am, we are taking a break to eat those you have there."

That produced a smile on her face, then laughter. "I had a husband once. Frank was a good provider. He left me too early. His heart quit him. We had two sons. Johnny was killed in a logging accident at sixteen. Ira lives in Texas now. He writes me letters, wants me to come to Fort Worth. He has a large mercantile business there. He joined his wife's Methodist church there. I have two grandchildren—I have never seen them except in pictures."

"Why don't you move there?" Chet asked.

"I guess because I am safe here. Or in the past it was safe. I have been a Mormon all my life. I cling to my faith and I fear leaving it. Oh, the elders think I should remarry. But I don't need another man—I am not child bearing and I had a good man that God will rejoin me with, I hope, in heaven. Enough of that. You all eat."

"Edie. Thanks. My first wife died in a horse jumping accident. That was her thing, to jump horses, and she was good. But over-achieving took her from me. Elizabeth was a lady who wanted to buy some of my claybank horses. She came by my place in southern Arizona to buy them when she heard I was there. Came in a fancy coach—widowed, she ran a large *hacienda* in Sonora. We met and soon were married. She is a delightful partner in my life, and if it had not been so cold she would have been here today."

"Thank you for sharing. You have a wife, Jesus?"

"Yes, it took me a long time to convince Chet's wife's maid, Anita, to marry me. But we are married and she is coming out of her shell. It is hard to feel like an equal when you have been a worker and now you are an equal, but she is accepting that."

"Miguel, tell her about your wife."

"Edie, we all owe a lot to our boss. He rescued a young lady who was being held by some outlaws and he brought her home to the ranch. The first time I saw her I said, 'Miguel, you need her.' I didn't know her. I was afraid to talk to her in fear that it might turn her away.

"The reason that I came to Preskitt was a woman I loved was killed in Mexico by bad men. I settled that score and was restless, so I went north. I did not want to farm or work in a mine so I got a job as a *vaquero* at Chet's ranch. No woman had turned my head since I lost her—five years ago, or longer, until Lisa came there.

"I knew that she had been mistreated, held against her will by bad men. She had an edge to her I had to soften. I asked Raphael, our foreman, for a day off if I could talk her into going on a ride with me. He is a great man. He gave me the time and I asked her. At first she frowned and I told her I was not there to use her—you know what I mean?"

"I can imagine, yes." Edie smiled as Miguel poured his heart out.

"I picked an easy horse for her to ride. She made lunch. We rode around and went over on the mountain edge to look over the whole Verde Valley far below. She asked me what were my plans? I told her to become a ranch foreman."

"Not a helper riding with Chet?" she asked.

"Oh, no. He had plenty of helpers. I never expected that to ever happen. I got through Lisa's shield after several picnics. I asked Raphael if I married her could I still work there and could I get us a *casa* for us to live there. He said she could probably get one, he didn't know about me getting one."

They all laughed.

"He told me that they'd have to build one. You know how you want to be married once you asked her or in your case after he asked you? It required months. I thought it felt like years. The priest was ready to marry us. I was ready to marry her. She was ready to marry me. But the *casa* was not ready to live in.

His wife, Elizabeth, bought her a very expensive gown to get married in. I have a picture of her and me I will show you tonight. Finally everything was ready. We had a weeklong honeymoon at Chet's apple ranch and came home riding the clouds."

Smiling, Chet said, "Edie, that is the longest story he ever told in his life."

She dabbed her eyes. "Tonight you'll have to tell me how you got to ride with these two."

"Can we do your dishes?" Chet asked.

"Heavens no. You men have work to do today. But I will treasure your life stories forever. Thanks for making my day."

"No, we have to thank you for your wonderful food. And now we will go to work."

"I prepared a picnic basket for you to take. It has boiled eggs, sliced bread, prickly pear jelly, pickles, and cookies. Not a manly lunch but enough until you get back."

Chet kissed her cheek going out. "We love you, Edie."

Miguel went for the horses and Chet and Jesus went on to meet Deputy Knowles.

"Last night, a man named Sam Thomas offered to ride with one of you if that's okay?"

"Fine. Jesus will ride with him."

"Certainly. He'll be here shortly."

"Good. Miguel went for the horses. He can ride with us. He is my new man and learning how we do things. Jesus is a tracker and finds things."

"However you want to do things. I just want to know who the killer is and stop him."

"I know how you feel. It is your job to protect the folks up here. It may take a long time for us to resolve this, but in the end I believe we will find him."

They met Sam Thomas, a redheaded man about thirty, who had the hands and shoulders of a big Swedish lumberjack. He had a great smile and was as anxious as his pal to find the killer.

They split up. Jesus and Thomas rode off to the second site. Chet, Knowles, and Miguel went to the first scene, the Forester place.

It was frosty but the sun would warm things as the day advanced.

Knowles told them on the road, "One of the church members, Jim Jennings, came by my house last night to ask if he could get title to the Forester place, if he paid the taxes. You know the sheriff is the county tax collector. He wanted it if it was cheap enough. As an investment, he said. I wrote the office in Preskitt to see what could be done. My wife is going to mail it."

"It isn't farmland, is it?" Chet asked.

"No. But if the homestead part has been completed it would be a cheap starter place for a newly-wed couple. The church sends lots of them down here from Salt Lake. Jim's a man in his fifties and stout. He's made some good investments and is a rather rich man by Snow Flake standards."

"He have more than one wife?"

"You know I have to live here. That federal law has to be enforced by your marshals so I'll let that dog lie."

"I understand. I am not looking for a criminal investigation, I am simply curious."

"Thanks. Let's not talk about that. I want to solve these cases. They keep me awake at night. I have run out of leads. I am so glad you came. I've been looking for apes in the woods I guess. I did think about your notion last night and it made me sick, the fact that the killer could be among us here. But you are right; he has to be. No drifters would keep coming back just to kill."

"You ever think about using a water witcher on these sites?"

Knowles chuckled. "What could he do?"

"I was in Fort Worth once and heard about a man who lost a pocket watch on a picnic in some tall grass prairie. He hired a man who witched water wells. He witched for two days with a peach tree fork and found it."

"How would we know what to tell him to look for?"

"It's a real wild thought, but we have no clues to point a finger at anyone, and maybe there is nothing for him to find. But it could be worth a try."

"Let me think about it."

"We are desperate and we do need a lead on something."

They walked around the site of the murders. The shack of a house had more cobwebs, Chet figured, than six months earlier. Old bloodstains were black. Someone had stolen the bed Knowles told him about. Chet stood on the rise to the north, wondering if the killer had stood in this same spot and watched the family while making his heartless plans to rid the world of these unbelievers. With the leaves on the trees, the watcher would not have been seen. Or perhaps he rode up like he had presents or food for them. No matter what he did, he brought cold-blooded death to four humans.

"I've seen enough," Chet said with still no answers.

Knowles, mounting his horse, agreed. Miguel kept quiet. They rode in silence for several miles.

"Now I have seen the place. What would be the tax price he'd pay for it, this guy you wrote the letter for who wants to buy it?"

"Less than a hundred dollars."

"The house is a shack that leaks whenever it rains. I saw no garden spots. I dropped a small rock in the well. There is water at thirty feet but not much of it. No fences. No timber. Why would anyone want this place?"

"He said as a future investment."

"He hasn't eaten any funny mushrooms or smoked some weed in a pipe?" Chet asked.

"No. He is a strong church member. I doubt he'd ever do that. I think he may have been trying to buy it before the murders. That cowboy that reported the deaths said he'd seen him out there checking around."

"Before or after the murders?"

"Both sides of that happening."

"Strange to me why anyone would want it at any price."

Back at the office, Jesus and Thomas had returned as well from the number two site.

Jesus shook his head. "We found nothing out there."

"Tomorrow we look at number three and four." He looked at Knowles, who nodded.

Their horses put up, they walked the dirt street back to Edie's house. Winter-like weather kept hanging on. He needed to write his wife. This was going to take much longer than he originally thought.

"Well the investigators are home," she said, meeting them at the back door.

He laughed. "Sure not much more than lookers."

"You three will solve it. I have the faith. Any new clues that you could list for me?"

Chet shook his head, drying his hands. "The food smells good."

"You three ate since breakfast?"

"Miguel, Knowles, and I had the picnic basket you gave us. Jesus, you and Sam Thomas just had the jerky you carry, right?"

"Tomorrow you'll have another basket. Two since you go in different directions."

"Hurrah," Jesus said.

After the meal, Chet wrote Elizabeth a short letter. Told her that the crimes were unbelievably bad, the clues had evaporated, and they had no suspects. That he'd be home when he could and he loved her.

The men were gone to bed. Edie said she'd mail it for him.

"Not a word, but you can help me with some information. A man called Jim Jennings keeps coming up. Do you know him?"

"He has three wives and I am glad I am not one of them. Is that enough said?"

Chet nodded. "I had to ask."

"He's very outspoken."

"Thanks. What does he do?"

"His wives milk cows. Sell some. They make butter and cheese and have babies. In the summer they raise crop-size gardens. He sells the produce. They never say anything at socials and never have time for quilting—because that is a woman's event and at them women talk to other women. He doesn't want that. There is an old adage he must use. Women are to be seen and not heard."

"Thanks. I better get some sleep. I hope we are not wearing you out."

"No. I want you to find the guilty party. There is one more man that you should know about. Grant Colby. Both his wives divorced him for his severe abuse to them. That, in my church, is unheard of, but it was so bad the church elders excommunicated him."

"Where does he live?"

"In Randolph Canyon. He is a snarling bulldog sort of guy. The church board and bishop never went over there where they weren't armed with shotguns."

"I wonder if Knowles ever questioned him."

She shrugged. "I have no idea."

"Of course not. Don't tell a soul. I'll look into it. Have any of Jennings's wives complained about him?"

"If they have I have not heard about it."

"Good night, Edie, and thanks again."

In his own bed later, he wondered about both men. He had to know more about both. It may not be either of them, but they were the only ones he had for the moment. He rose up, fluffed the pillow. Be a damn sight better being at home right now . . .

CHAPTER 18

The next morning before Thomas arrived, while his men were getting the saddle horses, Chet asked Knowles about the Colby guy.

"I talked to him with two witnesses. We all had shotguns across our laps and we never dismounted. He said he was on his own place at the times I listed concerning the murders. He yelled that I had no right to question him and to get off his ranch property. I really think he told the truth. Why would he kill people he didn't even know? His neighbors can mark the times he rides in and out of there. They dislike him and watch any activity he does real close. They had not seen him ride in or out except once every month or six weeks when he makes trips to town for supplies. And those times were not the times of the murders."

"Well, there goes another theory."

Knowles agreed. The two of them rode to another scrubby place where a man, his teenage son, and his wife were all murdered the same way as the others. Beheaded and her violated. Nothing outstanding showed up. The others had no reports on number four where a widower and his grown daughter were murdered in the same style.

Jesus said it was as shabby as the rest of the sites.

"It is almost like he was cleaning up the country-side," Miguel said. This time he had gone with Jesus and Thomas.

"That's right," Thomas said. "I wonder who else he plans to cull out."

"No telling, guys. Grady Burton is a well witcher. I talked to him last night about coming out and doing a search at one of the sites. He says he once found a ring for a woman but promises that there may be no results. Where do we start?" Knowles asked.

"Number one place. Let's scour it tomorrow. What does he cost?" Chet asked.

"He is superstitious about that. He won't charge us a thing."

"That is pretty nice."

"He's like most of the residents up here. They want this madman captured."

"What else can we do, Knowles?"

"I have no idea. But I would think that after all that slaughter the killer must have had blood all over his clothing."

"Right," Jesus said. "Like a butcher has."

"Yes," Chet agreed. "And if he took them home, his wife, if he had one, would notice."

"But if he had control over her, she'd never say a word."

Chet agreed with him.

More unending thoughts about the situation that led nowhere.

Back at the house, Edie handed Chet a letter from Liz. It had been forwarded from Holbrook.

Dear Chet,

I know you are real busy working on solving crimes. I am fine, and Monica with Lisa send their best wishes. We are all busy helping the less well-off folks in the church by sharing some canned food. Raphael also took two sacks of frijoles to the Methodist church. They said they had enough canned goods and the frijoles would help. Lots of people are out of work. Many blame the economy being so bad. Hannagen wrote you that they are holding up the government support money for the wire due to the economy. He said he would be in touch with you when he saw an opening. The ranches are doing fine.

Come home when you can. I miss you so much.

Elizabeth.

"Is everything okay?" Edie asked, putting a full plate before him.

"Yes. No word on the telegraph starting yet."

"Good," Jesus said, and began eating.

"Oh, Miguel, Lisa sent word she is fine. Liz never mentioned Anita, but she's in town."

"She doesn't write, either. I can send her a letter and they will get it to her," Jesus said.

"Maybe write one for me please?" Miguel asked.

"We can do that," Chet said between bites of delicious food.

"Someone can read it to her?"

Miguel smiled. "No. Lisa can read. She is the one teaching me, but I am not that good at it. Besides she doesn't know where I am."

All four laughed.

Late the next morning they met the gray-haired short man, Grady Burton.

"We appreciate your agreeing to help us find a needle in a haystack," Chet said, and introduced his men.

"I don't know if I can do you any good. But we can try. This killer must be stopped."

They went to the Forester property and started going over the ground. Nothing.

Chet brought sandwiches and more cookies Edie had made for them. They ate them for lunch and then went back to searching.

"Hey," Jesus shouted. "We found something."

He stood with Burton in an open spot in what Chet considered part of the side yard.

"What is it?"

"Someone burned a coat here. We have a small piece of material that did not burn. And a gold ring."

Chet looked hard at it. "It is tarnished gold."

"Forester never had a gold ring in his life," Knowles said. "Or he'd have pawned it."

"I don't know what it will point to, but I think it's the killer's clothing that was burned here."

"I saw the spot when I first came here and thought that this was where they burned their trash."

Miguel had polished the ring some. "There is writing inside."

"What does it say?"

Knowles held it toward the sun to better see it. "E-m-i-l-y."

"Emily."

"Who is that?"

Knowles shook his head. "There are some women in our community named that."

Burton nodded. "Several women, old and young, that I know of. But how did it get here?"

"Using the traces of burnt material I'd say the killer burned the bloody coat, forgetting he had that ring in his pocket."

"I was over it twice," Burton said.

"Up there, on that rim, it is grassy and weedy. I bet when the killer was here he stood there watching. Try it next, Grady," Chet said.

Knowles was still polishing the ring. "Somewhere, someone knows this ring and who it belongs to."

"Well, the killer won't tell you. That's for sure," Chet said as he headed up after Jesus and Grady.

Grady stopped and Chet did, too.

"What is it?" Chet asked.

Jesus was on his knees digging carefully with his jackknife. Then dangling on a chain, he held up a dirt-packed pocket watch.

"Oh, my God," Knowles said, joining Jesus who was polishing it on his pants. "How did it get there?"

"The earth must have been cracked open here. It fell in the crevasse and the monsoon rains closed it up again," Grady replied.

Knowles shook his head. "I know the owner of that watch—James Jennings. How do we prove it?"

"I am thinking he knew that watch was here

somewhere, couldn't find it, which is why he wanted to buy the place."

"How does the ring fit in?" Knowles asked.

"I am not worrying about that for now. What we need is a confession out of him to cinch this case."

"You're right. A good lawyer in court could twist this around saying he simply lost it here."

With all of them gathered on the steep hillside, Chet warned, "We must be quiet about our finds. He can't know a thing ahead of time that we have these two items. This is good evidence, but we still need his confession to close the case."

"If I'd have lost this good of a watch, I'd been on my hands and knees looking all over for it," Thomas said, and laughed. Then, sober faced, he said, "But for the life in me I can't imagine anyone murdering those children. They did no harm."

"Will his wives testify about him coming home with his clothes being bloody at any of those times?" Jesus asked.

"If he can't reach them to shut them up," Chet said, "I bet they would talk."

"They damn sure don't talk in public now," Thomas said.

Burton nodded. "You'd think they don't have tongues."

"If you arrest him, would the bishop go with you to talk to them about testifying against him?" Chet asked Knowles.

"I think he would. He wants these crimes solved and the thing put to rest."

"Keep looking. Knowles has the evidence. We will

ride in quietly to see the bishop. No shouting when you return later even if you find more evidence."

Chet shook their hands. He saw both his men had relaxed a lot. Even Thomas and Burton looked relieved. But they still had some narrow bridges to cross before they had Jennings locked up forever. A lot would depend on his silent wives' help—Chet knew they would be hesitant to testify. Maybe the ward leader or bishop could convince them to overcome the fear that talking could get them hurt or even killed.

The whole thing was fragile.

They stopped at the bishop's house. They found him working on his business books. He removed his reading glasses and stood to shake their hands.

His wife closed the doors to the study. The winter sun beamed in the southern windows as he showed them chairs.

"How is the investigation going, Knowles? Nice to have you here, too, sir. I understand you are here to help get to the bottom of our murders."

"We made a find today."

"Good. What is it?"

"Grady Burton witched at the Forester place for any item he could find. I know we didn't need water up there. He had some luck finding some jewelry wrapped in burned suit material. It is a tarnished ring with the name Emily engraved in it."

"Who lost it?"

"Let me show you the second find." He drew out the watch. "This was found at the same site above the house in a crack in the earth that we think the monsoon rains sealed. These rains I understand came some weeks after the first murder."

The bishop nodded, looking somberly at them. "I know who carried that watch. Is he your suspect?"

Chet and Knowles both nodded.

"Sir, we think if we arrest him, you could help us convince his wives to testify that he came home bloody or he brought bloody clothes home after one of the murders."

"You are certain your evidence points to him?"

"Yes, sir."

The bishop shook his head. "Well I know this from before. Emily was his first wife. Her disappearance in Utah made some people in Salt Lake, ten years ago, suspect he was involved in her disappearance. If that ring was not on her finger, then she didn't disappear with her ring on, did she?"

"They never found her body?"

"No trace of her. I have thought for years she might have run away. That ring is grim truth that she didn't. Yes, I will speak to his wives. We know they have lived under his thumb for years. If he is guilty and they knew they could escape his hold, they might testify."

Knowles nodded. "Then I will arrest him and charge him with murder."

"He may hire some big lawyers?"

"Without a doubt. But with good evidence and, hopefully, testimony from the wives he will be found guilty."

"Amen. Why would anyone do such a horrible thing?" The bishop shook his head.

"He could think God empowered him to do it."

"I guess so. But your hunch, finding that ring from his dead wife, really makes me sick. If people had checked more and found out what really happened to her, we'd never have had this horrific disaster here."

Knowles nodded. They stood up and shook his hands.

Chet and the deputy rode over to Jennings's house, hitched their horses at the yard gate, and went to the front door. They knocked. It took a long time for a woman with gray-streaked hair to answer.

"We need to talk to Jim Jennings."

"What for?"

"The matter is with him. Is he here?"

"No."

"Stand aside."

"I won't."

Knowles took her by the shoulders and moved her aside. "Better tell us where he is at."

Tears began to spill down her face. "He said not to."

"Where?" He shook her.

She glanced at the staircase. "Up there. May God protect me."

"He will," Knowles said. "Better draw your gun, Chet."

He nodded and did so, then moved a little to the right as they started up the staircase. At any minute he expected a door to open, a handgun to stick out belching lead, fire, and smoke.

"I am unarmed. My hands are high. Knowles, your enforcing federal law about polygamy will end your career in law enforcement I promise you." Jennings was standing at the top of the stairs.

"James Jennings, my warrant is for the murder of the Forester family." Knowles handcuffed him. "Now march downstairs."

"Murder? I never murdered anyone."

Chet knew Knowles could not resist his next words. "Your late wife Emily may finally rest in her lonely grave when you hang for her murder."

"What are you talking about?"

"The ring you removed from Emily's finger when you put her in her grave."

"Huh? I never killed Emily."

"No, you killed her and removed her ring at the burial site in Utah."

"Damn you. She was my wife. I loved her."

"You killed her and then knew they'd hang you, so you went looking for a shallow grave to put her in but you saved her ring."

Jennings looked around. "Where are we going?"

"We are walking to the jail. You will be transferred to Holbrook and then to the Preskitt court. There is no bond for murder."

"But my business; who will run it?"

"You won't need to worry. You won't see the outside of prison except on your walk to the gallows."

"You can't prove I killed anyone."

On their way to the jail Knowles slowed and turned toward Jennings. "Where are the bloody clothes you brought home after the murders?" he asked.

"Who told you that?"

"Your wives."

"My wives told you nothing."

"They will. I am taking their testimony after I put you in the cell."

"Where did you bury Emily in Utah?" Chet asked him.

"What are you talking about?"

"We have the ring that you left in bloody clothes you burned at the Forester place. Where did you plant her? You said she ran off and left you. She never lived to run away. You caught her and killed her and took that ring off her finger and didn't dare use it because your next wife would know it was hers."

"Liars!"

"Show him the evidence," Chet said, shoving him into the sheriff's office and toward the cell.

"You can't prove that."

"It has her name inside it."

"I want a lawyer?"

Knowles unlocked the cuffs.

Chet made him widen his stance and found a derringer strapped to his leg. Then he took a large knife, in a scabbard, from behind his back and tossed it aside.

"You cut Mrs. Forester's throat with that after you used her?"

"I don't know what you are talking about."

Knowles shoved Jennings into the cell, then shook his head. "I guess I am getting stupid after all this time."

Chet put his hand on the man's shoulder. "No you are a patient man who has struggled to do the impossible. I am going to go to supper with Edie. We will share guarding the jail. I will send one of my men back after we eat, and then we will change shifts again tonight."

"Thanks."

He lowered his voice. "We need to keep pushing him about his crimes so we can break him and make him confess."

Knowles nodded. "Thomas is coming in, so when he does, I will go with the bishop to get the testimony from his wives."

Chet nodded. "We can support him. Good luck. That sister, who answered the door, will be tough."

"I know all about that. I spent nine months trying to solve this and in less than a week you turned this case around. I heard lots about you, Chet Byrnes. I can see now that many were damn lies. You ever need help you can sure call on me. I'd be proud to help you."

"Oh, you did lots of work and the rest we did together."

"Thanks."

That evening they told Edie all about finding the ring and watch. Chet added what the bishop said about the ring and swore her to secrecy.

"I guess now I'll lose my boarders?"

"We need to get back to Preskitt, Edie. I imagine someone else will need us to help them at some time."

"I have heard so much about your home, your wife, and your life I feel like I am part of the family, along with these two men that belong with you. Not many men would trust his life to two young men from Mexico. I know why you do that. You trust them and you know the dedication they have for you. They are not just your bodyguards. You three men are brothers, and thank God for you looking over all the God-fearing people in the territory."

Chet kissed her forehead and hugged her. "The worry, fear, and distress is over and we so appreciate all the little things you did for us while we were here."

"Oh, Chet, tell your wife from all of us, we so appreciate her sharing you with us to find this madman."

"I will, Edie. You know where we live if you ever need us again. We will come riding."

"It has been a very exciting time in a sleepy town to have three U.S. marshals staying with me. I guess my reputation is safe."

"Oh, yes. Three married men."

"Those ladies have lots to look forward to upon your return to them. I will envy them. My husband would go on trips for the church to help somewhere, and I always thanked God when I saw him riding up the lane and we could renew our love and life."

"Edie, we sure thank you. I am going to pay you for our board and room. We'd have had to pay for a hotel and café otherwise. We get our expenses paid for by the marshal service. What you do with the money is your business."

"I had no plans to charge you. I will find someone needy to give to."

"Thanks. Good night, Edie."

"Good night, my friends, and thanks for bringing some sunshine into my life. I'll have breakfast at six so you can get an early start." A knock sounded from the door. "I'll go see; it may be for you."

They waited in the room and when Chet saw the

deputy with his hat in his hand, he knew something was wrong.

"I have some news. Thomas and I stepped out of the jail tonight to get a bite to eat. Jennings did not act strange or say anything to make us think something was going to happen. He used a blanket for a noose and strangled himself to death. Sure was a helluva way to die."

"I am sorry that you had to go through all this, Knowles."

"Chet, I have to admit I was worried about arresting him. But we had him by the evidence. I know it will leave some people thinking we may have arrested the wrong man, but I want to tell you his second wife Sarah told the bishop and me, tonight, that he came home twice in bloody clothing around the time of the murders. His first suit coat disappeared after the Foresters were murdered. We had the right man. He knew it and took his life."

Chet had a hard time falling asleep. Criminals upset him, but few of them killed people because they believed their victims were not religious enough in the eyes of God to live. Bad thing to ever happen . . .

CHAPTER 19

They pushed hard and by noon on the second day made Holbrook. Winter let go a little but the calendar said there was still some time left. They stopped and told the new deputy, Joe McCarthy, about the Jennings situation. He agreed it was good to have it settled. Joe had not heard anything about his predecessor's whereabouts. He told Chet he felt Randall Cates was GTT. In other words—Gone to Texas.

The next stop was three days later at Windmill Ranch. Susie and Sarge, along with their crew, sat around the fireplace and Chet told them a less grizzly story about the murders and how they eventually found the evidence. Everyone shook their heads and a few said they should have hung him right away.

"Oh, we need to present a better picture than that. People back east feel we are all as mad as Jennings. We need law and order to prevail if we ever want to become a state."

Later he and Susie spoke privately in the kitchen.

"Chet, does anyone really know what all you do for the territory?" she asked.

He shook his head. "That doesn't matter. I have ranches to run, and people count on us to provide them a life."

She shook her head and hugged him. "Brother, I shudder every time I hear that you and your men have ridden somewhere to stop crime or arrest an outlaw gang."

She put her finger on his lips to silence his protest. "You don't have to tell me someone has to do it. But as far as I am concerned, they need to get someone else besides my brother to do their calling for help."

The next morning, he kissed her forehead good-bye, picked up her son, Erwin, and told him to take good care of his momma. He'd noticed the close relationship the toddler had with Sarge, but he sure looked like his real father. Mounted on his roan horse he waved good-bye to Susie, and his three-man outfit, along with their packhorses, rode for the Verde Ranch.

Rhea and Adam met them at the front door of the big house. Jesus told her that he and Miguel would put up the horses and be back.

She hugged him, and with Adam in his arms they went inside the house. The boy jabbering about some lamb he rode and Rhea filling him in on the latest ranch news. Almost home . . .

Tom came over and had to hear the stories. Asked about his daughter and son-in-law. Chet gave him a good report on them. Nothing wrong at the Verde

River Ranch. Rhea made them supper and they slept, overnight, in the big house. Up at dawn, they rode up the mountain and by mid-morning they were ringing the schoolhouse bell. The boss was back and everyone hurried out to welcome him home.

Lisa came on the run for her husband. They hitched a team to the buckboard to take Jesus to his wife Anita who was waiting in town. Smiling, and looking great to Chet, his wife came to hug and greet him.

"Oh." She swept a curl back from her face. "Good to have you back, big man."

Monica was on the back porch, arms folded, and when he waved she shook her head and went back inside.

Chet shook Raphael's hand and answered him when he asked how the new man was working out.

"Super. He's learning the way fast. We had lots of work to do and many miles to cover, and Miguel did very well. I will tell you more about it and how we solved all the problems."

Chet thanked everyone still standing around, told them he was glad to be back at the ranch, and for God to bless them all. Then hand in hand he went into the house.

"How was the trip?"

"Long and tough, but we solved the crimes at both places. They were two different crimes. One at Holbrook was a neighbor killed a man for his wealth and ranch. At Snow Flake the murderer was one of them and he committed suicide after we arrested him. Both were very black crimes and hard to understand. One stole and killed, and the other thought

God had sent him to kill less religious people. With the second, we found that he probably murdered his first wife years earlier in Utah. If that crime had been solved back then he'd not had a chance to murder four other families."

"I am sure glad you are home."

"Liz, I am, too. Anything wrong?"

"Lands no. I simply missed you." She squeezed his arm.

"I did, too. I'll tell you more after a while. No problems here?"

She threw her head back and laughed. "Nothing that you can't solve later."

"Good. I can do that. How is Cary doing?"

"Fine. She writes she is helping teach children down there, found that she can teach. Last Saturday, for the first time, she attended a dance and young men danced her feet off. None of them had danced much with her before at other dances, so she felt she was now being accepted back in the community."

"We figured she'd recover. Sounds good, doesn't it?"

"You stopped and saw Adam. How is he doing?"

"Fine. He talked about riding sheep the whole time. Rhea is raising him right, I guess. No. I know it. She tries hard and of course he is her pride and joy."

"Did you ever think maybe we should have both your boys together, here, at the ranch?"

"I say no. In the first place, you'd break both women's hearts. Second, you'd be tied down and couldn't do all the things you get done with the help, or come riding with me."

"Can we can talk about it more, later?"

He agreed. He realized she said this out of the feeling of guilt that she might be neglecting him not having the boys there all the time. Shame they lost the baby, but there was nothing anyone could have done about that. The boys were fine where they were.

"Well, stranger, I see the cat came back," Monica said, putting a plate of food before him.

"Yes, ma'am, how are you?"

"My usual self."

"No big cowboy came to court you while I was gone?"

"One big cowboy is enough. I damn sure don't need another."

Liz put in, "We share you. She gets to feed you and I get to do the rest."

"You ladies are the diamonds in my life. You both sparkle."

"Eat your food before it gets cold. This is a lonely house when you aren't here to upset it. I am as always glad when you tromp back here from God knows where and she doesn't have to worry about you being shot or hurt on your travels."

"Thanks, Monica. I had Susie tell me what to do for years, and you fit her shoes just fine. By the way, I stopped and saw her, Erwin, and Sarge coming and going. They are doing great. Tom's daughter, Sandy, and Cody are making it fine with Sarge herding cattle to New Mexico. Don't ever tell anyone, but Erwin really looks like his father. He and Sarge are real close buddies, but I could not get over the resemblance."

"You look tired," Liz said. "After lunch why don't you take a *siesta*? There is nothing pressing on your desk."

"Sounds good. Your food is still the best, Monica." Good to be home, too, that was for sure . . .

CHAPTER 20

Home. For a week they had some light snow, nothing the sun wouldn't melt by noon the next day. He'd ordered mowers for all his ranches and Ben Ivor promised him he'd do all he could to get them there. Kathrin, Ben's wife, was there with both of their small children. They chatted a bit before she ran off with them to do something.

Ben shook his head. "I never dreamed at forty I'd have a new family. I'm so glad you found her, that you saw the saving graces that woman has. Chet, my business exceeds most mercantile stores in the territory thanks to people like you. And I thank God every night for you, it, her, and the kids."

"Ben, you treat everyone of your customers like family. She is the star in your crown, and it is no shame for a man to have a lovely wife and children."

"She said she never had any life before she married me."

"God did that, huh?"

"He must have. My first wife and I never had a

child. Come to think of it, she did lose some. I hate to think bad of her, but that might have been intentional."

"You did good this time."

"I hope I can get all this mower gear for you by haying time."

"All you can do is try, Ben. I trust you."

"If I can't, I might be able to get some used equipment to get you by on."

"We have to do what we have to do. Thanks."

He found Bo was his usual smiling self when he caught him in the land office next. "I found that nephew of yours, Ty, some more land out there."

"Worth the money?"

"I think so. It has an artesian well to water twenty acres of alfalfa. The whole eighty is close to him and costs eight hundred dollars."

"You buy it?"

"Yeah, because I can sell it for more than that if you and Ty don't want it. But what do you think?"

"I'll buy it. He can farm it. He gets on his feet, he can pay me. I'll need the location. How did you ever get it?"

"A guy in Illinois inherited it. He wanted a quick sale and I made one by mail."

"Thanks. I know the place. I'll go tell Ty."

"Thanks. Your family doing all right?"

"Yes, except my poor wife is pregnant again. Guess that happened like on the tenth day you breed a mare, huh?"

"I don't know, Bo. I am not that lucky."

"Sorry. She was married to her first husband for ten years and they never had anything. Now—"

"Like Ben Ivor when he married Kathrin and now they have two. She'd never had any kids before she married him nor did he have any with his first wife."

"I am pleased. Hadn't been for you sobering me up, I'd probably died of exposure out behind Whiskey Row. When do you get possession of this eighty?"

"The lease on it ran out first of the year. You and Ty can have it now."

"I better go see how his mowing equipment is. I ordered a dozen mowing outfits for several places today. He may need one, too. Where's Liz?"

"Teaching school with Lisa out at the ranch. They are teaching English to the children so they can attend regular school."

"If it isn't reforming drunks you are into that. My buddy Chet Byrnes. Come by and visit and bring Liz with you."

"I will do that."

Chet finished up his business and stopped by to talk to Jesus and Anita. Jesus was splitting firewood for her range and welcomed the break. Chet quickly noted how Anita had taken on the role of wife and not servant.

As they enjoyed a cup of coffee, Jesus teased him about when they stayed with the Mormon folk and not having coffee to drink.

"Tell him what we talked about, Jesus?"

"Anita and I went to see Bo about getting a place of our own. He asked if we had money to buy a place. I told him maybe not a big place, but we could afford a ranch and we wanted it between here and your place."

"I think it shocked him that a Mexican family our age had that much money," she said.

"Does he have a place listed?"

"We get to go look Friday at a place he said that is like what we described."

"I will still be here then?" Jesus asked.

"I have no plans for now. Hold his feet to the fire. Other words don't pay the first price he tells you."

She laughed. "We told each other that."

He went on back to the ranch house and his bookkeeping chores, still amused by Anita's response. Those two, in time, would make a great team if not ranchers on their own. No matter they would rise to the occasion.

Jesus and Anita would get themselves a ranch. But for now he had two good men to support him. He was still busy looking at invoices and bank deposits when Liz came in.

"How are we doing?"

"All right. JD is selling more beef. He makes his own way now, selling enough beef to cover his costs. I think by next year they will find even more markets for their cattle than they have now. And in the future his citrus and grapes will make money, too. The upper ranch at Hackberry has made money. The Windmill Ranch and our sales to the Navajo Agency is the greatest source of our income. Tom's big operation has moved ahead of the other ranches since it is the largest. The Hereford division will really make us money now we have the bulls we need. Toby's ranch and the Oracle place will take a few years before they even make a nickel, but they will make it and be good sources of income."

"Good. You need to go to Oak Creek and do something nice for them. They send us peaches, apples, strawberries, and vegetables all summer long."

"I will ride up there and see what they need. They do make money with that operation."

"I think the fruit and produce they bring us is worth a lot."

"That is all my end. I see you and your school project have moved six students to the real schoolhouse and they are all doing well there. Everyone is making a big fuss about them and that will encourage more to go there.

"You seem to have something on your mind, Liz. What is bothering you?"

"I am just tired of winter I guess. I know you have lots to do to keep you busy and the telegraph business is waiting offstage. But I'd like to take a trip somewhere with you."

"I'll see what we can do. Just give me a few days to catch up here."

"Oh, I am not rushing you. You get time, I'll be ready."

"I am thinking I want to go up and see Toby and Talley. They have been pushing hard to make that place a ranch and I don't want them to quit. We can go down to the Verde and spend the night at the big house, then get up the next morning and ride to Toby's before dark. Does that suit you?"

"Wonderful. When?"

"Next Monday."

She kissed him on the cheek and left him to deal with the rest on his desk.

Monday rolled around quickly. That morning his men were ready and had packhorses loaded in case they had to camp somewhere along the way. The weather looked open and mild. The four rode out the gate with three packhorses and the trip began.

By noon they were at the Verde Ranch. Rhea and Adam welcomed them to the big house. Miguel and Jesus rode off, after unloading the packhorses and grabbing her flour tortilla–wrapped beef and *frijole burritos*, to go look at the Herefords.

Adam and Liz talked about sheep riding. Chet walked down looking for Tom. Millie came to him and said, "Tom's went somewhere to check on something. He never said where or what, but he'll be home by dark. We'll come over to talk to you both when he is back, but I want you to know something. Tom and I have talked about it. Today, we think you did the right thing for Cody and Sandy, but I could have killed you when they got married."

"I wore a steel vest that day."

She broke out laughing. "You needed one. Chet, that girl of mine writes me a nice letter every week. And she is learning a lot of things about cooking and how to do things from Susie. I am pleased with her and him—growing together."

"That would be great. Do come over. Liz was fed up with winter lockdown and came along to check on Toby's progress. As for Sandy learning from Susie— You know Susie was my mainstay in Texas. I knew you two became close friends when she lived here at the big house. I have nothing for Tom; just was going to visit."

"He loves to talk with you. I recall coming back here when you took this ranch back from those crooks. I never thought you'd get it done. But you prevailed and thank God for all of us. Tom, Hampt, and Sarge were the only help you had."

"We've come a long ways."

"Oh, much more than that. I'll be up there to the big house when Tom gets here."

On the way back to the house, he spoke to a few cowboys coming in.

"We've begun calving and so far this open weather sure helps," a hand called Ruff told him.

His partner agreed.

"Keep after them, guys. Thanks."

"Hey, we all like this outfit. You keep it going and we'll worry about calving."

"Thanks."

His two men were still off looking at the Herefords. Rhea and Liz were playing with Adam when he walked in.

"See Tom?"

"No, he's off checking on things. He'll be back later. I'm taking a nap."

Liz stood up. "We are planning a meal and Adam is helping us."

"You have things under control. How is Victor?"

"He's fine. Went to check on his fencing project at the new farm."

"Okay, all is good. Just wake me up when Tom comes."

She winked at him and he went to find their bed

upstairs. His boots and gun belt off, he lay down and soon he slept.

Over supper Tom and Millie joined them. He'd gone to look at some cut fencing his men reported. They'd fixed it and came in and told him they thought someone probably wanted to ride across their fenced pasture as a shortcut. No cattle had been driven through the opening.

"Made me mad that someone cut my fences. We have gates at intervals. A guy cuts your fence thinks he can. We only have fences on land that we own."

"That sure has you stirred up," Chet said.

"If I catch him I'll kick his butt, hard."

"No idea who he was?"

Tom shook his head. "Just some jasper passing through I'd bet."

"We're going to see our man at the eastern division and how he is making it."

"He told me next time he came to town, he was bringing his wife to visit us."

Chet smiled. "I told him to go easy on the work and do that."

"He is real serious about making it a good ranch."

"He and Spencer are both trying too hard. I told him not to push too hard. Told them they need to take time with their wives."

"Spencer's is Hispanic, isn't she?" Rhea asked.

"Yes. She has two small children. Her husband was killed in a horse wreck last year at the Diablo Ranch."

"I thought he took a woman out of a—a house?"

"He did. She didn't want to live on a ranch so he gave her the fare to go back home. She never left

Preskitt and now takes care of some man who is in bad health."

"Lucinda Marcos is Spencer's wife and she is beautiful," Liz said. "I met her. You'd love her, Rhea. Her children are very sweet and they love Spencer."

"Did you like the site they are building on?"

"Yes. But I don't want to live down there. Preskitt's summers have spoiled me."

All around the table laughed.

Chet spoke up. "Rhea, you fixed a great supper and we appreciate all you do with Adam."

Everyone agreed.

They rode out early. Chet was feeling good. Miguel's horse bucked some. Nothing fancy, simply feeling he had a few kinks in his back to get shed of. Miguel could ride almost anything, never got mad at an animal and somehow managed to make it behave. A good sideman to ride with. He matched Jesus.

They made the T Bar X Ranch, but when they came in sight of it no smoke was coming out the chimney. Chet held his hand out and stopped Liz. "Something's wrong here. That front door is wide open."

"I'll go check it," Miguel said, and jobbed his horse to charge up there. Chet and Jesus drew their handguns. They looked to the pine-clad slopes for any sign of threat. Liz had her .30 caliber Colt in her hand.

Chet shouted to Miguel, "Watch yourself. They may be lying in wait."

"Where is Crystal Hayes at? She usually stays home."

"No one seems to be here. But they trashed the house."

"What do you think is wrong?"

"I have no idea. Something is bad wrong here. I hope Miguel doesn't find any bodies."

"Oh, that would be horrible."

"Liz, you and I know this is still a raw country. Anything can happen, isolated as this place is."

"Ain't no bodies. But they sure made a mess of the house," Miguel said, reaching them. "Looks like the work of some drunken Indians to me."

"Good enough. Jesus is checking the rest of the place."

Just then Jesus came from the back of the house. "Whoever they are they stole the horses that they had."

"Oh, my."

"Time to move on. Nothing we can do here. Better see how Toby is getting on up ahead. Liz, bring the packhorses. Someone needs to ride point. Let's hustle. I don't like this one bit."

"Go," he said to her, and went to beating on the packhorses to run.

Jesus took the point and Miguel dropped behind him. All four of them were looking everywhere while loping their horses for the ranch road that led into the old rustler's place.

A million things flew through Chet's mind. Most of the Apache renegades were down in Mexico. But who knew anything for sure? Why didn't they burn the ranch house? They used to do that every time.

His roan horse was running smoothly and Liz was holding her horse back. He slapped the slowest packhorse with his rein to make him go faster.

She nodded her approval and they pushed up the road. Chet worried about an ambush where the road went into the pine forest. In the clear open country they could see anyone coming, but the forest offered cover and the road into the ranch was heavily tree lined.

They reached the ranch sign and turned north onto the narrow road leading into the ranch.

"If we get attacked, let loose of the packhorses," he said to Liz.

She nodded grimly. If it was only him and his men he'd feel a helluva lot better. Now he had her safety to defend, but no need to regret the trip. They'd been lucky thus far.

Some hatless riders appeared on the road. Jesus shot his pistol at them. They panicked and fled north. Had they burned the ranch and killed his crew? Miguel spurred his horse past Chet and Liz and also shot at the fleeing riders.

"Let the packhorses loose."

Determination showed as Liz bent over, urging her horse on, and she shook her head. "Not yet."

"Damn it, turn them loose."

No reply. He rode in to press the packhorses to run faster. He could see the ranch house and new barn structure. The braves had ridden off to the west to avoid the new barbed-wire fencing on the right side of the drive.

He heard someone shouting and waving for them to come on up to the house. It was Toby with a rifle—at least he was alive. Then several men and women came out onto the porch.

"Look there's some of his neighbors," Liz shouted, a smile replacing her grim look.

Chet slid his horse to a stop and Toby ran to meet them. "Thank God you came. It's been hell up here. My neighbors all came here when things broke loose, knowing me and my brush cutters had plenty of rifles and ammo."

Folks were hugging each other and some of the women were crying.

His wife, Talley, wet eyed, said, "I kept saying if only Chet could come save us like he did me before. And you did. God I love you, Chet Byrnes."

"Hey, let me help them unsaddle the horses."

"No," Jesus told Chet. "You take everyone back into the house. We can do this."

Liz had his arm. "You hear your guardian tell you what to do?"

He smiled, shaking his head. She steered him across the porch to the front doorway. Inside he unbuttoned his heavy coat and Cecil Hayes began telling how they learned there was a war party roaming the rim. "A friendly Apache came by and warned us they were coming. We decided there were more guns up here than defending our places."

"They ransacked your place," he said to Crystal. "But didn't burn it."

"No," she said. "That would signal the army to find them."

"The army is up here?"

"We understand they are."

Her husband, Cecil, shook his hand. "Damn sure good to see you."

"I am glad to be here. We haven't had any Indian problems since Cole shot an Apache that we captured herding cattle to the Navajo. That was over three years ago."

"Well, we have it again."

"Have they attacked you here since you came over here to Toby's?"

Cecil said, "They tried but those Mexicans working for him laid down a barrage of rifle shots that stopped them. They lost some horses and bucks. They have not tried anything like that since. They did burn some of his brush piles out on his meadows, which saved his men doing it. I want to tell you I thought you'd hired a kid. But he's serious and knows what to do."

"I thought he'd make the grade."

Toby, Jesus, and Miguel came in and the women serve them cake and hot coffee.

"Boss man, we have done all we can. Those Apaches got a good taste of .44/.40 ammo two days ago. I got some boys than can sure use gun sights. You see the army?"

"Didn't see anyone on the road."

"We thought they were coming," Crystal said.

Chet shrugged and turned to Toby. "How is your food supply, Toby?"

"Good. That big snow storm taught me to have a good supply on hand in winter."

"You've done well. I'm proud of all of you. We

were just coming to see your progress. Never dreamed to find this."

"When Cecil Hayes and his wife came over and told me about them bucks being on the warpath, I told him I had some sharpshooters and plenty of ammo. Those men all fought shoulder to shoulder to turn them back. Those Indians never expected that kind of firepower. No one of us was even scratched."

"I think they were mostly young bucks. We are lucky Geronimo is down in the Sierra Madres," added Hayes.

"Lucky or not, these boys have really been a big help."

Chet smiled at him. "I saw all that cleared land. Looks great. Your mowing machines are ordered."

"I won't be settled until we find mother cows for this place."

"Keep working. They will come."

"I know. Just anxious. Thanks."

The barn builder Harold Faulk came over. He shook Chet's hand. "Things have been pretty busy up here. Me and my family sure appreciate the work you give us."

"I may have another job down near Oracle. We are building a new ranch headquarters on a new place I bought, and they will need corrals there."

"We'll get the barn done here and we'll come over to Preskitt and make the deal. Save it for us."

"I will. Coming here I certainly didn't expect an Indian attack. Glad no one was hurt."

Things were crowded with everyone sleeping on the floor of the main room heated by a large wood-burning stove a ranch hand kept going. No one complained. Two men stood guard even though everyone knew that most Apaches were so fear filled about being killed in the night and not going to their heaven, that they would not attack.

They ate well the next morning. Jesus and Miguel did some scouting and found no fresh signs, but that didn't mean they were gone, merely being more guarded about their movements. Still the pair found nothing but empty camps where the Indians had been.

A company of the black cavalry came by the ranch and the white officer told them they could all go home. The renegades had been disbursed. The danger was over for the moment.

Thank God . . .

CHAPTER 21

Chet decided to take a course northwest the next morning and go to the Windmill and then home by the Verde Ranch, so after a quick breakfast, Chet told everyone thanks and they headed for Susie's place.

They made it halfway, found an empty soddy to sleep in out of the cold, fed the horses grain, and ate a supper of elk steak that Toby gave them. Oatmeal for breakfast and then hit the windswept rolling grasslands for the Windmill.

Liz had a scarf wrapped around her face against the cold, but never complained. Long after dark they reached the ranch and Susie met them with a lantern. Hands showed up and put up the animals. Her boy Erwin was excited about Liz being there. He commanded her full attention.

Susie ran them baths and Chet shaved. He felt alive again. The women made a big meal. Chet sat in the warm living room and talked to Sarge's man about things. Sarge had left early with the herds in case of snow.

They had to tell everyone about the Indians, how Toby was doing with the new place, and about the Oracle Ranch and their plans for it.

"You four need to stay here another day and get rested," Susie said at bedtime. "Besides, Liz and I have not finished our visit with each other."

"We will do that, sis."

Liz smiled. "I didn't think they would argue with you about that. It has been quite a trip. I heard my first war cry and it gave me goose bumps."

They turned in. Chet and his wife shared a double bed and slept in each other's arms like newlyweds. There were no threatening dreams or nightmares. Susie's house was like being home.

Up early, he found Susie in the kitchen feeding her foreman and four hands a breakfast of oatmeal and flapjacks. Just like Texas, he reminisced. He had a nice conversation with them. Jesus and Miguel went with the crew to feed hay.

"What next, brother?"

"I am waiting for the wire to string a telegraph across the territory."

"Oh, my God. I hoped that was put off. You don't have time to check ranches and do that."

"Susie, that line will open the northern part of Arizona. We need these features to ever become a state."

"All right, empire builder. I should be used to your spreading yourself out. You've done it since we came from Texas. I see why you brought Liz along this trip. It may not have been a real vacation but she needed getting out, didn't she?"

"I thought so."

"It was good for her, even with the Indian scare, since nothing happened. There is something in her that makes her need these times to ride with you."

"When I can I do it."

"I don't need that kind of thing. I am an old hen who needs her coop. I made one trip to New Mexico and I saw it all. I ate enough dust to do me a lifetime. Those poor Navajo women live such a very gritty life. If Sarge needed me I'd go, but I like my house."

"I guess I never thought much about how different women think about those things. I am always glad to be back at Preskitt, but I can leave it long enough to settle a problem or two."

"When you have a mission, you saddle up. Like finding those two women. That was so nice. Few men would take the time you did."

"And solving murders. Someone needed to solve all four of them, and if I was needed I'd saddle up again, but I have been thinking, I should be out feeding cattle with the others this morning."

"No, your boys are doing that. How is this new man?"

"Miguel. He's like a twin to Jesus."

"How is Jesus's marriage going? She put him off forever."

"Anita? I think she dreaded becoming an equal of her former boss, but she is learning how to live as a wife and equal. They are looking at a place Bo has between the ranch and town. I don't know which one, but he has saved his money and they can have what they want."

"Amazing. A few years ago he was a tracker, and now there is no one any more loyal to you."

"Oh, Cole and him were a great team."

"I know and now he runs the stage line. I thought my brother would not find another good man. Jesus chose Spencer and you now talked him into building a headquarters. Where did Miguel come from?"

"Raphael told me he was going to pick a man to replace him some day. Could he ride with me to learn? I said yes and I am seeing how, by riding with me, he could become the man to replace him. It would not seem right to appoint a foreman from the ranks of the *vaqueros*, but, after having ridden with me, that would work."

She nodded, hugged him, pleased that she didn't have him to worry about.

The ride to the Verde Ranch the next day was sunny warm and they made it after dark. Beside Rhea, at the front door, Adam shouted, "Momma Liz is here."

Not Daddy is here. Momma Liz is here.

The women fixed supper. Victor was at home and after eating, played his guitar and sang for them. A nice easy evening that brought back memories to Chet. Victor had cooked for him and his first wife Marge on their honeymoon where they found the ranch that Bo had handled for them. Lucy was their guide, for exploring the large tract of deeded land that became their north ranch.

After hugging his son the next morning, as he started for the horses, he heard Adam say, "Momma Liz, come see us more. He don't have to come."

"I think you have a new admirer," he said to her under his breath, swinging into the saddle.

"A good one, too."

"He's growing up."

"Way too fast."

They rode home in the shadows of the deep canyon and at last topped out on the mountain and rode west. Be good to be home at last. They rang the bell and the bundled-up women came to welcome them home.

Lisa came to kiss Miguel and like newlyweds they left. The stable boy hooked up a buckboard to take Jesus home. He hugged Liz, thanked Chet, and was off for Anita until he was needed again.

Raphael went with the boss to the house to listen to the Indian stories. Monica served them lunch and after his foreman left, Chet read his mail. Hannagen wrote that the telegraph situation was still hung up, but he expected them to have news shortly.

A U.S. marshal wrote him a letter about a man who embezzled a large sum of money from a small town bank and might be headed his way. Theodore Danbury had disappeared from Wall City, Utah, leaving the bank vault empty of several thousand dollars that belonged to the local depositors. Danbury was described as a man near forty, brown hair, mustache, five-nine. He might have been accompanied by a female, Regina Porter, twenty-three years old, brunette, near six feet tall, very attractive. There is a photo enclosed of both Danbury and Porter.

The letter went on to say that the marshal had heard Chet was a very dedicated law officer and that he knew northern Arizona. It was thought that the two probably took the Honeymoon Trail, what they

call the road out of Utah, that they would cross the
Colorado at Lee's Ferry and go south into Chet's
region. The letter writer added that he would appreciate any assistance Chet could give and be in touch
if he heard anything about their whereabouts. It
was signed Chief U.S. Marshal for Utah, Kenneth
Manhattan, Salt Lake, Utah.

Chet wrote Cole Emerson to be on the lookout
for the couple and to spread it down the line east
and west. Then he wrote Manhattan that he would
look for them.

Chances of finding them he counted as little to
nothing, but he would make an effort anyway. They
had to be somewhere. Then he busied himself with
doing ranch bookwork. Lots of expenses were coming
in from the Oracle Ranch. Plus Toby's payroll had to
be met and the feeding bill paid. But Toby and his
wife would succeed. The bank had cashed another
Navajo beef check.

Shawn wrote him a long letter about how well
things were going for them and how many calves
Spud saved. How fast Clem was growing. How neat it
was to be Lucy's man and how he owed Chet his life
for all he did for him to make his life so wonderful.
Plus he thought with all the land they had deeded
they could run nine hundred mother cows, would
Chet think on it.

The letter made him smile. All that talk to lead up
to nine hundred cows. Well, the boy was doing more
than sleeping with her. Then he laughed. That boy
would make it big someday and he had a good partner to help him.

Chet read the next note. It came from Texas.

Dear Chet,

My name is Salty Hogan. I met you a few times when you were in Texas. You probably don't remember me. Anyhow a crook stole ten thousand dollars from me. He sold me a salted gold claim out by El Paso. They say he's staying near where you headquarter at a place called Horse Thief Basin.

There is a warrant out for him from Texas and a five-hundred-dollar reward for bank embezzling. I'd split my ten thousand if you can get it back.

I enclosed a photo of him and you'd still have the five-hundred reward if you can't get my money back. The bastard's a mean devil. But I seen you in Texas clean up on two big guys at a dance who insulted a lady friend. Ralph Sutter won't be hard for you to handle. Five-nine. Green eyes. Two hundred pounds. Right cheek has a red scar on it.

> *Salty Hogan*
> *Northfield, Texas*

Strange letter—get my money back and you can have half. Salty Hogan did not mean anything to him that he could recall. Hogan might want this guy killed or have other reasons for planting him. No county court was mentioned where he was wanted for embezzling so that could be a hoax, too.

He'd send a wire to the U.S. marshal in El Paso. Be the quickest way to find out about Sutter's real worth. He'd do that in town in the morning and have an answer in two days.

Liz came in. "What is it? You look perplexed."

"I got a letter from Texas. Said we met a few times and that some bank embezzler is over at Horse Thief Basin. I'm wiring a marshal in El Paso in the morning to see if there is any truth to it."

"And if it is?"

"I will go and arrest him and collect the reward."

"No, you won't. You don't collect rewards. You give them to your men."

"Might do that, too."

"You will. Part of your code of the West business."

"You short on anything around here?"

"No."

"Then I'll split it with them." He swept her up and kissed her.

She finally broke the kiss. "Times I could kill you, Chet Byrnes."

"No, don't think you could. You recall the dizzy day I dried your feet down on the Santa Cruz? The same day I bathed you and in the night we swore our souls would never part."

"Damn, cowboy. You have a good memory."

"I can still smell hay like it was here today."

"I have no plans to leave you or make love in a haystack, either."

"Good, get your town clothes on. We're going to town and I am taking you to supper at the Palace Bar, get a hotel room, and have a honeymoon."

"I won't be long. Get a buckboard ready."

When they got to Preskitt, he wired the El Paso U.S. marshal regarding one Ralph Sutter and the charges and rewards on him. Then he drove down to the livery. His pal Luther Frey wasn't there. He had the swamper put his team up for the night. Then, the lady on his arm, they walked the boardwalk. He sent a boy to the Adams Hotel to reserve a nice room for him and his wife for the night. Told the boy they would be along after supper and started to give his name.

"I know who you are, Mr. Byrnes. You are the most famous man in Preskitt."

"Thanks. What's your name?"

"Fred Brown, sir, and I will have that room reserved for you. You don't need a boy to help you, do you?"

"Can you read and write?"

"I can, sir. I wouldn't need much pay. I don't eat a lot. And I could do things for you like step and fetch things." He swallowed, twice. "If you could use one?"

"Fred Brown. Be at the hotel at eight a.m. I'll put you to work. Here's a quarter."

"You mean I am hired?"

"Yes."

"Oh, yes, sir. I'll get that room and see you in the lobby at eight."

"Thanks, Fred Brown."

"Mister Byrnes—"

"Fred, you work for me now so I am Chet."

"Chet. I can learn that."

"You better tell your mother you are going to work for me."

"I can't do that, sir—I mean Chet. I am on my own. I have been for two years."

"Is she alive?"

"I think so—"

"Well, we can resolve that later. See you tomorrow, Fred."

Liz had been silent. She caught his arm as they continued their way to the Palace Bar. "Is he an orphan?"

"We'll find that out tomorrow I guess."

She was chuckling and shaking her head. "Big man, you can sure find them."

"At least they ain't dogs."

"No. But who else hires a boy for a chore and then hires him to work for him?"

"Me."

Seated in the restaurant, he told the waitress, "I want a nice steak, knock off his horns and cut off the tail, cook it real quick on both sides. My wife wants one done and smaller."

"You two on a honeymoon?"

Laughing so hard Liz could hardly speak, "Honeymoon is right."

"I thought so. I will turn your order in, but if it butts you don't blame me."

She left them, laughing.

"How did I ever find you? Oh, it was at your granite office building south of the Spanish Capital of Tubac."

"You won't ever forget I only had a canvas shade for a roof over my office."

"I won't forget how Maria blushed when I said, "He needs to see me. I will bathe and get him to wash me."

"Not near as much as my face heated up when you asked me to do that."

"Oh, I knew it was bold. But what the *hey*. It worked."

It turned out to be a great night. And after breakfast the following morning, they took Fred Brown to the mercantile and bought him two new shirts, two pairs of jeans, underwear, a jumper, and a pair of cowboy boots.

"If you are riding with me, you need to look as good as my other men."

When the boy didn't answer him, Chet looked over at him. "I never asked. Can you ride a horse?"

Tears streamed down his face. "Chet, I can't help it. They're just running 'cause I never had any new clothes in my life."

"Good way to start a new life. You need a haircut."

"I can do that at the house for him," she said.

"She's your barber I guess. Get a tight-fitting hat. One you like."

Fred tried on a gray one. "How does it look?"

"Good." Chet put the hat on the stack. "Tell Ben I was by and didn't need anything from him."

"Oh, yes, Mr. Chet, I will tell him, sir."

"Let's go to the ranch," he said to them. His things in a roll, Chet stuck the hat on the boy's head.

Fred and his wardrobe secure in the back of the buckboard, they drove to the ranch.

At the house they introduced him to a stern-faced Monica as the new man on the ranch.

"Nice to meet you, Fred. We eat breakfast at six a.m., lunch at noon, and supper at six. You miss them you starve."

"Yes, ma'am. I can do that."

"I thought you could."

"Fred, there is a bathtub upstairs. There's hot and cold water. Mix them to suit. Wash with soap and rinse. Then scrub your head twice and dry it on a towel. When you come downstairs I will cut your hair. Those hand-me-downs you wear need to be thrown away."

"I could—"

"No. Men who ride with my husband don't wear rags even if they are clean."

"I understand."

"Fred, I know this day is hard for you, but I believe you will survive."

"Thank you, missus."

"It's Liz or Elizabeth."

"I will try."

"No, Fred, you will prevail."

"What is that word?"

"Says you will succeed."

"Thank you."

"You do not have to say thank you every time. Just nod is enough over small things. Change up your words. Say I appreciate you doing that. Even say that was good. Mix your speech up. Makes you sound stronger. Listen to Chet. Don't use his expressions. Find your own."

"Liz, thank you. I will learn."

Chet heard it all and smiled. She had a student.

His bushy hair, cut and plastered down, changed him somehow. To Chet he looked very serious. He hoped the boy would make it.

CHAPTER 22

In the morning, after breakfast, Chet told Fred to find Miguel at his *casa*. "Shake his hand, give him your name, and tell him you are the new man on our team."

"I can do that. He will know looking at my clothes I am new I am sure."

Monica and Liz snickered and agreed with him.

"Tell him anyhow. Bring him here and you can learn how to drive a team and a buckboard today. Be careful. At noon, be here, wash up for lunch, and then hitch a new team and drive them until time for supper."

"Thanks, Chet. I always wanted to do that."

"Good luck."

"Yes."

Fred returned with Miguel in a few minutes.

"Miguel, you need to show Fred how to harness a team and teach him to drive a buckboard. After lunch he will harness another team and you shall observe him. When he gets good enough at that, take him to the firing range and teach him how to load and shoot a pistol safely. Then a rifle. Fred has lots to learn."

"Let's go, Fred," Miguel said.

"I'm coming."

In the next week, their new man learned how to harness and drive a team. Chet read the wire from the marshal in El Paso. The warrant for the man Ralph Sutter came from Llano County Court, Llano, Texas. His crimes, found by the grand jury, were bank embezzlement, falsifications of document, and fraud. He was last seen in El Paso, but the marshal could not locate him before he left. The rewards on him are valid by authorities in Llano for a sum of a thousand dollars. The wire was signed by Chief U.S. Marshal Tom Brooks.

"Salty lied to me about the reward or they may have raised it. I will ride down to Horse Thief Basin and find him."

"With your men?"

"Of course."

"Is Fred ready to go along?"

"He may as well. He has to learn. He can hold the horses and help Jesus cook."

She nodded. "He will come back from there six feet tall."

"He's not lied to us about one thing. He can harness and drive a team, shoot a rifle, and a pistol. He needs one—"

"He could handle mine. I shall loan it to him."

"That is fine with me."

"You be careful."

"Of course."

They took two packhorses. Chet found a smaller

saddle for the boy, selected a roan horse that Liz rode, and they left early. Fred led the packhorses and took some teasing. They took the back way going by the Iron Mountain Camp. Since mining operations were spread all over the Bradshaw Mountains, they'd have a tough time finding Sutter if he was even in the area. The picture wasn't great, but they had an idea what he looked like and if he was with the woman, they might be easier to find.

Chet rode side by side with Fred for a while. "In case of trouble, try to keep your head down, hold the horses, but when things get hot find cover. We can get more horses, but finding a new boy may be a big problem for us."

Fred nodded. "I savvy."

"Until you've been in a few shooting scraps, I don't want you shot. Most people we arrest will shoot back if given a chance. One group of rustlers fought till they all were dead rather than go to prison again. So, until you get some experience, lay low. Jesus and Miguel are experienced at this business. Any time things get tougher than you can stand, then bow out."

"Chet—I been on my own for two years. I been begging and doing odd jobs to survive—this chance you gave me I won't squander—that's the word, ain't it?"

"Yes. A good one. Where did your parents go?"

"Dad got drunk one night. They say he fell in a creek and drowned. I think they drowned him. Six months later, my mother threw me out. Said I was big enough to shift for myself, so she got on a stage to go become a whore in Tombstone where she said they paid in real gold."

"You never heard from her again?"

"No. I was fourteen when she left. I'd been doing errands, swept the boardwalks for nickels and dimes. Sold newspapers. Went and got folks horses. Worked in gardens for my food. Shoveled horse shit out of small stables and caught stinky pigs. I did it all. But I never stole anything or did anyone harm. There's some tough kids around town; they beat me up a couple of times. Gangs of them hang together. I got a bat-size club and settled with them. They never picked on me again."

Chet nodded as he rode beside him climbing the steep mountain road. "I think we see your side of things. I know how tough it must have been."

"I'm sorry. I ain't a crybaby, but I thought that night in Preskitt—I thought you needed a slave. I would have been one had you needed one, but all night my belly cramped. Then you and her took and bought me new clothes, brought me to your house, gave me a bath. She cut my hair and let me sleep under your roof in a real bed. Eat real food at your table—I ain't feeling sorry for myself. I got over that years ago. I just can't believe what you done for me—that's why I cry sometimes."

Jesus had dropped back to ride on the other side. "You have a tough story. Tougher than my own, but, Fred, you are among *amigos* here. We care for each other.

"You met Miguel's wife, Lisa?"

Fred nodded and smiled.

"An outlaw was holding her in bondage when we ran them down. A rich man's son turned outlaw. She went through hell. Like he did you, Chet brought her to the house and his wife helped her overcome all she went through. She was not as pretty as she is now. She trusted no one and she swore a lot, but Elizabeth showed her a better way to live. She went back to church. This *vaquero* that rides with us, he courted her. You've seen her. She's a lady now."

"I know I am lucky to be riding with you three, and I am so glad that sometimes I get sad at my good fortune."

"Oh, you will be fine and cussing the days we have to be out looking for criminals," Chet said.

"Isn't he close to the age of your nephew Heck?" Jesus asked. "I never met him but Hampt told me that sad story."

Chet nodded. "One of the saddest days in my life. I had bought the Quarter Circle Z. Fought to take it back from a crooked foreman. Heck was along with me because he was giving grief to his mother, May, now Hampt's wife. We were going back to Texas where my family had been in a bloody feud, and my plans were to bring everyone out here from Texas. We were on the Black Canyon Stage headed for Hayden's Ferry at night and were held up and robbed. They did not recognize me in the dark or I am certain they'd have killed me. They took my nephew as a prisoner so as not to be followed.

"I took the stage guard's rifle and then took out a team horse and I rode him bareback after them. I don't think he'd ever been rode before, but we got along.

"I rode all night and found them in a camp thinking they'd eluded everyone. I took them on and shot them until only one was standing. He gave up. I tortured him to tell where that boy was. He finally said, 'We cut his throat aways back and threw him off the mountain.'

"I was so mad, I must have shot him five times. A couple hours later I found Heck's body down in a canyon. I carried him up to the road. The posse came by and I told them the outlaws were all dead and the loot was up on the mountain in their camp.

"I went back to the stage robbery site with his body. I was lost about what to do next. A woman, Marge, who later became my first wife, had come down there in her buggy. I think she heard about it on her way into town and rushed to my rescue.

"I don't think I would have survived except she took charge and arranged everything, funeral and all. That boy had made great changes in his life on that trip. It was a damn shame.

"I had told Marge that I was promised to a woman in Texas. Didn't matter. She got me through those black days. I went back to Texas and the lady I had promised to marry could not leave there because her father's health was too bad for her to move him.

"I brought my entire family out here by a wagon train. Marge was there to greet me and I told her I was single. It never changed her stride; she went on taking care of me—until I felt so guilty I married her."

"You didn't tell him that she had first paid all your bills including at the bathhouse so you could stay in town that first time." Jesus laughed.

"I had to tell her it was not my way to take money or let someone pay for me. Paid her back for all that.

She wanted me to settle there. After we were married, we had a son Adam and then she was killed in a horse-jumping accident."

"Lucky thing huh for me that you're still here? Guys I am ten feet tall riding with you. Thanks for the history lesson. I will try to live up to the ways you three do things best I can."

"Don't try too hard. You will fit in," Chet said.

There were some false front stores and large tents set up for business in the community of Iron Mountain. Some were bars, others offered gambling, and two had scanty-dressed women who came out in the street and offered their services openly to Chet and his men.

Chet noticed Fred got a little red faced at their bawdy offers. He told them no and the four rode on to an open place with ropes for hitch rails between pines.

"Fred, watch our horses. We are going to split up and see if our man is around here. Jesus, you take the far tents and Miguel and I will start from this end."

They left Fred, and Chet and Jesus walked to the nearest gambling tent. There were several filthy miners inside with shaggy unkempt beards and soiled clothes gambling at cards and the faro wheels.

"What can I do for you gents?" A young woman in a low-cut dress confronted the two of them.

"I am looking for a guy. Ralph Sutter, you know him?"

"I might. How much will you pay me?" She shifted her hip at him and pursed her mouth.

"I have a ten-dollar bill. I'm going to tear it in half and give you one half. If I find him on your information I will give you the other half and ten more."

She looked around and quietly said, "Come out back. I can't talk in here." Then she raised her voice. "Why sure, mister, I can take care of both of you. Right this way. Bargain prices in the middle of the week."

She led them out of the tent to another. Once in her canvas-partitioned room with a bed and two trunks she swept her hair back from her face. "I need four dollars to split with my boss for turning a trick with you. Your man Sutter should be dealing cards in the Crazy Horse Saloon in Horse Thief Basin."

She held her hand out for the four dollars.

Chet paid her and gave her two twenties besides the other four.

"You mean you trusted me?" She blinked her blue eyes in the subdued light in the tent.

"You said it all straight faced. Thanks."

She cast her look to the ground. "Sure you don't need my services for all this money."

"No. We're lawmen looking for him. You probably saved us a week of looking."

"Well, mister, go out the back way from here, so they think I did you both a favor in my bed. And thanks. Come back again. I never caught your name?"

"Chet Byrnes. He's Miguel Costa. We live at Preskitt."

"Oh, I've heard lots about you, sir. Nice meeting you, sir."

"Thanks for the information."

She shook her head and waved the money at him. "Best trick I've turned in weeks."

Outside the back way, he sent Miguel, laughing, to find Jesus. They had a good lead. Her cheap perfume was still in his nose. It sure didn't smell like hay. How did girls like her get locked up in that trade? Like Bonnie and others had been, they wanted wild times to celebrate and have money. Oh, well, he couldn't worry about them all.

He found Fred seated on the ground rocking on his butt. "You find out where he was at?"

"Yes, Miguel went to find Jesus. Our man is at a saloon in Horse Thief Basin, dealing cards."

Fred got to his feet and brushed off the seat of his pants. "That's easy, huh?"

"May have saved us a week looking for him."

"Who told you?"

"A lady of the night for a few dollars."

"You didn't?"

Chet laughed. "No. She was willing but I don't mess around."

"I thought not."

"Here comes Jesus and Miguel. Let's mount up. I don't want him getting word we're looking for him."

Fred agreed and handed the reins out to the men.

"Boy, you got lucky," Jesus said about the information.

"Yes. Let's trot some. We can eat some of Monica's food on our way."

The sun was down by the time they reached Horse Thief Basin. The saloons were perched on the hillside side by side with a hundred steps to climb to reach the porch and the swinging doors.

Crazy Horse was the noisy second one. The racks were crowded in front with hipshot horses.

"String a lariat between two pine trees across this street, Fred, and we will use it for a hitch rack."

"Yes, sir. I got it."

The horses hitched, the three checked their pistols turning the cylinders to the light shining from the businesses upstairs.

"I have the horses secure."

"We'll be back. Preferably with him."

Chet crossed the dirt road and scaled the stairs to the saloon, his two men watching all around them. They paused at the top and stood for a moment before the swinging doors. Chet strode inside and adjusted his eyes to the brighter lights in the sour-smelling smoke-filled barroom.

There were several tables of players, and like he figured, his man would be facing the front door. He noticed the scar on the man's cheek as he dealt cards two tables back.

He strode by him for the bar. When he reached it he leaned toward the bartender. "I am a U.S. marshal. Give me, very easy, the sawed-off shotgun from under the bar. I assume it is loaded?"

The man gave a wooden nod and he slipped the sawed-off gun out to him. Chet whirled with it in his hands and pressed both barrels to Sutter's back.

"You are under arrest, Ralph Sutter. You can live or die right now. Everyone, I am a U.S. marshal. My name is Byrnes. Those two with their guns drawn are my deputies. We are only here to arrest this man. No one will get hurt if you all remain calm. Rise, Sutter."

The man grumbled but obeyed.

"Miguel, come put cuffs on him and liberate his guns and knives."

His man removed a short-barrel sheriff model Colt plus two smaller guns and two knives from the prisoner.

"That your money?" Chet pointed at the pot on the table.

"Yeah."

"Rake it off in his hat, Miguel. He won't need it where he's going."

The crowd laughed.

Chet swung the shotgun around and that silenced them. "Miguel, take him outside. No one make a move."

With Miguel out the doors and Jesus still covering everyone, Chet slowly set the triggers down, cracked open the gun, and extracted both shells. He gave it back to the bartender, set the ammo on the bar, and paid him with a ten-dollar gold piece.

The man thanked him. He went to the doors and told Jesus he could holster his gun. "There ain't no friends of Sutter in here."

The crowd laughed.

They took the stairs down quickly and went across the road. The prisoner stood bare headed, while Fred took the money out of the hat and put it in the saddlebags. Then he put the hat back on him.

"Where is your room at?" Chet asked.

Sutter gave a head toss south. "Fred, bring half the horses. Miguel, the rest. We are going to find his place. One bad step, Sutter, and you won't ever see anything again. You hear me?"

"Who sent you?"

"Salty, who you cheated on a salted gold mine according to him."

"That son of a bitch deserved that. He cheated a widow woman out of that money."

"I don't have a warrant on him. I have one on you."

"Jail me. They won't send anyone after me. I'll be loose in three months."

"No. They raised the reward to a thousand dollars. They will come get you. Now where is the money you cheated him out of?"

"I spent it."

"You are not living that high up here. I can get the hideout from you by holding your head under water until your memory improves or you drown."

"You can't—" Chet stared him down. "All right. It is at the cabin I am living in."

They were walking down the road shadowed from the stars by the tall pines but still visible enough to see things. Chet noticed the crowd had come out on the porch trying to get a look at them, but they were out of the line of sight. The knowledge there were four marshals should keep the greedy ones from trying to jump them he hoped.

The low-walled log cabin was up a holler and a horse nickered at theirs. Good, he had transportation.

Chet stopped him outside. "Who is inside?"

"A doxie named Judy."

"Wife? What?"

"She's just a whore."

"No tricks. Stay here." Chet drew his Colt and pulled the drawstring that lifted the bar. Quietly he opened the thick door. Gun in hand, he went to the table, lifted the chimney, and lit the lamp. All the time watching the figure under the covers in the bed for any movement.

At the light she sat up, groggily, in her night shift and threw back the covers. "You are back early. How many did you bring for me to entertain tonight? Holy crap—you aren't Ralph. Why are you coming in here uninvited?"

"We are U.S. marshals. Get some clothes on; then you sit on a chair and keep your mouth shut."

Cussing like a sea captain, she purposely dressed with little modesty and took her place where he said. When she started to say something, he shut her up.

Chet called to his men to bring Sutter in. They pushed him onto a second chair.

"Now where is your money?"

He shook his head. "I ain't got any."

"He's telling you the truth. He has to sell my body half the time to play cards."

"No, he lied to you. Now shut up."

"There's enough water in that horse's trough to drown him," Jesus said.

Chet gave a head toss. "Do it."

"You going to drown him?" she asked.

"Unless he tells us where the money is at—yes."

"You guys are lawmen! I never heard of that before."

"Stay seated or Fred will tie you up."

Out back he heard Sutter gurgling and finally in a garbled scream shouted, "I'll tell you all about it."

"All of it?" Jesus asked.

"Yeah."

They brought the dripping outlaw back inside. His hair was soaked and water ran down his face.

"Where?" Chet asked.

"Under the false bottom in the trunk."

Fred emptied the clothing and things out of it.

Chet leaned over. "Use your knife to cut that seal and lift the false bottom out."

Fred did as he was told. He lifted the thin board out, and stacked in side by side was money all wrapped up in paper bands.

"Holy cow!" she shouted, "you lying bastard, and you been making me do it for your gambling money."

Chet shoved her down in the chair. "Now, where is the rest?"

He shrugged. "There ain't no more."

"Take him back out there."

"No, no. You will need a crow bar. It's in tin candy boxes under the floor, over there." He pointed to the corner of the room.

"Where else is it?"

"No more."

"Bank accounts?"

"I got seven hundred dollars in a bank in El Paso. That's all I have got. I swear to God."

"Write her a cheek for the full amount."

"Huh?"

"Where are your checks?"

"In the trunk."

"I've got it." Fred brought it out of the pile and handed it to him.

"What's your name?" he asked her.

"Judy Sacowski."

"Spell it for him."

She did and he wrote it in and the amount plus his signature. Then held it up with both hands for him to give to her.

"Now how do I get it cashed out here?"

"I am sending you with a note to a Mr. Tanner at the First Territorial Bank. The note will tell him to present the check to the El Paso bank by mail. You can wait for it to come back to you. May take a month. Here is twenty dollars to live on until it gets here."

"Any of you guys need a live-in until then?"

"No, Judy. You will make it and I don't need to be kissed."

Turning back to his men, Chet told them the next step. "Now put him in leg irons. We will chain him to a tree. We're going to sleep out under the stars, have breakfast in the morning, and ride home tomorrow."

Miguel found a claw hammer to pry up the boards. There were eight metal candy boxes under the floors full of hundred-dollar bills. They put all the money in the trunk and carried it over to where they were going to sleep. Jesus chained up the prisoner away from them, and he was given a blanket to get under for warmth.

Next morning they ate oatmeal with bugs. Jesus made a big pot of coffee. Chet wrote Judy a note for his banker regarding the check.

She put everything she wanted in a sheet. They did that with the money, too.

Then she talked them into letting her ride double behind Sutter on his horse back to Preskitt. That sure drew laughs from bystanders, them riding double going through both Horse Thief Basin and Iron Mountain.

The dove that informed him ran up to them and walked beside Chet's horse, talking in a low voice. "Well, you got your man. Ever need a real woman, come back here. I'll be here as long as the gold lasts."

She slapped his leg and then winked at him.

He never said a word but was amused.

When they reached the edge of Preskitt, Chet told them to stop and dismount.

"Miguel, take that rope off Sutter's horse and put it around his neck."

"What are you doing?" she asked.

"Giving you a bill of sale for that horse."

"Well, Marshal, bless your soul. You sure do know how to treat a female right. Better than that old sumbitch ever did me. You ever get out of jail, don't come looking for me. By then you will be too old to do anything anyway. Thanks again, boys."

Bill of sale in hand, a flash of her legs as she settled more comfortably in the saddle, her sheet tied on the horn, she beat her new horse's ribs with her heels and she left them laughing on the hill.

Miguel handed the rope lead around Sutter's neck to Jesus, who asked, "Do I need the telegram from that marshal that you have, for the sheriff to hold him?"

Chet got it out and handed it to him. "Tell Anita hi for us. We're going home."

"I will. See you in a few days. Fred, don't let them pull your leg going home."

"Thanks. I will try to prevent that."

That boy was making better conversation already.

The last three quarters of a mile to the ranch they had a horse race. Miguel won. They rang the bell that the boss was back. His wife came running to hug all three, Lisa not far behind for Miguel.

"Good to be back here, Liz," Fred said, a little red faced while Chet kissed her hard.

Fred stared at the two of them. "That's all I need now."

Chet turned to him. "What's that?"

"Well Miguel kissed his wife. I bet Jesus kissed his, and you kissed her. All I need is a wife for me to kiss."

"No rush on that, partner. None at all."

"Come on," Liz said, "Monica has your food waiting. She doesn't need a kiss."

CHAPTER 23

Late as it was in the season, it snowed the next day. Fred busied himself building up the firewood supply for the various fireplaces. Chet read the *Miner*'s latest issue. Not much news in it.

"Snow stopped yet?"

"It never really started," Miguel replied as he finished loading the office fireplace.

"Hitch a team and we will take all this money to the bank and have it counted."

He stopped before going for another load and buttoned his wool coat. "You trust me to drive?"

"I have to start sometime but not today. Strap on your gun. You run the guard part today. Wait? How many cartridges do you have for it?"

"Five."

"That little ammo won't get you out of the batwing doors of the Palace Saloon."

"Then I should fill the loops on my belt."

Chet nodded. "And keep the rest in your saddle-bags. We will stop and buy more in town."

"I'll only be a minute."

"I have time. Send word when you're hitched and ready."

He sat back down, reminiscing, wondering if he had to learn all these things when he was young.

His father had come back home, out of his mind, from staying out too long without water or food looking for Comanche captives In truth he didn't come home by himself. Two Texas rangers brought him home on a travois from out there on the Llano Estacada. They said the Comanche thought he was mad and they would not harm him. But he never found his children that they had taken away. He lost his senses in those months searching non-forgiving land the heartless Comanche thrived in.

At the time, Chet didn't sleep more than a few hours each night. How could he hold the ranch together? He wore out two Colt pistols shooting targets in the canyon beyond hearing. No one was helping him learn anything. He taught himself.

He was looking for some cows he'd not seen in several days. From the ridge he rode on, he watched buzzards circling and rode down through the cedars and live oaks on some old cow-winding trail to find death. Then he saw a red-dyed half feather. His heart stopped—*Comanche.*

The dead cow was a trap set for him to ride into looking for the deceased animal so they could ambush and kill him. His mind began to inventory his guns and bullets on hand. His .30 caliber Colt loaded on his hip. Powder in a horn. He shook it. Not a lot. Two dozen bullets in the purse on his left hip. A box of caps for the nipples and half a box of rim fire .50 caliber cartridges for the lever-action rifle in his scabbard.

Off his horse and on his knees, he prayed to God and promised him if God let him live that day, he'd never leave the house again without being fully armed. He hobbled the fine gelding, and with his hunting knife in his belt, his six-gun in his holster, and the heavy rifle in his right hand, he ran in his knee-high soft leather boots. Busy dodging from tree to tree he saw more barefoot pony tracks. How many were there?

He heard the soft fall of an approaching unshod hoof. A distinct sound in his ears. How many more? He crouched and when the war-painted buck rode by he shot him in the face and moved. He heard their guttural talking. As he reached another thick tree, two rode past him and he shot both in the back. He had two shots left in that pistol. Then he saw the outraged screaming face of another war-crazed buck holding a lance. He shot him twice and somehow the Indian's spear point missed his body because the sound of the shot had caused the painted horse to buck.

Were there more? They came at him through the trees busting brush on high-flying horses. His rifle's first bullet struck the center one's horse. Hard hit, he stumbled and the buck's spear plowed in the ground. When the buck scrambled to his feet, Chet's second shot blew a hole in his war-painted chest and threw him on his back.

The Indian on the right had to jerk his horse

back, and the third shot from the long gun blew him off the horse.

Whirling in a crouch, Chet levered the empty cartridge out, jammed a new one in the chamber, raised the muzzle without aiming, and blew another buck's face apart not twelve feet away. Then, frozen, he sat down on his butt on the hard ground.

Crows were calling. Probably about the dead roan longhorn cow that he had found speared, lying in the open grassy spot.

Standing, he went to his horse, found the whetstone, and sharpened his big knife. It took a while to get it sharp enough to suit him. Then he scalped each Indian, mounted each one's hair on the shaft of one of the spears. He walked to the top of the hill and drove the spear into the ground. He mounted flat rocks around so it would stay longer. Now any Indian who came by would see it and be warned.

He mounted his pony in the red flair of sundown. The Indians' blood had dried on his hands, making them stiff. His shirt was all bloody and his good silk neckerchief was stained.

He almost fell out of the saddle when he finally reached the ranch. In the dark he stuck his head into the water of the horse trough a couple of times. The stinking buffalo grease of their hair still clung to him.

Susie wasn't even twelve then. She came with a lamp and she brought the little Mexican Adeline who cooked for them and cleaned house.

"Oh, my God, you are all bloody, brother. How did you do that?"

"Comanche killed a cow to trap me. I killed them all—six or seven, I don't know. Then I scalped them, tied their hair on a lance—ah, spear—and planted it for all them red devils to see when riding by."

"You aren't hurt? No wounds? How did you do that?"

"Sis, gawdamn it, I just had to."

Those two girls hugged him and they all cried.

He finally fell into bed. In the morning, at breakfast, his younger brother got real mad. "You're nothing but a damn killer, Chet Byrnes. Why, if you'd have shot two of them the rest'd run away. But five or six; that's damn murder."

"Dale Allen, I had no choice. They kept coming after me."

"Where are you going to now?"

"To town. I promised God that no one would get after me again where I wasn't better armed. And I soon will be."

He bought a Winchester .44/.40 and a .45 caliber Colt. And plenty of ammunition.

An hour later after Chet came back from reliving that part of his past in his leather chair, Fred drove him and the proceeds of the Sutter arrest to the bank.

At the bank, Tanner met him. "That woman you sent has her money. I wired the details to El Paso, said a U.S. marshal guaranteed he signed it. They wired back the check was good. She paid the fee and went out the door with her cash. Oh, and she said to thank you, too."

"Good. Now I want you to meet Fred Brown, my new helper. Fred, Mr. Tanner."

Fred shook Tanner's hand and handed over the money still in the sheet. Two employees came out into the lobby, took it, and they said they would have it counted in a couple of hours.

Chet and Fred left the bank. Fred was laughing.

"What's so funny?"

"In this outfit and all cleaned up he didn't even know me. I did lots of work for him."

"See, Fred. Don't let your head get too big, but this proves you are moving up the social ladder around here."

They laughed all the way to the buckboard. They went by and introduced him to Bo who showed Fred the land that Chet owned across the territory.

"Aren't you the boy that did odd jobs around town?" Bo finally asked.

"Yes. I am. Though most people don't recognize me, now, sir, thanks to Chet."

"I thought that was you. Let me tell you a story. I was drunk when I came here and he tried to sober me up. I did not want to be sober. He hired two tough men to work night and day and made sure I didn't drink for three months. I don't drink anymore. I have a pretty wife with one baby boy and another one on the way. I live in a damn nice house. I have a damn good land business. All thanks to him. So you listen to him; he's a real good teacher."

"Bo. You don't know how proud I am."

"Where's your folks?"

"My dad died back a few years. My mom told me two years ago that I was old enough at fourteen to make it on my own, and last I heard she was working in a cathouse in Tombstone."

"You've got a real education then?"

"I sure did."

"How did you meet Chet?"

"I ran an errand for him and his wife, and he told me in the morning to meet him and I'd have a job."

"Where did you start? Shoveling pig shit?"

No. I started with Jesus Martinez and Miguel and we went and captured this outlaw at Horse Thief Basin who had this money. His name was Sutter."

"Any shots fired?"

"No, sir."

"Sounds like you started at the top of the ladder."

"I believe I have and I pinch myself every morning to be damn sure I ain't dreaming."

"Good enough. Lots of luck. You sound like a young man going places."

"Thanks for the compliment. I'll stand back now. I bet Chet wants to talk business with you."

Chet shook his head. The boy was learning fast. "Bo and I meet all the time. I support this office buying abandoned homesteads."

"He steals them."

Chet shook his head. "Lots of people come out here to hard scrabble to make a homestead. Then they give up. They can't make it or only eke out a living. It's a thing called the economy. You need markets and jobs. Arizona is sadly short on both of them."

"What about the mines?"

"There are not enough of them. Oh, like Tombstone, it is flourishing today. But they haven't found many more mines or districts that rich."

"You think they ever will find some more rich mines?"

"Anything can happen. Railroads will connect us and help. But this is a dry arid country. We got more rain in Texas than they get here."

Fred nodded. "Thanks, I learned more today than I have in a year. I never thought about any of those things. So damn busy eking out my food every day and finding shelter."

"Who was the guy you brought in to jail yesterday?"

"Jesus brought him in. He lives in town now with his wife. The prisoner's name was Ralph Sutter. He embezzled bank money and who knows what else. I got the warrant information from Texas. He beat some guy out of ten thousand dollars in Texas over a salted gold mine. He offered me half if I could recover it."

"Did you bring in a lot of money?"

"More than Fred and I wanted to count. The bank is doing that now. And we don't need any publicity, either."

"Oh, I know that. Fred, good luck. You be sure you don't let anything happen to him. I've got more land to buy for him."

Next Chet took them by the saddle shop. Fred met

McCully's daughter, Petal. Her father was bedridden but improving and she ran the sales.

They sat down with his best saddle maker, Gordon. He showed Fred all the features of the saddle that would be good for him. The seat Gordon recommended should be sixteen inches.

"You will grow that big. Too big now but not too big in five years. Our saddles last a long time. These swells are for riding bad bucking horses. You don't need that much swell—more like this model."

Fred followed him to another style. "This back is too tall. You have to throw your leg over it with chaps in the cactus country. That gets to be work in a long day. That horn is for ropers. A smaller one will do you."

"How much will this cost me? Don't you have a used one?"

"You work for Chet?"

Fred nodded.

"The price would be sixty-five dollars to you. Anyone else add fifteen dollars."

"I have been a burden to Mr. Byrnes since I came—I have a saddle at the ranch I can use. That's good enough for me."

"Gordon, make him the saddle. He will pay you."

Fred dropped his chin and shook his head. "Yeah, maybe in two years."

They left the saddle shop. The saddle would be ready in three weeks. Fred took the reins in his hand. "How will I get that money myself to pay for that?"

"Let's start like this," Chet said, turning to face him. "There is that five-thousand-dollar deal being counted that that Salty Hogan man offered me for finding his money. I figure two thousand apiece for Jesus and Miguel and a thousand for your part. Then split the thousand-dollar reward money coming for Sutter, by thirds. Another three hundred some dollars."

"Three hundred thirty-three, right?"

"Exactly. Today you start a bank account. We don't talk about that to anyone. It would cause jealousy among the rest at the ranch. You were there and took your chances. It could have been a shooting. Jesus has enough money to buy him and Anita a ranch. They may do that shortly."

"Chet, I've never had thirty dollars to my name, let alone sixty-five. I see now how it works. Thank you." He clucked to the horses and they went back to the bank.

When they walked into the bank, Tanner's assistant showed him into his office and left closing the door.

"This man did more than salt mines. He must have robbed people wholesale," Tanner said.

"How much money did you count?"

"You two sit down. There is over eighteen thousand dollars here. What next?"

"Five is to be split. Fred here gets a thousand and opens a new account. Jesus and Miguel get two apiece into their accounts. I need five thousand shipped to Salty Hogan in Texas for that bad mine deal. That leaves a thousand reward to be split three ways between Jesus, Miguel, and Fred."

"That leaves seven thousand plus left."

"Wire the banker who he embezzled the money from in Llano and ask him if, after the reward is deducted, he would take half that amount returned to him, no questions asked."

"I can do that. He will accept it. I know he thought he might not get even a dollar of it back since it is over state lines and all. How will that be split?"

"Three ways my men as before."

"Fred Brown, welcome to my bank. You can draw money at the teller window or write checks on your account after today."

Fred only nodded. He never said a word. Motioned he was going outside and left the room.

"That boy all right?"

"He will recover. He's never been this rich before."

Chet found Fred later leaning against the newspaper office staring off into space.

Chet stopped before him. "You all right?"

He barely bobbed his head. "Gawdamn it—I was about ready to cry in there. I been thinking you got some money and I could borrow on you."

"Sure, how much?"

"I don't know yet but if that Navajo woman out there at the fork of the road, going home today, is there selling blankets, I want to stop."

"We are finished. You can go now."

"Good. Load up. You'll see."

Chet saw the woman's old wagon and the paint horse pulled off it and grazing on a long rope. Fred stopped, tied off the reins, and went around to squat before her to buy something. At first they had trouble conversing, but she soon removed her silver and turquoise necklace from around her neck.

He turned to Chet. "I need to borrow thirty dollars?"

"Who are you buying that for?" He dug out the money and Fred paid her.

When he turned back he said, "Well, sir, I don't know a damn thing that you need, but your wife can wear this I figure."

"I guess I'd never thought about buying that jewelry for her. I bet she cries."

"I didn't aim to do that."

"She will be fine. Thanks," he said to the woman, and tipped his hat to her.

She smiled big in return.

They drove onto the ranch grateful it had warmed up.

"Will you put it on her since she is your wife?"

"No. That is your gift. You tell her to shut her eyes and you place it on her neck."

"You ain't much help at times."

"Not when it's your plan and you have to pay for it."

He reined up at the steps. A boy came running to take the team. Liz stopped at the edge of the porch.

Chet told the boy to take the team and waved Fred over. "Honey, your boy has something he bought for you today. It was solely his idea, so close your eyes. Fred, do your thing."

Fred placed the necklace around Liz's neck. "What is it? It feels heavy."

"It sure isn't a rock to weight you down in the water," Chet teased.

"Fred, what is it? May I look?"

"Yes, you sure may."

Running into the house, she stopped at the front hall mirror, the men following her in, smiling.

"Oh, my heavens. Fred, why did you buy this for me? It must have cost a fortune."

"Liz, I never had anyone in my life open their house to me like you and Chet have. The past two weeks have sped by. He ordered me a new saddle today. I'll pay for it, but I never had any new clothes before to wear. Boots, hat, you name it. That was the only thing I could think of to buy—he has all he wants. I wanted to really show my appreciation for everything you two have done for me."

She hugged and kissed him. "You certainly did that. I need to show Monica. She almost has supper ready, so you guys come wash up."

Chet Byrnes shook his head. That boy would make a real hand someday.

CHAPTER 24

Word came by telegram. Construction could commence on the Northern Arizona Telegraph line when he got up there to Gallup. He had lots to do and a short time to get started. Hannagen had started the ordering. Next he sent word to Harold Faulk and his family who were working over at Toby's eastern division to get done on the barn and report to Preskitt. They had a line to build. He sent a young man to ride to Center Point and tell Cole he needed several teams to cut the needed poles and to find the transportation to bear them eastward for a start.

They were off and running. By telegraph, he learned part of the glass insulators were at Gallup, more were promised. The bolts to screw them on the poles had been back-ordered due to the demand of the expansion of lines all over the nation, but there were more sources where they could be gotten. Might have to string them in leather carriers like early ones did. No, Chet decided, he wanted a sure line. It all rode on when they got all the poles they needed.

Ranch calving time was on them, twenty-four-seven, and all the ranch hands were busy checking for cows who needed help delivering. Jesus, Fred, and Miguel all rode for Raphael.

Chet stayed at the house, where each day kept him busy getting telegraph wires and answering them plus placing orders. The man came back from Center Point and said they still had snow but Cole had teams of men cutting and peeling poles for shipment. He had over two hundred and fifty ready to ship east, and another five hundred in two weeks.

Chet read Cole's letter and decided that was the best he could do. He knew that when he went up there to check on things, he would have less contact with everyone at Preskitt.

He was at his desk behind piles of paper when a man came by the house and said there was a dead man's body on the mountain road halfway to Camp Verde. Jesus came by about then with some more mail from town and Chet asked him to go investigate the matter.

Chet was busy calculating the number of poles he'd need delivered to start a large crew on the east side when Jesus came back hopping mad.

"What's wrong?" Jesus never was angry.

"You know Sonny Carlisle?"

"No, who is he?"

"A damn deputy out of the courthouse in town."

"What did he do?"

"He came along while I was gathering the information about this dead man and told me it wasn't none of my damn business, being a U.S. marshal. Then he threatened to charge me with messing with county justice. I could not tell him a thing. He had them load the corpse of the man, never took any notes about the area where he was, and took him to town."

"What did you learn?"

"A passerby said his name was Phillips. Raymond Phillips and he lived with a woman named Caruso at Camp Verde."

"What killed him do you think?"

"We may never know since it was none of my business."

"I'll go in and find out tomorrow what they did. I have carefully avoided a war with the Yavapai County sheriff, but they had no business threatening you."

"You know what I think?"

"No? What is that?"

"I think we need to go get Spencer, put his ranch-building job on hold down there, and use him on this telegraph line building. I'm not saying you can't do it, but you had Cole head the stage line business and he got it done. Spencer is the same way as Cole. He knows how."

Chet sat back in the chair. "It took a dead man in the road to give you that idea?"

Jesus pulled off his goatskin gloves and sat down. "I've thought that for several days now. We make a good team to capture outlaws, solve crimes, like we did over east. But neither Fred, Miguel, nor I are much good at building things. I think Spencer is the man. His new wife and the children can go along. She isn't a fancy woman. She left Diablo and went up there to be with him. You can hire her a woman to help with the kids while they are camping on the road. You can supervise from here. Hannagen's men won't run over him like they tried on Cole."

Chet frowned. "He must be two hundred miles away."

"Take a stage to Hayden's Ferry, rent some horses, and we can be there in a day's ride."

Chet said, "The manager Frisco can keep things going. Let's take the stage at midnight. Take saddles and get horses down there. I will get word to Miguel and Fred. We can do that. You go home now and tell Anita."

"What is up?" Liz asked at the door.

"Jesus is going home and will meet the rest of us at the stage tonight. We are going to go get Spencer to run the telegraph crew."

"What about his new wife?"

"Jesus suggested we get her a helper as they camp along the way."

"Helper is fine. What if she balks?"

Jesus said, "We think she is flexible. She married him."

Amused, Liz shook her head. "Thank you, Jesus. I get my husband back."

"I need to get those two to come in to get ready for tonight." He rose from his seat and headed out.

"A boy can go find them," she said after him. "Lunch is ready. Jesus, eat with us before you leave. I will be right there."

Chet came back. "I sent a stable boy."

He washed his hands with Jesus. "We get smarter, don't we?"

"Yes. A few years I'd never told you that. But I know how we all operate now and it made sense."

"With that pile of paper in there I was buried in a dust devil I could not escape. Obviously not one of my finer situations."

"It showed."

They finished lunch and Jesus left before Miguel and Fred came in onto the porch.

"Tell them I have lunch," Monica said to Chet.

"Come eat. She has food."

"Jesus was here?" Fred asked, coming in.

"Yes. He went home and we will meet him at the midnight stage. We are going to see Spencer. Jesus says we need him to build the telegraph line and let Frisco deal with the ranch house building."

"That sounds good," Miguel said.

"Will his wife go along?" Liz asked them.

"Oh, yes, she never had a life so good," Miguel said. "She was a *vaquero*'s widow, not a supervisor's wife. Big difference."

Liz laughed. "You men are so sure. But I think the idea is very good. He is a construction man. My husband is a cowboy and marshal."

"I think Frisco can keep the project going," Chet said. "Go grab a nap, men. You will need it. We will need to move to get this job done."

Liz shook her head. "I'd say not to worry. Hannagen and his bunch can't do it without you. They wear low-cut shoes. They did at our meeting at Windmill. A rattlesnake would bite them the first day on the drive to put up poles. Spencer will get it done. They won't and they know it."

Chet hugged her and they went off to take a nap, Chet shaking his head about the whole situation.

One regret. He wished he'd thought about Spencer earlier. But he was the right choice for this job. Frisco could see to it that the ranch down there progressed.

CHAPTER 25

His crew dressed for winter, they reached Hayden's Ferry in the near eighty-degree heat of mid-day. Getting off the stage they laughed. "It's summertime down here."

Jesus went to secure horses. Chet promised to order him food at the café and they wouldn't leave without him. The stage office man agreed to watch their gear and promised it was safe there.

They ordered food in the Mexican café and told the waitress who asked about him that Jesus was coming.

Chet called to her. "I must tell you, he is married now."

She made a sour face and then laughed. "Too late, huh?"

He nodded.

Jesus came in and told them they had four good horses this time, and the man was excited they were the men renting them. The food arrived, and the plan was to ride to Mesa and get a room for the night.

After lunch they rode, finally reaching the irrigated citrus orchards and cotton fields plowed for planting later. The wide streets of Mormon town were laid out with many empty lots. They put their horses in a livery, ate supper in a café, and went to the hotel for the night.

They were up, bought breakfast from a street vendor, and left the stables at sunrise eastbound through the saguaro desert. They crossed the Gila on a ferry and before the sun set rode up to Frisco's house on the ranch.

His wife, Rosa, came out, rang the schoolhouse bell, and laughed. "The boss man is here with a posse."

"Rosa, you met Jesus. That is Miguel, and Fred. How is your husband?"

"Good. He must be close to coming home. The boys here will put up your horses. Come in the house. I have coffee and there is enough food cooked for all of you."

"Thank you."

"Something wrong?"

"We need to talk to him about loaning us Spencer."

She laughed. "He might cry."

Chet nodded. "I have a telegraph line four hundred miles long to span northern Arizona that needs building."

"You are what?"

"Building a telegraph line."

She laughed. "I see why you came. He must be close to coming here. He seldom is this late."

"There is a horse out there," Fred said.

"That's him." She ran to the door and held it open. "Your boss is here."

"Oh, tell him I am coming. Let me wash up."

"He is coming," she said.

He came in and hung his hat on a peg beside theirs. "Nice to be home. What can we do for you?"

"We need your help. You know there is a telegraph company that wants to build a line from Gallup to the Colorado River on the west side? I am the person they are looking at to build it—I do a lot of things but I am not a construction man. Spencer is. I need to borrow him."

"I guess we can get along. He has some good men that can continue to do it. I will have to spend more time down there, but if you need him, yes."

"Good. We need to go convince him tomorrow. Sorry to impose on you both this way, but things are breaking fast and I really need him."

"I am so pleased you came to make this place a ranch. You know I support you on everything. Spencer is great man and I appreciate you loaning him to us because he cut a wide swath and I think we can take it from here and run."

Chet's men nodded in agreement as to what was said about Spencer. They ate supper and bragged on her food. The crew even washed her dishes so she could quiz him about Liz, who she loved meeting.

He assured her his wife was doing well and she didn't come because this was such a fast trip.

"You have a new boy with you?"

"Fred Brown."

"He looks young for such a job."

"I was younger when I took over the family ranch."

"You know my husband is very pleased you have taken the ranch on in a way he likes."

"We will keep doing that, I promise. I simply need Spencer's skill about jobs that I need done for me."

Frisco rode with them in the morning to Apache Springs. Mid-morning Spencer came out of the nearly completed bunkhouse looking stronger than he did when they left him.

"Well, what brings you all down here?"

"You are making some real progress here."

Chet dismounted. "That's Miguel. You knew him from Preskitt. The new guy is Fred Brown. Let's find a nice place to sit and talk."

"Walk away from those hammers and saws," Spencer said. "She's going to be a great place isn't she, Fred?"

Fred shook his head, gazing around. "They call such places oasis, don't they?"

"Yes. But this isn't a friendly inspection trip. Am I fired?"

"No. But we need you to ramrod another deal."

Spencer frowned. "Which one?"

"I need you to build the telegraph line across northern Arizona."

He stared at him. "I don't even know Morse code."

"We are just building it. My steering people say you are the choice."

"Those three hooligans?" He frowned at the others.

"Things are breaking fast. It needs to be up and operating."

"What will I do about Lucinda?"

"I will pay for her to bring a woman to help her. If she needs more help, hire them. She, and they, can live in a nice tent and move with you."

"She's waiting out here to live in the bunkhouse."

"Do you think she won't go with you?"

"No. She'll go. She and I want to be together. Guys, I have been in heaven here not only because of Lucinda but, see those boys. They work their asses off for me. They respect me, and there are no jobs in Mexico for them.

"Let me go talk to Lucinda. Damn. I have a spot here where I really like getting up every morning."

"Want me to go with you?"

"Hell, yes. And I thought I had a place where I would stay in one place for at least a year." Spencer started laughing as he walked toward a tent.

"Honey, you in here? We have company." She looked up in the tent's lamplight and stopped washing dishes.

"Oh, señor, why are you here?"

"Hi. I need you and your husband to go fix another problem."

"Please sit. Move? But I have two children."

"I know. I will hire a nanny to help you, and if you need it, a housekeeper, too. Then you can move with him down the line."

She blinked at Spencer. "What should I say?"

"If you want help with the kids and to chase me building a telegraph line, tell him yes."

Lucinda turned to Chet. "Yes. I will go. I love him and want to stay with him."

"Good. I want to take you, him, and the babies to Preskitt. Show him the plans. Then, in a few weeks, move you to the starting place. We can hire a trucker to move your things up there. If Frisco has a buck-board we can take you four to Preskitt immediately."

"You really want to get started that fast?" Spencer asked.

"Yes. We need you to make your decision. Lucinda has, and she knows it will not be easy."

"Oh, Spencer, I think this is a big deal. He has the confidence in you. We can manage being a little rushed."

"You will stay at our house at Preskitt where we will go over the plans. My wife will be your hostess."

"I hope my heart is strong enough for all of this."

"We will travel to Florence in one day. Mesa the next. Then over to Hayden's Ferry and a stagecoach ride to Preskitt."

Very serious, she nodded. "I will get things we need ready now."

Spencer went over and hugged her. "It will be worth the trouble. I will help you."

Now all Chet had left to do was move them to Preskitt. His men would help. And he'd be back home in less than a week.

Traveling, he and his team learned how to feed a two-and four-year-old, rock them to sleep, change diapers on both children, and how to move them with their minimum things. The four-year-old boy was Carlos, a cute dark-eyed boy, and the two-year-old was a pretty girl named for Bonnie at the ranch.

Chet decided that he and Miguel would go a day ahead to set up for their arrival. Jesus and Fred stayed with Spencer and his family.

Finally, leaving the stage, the buckboard was waiting for them in Preskitt. "How are she and the babies doing?" Liz asked him, concerned, on the ride home.

"Better than the men are."

She burst out laughing.

"It wasn't funny." He clucked to the team. "They will be here tomorrow night. She is a very lovely lady. Spencer is lucky."

"What are your plans?"

"Bring them to the house. Show him the plans and work out a way to do it. We will hire her a nanny, and by the time we start the weather will be warm. We can move her tent along with construction so she will be close to him."

"I am glad you have it all figured out."

"Close to doing that. Any more telegrams?"

"No just more mail. How did the new place look?"

"He almost had the bunkhouse built. Frisco says he can continue but slower. No problem about that. The men agreed it would be a fine ranch headquarters. Just sorry that because of the children we couldn't travel like the men and I did. Faster. But they are sweet kids. He found a good woman like I did."

"Jesus found him for you, didn't he?"

"Yes. He had cowboyed for Tom on the Verde

Ranch but needed more money, so he was working on building the headquarters at Center Point. Jesus saw lots of things in him. He can certainly get things done."

"All these leaders you found started with Tom and Hampt, didn't they?"

"Sarge, too, and several good men besides them."

"Did you ever believe you'd have all this to do?"

"No. I came here at the right time. People are still discovering the territory. But figuring how to make it pay was the next step. Arizona will have more competition in the future, but it will hold as we are until the railroad comes to north Arizona. Then we can compete with the rest of the U.S."

"Ten years away?"

"I hope so or sooner."

When he pulled up to the ranch, in the dark, Raphael stepped up and welcomed him. "Always good to see you."

They shook hands. "It's getting warm down in the valley."

"Oh, it will be hot, but we will have better weather than that. You find your man?"

"He will be here tomorrow."

Miguel and Lisa had been kissing. He stepped over. "I am ready to go when you get ready."

"You have at least two days of putting up with him, Lisa."

"Thanks. I don't mind sharing him with you. The reunions are fun." They were off.

"Anything go wrong?" he asked Raphael.

"No."

"Then I am going to get some sleep. Talk later."

"Yes."

He herded her under his arm. "I wish at times I could fly. These trips take so long."

"You might fall off the eagle you choose," she teased.

"Probably would. But we will be getting back on track tomorrow after Spencer gets here."

"Thank goodness."

"I have some food," Monica said, standing in the kitchen before her range.

"Good. I am hungry. I missed your food."

"You're all set. I'm going to bed."

"Thanks."

He watched her leave. "Is she feeling bad?"

Liz nodded.

"Sorry."

"She won't go see a doctor. Nothing I can do."

"One more thing to deal with, huh?"

After eating, putting the dishes in the sink, he dragged himself upstairs and at last dropped into bed, hugged her, and fell asleep.

He didn't wake until noon. Took a bath, shaved, put on fresh clothes, and Liz fed him.

"Monica's in bed. That is how bad she feels."

"Wonder what she has wrong?"

"She won't talk to me about it."

"Should we send for a doctor?"

"She refused that twice this week. Chet, I don't know what to do."

He saw she was crying. "She's like a mother to me. She won't listen to anything I say."

"That is her way. You or I could not influence her."

Liz crossed herself. "I may ask the priest to come today."

- "Do that. It would help you and maybe her, too."

"That sounds so final."

"It is all you can do."

She sent a driver to bring the priest back to the ranch. The father arrived at dark and spoke to her.

His two men, Spencer, and his family arrived on the late night stage. The welcome was quiet.

Monica died in the night.

Lisa volunteered to cook breakfast with some of the other women in the morning. Liz accepted her generous offer.

Things were pretty solemn in the big house, except for the children who had no idea about the love for the woman taken in the night. Her body was carried from her bedroom, wrapped in a blanket, and taken to her church for burial that afternoon as she had directed.

The ranch's population attending the service, there at the church, had overflowed into the street. There were others there as well. She was laid to rest in the adjoining cemetery and everyone filed back to the ranch on every conveyance and saddle stock they had.

Chet hired some taxis to take the others who did not have rides. Lisa and her crew had food set out in the great barn back at the ranch.

Liz took the workers aside, thanked them, and told them they were a great tribute to her friend Monica and how much she appreciated them. Lisa hugged her and told her they all loved both Monica and her, and knew how deep her feelings were on her loss.

After a time, Chet and Spencer left the group and went into his office to go over the line building plans step by step.

"First we need a surveyor to stake the line and mark each pole hole."

"Sixty some feet apart except across hills that may require more to provide clearance," Chet told him.

Spencer shook his head at the numbers. "That means thousands of poles."

"Right. A glass insulator bolted on each one."

"It all has to be there. Workers, holes dug, and tamped in. Insulators on every pole standing up. Then wire stretched on each of them and secured to the insulators."

"One slip in supply and we pay for men to sit on their asses. If we start at New Mexico we will be two hundred miles from Gallup at Center Point. That's a two-or three-week haul to get it there."

"You will need a real supply person to keep that going," Chet agreed.

"Any break in the supply link will cost you money."

"We can't start it without half our needs ready to lay out. Then supply will really call for fast delivery."

"There are bound to be problems in delivery."

"Yes, but we must minimize them for this to work. When you get that many people working, it is the same as building a house. You need the lumber and nails there and ready."

"Look over this schedule they sketched out here." Chet handed him a new folder.

Spencer made a discovery. "They have a livestock

contractor to supply beef. Why not hire some hunters to harvest a few antelope or deer? That would be cheaper and a much easier deal the way we will move. We can hire a hunter for a dollar and a half a day."

"Good."

"When we get a week under our belt we may need to hire more workers."

Chet nodded. "What else can you see?"

"The lack of material; one item will suspend our construction."

"I will go over that with Hannagen. You will be there for that meeting."

Spencer said, "Cole has too much to do to work on our pole needs."

"I know. I have a man coming from Toby's outfit. Harold Faulk and his family are your kind and I think they can handle it."

"That the Harold and his family that built the pens?"

"Yes. He knows northern Arizona and the people. He would be worth talking to."

"I met him when we were running down the stage stop raiders."

"He works hard. After you talk to him, when you feel everything is ready, I think we need to go over to New Mexico and see if they can supply the material all the way."

"I'll read through all these reports again in our room. You moved Lucinda and the children up here so smoothly. Thank you. She even brags on you. Moving two small children can be tough, and you did a helluva job. I think this telegraph business will be exciting. You've done a good job starting to set this up."

"And now I've dumped it on you to get it done."

"Hey, I am honored to be here."

Lisa told them to come eat supper; the others were already at the table.

Chet thanked her, then, moving to Liz, put his arm around her shoulder. "You have a replacement for Monica?"

"Lisa and I talked. She will look for someone that fits. She told Miguel she wanted to handle it until we find a suitable replacement. Food may not be as good but she cooked with Monica for months before she was married. He doesn't mind. He gets to eat here."

"Good. It will work." When Chet came inside the kitchen he asked them to bow their heads, he would pray. He made it short, mentioned Monica and how she would be missed. Amen.

CHAPTER 26

Harold Faulk and his family arrived in two loaded large farm wagons the next day. Liz welcomed them to the house and more bedrooms were filled. Chet and Spencer worked more on plans, and they had a talk with Harold about procuring thousands of poles for the line.

Harold sat in the circle of three. He looked very serious and finally spoke. "I think we should start buying poles for cash. That would be the best way to get them. There is no work up there at Center Point. A cash price on poles will make folks bring them in."

"Can we get thousands of them?" Spencer asked.

"Price is right, they will bury you with them."

"Chet, what do you think?" Spencer asked.

"You went up there to work on the headquarters to make money. What else could you have done when you finished?" Chet asked.

"Nothing," Harold said. "That's why I drove down here to find work with you. We can get hand bills printed on wanting poles and my family will pin them up all over."

"What do you think?" Spencer asked.

"We establish a price. I think Harold can handle it. Then we'll need teamsters to haul the poles."

"They're around."

"My man Fred will take you into Preskitt tomorrow to get the bills printed. Think what you want to say. I'd say start at a quarter a twelve-foot-tall solid pole."

Both men agreed that was fair.

"Your wife may need to shop. Take her with you," he said to Harold, going for dinner.

"I bet she does."

"Your daughter might want to go, too?"

Harold agreed. "My boy Ray is riding with *vaqueros* today. He won't care. But Claire will be excited to go along."

Things moved along smoothly. They devised a way for Harold and his wife to handle the pole payments at the Center Point headquarters and for the collection to be there. There was enough land there to stack plenty of poles.

Fred took the three Faulks to town on a buckboard. Chet noted that Fred did not miss any chance to talk to the cute tomboy Claire. He kept his observation to himself until Liz mentioned it. "Your man sure liked that buggy-driving business today I bet?"

"Oh, yes. Claire is the toughest working girl he's ever spoke to in his life."

"You warn him?"

"No."

She laughed. "I guess he will find that out himself."

"They are just kids. I am not worried."

"What were you doing at that age?" she asked.

"Busy running a Texas ranch full time. My dad had already lost his mind."

"I bet you were looking for a female during that time."

"There were not many to see. Not working out there."

"Oh?"

"Not like we have here. A near full house," he said.

"We do. Lisa is doing a great job. She has talked to me about her doing it full time."

"What does her husband think?"

"She says they talked about it."

"I am not opposed. You want her, you hire her."

"I will think about it. She has a life to live, too. Monica didn't. So I don't expect the same from Lisa."

"Summer is close. I want to move on the telegraph deal, so we will be leaving again soon."

"I understand. Do railroads come next?"

He smiled as he shook his head. "I am not a big enough player to do that." He hugged her and kissed her cheek.

"I don't believe that."

"Thanks. I want to check on some things before I go to New Mexico."

"Tomorrow?"

"Planning for then. Or the next day. Might even be after that. I want to run up to check on Toby. I have a feeling something might be wrong over there. He's done well but I need to follow my gut feelings."

"Didn't Harold just come down from there?"

"I know, but before I get buried in stringing

telegraph I want to be certain those two kids are all right."

"Want me along?"

"I'd rather make a flying trip up and back."

"Who's going?"

"Miguel and Fred."

"Takes two days to get over there."

"We'll try and make it faster."

Chet and his two men hurried over on the General Crook Road to the eastern division. They went by the Hayes place, but they didn't stop. It was late when they got to the dark ranch house.

"Hello the house," Chet shouted.

A lamp come on in the house. "That you, Chet?"

"Yeah. Sorry to wake you."

"Something wrong?" Toby asked, opening the door.

"No. Just checking that you two were all right."

"Come in. One of the boys putting the horses up?"

"They are. Sorry to wake you and Talley. You haven't had any more Indian troubles?"

"We have not seen one since you left here." Talley stood by Toby in her robe.

"Go back to bed. They're bringing bedrolls. We'll sleep on the floor tonight."

"You three. Is there only three of you?"

"Yes, ma'am."

"I'll make some pancakes. I know you have not eaten. Why were you that worried about us?"

"Yes, I was. I must have had a bad dream to worry

about you two. I felt something was bad wrong up here. Strange feeling I guess, Talley. You both should know that Harold and his family got to our place. They're going to buy poles at Center Point to string our wire on. Spencer thought we could do that job as well, short as this country is. Paying twenty-five cents cash for a twelve-foot-long pole."

"Man, I know some guys would get after that," Toby said.

"How many will you buy?" Talley asked.

"Way over two thousand are needed."

Talley was still thinking about Chet's worry. "I appreciate your coming all the way here on your worry. As bad and hard as my life was, this man you have running this ranch is the greatest man on earth to me. I am living up here, wild Indians and all, in a real heaven. We never have a cross word. He keeps me in firewood and he really worries about me. I mean when I came up here, I thought more slaving and complaining. I don't have none of that and ain't nothing going to shatter that. Not renegade Indians, bears, or mountain lions. But I am proud you thought enough of us to come save us even if we didn't need saving."

She put down the mixing bowl and came over to squeeze his hand. "Thanks, Chet Byrnes. Tell that lovely wife of yours I won't ever forget that dress she gave me for our wedding. I am where I belong."

"Good. Then forget I came clear over here."

They rode back the next day seeing no sign of Indians.

"You think Jesus bought that ranch he was talking

about while we were gone?" Fred asked them while riding.

"I guess we will know when we get home."

They spent the night with Rhea, Victor, and Adam at the Verde Ranch. When they rode up the mountain the next day, Liz and Lisa were coming out of the house with two picnic baskets headed for the buckboard.

"Hey, ladies, where you going?" Chet asked.

"Jesus and Anita bought that ranch. Come along; we are having a picnic lunch over there."

"You want Fred to drive?"

"Lisa can do it. Oh, Miguel, you are moving to the big house when you get home. She wants to be the chief cook and bottle washer for a while."

He smiled big and winked at his wife. "I figured she would. Saves us buying food, huh?"

"That too."

From the Preskitt Road they crossed a small spring-fed creek and there sat the large white house with a barn and corrals at the end of the drive. All fenced and tight. In a bright new yellow dress, Mrs. Martinez stood waiting with her husband all decked out in a white shirt and vest.

"Welcome to the Triple M Ranch. We don't have much furniture, but we did buy some benches until we find some."

Everyone laughed.

"How were Toby and Talley?" Jesus asked him.

"Kind of like the Martinez bunch."

"How is that?"

"Damn proud of what they have. Talley told me

she was having the dream life she never thought she would find."

Anita came and took his arm. "I want you to bless this place. The priest is coming Sunday after church, but I have been around you a lot these past years and you have done this for many people. I want you to bless it for the two of us."

He felt a little short of words for a second, then gathered his wits. He took off his hat and the others did, too. "Lord, Anita and Jesus have bought this place to raise a family. A place of their own. They never imagined such a place as ever being theirs growing up, working hard, but you have helped provide this acreage. Let this be a holy place to raise a family, to put a ranch together, and some day pass a better place on to their children. Amen."

Mid-afternoon they went back home. Riding along with Miguel and Chet, Fred asked, "Why did it take Anita so long to marry Jesus?"

"She told him she feared becoming a wife."

"Hmm, she looks as happy as Talley did over there."

"Fred, you will learn a lot about women in the next few years. They're different and every one of them is different in a different way. Right, Miguel?"

"Boy, yes. Completely different. A lot of women would have grabbed Jesus in a minute. He had to convince her. They'll do fine, and she is coming out of the shell she was in. In Mexico there would have been no such a step up for her to make, from servant to home owner. You stay where you always were all your life. In Mexico I'd still be a farm hand."

"Guys, I have a lot to learn. I have been scratching

at a living to even eat before I joined you. I feel damn grateful riding with you all everywhere I go. I never spoke to a girl like an equal in my life until I met Claire. I sure didn't impress her, but it sure was nice to talk with her like I was one. You all taught me that."

"I know how you feel," Miguel said. "Bandits killed my first wife. I ran away from Mexico and Raphael gave me a job. I thought my life would be in shambles forever. This tall pretty girl who worked in the big house wanted no part of a simple *vaquero*. But when I took my hat off to talk to her, she looked at me like I was funny.

"Boy, she was as cold as the north wind in winter. Then Chet told me part of her story, how she ran away with a man who she expected would marry her. He didn't have her story right, but in the end she told me the details, and they were sad. I had to make her believe I was not there for that. I asked her to go riding on a Sunday. She got permission and we had what you call a good time but at a distance.

"When we got back, I said, 'Can we ride again?' I feared she'd say no. She said she would ask Elizabeth again.

"So we rode again on the next Sunday. Then we danced at a wedding here and all those *hombres* who had no wives danced with her, too. But she came and found me that night and told me she had saved the last dance for me. I knew I'd made a step up.

"I was living in the bunkhouse. She lived in the big house. If I asked her to marry me I needed a house. I asked Raphael if she would marry me could

I have a house. He laughed and said, 'Maybe not for you, but she could have one.'"

They all laughed at that.

"I am learning." Fred shook his head and smiled. "Lots to learn."

"Let's move it. When we get back to the house, we will have a lot to do. This telegraph business is about to bust open. Harold is going north to get set up buying posts. The family will tack up signs all over and hope a hundred loggers come running forth with posts. The four of us need to go to Gallup. In a week I hope it will all begin."

That evening Chet talked to Spencer and his wife about the plans. "Why not wait until we get started. Then we can move you, Lucinda, and the children to the main camp."

"I agree things will be more orderly by then. Who will move us?"

"Maybe Jesus. He understands moving and handles expenses well. I will supply him some good men."

"We won't have raiders like the stage line had?"

"I hope not."

Liz came into the room. "Lisa has supper ready; we better get in there." She caught him by the arm and whispered, "Did you see Fred sneak a kiss on Claire earlier?"

"No."

"They did it pretty private, I was upstairs, but I peeked and saw. It was very nice and cute."

"He said she was the first girl he ever talked to he was so busy surviving."

"I can imagine."

They had a wonderful supper. Lisa had a girl to

help her named Sonja. She was in her mid-teens and very bashful, but she, too, would emerge out of her shell. Chet thought the girl was very pleased in her new dress on her first day of work.

Miguel was very proud of his wife's cooking. He showed it in his beaming but never uttered a word until they all applauded her.

The next morning Chet's men loaded a supply wagon with wall tents, cots, necessary food items, bedrolls, and extra clothing as well as all the tools they might need. Fred was appointed driver. The plans were to camp the next evening on the far side of the Verde, on top of the Mogollon Rim. They had the ranch's best team of Percheron horses who had plenty of speed and power for the grades they faced. Fred had driven them around for two days, so they felt he was the man. One of Raphael's best teamsters, Tonio, was going to hitch a saddle horse behind and then ride to the bottom of the mountain to be sure that things went well, and then Fred would be on his own.

They had one packhorse that Fred could use for a saddle horse. He also had his new saddle, blanket, and bridle in the wagon. He and Tonio had left an hour early in the dark but the stars and moon were out.

Chet, Spencer, Jesus, and Miguel all left later but they expected to catch him before he climbed the north road up the far mountain. A cool, not a cold morning, their horses did some extra prancing—none bucked. Waving to everyone they left for Gallup.

They stopped for a short reprieve at the Verde Ranch to hug his growing son Adam and Rhea. He spoke to Millie. Tom had gone to the Hereford Ranch. Victor was off working on a farm project. With that visit done, they rode to catch Fred who was halfway up the north slope and smiling like a tomcat who'd just ate a rat when they rode up beside him.

The big horses were sweating but not too much. He said he planned to rest them on the next flatter spot for a few minutes.

"We'll go make camp and build a fire for supper."

"No problem." Then he spoke to his team who were lagging. They threw their heads up and pulled hard.

Trotting his horse, Jesus looked back. "He must have driven horses before."

"I bet he did lots of things back then to survive."

"He sure is a survivor and he learns fast. That boy even talks different than when he first came."

Miguel nodded. "He told me Liz told him to vary his words. He does that thinking about it a lot I bet."

"That's what it is," Jesus said. "He never says the same thing often."

Chet agreed. "He doesn't miss much that goes on. Doesn't cuss much more than we do when we get mad. But he has changed his words and how he says things since he came to the ranch."

"That moved him from a dumb boy to a real guy. I guess I never noticed the guys who say the same things all the time until lately, and riding with you guys I am learning a lot more to say and how to do that," Miguel admitted.

Spencer made his horse get up beside them. "I really missed Jesus's and Chet's talking, with me down there working them poor boys from Mexico."

They laughed and rode on.

Camp made and Fred arrived shortly with his wagon. They brushed down the big horses, then fed them and the saddle horses while Jesus and Miguel cooked supper. The ranch cook at the Verde had cut them some choice steaks to take along. That and beans made the supper.

Going north, they saw the printed signs for posts wanted tacked onto trees. Fred drove on while Chet and the men stopped to visit Betty and her baby. Robert was working so the riders kept on going north. They arrived at the Center Point compound. Val and Rocky came out to see the big horses. Claire showed up to help him unhitch, and the two worked like a team. After the horses were watered and brushed down, the other workers came by and watched as the two polished the animals.

Chet came and told them, "The food's ready."

And the pair came along, talking softly to each other.

"How was the second day?" Chet asked him.

"Even better than the first one. I got over the stomach cramps."

The two of them nodded at each other.

"You think he may make a teamster, Claire?"

"Yes, sir. I saw him drive in here. He's pretty da— I mean good at handling them."

"I agree. Your dad buy any poles yet?"

"No, but from all the promises we have, we may soon be buried in them."

"I hope so. We'll need them."

"I like your son Rocky. He's going to be as big as you are someday."

"He is growing. You going to eat with us?"

"May I?"

"Certainly. Show her the way, Fred. I'll have to sit with the others but you two don't."

"Thanks, Chet, we want to be right."

"You are." He went to join his other men.

"Fred isn't going to share her?" Spencer teased.

"No. They need some private time."

"Boy, back in Texas I saved my money from picking cotton, doing odd jobs, and had three dollars made from an entire summer's work. They had a box dinner auction and dance where you bid on a girl's box lunch. Sharon McIlhaney, the prettiest girl in Shade County, would be the highest one sold. I held out for her red-wrapped box to sell.

"Big Mike Hansen was real serious about her and I knew I had to out-bid him. The auctioneer said on the start the limit on bidding was three dollars and when it got there that bidder was the buyer. They'd been selling for forty to fifty cents a box. When they held up the red box lunch, Big Mike popped up and shouted, 'One dollar.' The whole crowd got real quiet. Then this barefoot boy from Siler Crick, jumped up, shoved his fist in the sky, and shouted, 'Three dollars!'

"Big Mike shouted, 'Ten dollars.'

"The auctioneer shook his head. 'Spencer gets the bid.'

"'He won't live to eat it. I'll kill that wormy son of a bitch here and now.'

"Some elders grabbed Mike, threw him outside, and told him not to come back. But my belly cramped eating her mother's fried chicken and dancing with her at arm's length. I could dance barefooted then, too. She was very polite to me and even asked how I got so much money to buy her lunch. I told her I earned every dime. I had a heavenly night. She danced with others but danced every third one with me. Plus she came got me for the last one. I had a good evening but as the end drew near I began to wonder if I'd live to see the next sun come up.

"I knew from my friends Big Mike and his thugs were waiting outside. Before the last dance, Jim Griffin, a buddy, came by and said he had his grandfather's mule, Jacob, he rode over here and how he was out of a Kentucky racehorse and nothing in the county could catch him. He said if I'd come out the back door and jump over the rail the Colonel would carry me away.

"Sharon kissed me good-bye on the cheek and thanked me for being so polite. I tore out the back door, bound over the rail, hit the saddle kinda hard, grabbed the reins, and never stopped running him until I reached Siler Creek."

They all laughed.

"That is not all the story. I knew Big Mike would not be satisfied until I was dead. I told my grandma who raised me that Jim would come for the mule. I had a skinny pony, a dry hull of a saddle, a blanket for a bedroll, plus one small iron skillet, and the next morning I left Shade County. She gave me seventy-five cents, which was all she had, and I was on my own at fifteen. I sent her money every time I made some until her sister wrote me that she died and how she appreciated my helping her.

"I saw in a paper where they hung Big Mike for murder in Fort Worth a few years later. I was in an El Paso house of ill repute a short time after that and someone spoke my name when I came in the parlor. Boys, I swear it was Sharon McIlhaney. I asked her why she was in there. She got teary eyed. Told me she married Big Mike and should not have, but when they hung him she had no choice but take up that profession.

"I gave her twenty dollars and she begged me to stay. I couldn't. It hurt too bad. I guess now you know why I don't get along with doves."

"Spencer, you have a great lady now in your life, a family, and you are a long ways from leading a shabby life."

"Thanks. Those two kids are cute. Heck, did you hear Claire earlier. She damn near said *damn* earlier." Spencer chuckled over it. "Guess she is learning like we all learned."

Miguel nodded. "My wife said she swore a lot when Chet met her. She doesn't anymore. She told me so."

"I'd sworn, too, if I'd suffered what she had. Guys, we're all lucky to be here. I plan to spend a day here talking to Cole, my son, and Harold. Then we'll head east to meet the company people in Gallup and get things on the road."

Val gave them all tents to sleep in. Chet and Rocky played until bedtime. Cole still wasn't back, but she said his job did that a lot to him.

"You handle it well," he said to her.

"Oh, Chet Byrnes, he's your twin. He rode so long with you, he never leaves anything unturned. I can

get a little mad, but he does things right for me. He
puts up with me and he is as loyal as you are to your
wife. That really means a lot to me and to Liz, too. I
know we have talked about it. He rose from a common
cowboy to a superintendent. He's your student and
he learned well. Like his mentor, he works double
hard at making it go right. How lucky can I be?
And my childless state doesn't bother him."

"I'll see you and Rocky at breakfast."

"Thanks again for all you do for all of us. Liz
coming sometime soon?"

"She'll come later when we get it all going."

"Good. I really love her. How did she take
Monica's death? I couldn't come. It was over by the
time we heard."

"I think she accepted it now. Lisa is going to do
Monica's job. She's started and it is working."

"That girl has changed, too."

"Yes. You saw how hard she worked at the wed-
dings."

"And she married your new man, Miguel."

"She also helped Monica, knows the house, what
and how we do things."

"How do you manage all this you do?"

"I simply try. Good night."

Morning came early. Cole, Val, and Rocky joined
him for breakfast at the big tent.

"You made it home after all."

Cole nodded. "It was late. One of our drivers got
drunk and busted up a bar. He did about fifty dollars
in damages. I made him pay for it and told him he
was laid off for two months. I told him he could

come back if he stayed sober and he'd still have a job, otherwise he was through."

"What do you think?"

"He's a good on-time driver, but if he doesn't straighten his life up I won't take him back."

"Real tough being a boss, ain't it?"

"I can't understand it. He has a job that pays forty-five bucks a month. Good cowboys make twenty-five. If he comes back he will only make thirty-five dollars until he shows he can be a real driver and not get drunk."

"You can't save them if they don't want to try."

"I agree. By the way, I think you have a winner in Harold. I don't have the time for everything, and I know how hard his whole family works. They will buy you the poles, amen."

Val clapped his hand on the table. "This is the first time he ever said the whole truth—about not having time for everything."

"He is busy enough. But the telegraph wire will save you a hundred trips."

"I know it will."

"She said you brought Spencer up here to ramrod it."

"This was more important than the ranch head-quarters. Frisco the foreman will get it done down there."

"To good times." Cole held his coffee cup up. "I wish I was back riding with you. You took care of all our worries. I simply had to ride along and help."

"You graduated."

"Yes. I love this job. It is those hard decisions that

kick me. But I know I have to do them along with the rest."

"Been there. Done that. Tomorrow we go east and set up. Just help Harold and his bunch get the posts bought. They can do it but if he gets stuck, help him and get them rolling east with every empty freighter going that way."

"Holler when you have enough."

"I can do that."

He stopped Jesus. "Where's Fred at?"

"Oh, he asked me if it was all right to go riding on our horses with Claire today. I told him this was a get it straight day here and saw no reason why not. They left before sunup to ride to some small lake with a lunch she fixed for them."

"Does her mother know?"

Jesus laughed. "I guess she does but that girl is pretty strong minded. Would decide for herself if she were going or not."

"Jesus, you think you know it all now. I don't know about you."

"Yeah. You do. You were young once, too. They won't get into any trouble."

"Harold and Spencer are meeting today. Going over the posts he can buy."

"I guess we go east tomorrow?"

"Yes. We leave at sunup. It will take over four days to get to Gallup."

"Fred will be back by then. I know."

"He better be or her mom will kill them both."

Chet went over the stage line books with the young man hired to keep them. Rick Simmons was some-one Hannagen hired and sent over. He was very smart about bookkeeping and he kept them accurately from all that Chet could learn. Rick was certainly not a rough-and-tumble hand like most of the men around there.

"How are things going?" he asked the new employee.

"Mr. Emerson is so hard working and a gracious man to work for. I have enjoyed myself working here for him. But aside from the Methodist church activities I really miss the library, the music concerts, and entertainment I enjoyed in St. Louis. Do you ever think there will be things like that here someday?"

"Rick, I believe there will, someday when the railroad comes through here."

"Oh, thanks. There is hope then."

"Yes, there is hope. We may have a telegraph here in six months."

"That will be a step up, sir. I have met a young lady since I came here. I guess I have the privilege to marry her if she'll have me and we can live in my small company log hut."

"Rick, if you get ready to get married and plan to stay here, we will build you a cottage."

"Really? How fine, sir. How much notice do you need?"

"A few months. But don't hold back. You can get married and live in your cabin until the house is ready."

"Oh? They said it was a bachelor's cabin. I thought I couldn't live in one married."

"You will be fine. We take marriage very seriously. We will help you in any way we can and even have a celebration for you."

"Oh, Mr. Byrnes, how nice that will be."

"Will your parents come from back east?"

"No. My mother thinks the Indians are cannibals out here. I tell her in my letters I see them all the time and not a one has bit me yet."

Chet did all he could not to laugh until he cried. But he managed to hold it in. Later he found Val and told her. She laughed. "He is kinda strange, but I'll tell Cole what to expect."

"He is a bookkeeper and, I think, a very good one. He is an easterner. But he isn't giving up his job and leaving even for the cannibals wrapped in blankets downtown."

"Oh, that is so funny. He must never have told Cole that one. That paint pony you sent Rocky is a little large for him. But he rides it in a pen and tells me he's all right for now, but he needs a horse like you and Cole to ride next."

"When he gets the paint under him and rides him, well, he can have one."

"You have plenty of time."

"Did you know that Ty has the Barbarossa horses? I bet he can cut out a shorter one and break him out for Rocky in, say, two years. He took this head-swinging, bucking gray horse that Ortega and JD sent to me and made him a horse I am proud to ride."

"Why didn't I think about that?" she asked.

"I guess my sheep rider at the Verde will need one by then, too."

"He can have his little pony."

"Do that."

Suppertime, the couple came back on horses, put them up, and joined the rest.

"Sorry we're late. We saw a bunch of elk, some deer, and one old black bear," Fred said.

"Your mother know that you're back?" Chet asked her.

"I told her we might be late but I'm going to head that way after I eat. I did enjoy riding your horse today. Thanks. Someday I want one like him. Oh, did you have a job for Fred today?"

"No."

"Good. He is a perfect gentleman. You know they aren't easy to find."

"Good. He works for me and I expect that from my people."

"I believe that. He told me his story and I see why he thinks you're special. My family does, too. Having a good job is important."

"I am pleased with the both of you. I just didn't want to be criticized for supporting anything your mother did not approve of."

"I swear we asked her and she said we could go riding."

"No problem. I have a fatherly way about those I am responsible for."

"I understand. Sometime I want to visit with your wife. We were there when things were kind of upsetting because of your housekeeper's death, so we didn't really visit."

"Liz will enjoy talking to you. She will be coming up here shortly to join me, so stop over and talk to her."

"Fred told me a lot about things that you and she taught him. I am impressed. But now I am

going to have to ask you to excuse me. Mother will
be wondering where I am."

"Claire, if you miss breakfast, we're heading out
right after, so thanks for talking to me."

"Miss breakfast? No, I will be there."

And she was gone. Chet decided she was pretty
grown up and sure on her feet for what he thought
was a backwoods tomboy. Wait until he told Liz.
She'd smile at his discovery.

In four to five days he and his men would be at
New Mexico and the games would start. He hoped
the supplies came through and there were poles
over there, along with the hardware, insulators,
and some bolts. Too many things clouded his mind.
He hoped he had not forgotten anything. Maybe
Spencer would remember them.

Sleep did not come easy.

CHAPTER 27

They were eating breakfast at six a.m. Harold's wife, Ann, stopped him at the line and took him aside. "I won't keep you long. I wanted you to know I approved of Fred and Claire going riding yesterday. She works as hard as any boy, and I have been very frank with her about a woman's place in life. I met Fred at your ranch. He is a gentleman. A girl like Claire, who lived in the wilderness, still needs to be courted, and I see this in Fred. I thank you for all your concern."

"Ann, they are dear kids. I only worried you might not know it all."

"I know you watch after him. I heard his story last night. He's lucky you found him. They are both good people. Now I only hope we can do right by you and keep you in poles."

The next morning after Fred pecked Claire's cheek, he climbed up on the seat, unwrapped the Percheron reins, and drove the high-stepping horses for the main road. Heading out with his men and the packhorse, Chet waved to Rocky and Val.

The trip was uneventful. They crawled across northern Arizona and in four days were at the Gallup headquarters. The horses stabled, they walked two blocks to the hotel and secured rooms. They took baths, shaved, and changed clothes. A Chinese man took their clothes to be washed and ironed. Chet led them to the Mexican restaurant they liked and were busy eating when Hannagen showed up with his male secretary carrying his usual tablet and pencil.

"You are all already here. Good. May we join you?"

Chet waved the pretty girl over to take their order. "Fix him and his man up."

"Thanks," Hannagen said. "You have a good trip over here? I have gotten reports about your progress from our stage drivers."

"We had no problems, and for us that is new and welcome. You have not met Miguel and Fred. You know Jesus and Spencer."

"Good to meet all of you."

"We are eating, then going to our rooms. We can be at your office in the morning."

"We can start at eight if that works for you."

"We will be there."

The real business began to unfold in a large room of people in the morning. A man called Cash Armand was introduced as the supply person for the company. Chet then introduced his supervisor Spencer Horne for operations.

"We understand we have or will shortly have a thousand poles here. I set up a buying station at Center Point to get more. I am paying twenty-five cents apiece for them."

Cash shook his head. "How come so cheap?"

"There are no jobs over there. People can make wages at that price. We have set a buying station there. That is where the others we have came from, but this buying station should get us more at a competitive cost."

"Mr. Hannagen, we have some poles coming in a shipment that will cost a dollar here," Armand said.

"How many did we buy?"

"Four hundred to start."

"Stop that contract. We can blend that price in with the lesser costing ones."

"Yes, sir. Chet Byrnes set up the stage stops at an unbelievably low cost. We are working as a team now. I know operating apart has been difficult but now we need to blend your procurement task and their construction efforts. He and his men get things done. Continue, Chet."

"Our biggest concern is will there be enough bolts, insulators, and wire to keep us running once we start?"

"My access to rail now is at Bernalillo. I think I have the material coming and enough freighters to get it over here from there."

"Remember once we start we can't afford, at that distance, to lose our supplies and then our help. Or pay them to sit on their butts."

Cash nodded. "We will do the best we can here. I understand the past supervisor was being paid for you to fail."

"Yes. But we made it in spite of his efforts."

"Today, I would like, when this meeting is over, to go over our current supplies and what we lack to start," Spencer said.

"Very good. We can."

"I think we know what we have to do," Hannagen said. "Chet, you and I need to talk about other matters. Spencer, since you will be construction supervisor, you and Cash get together. We need to get this show on the road shortly."

In his large office, Hannagen and Chet sat down in leather chairs opposite each other.

"I have corresponded with Emerson about the matter of stagecoaches; I followed the course you suggested concerning having them in good repair before they were driven up here. We were going to start hauling passengers three times a week. But those stages are in Fort Worth undergoing costly repairs and I am paying drivers to sit around and feed horses in liveries at high prices. I must have bought a pile of junk or they are skinning us alive. What else do I need to do? I do have a man hired to get to the bottom of this repair business."

"Get them out here. You said the railroad is to Bernalillo. Bring them there, load them and the horses on railcars to west Texas, then drive them over here."

"I will do that. Thank you."

"Anything else?"

"I have just met him of course, but this man Spencer sounds tough. I like Emerson but they are different people, aren't they? Will they be able to work together, do you think?"

"To run a construction crew you have to be like a ship's captain more so than a supervisor. That's why I took him off a project I had him working on, because I knew he could run this one."

"Chet, I trust your judgment. I know you have spent hours working on all this, and I appreciate your efforts. I also know it will work thanks to your involvement. Next time I will ask you to buy the coaches."

They shook hands. Sounded like they could start—his question was how weak were those links back to Bernalillo and their source of supply there.

After lunch they met the head surveyor who had already staked forty miles west. Hugh Yates and his assistants discussed what Spencer expected from them, and they were soon all talking on the same track.

There was a mountain of shiny number ten wire rolls stacked in the yards. It would roll out fast once they started. He also saw the glass insulators and the shiny bolts that would secure them to the posts.

"We need to drill them on the ground, attach the glass insulator to the post, and then set them so they face the right way each time," Spencer said.

"I thought—" Cash started to say.

"We can do it twice as fast that way than have a man climbing a pole and trying to get enough room to drill up there."

They went on and by the end of the tour Spencer thought they needed twice the material than what they had on hand to start. Chet backed him and they went back to eat supper and sleep on it. Next day they rode with the surveyor out to look at the first stretch.

Spencer liked his route. He later told Chet the man realized the road for servicing the line would be very important and while shortcuts saved money they would be more costly to work on the line and keep up.

Chet wrote his wife and told her he'd be glad when Spencer could run with it alone, but so far they were still setting things up and gathering supplies. Cole wrote him that the pole buying was really beginning to work. Wagons were lined up with poles and he had some freighters already hauling them back east. They had bought over three hundred poles and many more were coming.

Spencer told Cash and sent the word to Hannagen's office. They decided to build the first stretch to the New Mexico border at a distance of twenty miles to test everything. The route went down alongside a small river, and at Spencer's insistence they put it above the roadside in case of a flood. He'd seen big rains swell creeks and take out everything. The progress was slow but by the time they were ten miles along, their speed became much improved and the last half was done in a few days.

At the following meeting they decided to start the next stringing in ten days. Poles were arriving from Harold. A series of tents became the headquarters. They hired two hunters to test that system and they delivered the game. A tent for the two wives was set and two men assigned to move them. He sent a telegram to Liz to start in their direction from the

ranch, but only take their time since it would be a
long trip.

Meanwhile he received another letter, forwarded
to him from the U.S. marshal in Utah, concerning
the couple Theodore Danbury and Regina Porter
who had run off with the bank money. The marshal
thought that they might be headed through Holbrook for the Mormon settlements below there.

He spoke to his men at breakfast about their possible route. Spencer told Chet that if he needed to
go look for the couple, he had his situation under
control and would be all right without him there.

Chet, Jesus, Miguel, and Fred saddled up and
rode to Holbrook. The new deputy sheriff, Joe
McCarthy, had still not seen his predecessor who
had run away after cashing that five-hundred-dollar
bill. McCarthy had also not seen the pair they
wanted in his town.

Jesus learned, in talking to some Hispanic people,
that a six-foot-tall pretty woman and a dressed-up
man had been there but had gone south. The four-
some rode south checking along the way. At the
freighter's stop, where they served such bad coffee
and food, the freighter said he had seen the pair a
week before when they stopped by.

Chet paid the woman who served the horrible
coffee a dollar, and they left. Jesus had food and
coffee for them in their own camp.

That night, Chet found a freighter going north
who saw the couple a few days earlier on the road.

"Man, she's a real looker. Wears a veil but she's tall
and looked like a bed full to me." He pulled out his
corncob pipe to laugh.

"They mention where they were going?" Chet asked.

"Tombstone is what I thought they said they were going to."

"Thanks."

"You be wanting her body, huh?"

"No. They robbed a bank in Utah."

He pointed his pipe stem at his bib overalls. "She could rob me."

Chet thanked him and left him to go back to his own camp. She probably could rob him. Silly man. She must be trouble is all he could think about her.

It was a helluva long ways to Tombstone from here. But the outlaws needed to be apprehended.

"Where did he think they'd go?" Fred asked.

"Tombstone."

"We going there?"

"I plan to."

Fred nodded. "I'm fine. Never been there."

"Big place. Twelve thousand people live there," Jesus said.

"Wow. That is big."

They rode in and out of rain showers for the next two days. Hats soaked and slickers dripping, they reached a mining town in the mountains called Mogollon, boarded their horses, ate a café meal, and slept in hotel beds. Drug themselves out of bed the next morning, had breakfast, and rode on, a little more rested, down the spine of the mountains that ran on the New Mexico–Arizona border.

On the desert floor they rode west not learning much about the pair. It took three more days to reach Tombstone. They took baths and ate at Nelly

Cashman's restaurant. Chet found Virgil Earp who said he had not seen the tall woman or her partner in any of the saloons.

Jesus took the photos to the *barrio* and found no one had seen them there. Two days of searching without a clue and Chet was ready to go back north. They had supper at Nellie's again and came out into the night.

A scruffy-looking cowboy stepped over in their way on the dark empty boardwalk, chewing on a toothpick. "Which one's Byrnes?"

"I am. What do you need?"

He looked around to be certain they were alone. "You want that Danbury sumbitch?"

"Yes. You know where he is?"

"Yeah. For fifty bucks I'll tell you where he's at."

"How do you know that?"

"I knew him in Colorado. But I want the bitch traveling with him."

Chet shook his head. "She's wanted, too. She will be arrested and charged with him on bank-stealing business."

The man smiled. "What a waste. She'd bring a couple hundred bucks."

"In the white slave business you mean?"

"Call it what you want, mister. She'd bring a lot of money."

"She is a wanted criminal as is he. You telling me his location?"

"Yeah for a hundred bucks."

"Twenty dollars."

"You cheap bas—" That was all he got out; Miguel

had him by the throat and against the wall with his gun stuck in his gut.

"You talking or dying?" his man asked him through clenched teeth.

"All right. All right. Give me twenty bucks. He's down at the Hart Ranch outside of Patagonia. Anyone can point you there."

"Why there?"

"Hart's as big a crook as Danbury."

"What's your name?"

"That isn't important."

"It is to me," Chet insisted.

"Cy Boyd. I work for Old Man Clanton."

"Nice to know you. If you've lied to me I might have to have this money back and your hide." He paid the man.

Boyd took the money, tucked it in his shirt, and left in a huff.

Chet and his men stood there a while longer discussing the information. Chet and Miguel went by Alhambra Saloon and spoke to Virgil about Hart in private.

"Hart has a helluva lot of money for such a small ranch is all I know." Virgil smiled.

Chet and his man went on back to the hotel and met the other two. "We saddle up and ride down there tomorrow."

They rode southwest and by afternoon came to the side road that had signs pointing to Hart's ranch. When they reached an overlook, Chet used his field glasses to scope the place. He handed them to Jesus. "Not many working ranches have a guard with a rifle out front."

"No, but the tall woman just came out onto the porch, said something, and went back inside."

"Good. We are at the right place."

"What should we do?" Jesus asked.

"Go down and arrest them."

"Fine. Let me and Miguel handle it."

"No. I won't ride up and get shot like the other time. But if anyone threatens us, shoot him."

"All right. We ride several feet apart and do what we have to do," stated Miguel.

"Wish it was early in the morning."

"We don't have that option today, Jesus. That guard does not look like a hard case."

"It's what's in the house that bothers me."

"I understand. Fred, you get on the far right. This may get tough. Get off your horse if they shoot at us."

"Yes, sir."

They came off the hill and spread out with their rifles drawn and ready. The guard ran to the front door and shouted something. Three men came out onto the porch.

One man, in a white shirt, came forward to the yard gate. "What the hell do you want?"

Chet reined up. "We are U.S. marshals. We are here to arrest Danbury and Porter on a federal warrant from Utah."

"They ain't here."

"She is. We saw her already. If you are hiding wanted criminals, that is a federal offense and you will be charged. You do anything and my men will shoot you before you ever reach the house. Tell your man to put down his rifle.

He did so.

Still wary, his men had their rifles at the ready. Chet stepped off his horse and disarmed the man he suspected was Hart. Told him and the ranch hand to move aside and went up to confront the people on the porch.

"Which one of you is Danbury?" He knew none of them was Danbury but wanted answers.

"Now tell the Porter woman and Danbury to come out."

He heard movement inside the house that sounded like someone leaving the back way. "Miguel and Fred, I think they ran out back. You don't have to be gentle."

"Now I want names," he said to the others.

Jesus was off his horse while the other two raced around back after the suspect.

"John T. Hart."

"Cowboy?"

"LD is what they call me."

"LD Smith?"

"No LD Mayberry."

"Next?"

"Jasper Holden."

"What is your business here?"

"Land agent."

"Now of the three of you, who was assisting these fugitives in their escape?"

"None of us," Hart said. "We didn't know they were wanted by the law."

"Damn you, let go of my arm," the woman said when Fred hauled her around the corner of the house. She looked like she'd been dusted well and acted as mad as a wet hen. Miguel had Danbury.

"They try to avoid you two?"

"Chet, she wouldn't stop running so I had to tackle her and put her in irons."

Miguel was laughing. "That boy could wrestle a steer down. Just ask her."

"Hart, do they have mounts here?"

"Yes."

"Go show Jesus where they are at. Danbury, show me your luggage. Fred, you and Miguel watch these others."

"How much loot is left?" Chet asked the man, shoving him inside the house.

"I don't know—"

"I don't have all day. Those your bags?"

"Yes."

"Step back." Chet bucked the suitcase onto the bed unlatched it and looked at all the neatly packaged money. "Wasn't much place to spend it coming down here, was there?"

"Who sent you down here?"

"A U.S. marshal in Utah asked for my help in finding you. He suspected you were coming south from Holbrook. Sure enough you were."

"You're Byrnes, aren't you? I'd heard about you. Thought you were at Preskitt and thought we could go around east and miss you stopping us. A mistake."

"I was over east setting up a telegraph line and liked to never found you, but a freighter liked your lady companion and then it was easy to track you to here."

"That was a mistake, too. Should have ditched her."

"No, your big mistake was stealing all that money in the first place." He told him to go outside and wait.

Jesus came in and blinked at the money.

"No place to spend it between here and Utah," Chet said, closing it up.

Horses were gathered. Prisoners and their luggage loaded.

Chet leaned on his saddle horn and looked at the remaining men. "I guess Danbury came to buy a ranch from you, Jasper. Well, he didn't. Mr. Hart, you and him better sell this place and get out of the territory. I don't think your business here can stand much looking into, and I'll be back to do it if you don't leave. And you, cowboy, load your gear and get out of the territory, too. I catch any of you again you'll do two years in the county jail on my charges. So in three months none of you should be in Arizona. Now get to moving."

"You can't tell me—"

Chet drove his horse up to the yard fence. "This territory don't need you or Jasper, either. I will be back and I will be sure you three are not in the bounds of the territory. Am I clear?"

"Yeah."

"Good. See you do it."

Chet's lack of faith concerning the Cochise county jail sent them west to Tubac where Roamer and Bronc were in camp. They left them to deliver the two fugitives to the Pima County jail and they cut east to head back to Gallup and the telegraph line.

In a week they were back at the construction camp. Shaking her head, Liz came to greet them.

Spencer, looking a little weary, joined them. "We're making a mile to two a day."

"Your supplies?"

"So far we have enough we can do about a hundred miles. That's halfway to Center Point. Harold's poles are better than the New Mexico ones. The reports are Harold's buying plenty of them over there and sending them back here. I think everyone is pleased. Did you do any good?"

"We caught them down near the border. They are in jail waiting for Utah officials to come after them. We recovered most of the money."

"You guys have been to China and back."

"Almost. Yes, almost." He hugged his wife. It seemed that far anyway.

CHAPTER 28

Hannagen was thoroughly satisfied that Spencer was the man. So was Chet. Lucinda who was faced with moving a lot was happy being back with her man, and all the workers spoiled her children. The nanny was a big help and it was all working out so far.

Chet, Liz, and his men went by the Windmill ranch with three packhorses to see Susie. Grass was growing and he wondered about his hay outfits. The rains had sprouted thousands of desert flowers that they rode through getting there. Did more new machinery come through yet? He had some folks waiting even if hay cutting was weeks away.

Susie had no reports. But she and Liz had a great visit. With one of his lead hands, Chet looked over the cattle they had for future delivery. That looked good. The next day they rode to the Verde Ranch. It was late when they arrived and Adam was asleep. Rhea fed them and Victor had to hear the whole story.

Tom and Millie came for breakfast. Millie asked about her daughter and they explained they had not seen her because she was at the homestead they lived on and Cody was gone to Gallup with Sarge and the cattle. But Susie said she was fine.

When Chet asked Tom about mowers, he said he shipped two to Shawn and had two for Toby to come by with his wagon to haul them home. Ben Ivor promised Victor two more and he thought they would be there in time.

"So all is good?" Liz asked him.

"Yes. Except I have a feeling I may have forgotten someone."

They all laughed.

The ride home was filled with meadowlarks singing on the canyon road. When they came to the top, he felt good. Almost home and no big storms hanging over his head—the telegraph would be a reality by fall. The railroad would be the next big thing coming. It even sounded more like a larger reality than ever before.

Lisa and her house girl Sonja greeted them. A boy from the stables rang the schoolhouse bell. Raphael came, his gait stiff, something he'd acquired recently. Many of the wives came from all over to greet them.

His foreman sent for a buckboard to take Jesus to his ranch. Miguel hugged and kissed his wife. Then Fred, to celebrate, for fun danced with a few of the wives in the yard.

"Well," Chet began. "I am so glad to be home. Let's have a ranch party Saturday night."

Hurrah! There was the cheer. Liz squeezed his arm. "It is nice to be back here."

There were short letters and daily progress wires from Spencer about his gains and slight problems, but so far things sounded good. Spencer called spades, spades. So Chet felt if there was a major problem he'd inform him.

Among his other mail was a request from the Indian agent John McCarthy at San Carlos, the desert Apache reservation on the Gila River.

Dear Mr. Byrnes,

   I know you are a busy man with all your personal business but as administrator of the reservation I have a problem perhaps you could solve. My problem is the sale of alcohol to the reservation population. My Indian police have the authority to arrest anyone who is on the reservation selling liquor, white or red, however the tribal police cannot arrest anyone who is not an Indian selling it. My experience with the local law is that either these people are immune to arrest, or the law has turned its back on such violations due to either bribery or not enough help.

   I spoke with federal judge Howard Combs in Tucson recently about my problem and he suggested I request your services to help us stop these sales.

   I understand you have served other federal branches. I know many people think this agency is some sort of a zoo for killers due to some of the renegade leaders like Geronimo. Most of the population simply want to get along and survive. Liquor has enough power, it causes more trouble among the Apaches themselves, let alone the citizens outside.

   There has to be a way to control it.

   Thanks for your consideration.

                              John McCarthy

"What is it?" Liz asked.

"Whiskey sales to the Apaches at San Carlos. The reservation police cannot arrest anyone but Apaches off the reservation, and the law down there won't seem to help them stop it."

"What county is that in?"

"Gila County at Globe."

"Is the same sheriff there?"

"I don't know. But if not, the one there either has all his deputies out busy counting cows for taxes or in bed with the whiskey sellers."

"I suppose you need to go settle it?"

"I will do some checking and see what can be done. We will have the party here before I run off on you."

"That's good. I will send word to the Verde Ranch, Susie, Robert, McCully, Bo, Ben Ivor, Ty, the liveryman—"

"Frey."

"Yes, and May, your aunt, the Parkers, Jenn all of them. Sadly, it is too long a trip for Cole and Val or Lucy and Shawn. The letters would not get there in time, that is, unless we postpone it a week or so?"

"See how it goes. That sounds like the crew, though."

"Oh, Betty Lou and Leroy Sipes at Oak Creek."

"We miss them a lot. I bet they'd come. Bless their hearts they supply us so much fruit and produce."

"Good."

Fred came into the room. "Anything I should be doing?"

"Tomorrow I want to look at this ranch's calf crop

with Raphael and Miguel. Fred, you want to come along and inspect the new calves?"

"Yes, sir. I'm writing Claire a letter to tell her about the telegraph start."

Liz winked at Chet. "All business I bet."

"No, ma'am. Not all business but we have a neat friendship—that is what I call it. Something new in both our lives. She never went out with a boy and I never went out with a girl before." He sat at the desk nodding his head. "Kind of a nice experience."

"I bet it was."

"Sure different anyway. I was around kinda prissy girls in Preskitt. They'd never ride a horse except sidesaddle you know. She's a lot more down to earth and I bet she'd out-ride me on a bronc."

"Keep in mind, you have a lot more miles to go before you need a wife."

"Yes, ma'am."

Chet wrote the Indian agent he would consider the problem and see when he'd have the time to answer his call for help. Maybe he could get them a guide or an Indian to show them the country when they got there. All he knew about it was more desert mountains. This also sounded like a more involved operation than a few whiskey peddlers with a pack mule or two. The fact that if it were a widespread conspiracy, catching a few hired thugs would not end it.

Maybe he should start at Globe looking into the network. They didn't make whiskey around there because there wasn't enough grain grown in that region. They'd have to import it. He needed that source. Those people probably knew Jesus. He'd need to talk to Miguel about him, Fred, and another *vaquero* from the ranch going down there to see if they could learn anything about the operation. How the liquor gets there. And then they would know more about the entire setup.

Now that Miguel and Lisa lived in the house, he'd talk to him that evening.

After supper, he invited Miguel and Fred into the library to talk the matter over.

"The agent at San Carlos Reservation has a big problem. His agency police can't arrest white men off the reservation who are selling whiskey and he can't get the Gila County law, for whatever reason, to arrest the whiskey sellers, so he needs our help."

Both of them nodded.

"Now, I think that business has roots in Globe. Maybe. Maybe not. But those whiskey people may be paying off the law to look the other way or they are simply ignoring it. I don't think you can make whiskey over there. Ingredients cost too much. So they are shipping it in and I'd like to know the system before we charge down."

"What do we need to do?"

"They don't know you, Miguel. Now they'd kill you in a lamb's tail shake if they knew you were the law, but if we have an idea where and how it gets there, we could sweep in and arrest them all. It is not that far to the Pima County jail, either, if there is a connection to the county law there."

"They don't know me, either," Fred said. "I know how to live in the alleys. Why I knew every boot-legger in Preskitt who'd sell you a pint. I even delivered them."

"Good. I thought I'd send another *vaquero* with you two."

"Fine. I bet the three of us could learn a whole lot down there."

"You have a man in mind?" Chet asked Miguel.

"Josephie Cantrell. He'd be honored to be asked. He is tough as barbed wire. A good hand but I'd rather have him backing me any time than most men I know. You and Jesus of course are excluded."

"Just be damned careful. Ask him quietly. If he is willing, I will talk to Raphael about the matter. Remember, these people will kill you if they even suspect anything; they won't play games. This has to be a very profitable business and they will do anything to protect from losing it, no matter how many they have to kill."

"How widespread do you think it is?" Miguel asked.

"It may go to the top county officials. Even to some of the big mine management around there. I have no idea, but they are already using their power to hold off any legal action against the whiskey sellers. I think that shows it runs deep into the county veins."

"No idea of a name?" Fred asked.

Chet shook his head. "That will be your business to try and ferret out while not getting killed. If we go down and raid them selling it, we will get the donkeys is all. Fine them, six months in jail and they are out. We need the top rung to stop it totally."

"It may take some time."

"I realize that. But when you have enough information and need me, send Lisa a wire that says

'Time for a birthday cake.' Oh, don't leave until next Monday, after the *fandango* on Saturday. We will have one more meeting before you leave." They agreed.

In the morning he talked to Raphael who agreed that Cantrell would be a good man. He sent word to Tom that they needed three unbranded saddle horses to use. Fred was leaving his clothes and new saddle at the house. Both Josephie and Miguel were going to wear their old clothes and *sombreros* and ride on old ranch saddles.

Things were laid out and the celebration was about to happen. Liz had managed to put it off two weeks after all, to get it right. She wanted everyone who could come to get there and that meant Val and Rocky even if Cole couldn't. Everyone coming knew it was a ranch and friends' party. The ranch wives, sons, and daughters along with the men were all dressed up. The town folks joined in. No one missed coming.

Liz pointed out she thought Tanner's wife Kay looked pregnant when they arrived. The banker later privately told him she was and how proud they were.

Ben Ivor's wife Kathrin spoke to him. "It has been a long time since you brought me back from Utah. I thought my life was absolutely over, but you didn't nor did Ben. I am so fortunate and now I even have children. You just remember if I can ever help you in any way, you call on me."

"Kathrin, you have done many nice things for me. But your and Ben's union pleased me as much as anything. Consider the debt paid."

"Thanks, but no. My life as a woman hung by a thread and you saved it. I won't forget what I owe you doing that. The rest of the people you saved are doing well, too. I see that Jesus finally married Anita, didn't he?"

"Yes. They even bought a ranch."

"Ben told me he is getting a setup to raise Herefords."

"Jesus and Tom are talking about that."

She smiled. "I am happy for you. Now I am going to talk to Liz. You are fortunate to have found her."

"Yes, very fortunate."

Valerie and Rocky came. Cole sent his security man Roy Kelly with her and the boy. Everyone there was excited.

"Robert and Betty thought the baby was too young for the trip," Val said. "They gave you a big thanks for inviting them."

Susie came with her son Erwin and Sarge's man, Ron. Of course he was off to New Mexico, but she told him Sarge planned to use Cody to make the drives the rest of the summer. That made Chet proud and he knew the boy's in-laws would be impressed.

Hampt came by. "What are you up to now the telegraph is going up?"

Chet quietly talked about the problem in Gila County and his plans.

"Sounds to me like you have a big fish to haul in."

"I hope so. They know my face too well for me to go down there."

"First time I saw you, I could not believe you'd hire me and you'd take on that bunch on the Verde. Jenn told me who you were and I thought you wouldn't get anywhere against that tough bunch, but you did. Then you brought that family out here from Texas. I fell in love with that quiet sister-in-law of yours, May, the day she got here. Lord almighty I never dreamed I'd get to marry her, and here I am running a ranch, even got my own children. Them boys of hers grew up to be big stuff, and we are so proud. I get up every morning and thank the Lord for my blessings."

"Me the same."

"You know you need someone to ride with you down there, I am your man to call on."

"Jesus is here."

"Yeah, but you might need a big guy to help when you turn them up."

"Thanks. I appreciate that."

When they parted he saw Lisa and Miguel dancing. Fred was dancing with one of the ranch hands' wife. He fit well in the mix.

His nephew Ty and wife Victoria came by and told them the in-laws were on a trip so they could not come. He had three new Barbarossa colts on the ground and was expecting six more.

Bo came by and asked about the telegraph line.

"Spencer makes two miles most days. He has a large workforce and they work really hard. So far the needed things are getting to him."

"That is unbelievable."

"No. I knew he could do it better than I could."

"Someone may hire him away when he completes this job."

Chet nodded. "Bet he'll charge them more than I pay him, too."

"Oh, yeah. In time I bet they have those wires running everywhere."

"When you have time, I have a big ranch you might like down on the border. You've seen that country. I think the man would like someone like you to own it."

"Save it for now. I have plenty to do. I plan to try to stock the Oracle and Horse Rustler ranches this fall."

"I hope it works."

"Oh, it will. Come to think of it, I have not seen Toby tonight.

"Liz, did we invite Toby and Talley?"

"Yes, on his last trip to town he said they'd be here. Strange he didn't come."

"I'll check on him in the morning."

"Betty Lou and Leroy arrived. They had wagon trouble. Maybe Toby did, too."

He spoke to the couple who said they were pleased to be there. Leroy said he was all ready for growing season and his fruit trees were in bloom.

Jesus and Anita were there. His man knew about the San Carlos deal. He asked Chet how things were going.

"Telegraph smooth. The rest I don't know. I understand they delivered twenty-four registered heifers to your place this week?"

Anita said, "Oh, Chet, I went with him and saw them down at the Verde. They are even prettier at our house. And the new bull is coming in from New Mexico. Sarge and his men are hauling him back in a wagon."

"I hope he is all right. He cost enough," Jesus said, crossing himself.

Chet laughed. "Now he can worry like I have, huh?"

She hugged her husband's arm. "Yes. I used to think he worried too much about you. Now he has me and more things to worry about as well."

"I would not worry about you. You have found a solid place to be. You make him a lovely wife and do a great job of it."

"Thank you, Chet Byrnes. That was very kind of you after I waited so long to do it. I should have—"

He held his finger up. "No matter. You did and did it right."

Jesus smiled. "I have told her that a hundred times."

"She heard me now, too."

They parted and he spoke to Lisa. "This party went very well as usual. You did great.

"Oh, someone just got here?"

Lisa frowned, straining to see who it was. "It's Toby and Talley."

Chet went over and helped Talley off the tall draft horse. Toby climbed down from his horse and shook Chet's hand.

"Sorry we are late. We had a small accident. Totaled the wagon and had to break these two horses to ride. The one I chose was really wild. Talley has a sore arm and my head hurts but we aimed to be here on time."

Talley hugged Lisa and Liz both. "It has been an interesting trip."

"We're so glad you are all right," Liz said.

"What happened?" Chet asked.

Toby said, "A grizzly bear was chasing a cow down the road. We were in the way. I tried to hold the horses but in the whole mix-up the horses panicked and turned the wagon over. That threw us out of it. That's when she hurt her right arm. She says it is not broken. I was trying to find my gun and shoot the damn thing, but he and the cow were gone.

"After all that we were too far over here to go back home. I caught the horses, stripped the harness off them, and put her on the gentlest one. He was all right. Jim here had a couple of bucking fits, but I caught him each time and by the third round I rode him."

Talley shook her head. "It was kind of fun and we survived. We're glad to be here."

Everyone applauded them.

Toby told Chet, "We are still clearing hay ground. Tom sent us the nice new equipment so we are ready for it all."

"You sound busy?"

"We are and it is good. How is the telegraph coming?"

"Spencer says two miles a day."

"Wow, he must be good at that."

"He has the supplies so far to keep him going. Harold is buying him enough posts."

"That Faulk family are really hard workers and do a good job. I have the best corrals in the territory and that barn they built for us is super. I hope to have it full of hay this summer."

"I bet you do just that. Talley, do you think you should see a doctor about that arm?"

"No, sir. I am fine. A little sore, but sure glad to be here for this party. Being with Toby is great fun, and we have a wonderful ranch shaping up. To be quite frank I am very lucky to be here with him. I wouldn't have if you hadn't gave me the chance. I never expected to have such a fun life, wagon wreck and all."

"You two better go eat," Liz said, and herded them away.

"Different person, isn't she?" Jesus said privately.

"All of us have changed, haven't we?"

"I guess. I recall those two women when we found them. Why they'd spat at you like a cornered mountain lion and clawed you apart."

"In both cases we did good. You know sometimes you have to taste hell to know when you're well off?"

"They sure did. Oh, and I'll be ready when you want to spring that trap in San Carlos."

"This is Saturday. Miguel, Fred, and another are going down there on Monday. They will tell us when they have things ready for us."

That night he slept uneasy. He knew those men of his needed time to line it out from top to bottom over there on the whiskey deal, but the wait was going to be hard.

CHAPTER 29

Miguel, Fred and Josephie left for Gila County. It was now three weeks and no word. He paced the floor. How much longer could it be? Maybe they were dead. Damn he should have gone down there with them. No, they'd recognize him from arrests he had made and delivered there. The whiskey ring had so much to lose, and any threat to their golden cow would be fiercely fought.

Desperate situations existed for finding ways to make money in the territory. That factor drove men to crimes like selling liquor to Indians. And everyone got a slice of that cake from officials on down. An apple rotten to the core by greed. He didn't simply want only the donkeys in this case, he wanted them all, which was why he was waiting for word and not going down there now.

Any day. Any time the wire would come. He didn't want a bad one saying that his men had been murdered doing their job. Time would tell.

Finally, one day, a town boy on a lathered horse

rode up to the house. And shouted, "I have a wire for Lisa Costa."

He heard her shout from the kitchen. "Chet it came. It finally came."

"I am coming."

She was at the foot of the stairs by the time he reached the back porch. The envelope open, she read and held it high. "*'Time to bake a cake.'*"

He closed his eyes. "Thank you, Lord. Thank you."

The suspense was over at last. He had things to arrange.

"Can I take a message back, sir, to send?"

"Yes, let me write a message on the envelope. You know where Jesus Martinez's ranch house is on the way back to town?"

"The Diamond M?"

"Yes that is his brand."

Liz handed him a pencil. He scribbled on the envelope: "*We got this today.*"

He paid the boy two quarters, which made him smile and thank him. Then he spoke to the stable boy, Jimenez. "You saddle a horse. I need you to take Hampt a note in a few minutes."

"*Si, señor.*" The youth raced for the barn. Chet went back inside and wrote on some butcher paper: "*Word came today for us to proceed down there—Chet.*"

That would leave Hampt to decide if he could go. Jimenez was back with a saddled horse.

"Give my note to him. Say if he wants to go we leave at dawn."

"Where?"

"He will know."

"I can do that, señor." He stuffed the paper inside his shirt and left in as fast a run as the horse would go for his destination.

Chet turned to his wife. "We leave at sunup."

"I know that relieves you. Not me. You be very careful."

"Jesus will be here in an hour to select the pack-horses and things we will need."

"What about Hampt?"

"He asked to go help me."

"Poor May can worry about him then."

"I told you before you came to live with me, down at Nogales that first day, that I had things I must do. I warned you."

"I accepted those terms. I know what goes on inside your brain. But I still have the option of being a wife that worries something bad may happen to you."

"Yes, you do. But I have managed so far. Let's go get ready. Thank the Lord all three are alive down there."

CHAPTER 30

The first day started out cloudy. The men had their slickers or canvas coats ready in case it rained. That's how wet it looked. Six packhorses followed. Chet decided they were ready for a full-scale war—even blasting powder was packed away. The wives were there to see them off. Hampt waved at May and Jesus's Anita told him not to get wet. Seemed she'd even found a sense of humor getting married to him.

They were a long ways from Globe and the whiskey dealers, but they had what they needed and if his men had located the culprits this could be short and easy. They reached the desert the end of that day. Warm enough, and the rain threat gone, they didn't put up a tent that night.

In the morning they loaded up, ate Jesus's oatmeal in the company of bugs, had some real coffee, and rode off to cross the desert. They planned to cross the Salt River below a diversion damn, then a shallow canal, then by evening, get close to the ship of a mountain called Superstition. Chet was

concerned they might warn the enemy if they went
through Goldfield north of the mountain's base.

The next day they avoided the stage station at
Florence Junction. Chet saw someone familiar sitting on a large rock beside the road when they drew
near Claypool. In his ragged clothing, Fred smiled
and jumped to his feet.

"We need to take a shortcut through these hills."
He gave a head toss behind him. Then he took up
the reins of the paint horse he had ridden down on,
one without a Quarter Circle Z brand on him.

"How is everyone?"

"Oh, they're fine."

Riding side by side through the spiny cholla cactus,
he told Fred to stop. "Where are the others at?"

"At the Coulter's ranch. The foreman says he
knows you."

"What's his name?"

"Jerry Boyd."

Chet couldn't think of who he was, but if they had
a place to hide what difference did it make? "You
guys know who runs the deal."

"The guy who runs the whiskey is Nate Bunker.
He owns a big saloon in Globe and he has a warehouse south of town. He has some real hard cases
working for him. They make regular trips, openly, to
an area above the reservation, sell all the liquor they
have, and then drive back to the warehouse. It all is
in the clear and open. The sheriff, Frank Cranston,
does nothing about the sale to Indians. We wanted
to try and catch him getting a payoff, but that didn't
happen. I still think they must pay him."

"What do the others think?"

"They also believe he is on the take. At a sheriff's pay how can he own three racehorses? He gambles big, too."

"Sheriffs get ten percent of county tax collections. Behan made thirty thousand a year. He won't make that much but he does makes money."

"I think we did good but I sure miss a bath."

Chet smiled. "You all have done great. When do we get to this ranch?"

"About another hour."

"Good. My butt's tired. How did you find this foreman that knows me?"

"He needed some help. He couldn't pull a calf by himself. We were around, so we stopped and helped him. He took us home, fed us, and asked why we were here. We told him it was a secret. He bought that and wondered where we came from. We figured he was no threat and said, 'Preskitt.' Then he said, 'There is a big man up there I went to grade school with from Texas. Chet Byrnes.'"

"I don't recall him. He has a better memory than I do."

They reached the ranch and Chet did not recognize the man who came out and shook his hand.

"I'm Jerry Boyd. You and me went to school in the third grade at Yellow Hammer Creek School."

"Yes, Miss Freeman was our teacher." Chet remembered her.

"Yes, we moved to Oklahoma at the end of the school year but I never forgot you."

"Jerry, I guess I forgot you."

"There is a faded picture they took of our class in

the house. These boys say you have been busy since you came here from Texas."

"Yes, we have. I have several working ranches."

"I thought your dad had a big working place there back then."

"We did. Three of my family were kidnapped by Comanche. My father tried hard to find them, ruined his health and his mind staying out too long. Rangers brought him home but he never recovered. I was running the ranch at fifteen."

Jerry's wife had obviously overheard the conversation and came into the room carrying a piece of paper. "Here is the picture, Jerry." The nice-looking woman smiled at him.

"That was Miss Freeman. I remember her. Where are you?"

"That's me squatted down there. See yourself? You are in the top row second right."

"That's my hair sticking up. My brother is in it, too. He was in first grade so they would have enough kids for a class. There he is. He was murdered in the feud we had with the Reynolds bunch. That's him, Dale Allen."

"I remember him, too," Jerry said. "This is my wife, Twilia."

"Nice to meet you, Twilia." Chet smiled. "If you could get a duplicate of that done, I'd pay you for it. My brother has two sons and a daughter living and I am sure they would like to see a picture of their dad. We had a tough time in that feud. I came to Arizona, found a place, and then some others. I appreciate you putting up with my men. They told you why we are here?"

"No. They said a secret job."

"It is. But I trust you and can tell you. We are here to stop a bunch of bad people selling whiskey to the Apaches."

"Oh, I know all about that."

"I guess it has gone on sometime?"

Jerry said, "Two years ago when Frank Cranston was elected sheriff it started. Folks were afraid to tell him. One guy did and he disappeared. It's be quiet or not be here."

Twilia spoke up. "Those deputies of his came here, counted our cattle, and demanded we go find more. Jerry said he had no more and one hit him in the face while the others laughed. Thank God he stayed on the ground."

"What are their names?" Chet asked.

Jerry shook his head. "It won't do any good."

"It will in court. I am rounding them all up."

"You're going to have a jail full."

"I can buy chains to lock them up outside."

"Rymel Schultz, Herman Fountain, and Ray Bailey," she said.

"How many more ranchers or foremen will claim these deputies threatened them at cow counts?"

"We can get more."

"Keep that thought. I want this whole mess straightened out over here. It isn't only whiskey selling to Indians obviously."

Miguel and Josephie came in.

"Good to see you. I hope we did enough," Miguel said.

"There are lots of things happening over here."

"Yes, I am starting to see that. You guys found a stream of things going on wrong."

"They sell Indians whiskey like it was candy. Run over people counting cattle, and ignore murders."

Miguel said, "There is lots more. Demanding protection money from small businesses like the Mexican café we ate at."

"You have the man's name who did it?"

"A deputy named Schultz."

"I think we should arrest the men on the whiskey sales first. I bet they have some untaxed whiskey, which will make it a federal offense and give them a longer term in jail. Then we collect the rest of them. In the end get a grand jury to charge these bad deputies. Can we arrest then down there by the reservation?"

"Sure. They go down there real open."

"Tomorrow night will they go there?"

"Yes."

"The food is on the table," Twilia interrupted.

"How long have you been here?" Chet asked Jerry.

"Oh, five years. We ran the big Key Ranch in New Mexico. They sold it and Mr. Burns asked us to come over here to run this one. We would like to have a better one, but the cattle business is so hard in Arizona. Markets so poor, and, well, there aren't many good jobs, either."

"Shame we don't have something open, ma'am. I was doing day work five years ago before Chet hired me," Hampt said. "I run one of his divisions now and married his brother's widow. It is fun."

"I thought I heard you bought a big place down by Oracle?" she asked.

Chet shook his head. "Yes. The place is a mess and the cows are all old."

"How is that?" Jerry asked.

"Man who stocked it bought old cows. Bankers don't know cows. He even drove them all to another ranch to count them there, too. Make the place look good."

"Where is he now?"

"In Mexico stealing my cows over the southern border."

"That sounds tough."

"My men put seven rustlers in the ground already."

"Whew. We thought it was tough up here."

"The reason I am here today is Arizona has to get rid of these criminals to ever get statehood."

"I hope you win the fight," she said.

"Twilia, we are going to if I have any say."

Chet did not sleep well that night. In the morning, she fed them pancakes with homemade syrup. Jesus brought her some real coffee from his supply.

The day passed with them repairing everything and getting their guns cleaned.

"I never had a paint horse to ride before, but that is one tough s.o.b. that Tom sent me."

"Fred, you ready to go back to Preskitt?" Chet asked him, amused at his talking.

"I want to see this business finished and done. I miss your nice house and great woman. I don't think I could leave her if she was mine. That ain't talking bad about her. That's how I feel. But this bunch needs taken out real bad. I want to be in on this, but I hope I never go back to being a street bum like I have been these weeks here."

"You won't."

They ate an early supper. Chet paid her for feeding his men. She looked at the money in her hand. "I'd have fed them without that much money."

Chet shook his head. "You two ever get out of work, find me. After thirty years almost, I forgot going to school with Jerry but I won't forget the two of you now."

"I hope you and your men clean up this big mess. When that deputy slugged Jerry over them cows I wanted to shoot him and the others with him. I'd had a gun I would have."

That evening they left the packhorses and rode to the place where the Indians were buying whiskey. Chet pointed out the shotgun guard standing by the wagon in the fire's light.

"I'll get the other one," Fred said.

"Sure?"

"Sure."

"Get him. The rest of us will force the Indians to stay back."

Hampt came up behind the guard with the shotgun, grabbed the weapon away from him, and rammed him in the head with the butt. That made the gun go off and howling Indians ran in every direction.

Fred had gotten the other weapon away from the second man and had him on the ground facing the barrels.

"What happened to the Indians?" Miguel asked.

"Apaches fear dying in the dark. They ran." Chet

turned to the two clerks holding the money. "Put that money down. You two are under arrest for selling whiskey to Indians. We are U.S. marshals."

"You can't arrest us. This is Gila County, not the reservation."

"I can and I am. Selling liquor to Indians is a federal law you have broken. Chain them up and one of us will guard them."

"I will," Fred said.

"Don't bother to stop if they even try to escape. Just shoot them," were the sternest instructions he could give Fred.

They left Fred in charge and mounted up heading for town. Miguel led them to the Elkhorn Saloon. They dismounted and hitched their horses at the rack out front. Armed with his shotgun, Hampt went around back.

"The man we want is?"

Miguel said, "Nate Bunker. He has some henchmen around and he is usually in the office straight back."

"You two keep everyone's hands in the air. Go."

"U.S. marshals. Hands in the air. Bartenders, you, too."

At the commotion, a man came in from the back. "What in the hell is going on out here?"

"Everyone is under arrest. You, get your hands in the air."

"Like hell I will."

Chet's first bullet showered the big man with wood chips from the door facing. He stopped and immediately went to his knees holding his heart. Chet took no chances, keeping the gun on him in case he was faking, but when he saw the man's flush face, he shouted, "Some get a doctor. This man is dying."

He laid him out flat. Hampt with the shotgun came through from the back. "No one else came back there."

Chet bent over to be certain the man down had no weapons. His rasping breath sounded final. Chet looked up in time to see an angry face and a badge bust through the batwing doors.

"What in hell is going on down here?"

"That's the sheriff," Miguel said.

"Sheriff, you are under arrest. I am U.S. Marshal Chet Byrnes."

Hampt had his shotgun leveled on the man. "Don't go for that gun. You're covered."

"You can't arrest me."

"Yes, I can. Consider yourself arrested. Miguel, put him in handcuffs."

"I'll have your head for this. Who in the hell do you think you are?"

Chet, tapping his own chest, said, "I told you, I am Chet Byrnes. Ever hear of me?"

"You can't—"

"Start with malfeasance of office. I have charges a yard long against you and your men. Take them to the jail." He stepped outside and saw a procession filling the street. "What's going on out here?"

Fred rode up on his paint horse. "Citizens making arrests. We also found two more deputies and brought them along with the whiskey sellers in case you want them all here."

Chet stood on the porch with the light from the

saloon at his back. "Citizens of Gila County, thanks. We will have real law here from now on. I promise you. Can someone please tell me where the sheriff lives?"

"A house about two blocks from here," Jerry called, he and Twilia having come into town.

"Would you take Hampt and Fred there after they lock this bunch up? I want all his records before someone burns them. Miguel, get all this guy's books and records you can find. I will need them, too. And to anyone out here before we close down, the drinks are on me."

There was a rush for the door.

The doc told him there was nothing he could do for Bunker. "He will die in the next hour."

"Thanks. You did all you could."

"I did."

"Good night, sir."

Chet turned to go back in the saloon. Twilia stopped him at the door. "They got the one hit Jerry. There's two more but you did good. I am going to write and thank your wife and I will get a copy made of that picture."

She stood on her toes, kissed his cheek, and disappeared into the night.

It was daybreak when the last two deputies were found, arrested, and jailed. When Chet's men went after the whiskey wagon, they found many drunk and passed out Apaches. The wagon was completely empty. But the warehouse had lots of booze in it. They buried Bunker in an unmarked grave. Six prosecutors and several assistants came to Globe.

Proceedings began and a grand jury was held. Those arrested were charged with many crimes.

The governor sent a former Arizona sheriff to Globe to hold office until the next election.

The San Carlos Apache agent came by and thanked him. Several businessmen did, too. The lady who had the Mexican café and had to pay protection fees threw a big meal for them.

He got a forwarded telegram from Spencer. *"Meet me in Center Point in three weeks."*

Things looked settled in Gila County. He told the men he'd see them back at the house. He was leaving immediately.

Chet took the stage to Hayden's Ferry and then to Preskitt.

Past midnight, Liz met him with a driver.

"Welcome home, big man. Spencer wants you to come to Center Point. Think we can do that?"

"Yes, I know. I got a letter and I bet we can do that. How have you been?"

"Oh, fine. I read some of the accounts and your letters. Did you really attend school with him?"

"Name all the people in the third grade you went to school with."

"I went to a Catholic academy. I can't recall one of them."

"Me, either. But he is sending me a copy of a picture he has. My brother went to school that year at five so they would have enough kids to afford the teacher. I did not remember a photo they made, but he had one."

"Can you tell who you are in it?"

"Yes."

"I hope they send it."

"His wife, Twilia, will. One of those deputies hit him in the face after they counted all his cows and knocked him on the ground wanting the cow count higher. She said if she'd had a gun she'd have shot him. The night we arrested him she came by and thanked me. Promised me a copy."

"I might have shot him, too."

He was laughing and hugged her. "I bet you would have."

The driver laughed along with them.

"Jose, don't laugh," she said. "You ever hit my man run for your life."

"Oh, señora, I would never hit him. He is too big."

He drew a deep breath when the house lights came in sight. "What's happening?"

"We are having a *fandango* to celebrate your return."

"You are something special."

"No. I am the woman would have shot any man that hit you."

"No doubt. No doubt," he said, shaking his head.

"Why did no one come home with you?"

"I wanted to be here with you. We had horses and packhorses over there to bring back."

"One of them should have rode with you."

"I had enough. I wanted home fast."

"Next time don't forget."

"Yes, ma'am."

"We are glad to have you home again. A big party is already planned."

"I want another for my four men when they get back. They really did a good job."

"No problem. Lisa and I can have a party going in no time."

At the party, Chet found and apologized to his men's wives. Told them the men were fine, they did a great job, and were coming home on horseback. "I know you all miss Fred not dancing with you when your husbands don't dance."

They all laughed. The music began. It was the usual nice party, but he took his wife off to bed before the end. So good to be in his own bed with her. He slept in the next morning. Lisa made him a late breakfast and he went to reading back issues of the *Miner* newspaper.

"When will we go meet Spencer at Center Point?"

"When the men get back. They'll be here in three days. Let them have some rest and then we can go. We need to invite Susie and Sarge, Tom and Millie, Rhea and Victor and Adam, and send word to Shawn and Lucy to all come to Center Point."

"Maybe invite Robert and Betty with the baby? Better bring along Lisa, too."

"Yes, that will be good. The telegraph line must be working. He's sent a wire here from every stage station he has reached. I saved them all for you."

"Good. I think it will hurry the train and business development across the land."

"No one can do any more than you have for the region."

"Oh, we all can benefit from it. This territory

needs to be a state and I am pushing for it to get there."

"You know some newspapers down state have criticized your unveiling the corruption as working against statehood."

"Let them complain. Those people over there have the right not to be run over by bad politicians. When did crime need to be covered up? It needs to be uncovered."

"I am not the one. But people want to sweep things under the rug quietly."

"That will not get us anywhere. Some people don't want to shake the boat. Well, the people who came out that night to back us thought that the crimes should have been dealt with. I walked out of that saloon's front doors and there must have been fifty men on horseback with Fred and his prisoners. They'd arrested two deputies. And they testified to the grand jury what those crooks had done to them."

"I am simply telling you what is being reported." She came over to the chair and hugged his head. "They don't know you or love you like I do."

"Your boy Fred said he didn't want to be a beggar ever again. He looked like one when he was waiting for us on the road going there and took us to Jerry's ranch."

"Jerry and his wife were a big help to you and the men, weren't they?"

"Yes. I wish I had a place for them."

"Maybe one will show up. Do they have kids?"

"No they're our age. She never said. I never asked."

"It simply happens, people say. I am sorry we

don't but I know nothing I can do about it. Valerie is the same. Oh, well. We have such a large family and your two boys, we are blessed."

"Yes, ma'am."

He had just begun to worry about his team returning when they showed up. Hampt had ridden on home. Jesus said he'd ride the ranch horse home. Lisa was excited and Fred danced with some of the ranch ladies.

Liz told him welcome back and his clothes were laid out in the bathroom.

He took off his hat and asked if he could kiss her forehead, he was so glad to see her.

She told him, "Yes."

He did it.

"Liz, you don't know how I have missed you, this wonderful house, and Lisa's cooking. Playing a bum and putting up with some of that sorry trash they had over there made me thank you both even more and made me know, I don't want to be a bum ever again in my life."

"I doubt you will be."

"Thanks for giving me this wonderful chance." He was gone to bathe.

Lisa and her helper, Sonja, cooked supper.

While eating, Fred and Chet talked about the telegraph coming to Center Point.

"Did you hear about the negative articles in newspapers on our cleaning up Gila County, coming home?"

"Jesus heard about it. Made him mad. Folks wanted to cover that up. Made me mad, too. Those people who wrote all that had never been punched around for not showing more cattle than they had, or had not seen Rosa paying protection money so she could keep her café."

"We did the right thing."

"You ever think about Jerry and his wife working for you? That ranch is a dead end. They had a good job at the Key Ranch in New Mexico. He straightened that place up, the owner made a big profit on the sale, and he lost his job. He'd do a real job for someone. I love him and her. They're our kinda people."

"I know what you mean. Bo has a place south of Tombstone he mentioned. The man wanted someone to keep it together if he sold it."

"That where you arrested the bank robber and woman from Utah?"

"I think south and east of there."

"How did he hear about it?"

"We will go find out tomorrow. Liz, you want to go to town tomorrow?"

"No. I gave Lisa some time off to go to Oak Creek with Miguel for three days. I mentioned it to you."

"Yes. I forgot. I told him take a week. So you stay here; Fred and I are going to town to see Bo."

"I know what that means. Where is this one at?"

"South. Past Tombstone somewhere. I don't have the details."

"Good. You two can get out from under my foot. Just remember you are meeting Spencer in five days. That means no long trip until that is over."

"I hear you. We will go see him right after breakfast," he told Fred.

Horses were saddled and waiting for them to

finish breakfast. They rode in and found Bo, busy as usual.

He looked up from his paperwork. "Hello, U.S. marshals. You mopped up Gila County, huh?"

"You have a babysitter for this Saturday night?"

"Indeed I do. What do you want?"

"Get a chair, Fred. You have a place somewhere south you talked about?"

"John Davidson owns the BBR Ranch down there. He's in his seventies. His wife died three years ago. His only son or child was killed in a wagon wreck ten years ago. His lawyer wrote me a letter some time back and said if I knew anyone who'd let him live there the rest of his life, he'd sell them that place for a song—but he wanted someone he could trust not to sell it while he still lives there."

"I really think he wants the place to keep on after he was gone. That ranch has a valid original Spanish deed, and I am not certain of the acreage but it is a large one. He runs cattle and has grapes, I understand. I have a picture of the house, corrals, and outbuildings."

"What does he want for it?"

"Don't tell a soul. Two thousand a year until he dies."

"You sure he has not sold it already?"

"No. The letter was from his lawyer in Tucson and confidential."

"Do I need my lawyer down there to see about it, Bo?"

"He's the one that did the Diablo case?"

"Yes. He's well respected."

"I will write and tell him to contact, who?"

"Russell Craft. I will write and mail him a letter about it before I leave town. He found me the Oracle Ranch."

"This place will rival it, only it has the fancy head-quarters, cattle and all."

"Of course there is a chance we are too late?"

"I think this has been kept very low key. I asked that lawyer to hold it, that I had several good pro-spects to check out."

"Okay, Fred, you don't tell a soul what we are up to."

"Oh, I won't."

"Fred made friends while they looked into the corruption over in Gila with a small ranch foreman who needs a larger job."

"I will get to work on it fast."

"Good. Give me a pen and paper. Thanks." He wrote Russell.

They picked up the ranch mail and mailed the letter. Bo was planning to mail his letter later. The two rode home happy as meadowlarks dancing in the road dust.

Liz welcomed them and when they were going through the mail, she found a large envelope with his school picture inside. She looked up at Chet. "Your hair lays down better now than it did back then."

"You found me in that picture?"

"Brother, I could find you anywhere I looked." Then she pointed him out to Fred.

"That's him all right."

"This lady wrote me a nice letter, too."

It was Chet's turn. He had the ranch picture to

show Liz. It looked like as big a deal as Preskitt Valley. Two windmills, a large house, good barns, and corrals.

"Look at this place."

"Oh, where is it?"

"The place below Tombstone?"

"Did you buy it?"

"No, but we are trying to. It is a place where the old man who owns it wants to stay and die there, and then have someone continue with it."

"Expensive?"

"No. Two thousand a year until he dies; he's in his seventies now."

"How big?"

"Over six sections."

"More ranches, huh?"

"Yes. And then I write Jerry that we might have a job coming open."

"What if it doesn't?"

"I said might."

"Stage lines, telegraph wires, and ranches; you are a very busy man."

"They are building the railroad to Tucson and then California in two years. The cattle markets will be open on it in all directions. Cattle will be worth something then. Produce like citrus and the like will be worth growing. We are at the gateway to making money, my dear."

"How far is this ranch from your old buddy Weeks below the border?"

"Close but if push comes to shove we can get him out of the way."

She wagged her head side to side. "So he will be a problem to you and you will have to deal with that?"

"Dear, he's an outlaw. They don't last long when the law is on your side."

"Long enough to kill you."

Fred had been silent, but now he chimed in. "Miss Liz, ain't no one's getting close to killing him while me and others are around."

"Fred, you and Jesus let him come home alone from Globe."

"Yes, ma'am. We won't let that happen again. No matter how bad he misses you."

All three laughed.

CHAPTER 31

The big party was finally held for the returning men. Lisa came home with her husband from the Oak Creek Place a day early to help set things up. Everyone came and the music and beer flowed. Fred danced with about five hundred females by Chet's count. Several men and women talked about the Globe deal and thanked him. A few even complained about the newspaper complainers.

Hampt and May joined them with her daughter and both of the little ones. May thanked him for taking her husband along. "After being with you, Hampt always comes home in a good mood. He really likes to go with you. Even on that lost herd trip he made. I missed him but he will never forget all you have done for us. I almost didn't come out here, and it has turned out so wonderful. Ray is going on to become a professor and Ty is happy with Victoria on his own horse ranch. Their dad would thank you for all you did for them."

"May, there would be something he didn't approve

of. May his soul rest in heaven. I have to talk to you about it."

She went to laughing. "Yes, you are right. This young man Fred? I know he's too old for her but Donna asked me about him. She'll soon be fifteen. All of sudden, Donna doesn't wear overalls. She has to wear dresses to all events and have to fix her hair. Hampt taught her to dance. I remember that age."

"They grow up."

"Oh, yes, but I want her to do it slow like."

"Mothers don't always get their way."

"You need to know that Fred has been seeing Harold Faulk's daughter Claire. The contractor's daughter. Don't ask me how serious they are."

"Well. Thanks for telling me. I will make sure I am there if something happens and she gets hurt. It is part of growing up, you know. But good to be prepared."

With the party over, it was time to leave for Center Point. He rented three buggies for the trip north. They had the ranch chuckwagon, used at roundup, to go ahead and set up camp at the base of the rim. Most of the men and large boys rode horseback. Susie and Sarge with Erwin had their own buckboard. Bo's wife, Bo, and the baby rode in a buggy.

The second night's stop would be in the great meadow ten miles south of Center Point. Then they'd go and on the last day arrive at the stage line around mid-day. Liz rode horseback and so did Lisa. Rhea, the nanny, and Adam rode in one of the buggies. Vic and Hampt were on horseback. May, Donna, both babies, Anita, Millie, and her daughter from Windmill all rode in another buggy. Cody had stayed back to watch that ranch.

Toby and Talley decided at the last minute not to go. But several of their cowhands and *vaqueros* went along to help set up tents and cots plus secure firewood. Victor played his guitar and sang each evening.

Cole and Val rang bells and fired off guns as they rode into camp.

Rocky rode his painted pony out to meet his dad. That tickled Liz and she got off her horse to get him. "My, what a great horse you have."

"I can walk, too," he told her as she got him off the horse. He got both her hands and led her to Val.

"They all came to see you."

"Thanks, Rocky."

"It finally is going to happen," Chet said.

"Bet you are surprised it happened so fast?"

"No. I've gotten reports every day by wire since the first stage stop."

"Even when you were at Globe?"

"I didn't get them there. But they were sent to the house and Liz has them all."

"Anything else new?"

"Waiting on word about another ranch."

Bo stepped over. "I have a little something I want you to open."

He handed him a letter from an attorney in Tucson he didn't know.

Dear Bo,

*Your request from Chet Byrnes to buy the BBR
Ranch will be accepted by Mr. Davidson. I first
contacted you because we knew you handled
Mr. Byrnes's land deals. I was not certain he
would be interested since I know he owns lots of
land and might not want it, but John is a very
respected admirer of his work to make Arizona a
better place to live. The terms are acceptable, and
we can close when Mr. Byrnes has time to come
down and sign the papers. We will have a complete
list of all livestock, equipment, and buildings. There
is an older man, currently the foreman, who would
like to retire but said he could be available for
six months.*

I look forward to hearing from you.

> *Arthur Roberts*
> *Attorney at Law*

"Must be good news?" Cole asked.

"Where's Fred?"

"Coming, boss man. What is wrong?"

He handed him the letter.

Fred read it. "Well, your third-grade classmate has
a job, I take it."

"The telegraph will be hooked up today. I'll wire
Jerry and Twilia to be prepared to move and that we
have the large BBR Ranch below Tombstone for
them to run for the Byrnes outfit. I'll tell him you
will be there in a week to ten days to move them
down there."

"They will faint when they get your wire."

"They will have some time to recover."

"What's happened?" Cole asked.

"Oh, Bo and I have been looking at a large ranch below Tombstone. He wanted to wait until we got up here to tell me we had it."

"You did buy it?" Liz asked.

"The letter said so. Fred is wiring Jerry that he'll be coming there to help move them to the new place."

"Good news," Liz said. "They say Spencer is riding a different horse in here shortly."

When Spencer Horne, Telegraph Construction Supervisor, rode into Center Point, he had his saddle cinched over a fresh-cut telegraph pole, sitting on sawhorses in a wagon bed, and was waving his hat and beating the log while the wagon was being driven by a laughing cowboy.

Hannagen had found them and laughed hard at the float. "Don't ever send a boy when you need a man, Chet Byrnes."

"No, sir. Spencer is a gem of a man."

"Word gets out about this job, the success and speed we had getting here, it will be national news. You and I won't be able to afford him."

Chet agreed. "You be sure to tell him that. He's done one helluva job. He needs to go on to bigger things."

"He will. I guarantee you and I will help him."

"Now all we need is business on this wire."

"We will have connections coming from California and New Mexico as soon as we hook it up. Business will be no problem. I found three good stages, for a bargain, coming from California. So with the others we will have stage service three times a week. Wells Fargo will connect us on the east and west and we will get many coach tickets bought for our line. Chet Byrnes, do you have any idea how much more money we will make with the stage line?"

"I have no idea."

"I expect revenues in the next year to reach a quarter of a million dollars for you and I to split fifty-fifty. Can you stand that?"

"He'll only buy more ranches," Liz said.

"He can buy the whole territory, as far as I am concerned, Liz."

"Don't encourage him."

"You two are a strange match, you know that?"

"How is that?" Liz asked.

"I am not being a wise ass. He looks like a big cowboy and you look like Spanish royalty."

"I thought we looked like Arizona, his big hat and my Hispanic foundation."

"No, you two are lovely together. People told me that if I could ever make a stage line work across here, I had to get into business with this rancher from Preskitt. Well, I thought I don't need a cowboy. But the deeper I went, not knowing those people were hired so I would fail, and seeing no end to the costs I was incurring, I asked for that meeting at Windmill. We met and I could see Cole and him were doers right away. We had not even found one stage stop and overnight they found several of them. They bartered, traded, and fought a war to make them work. I can't even imagine what else they went through and resolved.

"Then he said we needed a telegraph; that it

would suit our stage business, too, and here he came with another Stetson hat in the form of Spencer. Before I knew it they rolled out wire like carpet. Elizabeth, I never had a partner like this man. I am glad you found each other for your sake and mine as well. Tell me, what do you need at your house?"

"I can't think of a thing."

"Well, I will find something special that you do not have, when I am in St. Louis, and ship it to you. Now, excuse me please. I am going to talk to some reporters that are here special for this event of sending the first message from Center Point back east. I know it is going to disappoint you, Chet, but I saw the Atchison Topeka and Santé Fe Railroad planned route map through to here. They are changing the name at this point on their proposed lines and calling Center Point—Flagstaff."

"I guess that will be the name, then, won't it?" she asked him.

He tipped his hat and left to talk to the reporters that surrounded him.

"What do you think, big man?" She looped her arm in his.

"I couldn't give one damn what they call it. This is done, and I have lots of other things to look after. Where is Fred? I need to check on the hay operations that will soon start. Make sure everyone is ready. Settle up on the BBR Ranch and get Jerry and Twilia down there running it."

"Fred and Claire rode off somewhere. May's daughter Donna went fishing in some small lake with three teenage kids from up here. They looked nice enough and they had parents we talked to. When I asked

Donna if she could fish she frowned at me and told me in a haughty voice that Hampt had showed her all about it."

"I bet he did. Okay, with Fred not here, I am taking a nap. The big party is tonight. Valerie, Lisa, and two Chinese cooks are in charge. I hope they don't cut off their pigtails."

Liz simply shook her head. "Chet Byrnes, I don't know what I am going to do with you."

"I guess simply keep me and put up with me. Wake me up in time for the party."